"Fast-paced, dark, and wickedly edgy, *Dire Needs* is a paranormal shot in the arm for the genre! No one writes a bad boy hero like Tyler."
—Larissa Ione, *New York Times* bestselling author of *Immortal Rider*

"Stephanie Tyler puts a unique, fresh spin on shape-shifter romance. In *Dire Needs*, she creates a raw, sexy world where werewolves make and break all the rules."
—Maya Banks, *New York Times* bestselling author of *Whispers in the Dark*

"Stephanie Tyler has created a story that kept me on the edge of my seat. With breathtaking danger, sizzling romance, and unexpected twists, these Dire Wolves are going to rock the paranormal world."
—Alexandra Ivy, *New York Times* bestselling author of *Bound by Darkness*

"Riveting! *Dire Needs* hooked me from the very first page."
—Shiloh Walker, author of *If You Hear Her*

Praise for the Novels of Stephanie Tyler

"Unforgettable."
—Cherry Adair, *New York Times* bestselling author of *Riptide*

"Red-hot romance. White-knuckle suspense."
—Lara Adrian, *New York Times* bestselling author of *Deeper Than Midnight*

"Sexy and witty." —Fresh Fiction

"Stephanie Tyler is a master." —Romance Junkies

DIRE NEEDS

A NOVEL OF THE ETERNAL WOLF CLAN

STEPHANIE TYLER

A SIGNET ECLIPSE BOOK

SIGNET ECLIPSE
Published by New American Library, a division of
Penguin Group (USA) Inc., 375 Hudson Street,
New York, New York 10014, USA
Penguin Group (Canada), 90 Eglinton Avenue East, Suite 700, Toronto,
Ontario M4P 2Y3, Canada (a division of Pearson Penguin Canada Inc.)
Penguin Books Ltd., 80 Strand, London WC2R 0RL, England
Penguin Ireland, 25 St. Stephen's Green, Dublin 2,
Ireland (a division of Penguin Books Ltd.)
Penguin Group (Australia), 250 Camberwell Road, Camberwell, Victoria 3124,
Australia (a division of Pearson Australia Group Pty. Ltd.)
Penguin Books India Pvt. Ltd., 11 Community Centre, Panchsheel Park,
New Delhi - 110 017, India
Penguin Group (NZ), 67 Apollo Drive, Rosedale, Auckland 0632,
New Zealand (a division of Pearson New Zealand Ltd.)
Penguin Books (South Africa) (Pty.) Ltd., 24 Sturdee Avenue,
Rosebank, Johannesburg 2196, South Africa

Penguin Books Ltd., Registered Offices:
80 Strand, London WC2R 0RL, England

First published by Signet Eclipse, an imprint of New American Library,
a division of Penguin Group (USA) Inc.

First Printing, March 2012
10 9 8 7 6 5 4 3 2 1

Copyright © Stephanie Tyler, 2012
All rights reserved

SIGNET ECLIPSE and logo are trademarks of Penguin Group (USA) Inc.

Printed in the United States of America

For Lily, because this story could never have existed without you

Horatio: O day and night, but this is wondrous strange!
Hamlet: And therefore as a stranger give it welcome.
There are more things in heaven and earth, Horatio,
Than are dreamt of in your philosophy.
                    —William Shakespeare, *Hamlet*

For the strength of the Pack is the Wolf, and the strength of the Wolf is the Pack.
                    —Rudyard Kipling, *The Jungle Book*

Chapter 1

Rifter needed a woman, Brother Wolf needed to run wild, and their appetites for sex and destruction mingled, rose with a hot howl as Rifter's Harley roared through the winter night.

Both knew which appetite would have to be sated first—the fucking, then the running. Rifter and his wolf were usually on the same page in that regard. Tonight was no different, and he slammed his Harley to a stop in front of Bite, one of the many bars along the strip, because he smelled danger. He stomped inside, ignoring the way the room stilled and everyone turned to watch him. After hundreds of years, that shit got old, and he was well aware of what he looked like.

He was also well aware that no one in this room would want to be him, if given the chance. He could only pray no one ever would be put in that position again.

No, he was already part of a pack of the last six living Dire wolves, who cursed their immortality and wore their ferocity on their sleeves because they literally had nothing to lose.

Created by Hati, son of a Norse god, and watched over by a mystical clan of Elders, Rifter was six feet eight inches of raw muscle and more than seven feet, three hundred pounds when he was Brother Wolf, which explained the pain of the transition.

Brother Wolf was part of him—when he was driving the ship, Rifter could request things, and vice versa, but they were both equal in power. It was the only way they could inhabit one body. He had a great deal of respect for his wolf, knew what Brother needed and when he needed it. Brother did the same for him.

If one of them died, the other would too.

We should be that lucky, he thought, and Brother howled in response inside his head, reminding him of why they'd come here in the first place.

Brother Wolf's biggest goal—beyond chasing moons— was to become Father Wolf. That could happen only by mating, and that shit was not happening anytime soon.

Rifter's main goal was to die, but again, he'd be waiting on that one forever.

One of the female Weres, laced into a black bustier, caught up to him when he was halfway to the bar and rubbed her body against his. "Where've you been, Rift?" she purred.

"Prison," he said as he pushed past her, semidisgusted that his response seemed to turn her on. Prison couldn't hold Rifter and Brother Wolf, and God knew humans had tried more than once over the last centuries.

He took in the human motorcycle gang and the pack of wolves who'd started their own version of Hells Angels, only far more deadly, and then his nose led him to the young woman sitting alone at the bar. She was doing shots and swaying to the music, and she'd caught the bikers' attention—human and wolf—neither of which was a good thing.

He knew immediately from the rumblings that she'd been here too long.

Typically, the wolves stayed among their own, but

lately, they'd been mixing it up with the locals, and that wasn't going over all that well with the weretrappers. This bar was owned and operated by a Were—but catered to humans as well. The thing was, most humans beyond the weretrappers didn't believe that Weres existed at all, and the Weres and the Dires had been able to pass as full human for as long as they could remember.

He could deal with a fight to get his blood going. But first things first. He moved next to her, watched her turn to him, look up at him. Her eyes widened—appreciation rather than fear, and yeah, what the hell?

"You're not in a good place," he growled over the music.

"I've got a seat at the bar—that's the best place," she told him, not slurring her words yet, but by the way she was motioning to the bartender, she'd find herself doing so soon enough.

She was human and he was drawn to her.

Making sure she's safe.

Right, because he was a goddamned Boy Scout. He didn't give a shit about humans—those who knew about the existence of Weres were either terrified or idiot groupies or hunting his kind. The wider the berth, the safer for all involved. But there was something that yanked him to her, a zing right to his cock that had him by her side, watching her lick the salt from her hand, down the tequila and suck on the lemon while staring at him with green eyes that were far from innocent.

"I'm Gwen," she said, her voice all hot and smoky sounding even though there wasn't a cigarette in sight. She leaned back and stared at him again and let a smile tug one corner of her lips.

"Rifter."

He knew she wanted to comment on the name, but she didn't. Instead, she reached out and played with a zipper on his black leather jacket, then let a long finger roam over the soft, smooth fabric. He could picture the black against her creamy skin.

"I want to wear this," she murmured.

"Later. Naked," he told her and she stared at him, her neck graceful, her body more so, and she looked like some kind of aristocrat, like she should be in a ballroom instead of here.

But she *was* here. There would be no female Weres for him tonight, even though more were already circling. He picked up on the low growls, because Dires never went for humans. Everyone was confused, and he was president of the club.

He expected this to be all over fucking Facebook within the hour. "I want to take you home," he emphasized, in case the naked part hadn't been enough of a clue.

Have to. Need to. Fuck, he felt like dropping to his knees and howling and it had *nothing* to do with the full moon.

She tilted her head and continued to study him.

"I'm not into anything beyond sex." Blunt for sure, but he had to make that clear.

A small smile played on her lips. "Don't worry—I won't be around long enough to stalk your tall ass."

"You're moving?"

"Dying." Rifter froze and she shrugged. "You're not going to let a little thing like that stop you from coming home with me, right?"

"You're joking."

"No, I don't joke about death. Well, that's not true—I'm a doctor—we have to. Gallows humor keeps us from getting too emotional."

"You're dying and so you've decided to pick up strange men in dangerous bars."

"It's like one of those bad game-show questions—if you found out you only had a short time left to live, what would you do?" She laughed but there was little humor behind it. "I have no idea what I want to do, besides not die."

She looked healthy to him—healthy and beautiful, with long blond hair, wearing leather, and she did fit in here, in a weird way. And Christ, he could think of nothing more he wanted to do than die, *I-fucking-ronic*, as Vice would say. "How long do you have?"

"At least through the night. And it's not catching," she added as an afterthought. "Are you worth it?"

He didn't know how the hell to answer that. So he did so truthfully. "Hell yes."

"Then let's go."

Rifter checked to see if Vice was hanging around, because women sometimes acted this way with his packmate, who was a walking ball of sin. But no, Vice was nowhere in sight and everyone was antsy.

Goddamned full fucking moon. Like a bitch with a whip.

He didn't bother to fight the urge to pick her up, and he slung her over his shoulder, caveman-style, grabbing her jacket off the back of her chair. He heard her startled, soft gasp, but she didn't protest as he walked out with her, daring any of the wolves to follow him.

They all knew what he was—they may not like him, but they sure as hell knew to respect his power.

When he got to his bike, he set her down and handed her the coat. Her hair tumbled over her shoulders, her black tank top had ridden up a little along her belly and her cheeks flushed from the cold. "Thanks for the ride."

"That was nothing."

She refused the helmet he offered, instead wrapping her arms around as much of his waist as she could, and off they went. Normally, he didn't give a shit about the icy roads, but his passenger wasn't as indestructible as he was. Though he gave the bike lots of gas, he didn't get stupid on icy corners and snowy shoulders. After a while, she was no longer holding on and had put her hands in the air, yelling into the wind. He went faster because it seemed to excite her.

When he stopped in front of her house, a pretty little Victorian in the middle of nowhere, she hopped off and he followed her as she walked up the path. Before she could get to the door, he took her arm and pulled her close and brought his mouth down on hers before he could stop himself. She tasted like sugar and cranberries—tart and sweet—and he wanted more. Wanted it all, and Brother Wolf seemed to agree, as he was ignoring the running in favor of letting Rifter take his time.

When he pulled back, her lips were swollen and she was breathing hard and he was glad about that. "Every guy in that bar wanted to take you home tonight. Why me?"

Her eyes flicked over him coolly. "You were the biggest."

He couldn't tell if she was joking.

Chapter 2

Gwen wasn't. He was huge. Really freaking huge—built like a brick shithouse, with long, shaggy dark hair, hard jaw, cut cheekbones and those eyes—holy hell, they were gorgeous. Gray and blue and black and brown, all speckled like a kaleidoscope that could pull her really far in.

She'd more than noticed him when he'd walked in—no, she'd felt him.

Rifter. Even the name tugged at her.

He wouldn't be gentle, and she was so tired of being treated carefully. She just needed to get through the next few hours without a seizure.

"Just give me a few minutes, okay?" she asked, and he nodded, his gaze raking over her as he stripped off his leather jacket and threw it across her couch. Looked between it and her, and my God, she already felt naked.

He made her already small house seem like it was made for dolls, but somehow, she'd fit against him surprisingly well, despite the height difference. Her lips felt well kissed and her body strummed in anticipation of more.

"Just a minute," she repeated and backed out of the room before she stripped down and jumped him. A little tequila and all her carefully held self-control obviously had disintegrated.

In the privacy of her bedroom, she downed a couple of extra pills, the newest in a long line prescribed by the neuro, but they wouldn't work. None of them ever worked for long, which was why she'd had to choose between med school and having a life. Well, more so than the average med student, because the damned seizures got in the way of everything and the meds made her stupid or silly or sleepy.

She was tempted to throw them away, but then functioning would be gone. She was already living with a death sentence, so why make it harder?

God, the morning's neuro appointment couldn't have been any worse. She'd demanded the truth and she'd gotten it.

"The seizures will kill you," he'd said. "You're close to OD'ing on the meds and they're not helping. The activity is everywhere. I've never seen anything like it."

The MRI film left little doubt: The length and increasing severity of each episode debilitated her—inside her brain was the perfect storm of electrical impulses.

"Feel free to use my case as a write-up," she'd told him, and the doctor's mouth had twisted in empathy and pain.

He'd been frank but not unsympathetic.

She'd gone straight to the bar from the consult.

Tomorrow, she'd go back to work for a twenty-four-hour shift because what else was she supposed to do? Stay in bed with this man for the next few weeks?

She peeked out at Rifter, the breadth of his back taking her breath away. The leather jacket lay on her couch and she shivered, thinking about the way she'd be wearing it.

There were definitely worse ways to go.

He was looking out the window, no doubt because there was nothing else to look at, unless he liked medical textbooks. For the first time, she saw her place through someone else's eyes and realized how stark it was.

The house was white walls, bare floors. Rented. Even the furniture wasn't hers. The linens were bought on the cheap—without much thought, at the closest store when they'd had a sale. Everything was disposable because she never wanted to get that attached to anything—or even anyone, something she admitted to herself only in moments of extreme honesty—again.

She didn't want roommates—didn't want to live in a dorm or an apartment with people. In the past years, being around them had made her feel crowded, like she wanted to jump out of her own skin.

No, the only thing that had given her peace over the past years had been her daily runs. Sometimes she went twice, if only to feel the freedom of the wind on her face, the road before her open, her feet flying across the ground.

She wondered what would happen if she simply continued running without looking back, running until she literally dropped.

She'd lost so much and now she was literally losing time, sand through an hourglass that slipped through her hands no matter how tightly she fisted it. And her house mocked her now, a blank slate, much like her life. She'd thrown herself into medicine, wanting a way to make people feel better in the way no doctor had ever really been able to help her.

At first, the seizures hadn't been an issue. They'd been well controlled, almost suppressed while she was growing up, but when she'd hit twenty-one, they exploded, and four years later they were daily occurrences. She'd been so good—slept as much as she could, ate well, exercised.

Being good was so overrated. No one ever looked back on their lives and thought, *Well, at least I was good.*

She'd bet even Mother Teresa had regrets about that.

And so, when she'd gone to the bar tonight, she'd been looking to feed those long-buried instincts, her nerve endings tingling as she'd downed the tequila, as if her body was thanking her for finally allowing it some enjoyment.

How long had it been for her? Felt like forever since she'd had to choose between medicine and men. She couldn't believe she was still a goddamned virgin.

She'd made her bed and now she was so ready to undo it and experience it all.

Funny thing—she didn't feel like a virgin. It was like her body knew what it needed, and now that she was finally giving in to that baser set of pleasures, it would guide her with touchstones every step of the way, starting with the man she'd brought home.

And so she went back out to Rifter. "Can I get you anything?"

"You." He tugged her to him without further preamble. She liked that—having spent her life dealing with logic and science, and with her disease these last years, it was wonderful simply to give in.

Tonight she'd worn black leather pants, boots and a tight black top and had felt more like herself than she had in a long time. But now she just wanted skin to skin—needed to strip all the clothes off and roll around with this man. She reached up to twine her hands in his hair, pulling his face to hers for a kiss.

He tasted better than any drug or drink—instant intoxication.

His hands skimmed her body, cupped her breasts and then lifted her shirt and broke the kiss to pull it off her. It flew over her head with a soft breeze as his hands cupped her ass, his arousal thick against her belly.

"Beautiful." His voice was husky, and for a minute she was sure she couldn't breathe, because he looked at her with such hunger . . . she'd never felt more wanted in her entire life.

She tilted her head up, sure he would kiss her again, or touch her breasts, take her pants off before she got more frantic, but he didn't.

Instead, he tilted his head, but only to look at her strangely. Narrowed his eyes and moved his hands from her ass to her waist, as if holding her up.

"I understand if you're freaked. But I'm not going to die in bed with you. At least I don't think so," she muttered.

"Death doesn't scare me."

"I suspect not much does."

He nodded his agreement but he still didn't move.

It took her another thirty seconds to understand why, and by then it was far too late to stop anything.

Brother Wolf caught the scent first—the bitter, cloying tang of trouble—and then Rifter smelled it as well. It was the odor of a shift from human to wolf form. But the shift wasn't his, and Rifter went on full alert, a low growl rumbling up from his chest. He tensed, prepared to bolt outside to find whatever stray wolf was prowling nearby, but a heartbeat later, Gwen collapsed in his arms and the scent dissipated.

Brother Wolf howled, wanted to pace restlessly, and it was then that Rifter understood.

Seizure. Shit, in all his years, had he really never been around a seizing human before to notice that a seizure smelled like a wolf shift? Quickly, he lowered her to the bed, kept her on her side facing him and watched her body struggle, fighting with itself for control. Gwen would hate him for witnessing this, but he couldn't leave her. And goddamn, that bothered the shit out of him, since he'd known this human for less than an hour.

He looked toward the night table, checked the drawer as he kept a hand on her and rifled through the pill bottles, wondering if any of these might help. But Brother Wolf was calming down a little now, and Rifter hoped that was a good sign.

She was still helpless—she probably hated that most of all.

The only thing he could do to comfort her was sometimes not a comfort at all. He had the ability to dreamwalk, which made him a sort of human dream catcher by default. He could hold someone's nightmare at bay or help them through it by absorbing the fear and pain.

His curse alternately freaked and pissed off the Dires, and the Weres who knew about it. But his pull was strong and there wasn't a whole hell of a lot his family of Dires could do about it when he would involuntarily walk through their dreams in order to capture their nightmares.

The pack hated being so vulnerable to him, hated that he was forced to carry all their fears, but that had been his ability since he'd been born. He'd learned to deal with the burdens he carried and the fallout that came with them.

As a child, he'd been confused by the ability, but as he got older, his mother explained, *It's a blessing*. It was only before his Running that he'd been told that he'd actually *been* cursed with the ability, not born with it, and that he'd never be free of it.

Still, it helped him to keep track of what was happening in his pack.

While Jinx didn't love it, he was used to it—his own born ability of being able to talk to ghosts and helping them pass over into the spirit world meant someone was always fucking with his mind, and he would typically tell Rifter to just *get the fuck out*.

Vice was usually too busy indulging in one of his vices to give a shit what Rifter did. The man was born with seven deadly sins rolled into one sinful-as-hell body that women and men—both human and wolf—couldn't get enough of. And although he couldn't be separated from the sins that ruled his life, his ability let him use those extremes to help others find their balance.

Stray's dreams were almost completely quiet—centered more on hiding and being caught—and Rifter often wondered if he had the power to block Rifter from them, but he never asked. No, Stray was jumpy enough, having been found fifty years earlier in some back alley. He'd been separated from the pack after what the Elders called the Extinction, when they had smote all living Dire wolves except for them during the Viking Age, and ended up nearly losing his mind from lack of pack company.

These days, he spent most of his time hanging at the house, listing to old-school eighties metal and keeping up with the latest technology. But man, Rifter would let Stray have his back during a fight any damned time.

If the man had an ability beyond being an immortal Dire, he hadn't let anyone in on it, although Rifter had his suspicions.

And then there was Rogue—Jinx's twin, who could contact spirits. Rogue, who'd been captured months earlier by the weretrappers, a group not unlike homegrown terrorists who wanted to experiment on Weres and Dires. Lately, there were rumors that the trappers planned to clone the Weres for some kind of superarmy to use for their own purposes.

The weretrappers were humans, but they'd made a deal with the witches—one of whom was Rifter's former best friend, Seb, and now the trappers had some powerful spells on their side.

The enemy of my enemy is my friend.

Rifter and the other Dires were charged with keeping the rest of the humans safe from the evil that could entail.

But he didn't want to think about Seb right now. Not when Rifter could close his eyes and still hear Rogue's howls in the night. They'd gotten him back, but not until terrible things had been done to him.

Rifter knew from personal experience what kinds of horrors the man and his wolf had endured. He'd been with Rogue that night six months earlier. Both had been captured and taken to separate cells. It took Rifter three weeks to escape and take Rogue with him.

By that time, the man was a shell of his former self.

Now Rogue remained in the attic of the house, as comfortable as they could make an immortal in a coma. Whether he would come out of it—and how he would be when he did—remained to be seen.

Rogue's mind was a terrifying blank, and Rifter couldn't get inside, no matter how hard he tried.

And then there was the one they rarely spoke of: Harm—aka Harmony—the Dire who could calm the masses or incite riots with his singing, who'd gone out on his own thousands of years earlier and most recently made a name for himself as the unpredictable superstar singer of a rock band and who now lived as a recluse. Rifter would rip his fucking head off if he ever found the man—rip it off every day for the rest of his miserable life for the danger he'd put all of them in.

Along with the six of them were the Weres they'd let into their Dire pack, mainly those who'd gone rogue from their own packs because they were too mean or rowdy or didn't follow direction well . . . or they were still moon crazed, like the young twins Jinx had taken under his wing.

They listened to the Dires. Had their backs. The Weres weren't nearly as strong as the Dires, but they were formidable powers in their own right.

And oh yeah, no female Dires, because there were none.

The female Weres they hung with as part of their group were cool, and they could handle the Dires moderately well, sexually and otherwise, if they weren't newly shifted. It took a hell of a lot for a Dire to be with a human. Rifter couldn't remember the last time he'd let that happen but suspected it was right after he'd shifted for the first time, the moon craze making him goddamned insane with lust and hunger, and Brother Wolf hadn't had any measure of control either. Slowly, the two of them pulled back, got some form of measured control and agreed to keep their shit together.

Brother Wolf tugged—rightfully so, because Rifter was encroaching on his time—but he couldn't leave Gwen now. She was still twitching, a restless combination of sleep and unconsciousness, and nowhere near peaceful. He remained firmly rooted in reality, not attempting to enter her dreams like he itched to.

The dreamwalking had become worse in the months leading up to his capture. Since Rogue's coma, it had only gone downhill. Rifter had always been able to control it, but lately, his own dreams had been stranger. He'd wake up speaking the old language, unable to remember where he'd been.

The dreams were draining him. He wasn't scared of anything, but they freaked him the fuck out.

Jinx did what he could to help keep the dreams at bay, which included the use of Native American dream catchers, while Rifter actively tried not to sleep. Much. And even though he'd promised Jinx and the others that he wouldn't do this because they couldn't be sure the new dreams weren't the insidious work of Seb and his witches, Rifter pulled off the dream-catcher necklace and put it around Gwen's neck instead. Then he prepared to put himself in a danger he'd sworn not to.

He closed his eyes, her hand in his large one, her skin soft and smooth and cool, and goddamn, it would feel good on his cock. But this wasn't about him, and he had nothing but time, so he could afford to be magnanimous.

He settled into a light sleep. The push into her subconscious wasn't effortless, which was strange, because in her state, there should have been no resistance.

But very few could resist him for long, especially humans.

Finally he broke through and began the dreamwalk — a combination of actually walking through the person's dreams and then influencing said dreams. A handy skill. Inside Gwen's dreams, he got sucked into a swirling mass of terror and confusion and . . . hope. Strange enough, there was more of that than anything.

Rifter didn't know how the hell it all worked, but somehow, with the dreamwalk, he was both by Gwen's side physically while his dream self walked with Gwen inside her mind.

In that dream state — suspended from the reality of her world — he took her away from the pain and fear and put his leather jacket on her, over her bra and underwear, even though she wouldn't really feel the cold, and holy Mother of God, she looked fine. He almost stayed on the bed next to her, but instead, he put her back on his bike . . . and because they were in the dream, he rode faster than he ever would with her in real life. She laughed, her hands in the air the way they'd been before, and the vibrations rang through both like a fever.

But Brother Wolf's needs were becoming increasingly

hard to ignore, what with the white round bitch hanging in the sky, and he needed to run. Had no choice but to take Gwen with him.

Rifter's skin tightened, and he didn't fight the change from man to beast. He reveled in it. Letting the wolf take over was sometimes the easiest thing in the world . . . would be so damned easy to let him take over full-time. And so he was now Brother Wolf both in Gwen's bedroom and in her dream, and Brother Wolf complied by keeping his paw on Gwen's hand to not break Rifter's way into her dream.

In the dream, though, Brother Wolf was free, and he stopped and howled, and Gwen was watching warily. He smelled the fear on her skin, watched her face pale and her mouth gape in a frightened O, because, yeah, Brother Wolf was a big, scary-looking motherfucker, although a hell of a looker too. He shook his head and the fur around his neck shifted, and then he bared his neck and howled, his way of telling Gwen she was safe, although she wouldn't know that. And obviously she didn't because just then she backed up and began to run from him.

He caught up to her and for a while they ran side by side, until he stopped smelling her fear . . . until he saw the smile on her face. Brother Wolf dusted up the leaves from the ground, and they swirled around their feet, crunching in the night. And when Brother Wolf sat, she even reached out—hesitantly—and patted his back.

He gave a contented whimper in response. Bastard.

It was after one in the morning when Brother Wolf conceded. Rifter stood naked in front of her as she lay on the forest ground on a blanket of old leaves untouched by the snow, thanks to the thick covering of trees. She could see pinpricks of moonlight coming from above, her body sated from the run. As she gazed at him as if he was the best thing she'd ever seen, it made him feel like beating his chest.

Father Wolf, Brother Wolf whispered in his ear.

His cock jutted out toward her, and in response she reached to unhook her bra and stripped it and her underwear and lay on the soft ground naked under the moonlight, waiting for him.

In the dream state, he was supposed to lead her through a higher reality, a place she couldn't get to herself. He wasn't supposed to gain pleasure from it, but he couldn't help himself, not when her nipples tightened into perfect buds the color of ripe berries, her breasts a little more than a handful. A perfect blond triangle between her legs.

She had a runner's body—lithe, long, finely muscled, and his hand dipped between her thighs, a finger exploring the wet heat. She would feel this to her core. Her hips already began to rock against his hand in response to his touch, her fingers moved across her belly and her body thrashed, this time for pure pleasure.

He couldn't remember wanting a woman this much. He wouldn't take her like this, felt bad about doing this to her, but judging by the length of her orgasm, she needed it.

She'd remember none of this—if she had a vague memory, she'd think it was a hot dream.

He'd remember everything and it would haunt him for a hell of a long time.

Chapter 3

Vice slammed into the bar, intent on finding the assholes who called themselves the outlaws and decided they could take over this town and fuck up the wolf thing. Stray was by his side, primed and ready for a beat-down.

Separately, they were terror—together, fearsome, shit-kicking Dire wolves whose existence was a mix of myth and truth. The full moon tugged at them, a terrible, awesome pull, and they were more than ready to shift. Overdue.

But the call had come in less then twenty minutes earlier, one of the local Were bartenders telling them about rumors of a fight brewing between two different werepacks. The weretrappers were circling, and it was up to the Dires, the fucking police of the Were world by default, to stop the trappers without getting themselves captured.

The Dires, especially Vice and Stray, had been hunting down the outlaw wolf pack for days. The Dires tried not to get too involved in the werepack wars, but when Linus, King Alpha of the New York City pack, called them back from Europe six months earlier, the Dires willingly came to help advise Linus and, if necessary, help quell the rebellion.

Of course, that's when Rifter and Rogue ran into their own trouble with the weretrappers.

Linus had been able to quiet things down since the Dires returned, but obviously not enough. The king had been murdered by his own once loyal wolves days earlier, and now chaos ensued. Manhattan was in an uproar and Linus's son was missing, rumored to have died at the hands of the same outlaw wolves.

But as far as Vice could see, there were no outlaws in the bar and everyone appeared to be at peace.

Well good for fucking them.

"There are twenty weretrappers out back," Stray reported as he stopped to smell the air, then muttered, "Suicide mission."

"I wish," Vice muttered, stomping ahead. "Just gonna hurt like hell, and in the end, we'll all still be alive."

"We've been wanted since what feels like the dawn of time—you'd think we'd be used to it by now," Stray grumbled.

Vice's eyes glowed. "Let me take care of them once and for all."

"Rifter'll kill you—just do what we came to do and let's get the hell out."

Stray was *never* any goddamned fun.

Then again, neither were the weretrappers, who were humans, armed to the hilt with all kinds of silver shit, which was deadly in large quantities to regular Weres but could do nothing but cause extreme pain to the Dires. They could fight through the pain—and would—but it would be far easier to avoid contact with the stuff to begin with.

The weretrappers targeted all wolves—especially the Dires lately—not to kill them, but to hold them for experimentation. The horrors they inflicted on wolves, the majority of whom stayed as far away from humans as they possibly could, were unspeakable.

Vice had seen some of them firsthand on both Rifter's and Rogue's bodies, and his gut twisted at the thought of what they'd gone through.

He just wanted Rogue to wake up, no matter what state he was in. Slept on the floor next to the man just in case. So it was for Rogue that Vice was on the rampage, out to destroy as many weretrappers as he could without getting himself caught or drawing too much human attention to the packs.

Howlers was packed to the damned rafters, just the way he liked it, with wine and women and various other vices that would for sure lead a man astray.

Vice *really liked* astray, so much so that his entire life had been molded around it. The music slammed through him — the smells of Were and sex and smoke and whiskey washed through his senses. When Stray turned back to him, his eyes had already changed.

Vice knew his had too. It was controllable, but here, where there was no need to control, he let something be goddamned easy. And when a stripper — Were — slid by him, tits against his chest, and he smelled her want, immediate and strong, he wanted nothing more than to pick her up, carry her to the back as she wrapped around him, telling him he'd be so amazingly good.

He would be too. Fact of life and breeding and many, many years of practice.

But Stray the killjoy simply shook his head, reminding Vice they were just cutting through the bar and not supposed to be enjoying themselves. But hell, turning it off was never that simple.

Misconduct, misbehaving and sin — yeah, those were a few of his favorite fucking things . . .

Vice made it his life's work that all the people he'd come in contact with found their favorites too, because what the hell was more fun than that? He was born to lead people astray, take them off the beaten path, travel the road not taken.

Den of iniquity was tattooed across his back because his entire being was one, along with the words *mayhem* and *deviant.* They didn't stop the women—and the men—from wanting him. The wolves all knew better and gave him a wide-as-hell berth. They didn't want to be pulled into his world of sin, and Vice knew it was better they weren't all in the damned gutter with him.

"According to Facebook, Rifter left the bar with a human." Stray was checking his iPhone as they pushed through the crowds. "Twitter confirms."

"I fucking hate social media." Vice lit another rolled cigarette, the wafting of the special blue smoke hovering around both of them like a heavy embrace. "No one can just fuck in private anymore."

"Rifter went home with a human and that's what you're worried about?"

"Ah, Stray, come on. Probably just a rumor." He stared up at the full moon, the pull that much stronger because of this time of year. Mating season made them all edgy and way too unfulfilled, even after hours of mind-blowing sex. They couldn't get everything they needed, and neither could their wolves, and that made for some very unhappy dual-natured creatures.

If Rifter had taken a human home, she was in big goddamned trouble. That made Vice smile. "Let's get this shit over with."

He looked through the small window on the heavy back door and saw the open, tree-covered field behind the bar. When he opened it, the smell of snow—and human—would be unmistakable. "They're out there."

"Shift?" Stray asked, sniffed the air himself, and, yes, that was certainly the best option. Much easier to let their wolves run wild and leave their faces a complete mystery.

They eased out the side door so as not to be spotted, and in the small alleyway, they stripped, left their clothes behind as they let the change take over their bodies.

There was the familiar creak of bones and stretch of skin as Vice allowed his Brother Wolf to take over, pushing him to all fours as he shifted from man to beast.

It wasn't pleasant, to say the least, but as his old Marine sergeant used to say, *Pain is just weakness leaving the body.*

Vice *really* liked the Marines.

And when the shift was complete, their wolves were far bigger than most Weres and regular wolves. When you looked at a Dire in any form, you knew you were looking at something that wasn't entirely of this world. It was the height, the build, but especially the eyes—Vice knew his looked silver when he changed, and they were nearly silver in human form.

Time to kick some ass.

But as their Brother Wolves bounded for the hills, their wolf vision sharper now, their huge paws punching silently through the snow, something other than the cold made their hackles rise. The scent of death hit Vice hard. Human. Lots of blood. His mouth watered, his lips peeling back from sharp teeth, but no, eating humans was not cool.

They both slowed to a trot, crouching in the underbrush, which caught on Vice's pure white fur—and yes, he understood the irony of that color being on him—and left burrs in Stray's shaggy black coat. Vice's sensitive ears twitched as he listened for movement, and when he heard nothing but the icy wind cutting through the pines, he rose slowly to his seven-foot height on two strong legs, and Stray joined him. At the sight ahead, neither wolf could stop from howling desolately into the night— a cry of both victory and frustration, because they knew they had to shift to human form now, even though the moon's hold was fierce.

And they did, the change back just as painful as the wolf retreated and the man returned, Vice finding himself still on all fours, shaking his head to stop the ringing that always remained for a minute or so after the change.

Finally, he got off his knees and stood next to Stray.

"This was a trap . . . and it wasn't for us," Stray said.

The men stood there naked, surveying the carnage. The weretrappers were dead—twenty humans, scattered along the ground—and there was an eerie silence along with the metallic scent of blood drifting through the air. "Gotta bury them."

"Before anyone sees," Stray finished his thoughts. "Call the twins."

But Stray was already doing so, calling forth the young Weres who'd gotten kicked out of their own pack for being moon crazed. Jinx had taken them under his wing, and subsequently they'd moved into the Dire house. They'd gained some semblance of control, but they were still both like lanky teenagers, their wolves barely contained.

Within minutes the young Weres came bounding up, identical to each other in both human and wolf form except for the color of their eyes—Cyd's green and Cain's amber, closer to yellow than brown, their dark hair short and messy, dressed like they'd walked out of Abercrombie & Fitch.

Tonight, they were thankfully still in human form, although they were restless. These young Weres would have a hard time keeping it together unshifted with the scent of violence so pungent. For Weres, the scent of blood was enough to drive them to shift, thanks to their prey instinct.

"Jinx is coming . . . whoa, what did you do?" Cain asked, staring up at the full moon like she was calling to him—which, of course, she was, while his brother, Cyd, remained characteristically silent and just went to work hauling the bodies into the woods.

"Definitely the work of a wolf," Viee said as he studied a body and then pulled up short because he smelled . . . a Dire, and it wasn't Stray. No fucking way. "Is the outlaw pack stupid enough to do this out in the open?"

"None that I've heard of," Stray said, and then they both stopped short when they heard a rustle behind them. One of the bodies was moving, the man attempting to get up.

"He's mine." The smell of the unknown Dire got stronger, and Vice could still feel Brother Wolf's incisors, and he bared them viciously as he went over to the man who'd just shifted from wolf, prepared to do lots of harm.

But when he caught sight of the face, everything changed, and he wasn't sure it was for the better.

Harm.

All the Dires had been hunting this particular Dire wolf for years—and for good damned reason.

Harm mumbled something. The silver had done a number on his ass and they'd have to get him back to the house before they could get anything resembling an explanation as to why he'd taken on the weretrappers himself—why he'd led them into this homemade trap to begin with . . . why he'd let his fellow wolves down.

Harm was the reason Rogue had gotten captured.

Stray was next to Vice, a blur, half changed and howling, and Vice had never seen him so worked up, not while awake, anyway. The nightmares did a number on him, but Vice and the others were always quick to wake him, mainly to stop his screaming.

Vice heard his own Brother Wolf growl and knew he was in real danger of losing it, found his hand wrapped around the back of Harm's neck as he brought his face forward to rip out his goddamned throat . . .

"He's mine." It was Jinx, yanking Vice out of the way and baring his own teeth to Harm as the man struggled to stay on his feet. "When you're healed, brother, we're going to fight and you're going to be the first fucking Dire wolf to die and stay dead. And that's a motherfucking promise."

Chapter 4

Brother Wolf was tugging at him before the sun came up. Rifter reluctantly pulled his hand from Gwen's and his mind from her dreams and covered her with a blanket. She was calm now, satiated, if the small smile she wore as she slept was any indication, and Rifter had more pent-up sexual energy than he knew what to do with.

But Brother Wolf wasn't tugging for his run—no, something was happening there. It took Rifter a second to realize that Brother Wolf had set Father Wolf chomping at his heels.

It was the second time his wolf had brought up that goal in less than twenty-four hours.

"Not. Happening," he told his wolf, who bit out a howl so fierce, Rifter's eardrum ached.

It's already happening, Brother Wolf argued. Brother Wolf should know better than that, and Rifter told his wolf to shut it.

For maybe the first time ever, their goals were in opposition to each other, and neither liked it.

You like her, Brother Wolf told him, and Rifter couldn't argue, so he didn't. He didn't want to leave her, but both he and Brother Wolf knew that daytime and

Dires didn't mix all that well. No, they were better suited to nighttime, when it was easier to fight the weretrappers and avoid the law.

The Dires were too well-known and unmistakable to even try to hide themselves in human form from the Weres, although Stray was a tech wiz who made sure to either pull down pictures of the Dires that ended up online or alter them to avoid detection. Now, thanks to Sebastian's pact with the trappers, many of the humans knew what Rifter and Rogue really looked like, but the others were safe.

It just meant that Rifter had to be more careful—but he refused to have the other Dires bodyguard him, like they had right after he'd escaped with Rogue. He had his own set of tricks—plus strength—and it would take a hell of a lot for them to fell him again.

Now he left his jacket behind because Gwen was still wrapped in it and she looked damned fine. He noted her hospital badge by the front door near her keys. Doctor Kadlin.

A dying doctor. Talk about irony.

He stroked a thumb over her picture—how she managed to look sexy and serious at the same time was a mystery to him. He glanced back toward the bedroom and put the ID back down, then slid out the back door. When he checked his phone, he saw several messages from Stray. Important flagged ones that all but demanded he check in.

The only dreams he'd felt tugging at him last night had been Rogue's, which meant the others hadn't slept yet. Normally, that wouldn't mean much—they were as much creatures of the night as vampires, although both Dires and Weres could go outside in daylight with no ill effects.

It was one of the major reasons the weretrappers focused on them for their experimentation and not the vampires. Sometimes Rifter wondered about creating an alliance with the vamps, but, like wolves, they were an insular group that didn't trust easily.

After the betrayal of the witches, Rifter didn't either.

But no sleep coupled with the messages meant something.

Or it could just be that you were spotted with a human.

A human he'd wanted with a desire that burned through him like a goddamned house on fire.

He pushed the bike faster down the icy road, felt the wheels spinning and didn't care. His breath came in clouds that flew past his face, and he remembered the feel of Gwen's arms around him as he drove her home last night.

He was an idiot. He could've hurt her.

Dires were not gentle—never had been, never would be. It was the reason they didn't hang with humans—especially females—any more than they could help it.

Last night, inexplicably, he couldn't have helped it. When he'd thought about how close he'd been to taking Gwen in the leaves. Claiming her. Fucking her . . .

His cock throbbed and Brother Wolf was growling, and he pulled his bike into the woods, where he could hide it easily when he shifted and ran. Both needed this outlet, because the dreamwalk had served only to heighten his arousal instead of taking the edge off.

"You have an hour before the sun comes up," he muttered, stripped impatiently, the cold no more an annoyance on his skin.

The flakes that hit him caused steam to rise from his body. His temperature was always warmer, his metabolism more wolf than human, but even by wolf standards, he was overheated.

You let a human do this to you. He'd been wrapped and twisted up in Gwen until he couldn't think straight.

Usually, after he'd been with someone, the clawing lone-liness was worse. Hell, it was worse when he was with them most of the time.

With Gwen, the loneliness had been gone.

She was dreaming—none of that was reality.

Except for him—the dreamwalking was always and only real just for him.

He could still smell Gwen on him, even though the cold wind should've whipped her scent away. He put his clothes and the keys in the back, combo-locked compartment of the bike. And then he tugged his cock a few times, hard pulls because he needed that.

The pain after orgasm would mingle with that of the shift, and then he'd revel in the loss of control while Brother Wolf took the reins.

He'd wanted to taste her, the urge to dip his tongue to her sex almost unbearable. He'd settled for his hand because he was too worried about her human status.

He was afraid if he did more, he wouldn't be able to stop, and that had never happened to him, as he held himself to a control that was almost brutal. Pleasure was supposed to hurt—the fine line between it and pain was something he'd learned as a young boy, and later, as his wolf emerged, it became all balled together until it was impossible to pick it apart.

Last night had been worth the howling, tight pain that seared through his cock when he hadn't allowed himself to come. This morning, it was impossible to ignore.

He caught his dick in a left-handed, steady rhythm, threw his head back and closed his eyes. As he stroked, he thought about her . . . found himself in her dream again much too easily. And she was watching him. Strok-ing herself in time with him, her legs spread, underwear half down and fingers playing along her sex, a smile on her face.

God, she was beautiful, her body ripe and ready, no shame on her face like you might see on a typical human in her position.

Everything inside of her was blooming—she was opening for him like a hothouse flower, smelled like the dianthus that bloomed every spring in his old village in Norway. As a young boy, he would run through the fields there, the flowers' scent rich and spicy, the fragrance stronger at night, and he'd think about who his mate might be. Now those thoughts mingled with his desire as he pushed himself to the brink of climax along with Gwen.

Gwen roused with her hands between her legs, her body shuddering from a powerful orgasm that made her belly tighten with absolute pleasure. The aftershocks kept her muscles pulled tight, and she whimpered as the blanket grazed her exquisitely taut and tender nipples. She'd come hard, and Rifter had been watching her—she'd been so sure of it, could almost feel his hot gaze raking her mainly naked form even as she shifted from sleep to consciousness.

You're going insane.

Or just dreaming. She blinked several times, realized she was breathing as if she'd just had actual sex. She moved her hand from her sensitive flesh and let herself revel for several minutes in the completely satiated state.

The goal was to have a man do that for you.

Hadn't he, though? She could smell Rifter on her, his scent filling the room, intoxicating her again.

Black leather and underwear half off, bra unsnapped. God, if she wasn't humiliated enough, she had to find a way to give the man's jacket back.

Maybe. Or maybe she'd keep it to masturbate in.

Yes, definitely insane.

Her radio alarm blared in her ear. She reached out and shut it quickly, and as the orgasm faded, she realized her body was sore and her head ached from the strange dreams. No doubt Rifter had left at the first sight of her falling to the floor and thrashing around.

But he'd put her on the bed, left her in his jacket, which meant either that he was giving it to her or that he'd be back for it. God, he could've done anything to her when she'd been in that vulnerable a state. And maybe he had.

She closed her eyes and remembered running. Remembered his hands all over her—she'd had several orgasms before this last one; she was sure of it.

And the wolf . . . don't forget the wolf.

No, it was just a dream. Her sex drive had kicked into overdrive these past months. The seizure meds were known to suppress libido, but somehow, they were having the opposite effect on her.

It was almost embarrassing, although she suspected that if she'd been a man it wouldn't have been that bad.

God . . . *wolves.*

She needed to get to work—and fast—before her imagination drove her crazy.

She turned her head toward the clock and heard a soft crunch. She sat up and stared at the leaves on her pillow, touched them as though they were a hallucination and might not actually be there. But one crackled in her hand, and she stared at it before crumpling it in her fist and letting the pieces fall back onto the sheets.

Chapter 5

Rifter came with a howl that echoed through the darkness, staggered forward and rested his head against the nearest tree trunk as he was abruptly yanked from Gwen's dream.

And back to reality.

He breathed deeply, his body shuddering, the orgasm twisting him inside out, his nails raking the bark as the ecstasy mixed with agony—not nearly as bad as it was with actual sex, but not nearly as satisfying either.

Gwen was awake and his connection to her was efficiently broken. As it should be.

There was a danger inherent in dreamwalking—not wanting to come out of the dream at all, because it was easier to live someone else's dreams than his own life. But this felt different, like she'd walked into his fantasy. Which wasn't possible.

A growl from inside his head reminded him that he owed his wolf. Brother hadn't gotten what he needed the night before, although he'd had fun. And so he gave the word to Brother to take over, let the shift begin.

It felt no different than it had every other time except the first three, which were by far the worst and most dangerous. Only half the Dires survived the intensity of those early changes, and Rifter had gone to a lot of funerals as a young boy.

Letting your Brother Wolf out was something to be revered and feared. Those who made it through the transition were stronger than they could have ever hoped to be.

The shift was a nearly indescribable combination of bones crunching and skin stretching, and an uncontrollable howl left his throat as an invisible weight pushed him hard to all fours. Brother Wolf whispered the ancient language in his ear to calm him as his breath caught and stopped for a moment during the worst of the change.

And then it was done. Less than thirty seconds from start to finish, and it felt at times like an eternity.

Rifter let his wolf travel into the deep darkness of the morning in the woods. He rushed past the life stirring, off the main paths, jumping and running and stretching muscles. These woods were not his natural hunting grounds, but reality—and his brothers—would interrupt him too soon if he ran closer to home.

Brother Wolf ran until Rifter stopped thinking, until they'd merged as one beautiful, primal beast, predatory and sleek, built for extremes—and for battle. The smell of pine and snow, the pull of the moon readying to give up her throne to daylight, all mixed in his nose as he sped along the slick forest floor, hunting for something he could never find.

But Brother Wolf would never give up.

It was nearly time to turn back. Brother Wolf sensed the incoming daylight, his signal, but instead of doing so, he suddenly stopped short and froze.

Danger.

Before he could turn tail, an arrow whizzed past his head, narrowly missing his ear. He ran a little farther until he found a spot to squeeze through the brush and cut around silently, ending up behind the woman who'd tracked him.

Both he and Brother had been too distracted to notice she'd been following him. Tracking him, really. But now they could see the axe in her hand.

Weretrapper.

Brother growled behind her and she whipped around, brandishing the weapon as she ran toward him.

Bold. And stupid. She swung and he ducked, weaved his massive body around hers easily, because Brother Wolf was sleek and strong. And angry.

She dropped the axe and pulled a syringe out of her pocket, and that was all it took for Rifter to flash back to being held captive by the weretrappers. Brother Wolf sensed the anxiety and struck, biting into the hard muscle of her thigh, bringing her to the ground with a hard back-and-forth shake of his powerful head, even as she managed to jab a syringe into his side.

And then he spat her to the ground even before he felt the tingle from the drugs.

Witch. They tasted different, and while Brother Wolf liked rare as a rule, he didn't like witch at all.

Trap, Rifter told Brother Wolf sharply when he went to grab her. *Let her go—good wolf,* Rifter urged, and Brother never wanted to be caged again and so he listened.

She was a young one—they were being recruited before they were even out of high school now—and Rifter needed to kill her. But she wasn't alone—he could smell both weretrapper and witch on the wind, and he couldn't fight as well with drugs on board. Drugs and wolves didn't mix—wolves metabolized differently, and in larger doses drugs could be fatal. They had been what kept Rifter and Rogue prisoners. There was no way the weretrappers would've been able to hold them as long as they did otherwise.

Modern medicine was fucking the Dires royally. They used to have to worry only about silver ill. When he was captured, his body had thankfully gotten used to the massive quantities of drugs they'd injected him with.

He would have to let her go now and find her again by the scar she'd wear. The bite of a Dire couldn't be healed by a witch's spell. Rifter had made sure of that years earlier. Seb wasn't the only one who could cast spells.

Run, he commanded Brother Wolf, and he did, fast and strong, while the girl couldn't do more than hobble in the other direction, where Rifter saw a car parked close to where his Harley was hidden. He'd have the twins pick it up later, if the trappers didn't take it. The agitation began to mix with sluggishness as Brother Wolf navigated the still-dark woods easily, his pace slower than it had been earlier, even as Rifter urged him along.

He breathed the winter's air deeply to try to clear his head. Gwen's scent called to him—carried along the wind—as if she could heal him, which was ridiculous, but he was in no position to fight it.

He needed to get somewhere safe to sleep off these drugs, so he sent the wolf toward Gwen's—the closest safe haven he could think of. It was a struggle to keep the big wolf moving, but he managed.

He ended up in the back of Gwen's house fairly quickly and without incident.

Not followed. His wolf stumbled hazily, and his brothers in arms would kill him for being so foolish.

But what was the point of living if all he could do from now on was hide in the house on the hill that was spelled to keep the weretrappers out?

Rifter shifted back—barely able to do so with the drugs running through his system. His human form would absorb them better than his wolf's, and he jerked the needle from his side and shoved it into his pocket.

He watched and waited until Gwen's car pulled out from the garage about ten minutes later, a good thing, since he wasn't prepared to explain why he was like some kind of giant, naked Goldilocks and the Big Bad Wolf huffing and puffing combined, prepared to crash in her bed.

Her back door was disturbingly easy to unlock.

He was shivering as he went toward the bedroom. Brother Wolf was already out, unable to guard him while he slept. Rifter felt the steam from Gwen's recent shower still hanging, rich and fragrant, in the air, and their scents still mingled on her sheets. He pushed his jacket aside, curled up on her pillows with the leaves around him, and remained in a daze, unable to fully lose himself in a deep sleep.

He thought he'd be pulled into one of the Dires' dreams, but *still*, none of them had slept. That made for some fucking cranky wolves, and cranky wolves snapped easily. And hard. They'd no doubt remained up waiting for him, and none of his Dire brothers would be happy at this turn of events. Because Harm had deserted them, Rifter was their king—leader of this last remaining Dire pack—whether he wanted to be or not. And the Elders had made it clear that it was his brothers' duty to protect Rifter. They'd used the word *serve* too, but Rifter would have none of that. The remaining Dires were all alphas because at one time, each of them had been destined to lead his own pack. They willingly submitted to Rifter and Rifter alone out of respect.

They'd tried the separate-pack thing for a while, each Dire heading up a werepack, but it wasn't right. The balance was always off, and eventually the men found their way back to one another.

Five alphas under the same roof got tricky. They managed as well as they could, but all of them bore the scars from fights with one another.

Those were the only scars a Dire couldn't heal.

The Elders had put him in charge of a group of men who could damned well lead themselves—and filling Harm's shoes . . . well, it had pushed that wolf to go far off into the wild blue yonder when it was first suggested to him. Harm was never comfortable with his wolf—he related to humans, and given the first opportunity, he melded into that population when he and Rifter and the others were on their official Running, and he'd never looked back.

That happened when they were all twenty-one years old and newly shifted. Since then, Rifter and the others had all worked together to help the Weres, who were something like distant, more primitive cousins.

The wolf and his shifted male counterpart had too big of a disconnect for Rifter's tastes. Then again, so did humans and their inner beasts.

For humans, pleasures were guilty. In Rifter's eyes, that was the path to hell.

Humans were afraid of everything that wasn't like them. Sheep, lemmings. While he'd been told by the Elders that he should pity rather than despise humans, his experiences were too colored by the antics of the were-trappers.

Which had been born because of the excesses of his kind—his pack had been the ones that massacred the humans that would later form the trappers. Hello, circle of life.

Yeah, that was the rub for sure.

Chapter 6

Gwen still couldn't explain the leaves, and so she'd left them on the pillow for no other reason than she wasn't sure they weren't a figment of her imagination. She'd left the leather jacket there too, showered quickly and headed out, because exhaustion rode her and she was simultaneously nauseous and starving.

She had nothing in the house and stopped at the deli outside the hospital to order two egg sandwiches. Large iced coffee. Two brownies.

That should hold her for a couple of hours. But no matter how much she ate, she couldn't get her weight or energy up.

The ER was still bustling, which was never a good sign at five in the morning. Ever since the gangs had taken hold, the ER had been on constant overflow. Good for business, bad for the town.

"Leftovers from last night's full moon," one of the other third-year residents told her when she was barely three steps inside. He mimicked a vampire-fanged face. "Effing crazy."

God, she hated people who couldn't bring themselves to say the word *fuck* whenever they felt like it. "I think the moon brings out *wolves*," she said, and yeah, speaking of crazy, she was giving an awesome display and she was the president of crazy town. She'd fit right in.

She polished off the second egg sandwich and gulped the coffee, shoved the brownies in her pocket for sooner, rather than later, and attempted to head to the back room, where the lockers were.

Maximarius, aka Max, a nurse with a sleeve of intricate tribal tattoos and a face that made most of the male patients—and several female ones—fall into immediate lust, stopped her, took Gwen's bag and jacket from her hands and pointed. "Curtain three."

Gwen took a deep breath and realized she could taste the smells—the metallic taste of blood filled her senses, but above it all remained Rifter's scent. Spicy, clean … slightly smoky. For a second, she caught sight of trees and smelled the pine—and panic—and she wasn't in the sterile hospital environment any longer, her skin simultaneously hot and cold, and she shivered when a hand touched her arm.

"Hey, Doc, wake up—curtain three," Max said gently. Gwen looked around cautiously, saw the front desk and no trees, and things were back to normal.

Yeah, right. "Sorry—didn't get a lot of sleep last night. What's up?"

"She says it's a dog bite, but it doesn't look like that to me," Max said, a brow raised before Gwen pulled back the curtain to survey the at most eighteen-year-old with short dark hair and a quizzical look in her eyes. She wore her own shirt, her bloodied jeans in the corner, her legs covered by a paper scrub with the wound exposed to the air.

It was *not* a dog bite. She could tell that from several feet away, looking as she washed and dried her hands.

"When did this happen?" Gwen asked, moving forward. She sat on the stool and got up close and personal as she stretched gloves over her hands.

"About an hour ago. I don't have insurance."

Gwen would have to sew the muscle inside first and then try to make the flayed skin stitch up. If not, the young woman would need surgery. She glanced at the chart and saw that the patient was named Cordelia Smith.

She spoke briefly about the possibilities, of calling in Plastics to minimize the scarring, but Cordelia was shaking her head from the get-go.

"No surgery. Do the best you can with the stitches."

Most girls wouldn't want a huge scar on their thigh. But Cordelia shrugged, didn't appear to be in much pain. Gwen checked through the blood tests Max had attached to the chart, which all showed no presence of drugs, illegal or otherwise.

A high pain tolerance was one thing, but this was simply odd.

There was already an IV set up with antibiotics. Gwen shot Cordelia's thigh with lidocaine, and as she waited for it to numb out, she asked, "Do you know what did this? Because otherwise, you'll need rabies shots."

"I know."

"Look, between you, me and the wall, I know this isn't a dog bite. It's too big and deep—it looks like a wild animal tore into you. And rabies isn't something to fool around with."

"No shots," Cordelia insisted.

"Maybe you don't understand—there's no cure for rabies once you get symptoms."

"I get it. Don't worry your pretty little head over it, Gwen."

Gwen stared at Cordelia as an odd anger surged in her, caught herself fisting her hands like she was going to haul off and hit her. "Dr. Kadlin," was all she bit out, and she saw Cordelia clench her own teeth.

She pushed back off the stool and left the curtained area for a minute, using the time to both cool down and call Psych in. Gwen couldn't live with herself if someone didn't talk this chick into a series of rabies shots.

She downed a brownie before she finished the phone call, pretty sure the doctor on call wasn't appreciating her talking with her mouth full, but Gwen didn't give a shit. She went back inside the curtain, washed and gloved up again and set to work on stitching Cordelia up as best she could.

"Where were you when you got bitten?"

"The woods by the park on Central," Cordelia said. Her nails were short, painted black. She looked goth, had the tattoo of a pentagram on the inside of her wrist, and Gwen felt the anger dissipate as she remembered how young the girl was. Even when Gwen was eighteen, she'd never been young.

Those woods backed up to Gwen's house. There had been reports of gang and drug activity running through there. "It's not safe to be walking through Central alone these days."

Cordelia bristled again. "I know. That's why I was there—I'm part of a take-back-the-night movement."

"What are you taking it back from?"

"Monsters. Don't you know that this town is full of them?"

Gwen glanced up at her—she was so serious . . . so young. "Are you sure this group is on the up-and-up?"

"Yes. Are you interested in joining? Because I can get you in."

"No, thanks. I do my part taking back the night here." She'd gotten the bigger stitches in the muscle done—now it was time for the more delicate work while the numbing medicine she'd given earlier was still doing its job keeping Cordelia from feeling the pain.

"Not with the guy you were hanging out with last night."

Gwen forced herself not to react, since she felt Cordelia's eyes boring into her. Instead, she did a few more loops before she answered calmly. "Why are you so interested in me?"

"He's part of a gang."

Gwen could believe that—the bar she was in last night was a known biker hangout. But there was a sharp edge to Cordelia's tone, and Gwen barely looked up from her work. "Is he your ex or something?"

She snorted and shifted. "As if."

"Stay still."

"He's bad news."

"Most men are," Gwen muttered, refusing to look at Cordelia, seriously creeped out that this girl might've been spying on her at the bar last night.

"I thought doctors were supposed to know better than to let strange men into their beds."

Breathe, Gwen. She was sure there was at least one cop in the ER she could call in here to scare the shit out of this girl for stalking her. She chose not to answer, continued stitching until she had a row of black thread Plastics would be proud of.

But Cordelia wasn't giving up. "Do you know what this is for?" she asked, shoving her wrist with the pentagram in Gwen's face.

Gwen pushed back slowly on the stool and stood. "It's a symbol of purity—it represents the five elements."

"It's protection against monsters." She touched Gwen's hand and Gwen pulled away as if she'd been burned, a strange rustling in her ears as Cordelia began to chant, *"'The pentagram prohibits thee? Why, tell me now, thou Son of Hades, if that prevents, how cam'st thou in to me? Could such a spirit be so cheated?'"*

Gwen rubbed her wrist, fought a momentary light-headedness she attributed to a sugar rush. "What's your game?"

"Just looking out for you."

"Look out for yourself." Gwen's hackles rose—her voice didn't sound like hers—but Cordelia didn't look frightened. Instead, she smiled, which sent chills down Gwen's spine. She finished up the stitches but called Max in to do the aftercare.

God, she was twitchy as anything. The missed morning run, the lack of sex, the dreams . . . now she was losing it with patients. She left the room without a backward glance and got caught up in the remaining sound and fury of her shift.

One of the Dires had most definitely taken a bite from Cordelia. It was more massive a wound than a Were would've produced—and having been bitten on more than one occasion, although thankfully never by a Dire, Max recognized the differences immediately. That the Dire had let Cordelia go had been a stroke of luck for her . . . or a carefully planned thing on the part of the Dire.

Max wished to hell the Dire had simply ripped Cordelia's throat out instead, as she'd spent an hour avoiding the witch in curtain three like the plague—the woman made the hairs on the back of her neck stand up, and getting into a fistfight in the middle of her shift wouldn't allow her to keep this job. Besides, Cordelia had requested time alone with Gwen, and Max wanted to stay as far away from that as she could.

But when Gwen had called her in, she had little choice but to respond.

"You spooked her," Max said to Cordelia now as she bandaged up the careful stitches Gwen had given her.

"All part of the plan."

Max finished the dressing in silence and then stood. "You're all done here."

"Actually, I'm not. But I know you'll call me when necessary."

Max stared at Cordelia, wondering what lay underneath the facade. Her mind scrambled for a way to get out of this, even as she knew that would be impossible.

Cordelia seemed to know that. Maybe she knew everything, which scared Max more. This could all be a double cross, and Max would have no way of knowing until the end.

Cordelia pressed her for an answer. "I thought you wanted to remain free."

Max's stomach twisted . . . would she do this to Gwen? To be spared from the witches and clutches of the weretrappers who'd killed the wereking and his son . . .

She nodded and lowered her voice as she handed Cordelia a piece of paper she'd been holding on to for days. "Gwen's shift lasts until eight. Here's her car's make and license. If anything changes, I'll alert you."

She waited until Cordelia exited the ER before she locked herself in the bathroom and threw up.

When Max asked her to sign off on Cordelia's chart a few hours later, Gwen knew Psych hadn't gotten around to her. Cordelia would've been long gone anyway, and Gwen couldn't say she was too sorry about it.

"She didn't even wait for a script for her antibiotics," Max explained, and Gwen pushed the girl and the guilt out of her mind and continued her shift with a single-mindedness that would've impressed the hell out of the head of the ER if she hadn't seized in the middle of a late-afternoon case.

When she woke on a stretcher in a curtained room, she was a little fuzzy. Max was there, told her, "We gave you pheno to bring you out—longer than five and you don't react well to Valium."

Gwen had told Max about her allergies and her illness because their schedules seemed to mesh, and the nurse had certainly looked after her. "So I can drive, then, right?"

"Yup. Your shift's over, lady." Max gave her a tight smile and handed her a letter. "The attending doc asked me to give you this. Said it's not only about today."

Gwen took it and nodded. She didn't have to read the letter to know what it said, but she would anyway.

"Are you going to fight it?" Max handed her a ginger ale and Gwen gulped it, realized her stomach was rumbling again.

"I have a month to live. I'm done fighting," she told her and didn't get any argument, just a piece of paper with a phone number on it.

"Call me anytime," Max said, put her hand on Gwen's shoulder and gave a light squeeze. "You're a kick-ass doctor—I don't care if you don't have the piece of paper to prove it yet."

Yet. She wanted to laugh but she couldn't because she appreciated the sentiment.

"There's no need to rush out of here—stay until the IV fluids are done," Max told her, and she nodded. The second the nurse left the room, Gwen pulled the needle out, tossed it and opened the letter.

She'd assumed she'd work here until she couldn't. But the notice telling her she was deemed medically unfit to continue her residency made her want to scream and cry at the unfairness of it all.

And so she did both. Crumpled the paper but knew she couldn't rail at it as unjust, because the hospital's decision made sense.

She was medically unstable, which put the hospital at

further risk for malpractice claims. Maybe she was even emotionally unfit depending on the day, but what was she going to do for the rest of her short life? Time would slowly tick away, and God, she needed to get out of here. Travel. Stay busy.

She was starving. Angry. Restless.

Max had put her bag and jacket in the room with her, and now Gwen rifled through and found her prescription bottles.

She emptied them, one after the other, into the toilet and flushed. No more attempting to slow an unyielding process, no matter how terrifying the outcome was that loomed over her.

She felt gloriously, oddly free.

You have no ties to anyone or anything.

Her aunt always told her to look for signs to guide her along the way, and while Gwen had pretended she didn't believe in that, she did. But she followed a path because she wanted to help sick people.

Now she was one of those people.

She had no real friends in the residents here. Max would be concerned, and maybe Gwen would call her in a few days so she wouldn't worry.

But first, she walked away, out of the hospital and away from her illness.

Maybe she'd go back to the bar.

Or maybe she'd go home, strip down, put on the leather jacket and dream about Rifter and wolves and running again until the leaves covered her bed.

Chapter 7

The dream seized Rifter almost immediately, and he was in no condition to fight it or the sleep that dug him in deeply to this almost supernatural realm. He prayed that he'd end up in one of his brothers' minds—he could even handle Vice's twisted thoughts—but no. He was walking through a scene he recognized, but he was seeing it through someone else's eyes.

He recognized the old country immediately, the place where he'd grown from boy to wolf. He heard the music, noted that the full-moon celebration was in full swing.

At first, the familiar pull of the party made him smile as he walked through his village. The smell of the earth comforted him—fresh, fertile, showing signs of life, of mating. The music had a pounding beat, was as hot as the air. Most of the males were bare chested, the women in short dresses. Married or not, this night was all about mating. Procreation, flirtation.

He was aroused as female bodies brushed his, cool palms on his warm skin. He let the fingers skim his back. He wanted to stay, to dance ...

The screams started almost instantly. Hands fell away from his body, confusion reigned and he pushed through the crowd, which seemed to be running at him and away from an invisible enemy. The chaos made his head spin—although he was used to the heat of battle, this was one neither he nor any Dire could ever win.

But still, he wouldn't give up. He roared but didn't shift. Saw other men and women and children he recognized, grew up with, dropping to the ground, bleeding.

He swung his sword and his shield around wildly, seeing no one responsible for the destructive massacre surrounding him.

He was used to being in control—a warrior in charge of any situation. But the brutal force cast its dark shadow over him . . . and then he was running for his life. He looked back, tripped clumsily. Looked down, and the horror rose inside of him as he saw the bodies littering the ground. He willed himself to shift and couldn't, which was always the most terrifying part of all.

This isn't real; this isn't goddamned real . . .

He clawed the earth in his struggle. Invisible nails mauled him, ripped his chest, blood seeping warm and sticky on his skin.

There was no escape. He heard a voice come from his mouth—thin and reedy—begging for his life to an unseen enemy.

Not your voice . . . but whose?

He waited for it to end, for him to lie still on the cold earth. To feel the emptiness inside.

Waited for the dream to end. But something was different this time. He was . . . rising. He smelled burning incense, heard chanting, so loud he covered his ears. Bodies of other Dires rose around him, ghosts of their former selves and still wearing their most recent battle wounds, marched forward, dragging him with them. It was mass confusion.

It was hell, one he couldn't escape from. He still struggled to break free, and then, finally, the ghosts glided past him and he remained behind, still suspended from reality. One of the ghosts turned to him, took his shoulders and shook. *Save us, Rifter,* it said before floating away.

Rifter tried desperately to get out of this nightmare, found his feet on firm earth, and he ran in the opposite direction, looking for a way out. Instead, he found himself in Gwen's mind—a swirling mass of confusion and pain as well, but more manageable for him. She was in trouble—and she was pissed too. Another seizure—or maybe it was something more, because he could swear she was awake.

Either way, she needed his help. Whether she'd want it was another story.

His eyes shot open, and the harsh wheeze sprang from his throat and echoed through the room. He put a hand to his heart even though the steady throb rang in his ears.

The Native Americans thought that if you died in your dreams, you died in real life. For him, no such luck, although every single time before this when he'd had this particular dream, he did die on the ground in his old village. Since the ending of the dream segued into trouble for Gwen, he knew he had to help her.

He was also planning on never sleeping again.

"Where's Rift?" Stray called through the door when Vice paced for the nine thousandth time in front of the room where Harm was being held.

"Still not answering his goddamned phone." Vice's body was tight with frustration. The sun had risen and Rifter hadn't bothered to check in. The rest of them, plus Cyd and Cain, were holed up here safely. The house was spelled, unbreakably so, a gift from Seb to Rift before things got all kinds of fucked up.

Vice rested his forehead against the doorjamb and

wondered if Harm had stirred at Stray opened the door and assured him, "Harm's still out cold."

Vice blinked, and shit, he hadn't spoken out loud, had he? He didn't think so, and Stray looked confused too, but Vice didn't have time to delve into it because it was late afternoon and all they had to show for it was a text from Rifter from hours earlier saying that he was busy.

Yeah, *busy* with a *human*.

"How long do you think Harm'll stay down for?" Stray asked. "How do we know if he's faking it?"

"We'll know. But silver poisoning's a bitch." Harm had stopped mumbling minutes after they'd found him behind the bar and then sank into unconsciousness when Stray took him over his shoulder to carry him back here. Jinx had wanted to drag him by his dick but had listened to Stray and backed off. Eventually.

"Jinx tried to sneak in the window and cut his legs off," Stray said matter-of-factly.

That was exactly why Stray was watching over Harm. Although Stray was just as angry, he was by far the more tempered of the men and their wolves. And Rifter would most definitely want first crack at Harm.

By rights, Rifter was their leader, no matter how hard the man tried to pretend otherwise. It had been Harm's job, but he had refused to come back, even after learning of the demise of the majority of the Dires. Harm had been too busy fucking around. He'd been making music in lots of different genres and disguises. Take ten years off between gigs and then reinvent himself and reemerge. His latest incarnation was in a group intent on bringing eighties hair metal back into the mainstream. As of two years ago, when the band broke up, Harm had been on a giant stage in front of millions of fans, singing and fighting and screwing.

And doing interviews.

With that kind of media scrutiny, it was a wonder no one had discovered Harm taking a howl at the moon. And for years, Harm had reigned at the top of the charts, causing chaos wherever he went, trashing hotel rooms and the like.

But now Harm was here, and in no condition to do anything.

The Elders would have a field day with this one, but Vice knew he would never follow the wolf currently lying in chains on the floor of the basement, couldn't go anywhere near that fucker without ripping his eyes out. Instead, he slammed up to the third floor, where Rogue rested, seemingly comfortably, on the king-sized bed facing the window in full view of the moon.

Rogue hadn't moved, lay there like he was goddamned dead, and if his color hadn't been normal, someone would've put him in the ground already.

Vice's chest squeezed, the emotion coming on too strong, nothing he had control over. Excess roamed every part of his body, his mind, and he dropped to his knees next to the bed, the physical pain nowhere as bad as what Rogue or Rifter had endured, he was sure of it. But it was damned close, and for him, it had been a fact of life since long before he'd shifted for the first time.

Finally the pain eased, slightly at first before slinging full force back to pleasure. There was no gray area for him. Never would be.

Rogue understood that about him most of all.

Vice rubbed Rogue's hand—still warm. The man hadn't aged at all, looked exactly the same as he had when they'd left the house together for a night of leading people astray. But Rogue hadn't come back, and Vice remembered searching the streets for him, a growing terror in his throat. And it took an awful lot to scare the man literally made from sin.

Vice stroked a hand through Rogue's hair. They hadn't cut it, and the fact that it was still growing was a comfort to Vice. He stood, pulled Rogue's body toward him and stared down at the wolf on his back.

The eyes looked dull. Rogue's wolf was out of it too, both man and his Brother Wolf trapped inside a body that refused to work.

All the Dires wore their wolves on their backs. To humans, it looked like an intricate, lifelike tattoo, but it was actually a glyph that began to slowly appear on their skin sometime in the weeks leading up to their first shift.

The tribal wolf tattoos they had were real tats they'd all gotten together, a simple gift of solidarity toward Rifter, their king, and also to honor his dreamwalking curse.

When one of us is cursed, we all are.

And honestly, that held true. They just didn't happen to have a Native American shaman do so from birth.

"Damn it, Rogue, come on," he muttered, rubbing the tribal wolf tattoo that sat over his own heart.

Harm's return was probably not the best thing to share with Rogue, but hell, maybe the brother needed to get angry with him.

"Harm's here. Maybe he wants back into the fold. If you want your say, you've got to wake your sorry ass up."

Vice growled the words, but Rogue didn't so much as twitch.

Motherfucker.

Maybe bringing Harm up here in the flesh would help. Maybe Rogue or his wolf would catch a scent. Vice would do anything to bring Rogue back to life.

"Wanna smoke?" Vice lit up a rolled one, made with his special blend, and put it close to Rogue's nose, because one day he was going to wake this motherfucker up.

Rifter wouldn't even walk through Rogue's dreams

before their capture—said they were too fucked up. Now when he tried, Rifter couldn't get into Rogue's dreams. He couldn't be sure if Rogue was a plant from the sorcerers or weretrappers, and Rifter did not want to get trapped in his dreams.

So Jinx tried to figure out a way to wake his twin up while he continued his work dealing with ghosts and demons and other shit most humans believed happened only in horror movies and prime-time shows, although Vice had to admit that *Supernatural* was pretty damned good. He wondered if maybe he could get a consulting job with the network for it. You know, when his time freed up, since Jinx had snared him into helping him full-time on supernatural-activity watch to battle the dead and demonic.

It was certainly cutting into his fun time. The supernatural activity in the town had increased markedly over the past months, no doubt the work of Seb's witches. Although Jinx had yet to confirm the source for sure, Linus was worried about the possibility that the weretrappers were using Weres to capture their own kind. Rogue had been suspicious that it wasn't simply greed causing the Weres to turn on their own. He and Jinx had gotten reports that the spirit world in New York was suddenly quite active, and they knew that with the weretrappers working with the witches, anything was possible.

"If you sing that *Ghostbusters* song one more fucking time," Rogue would threaten him during the times Vice had worked with both twins on a ghost job. Now Vice whistled it, hoping to see any sign of life from the sleeping man.

Nothing. Just the steady beat of Stray's music. Metallica was the group of choice today. Hours of headbanging fun.

"Gotta keep doing your goddamned job since you

won't wake up." Vice blew smoke over his packmate and wondered if the man lying on the bed knew Vice was dying inside from this.

His phone rang, an unrecognized number. "Who the fuck is this?" he growled, and Rifter growled right back.

"Bring me some goddamned clothes." He rattled off an address and hung up without giving Vice the chance to ask any questions.

Vice plugged in the street address and pulled up the name Gwen Kadlin.

He was still at the human's house. Naked. Which meant he'd shifted and something had gotten fucked up. Vice finished his smoke and touched Rogue's forehead for a second. "You're safe here, brother. Just know that."

And then he went downstairs to share the news.

Jinx looked up expectantly. He held an axe in his hands, but Vice shook his head. "It was Rifter. Let's go grab him."

"Where is he?"

"Holed up at the human's house."

"What the fuck?" Cyd muttered.

The Were twins had been instructed not to breathe a word about Harm and what happened to the weretrappers to anyone. Now Vice added Rifter's current status to that list.

"Or I'll kill you dead," Vice intoned, stepping forward as if ready to do the job, and both Cyd and Cain nodded in silent surrender, each baring their throats slightly, a subtle sign of submission to the Dires.

They would make good warriors if Jinx could help them outgrow their moon craze. Some Weres never experienced more than a twinge of it when they were new. Others, like the twins, experienced such a wild pull for years after their first shift that they needed to be monitored closely for years during the full moon. They were dangerous—to themselves, to other wolves and, more important, to humans. They'd been known to murder indiscriminately and have no memory of why they committed the deed or the deed itself.

Slowly, Cyd and Cain had improved. Gained control. But until they passed their first five years, nothing was guaranteed.

It would kill Jinx to have to take them down.

"Jinx, you need to come with me to get Rifter and bring him back," Vice said.

"I think you should break the news about Harm to Rifter before he gets here. Otherwise, he'll try to kill you along with Harm," Stray called up the stairs, and yeah, when the hell would he admit he had a gift?

"I'm not dealing with that bullshit," Vice yelled back upstairs. *Or your mind-reading crap either.*

"Ah, fuck off," Stray told him and slammed the door.

Through it all, Jinx just sat staring blankly out the window, but his hand tightened on the wooden handle until his knuckles turned white. Vice sighed and wondered when he'd become the responsible, levelheaded one, because if that was true, they were all in a hell of a lot of trouble. "Fine, I'll break it to him," he conceded.

Jinx spoke for the first time in hours. "Good. Then Rifter will let me cut off his arms *and* legs."

Chapter 8

It wouldn't take Vice long to come and get him.

Rifter's body still felt heavy as hell, like he was glued to the bed, which was giving him a hard-on. Not being able to stop thinking about Gwen wasn't helping.

Gwen.

He didn't have a bond with her, but he still dream-walked with her without touching her. And it didn't work like that—at least it never had before.

But trying to figure out why it happened was getting him nowhere. Instead, he stumbled around her house a little more, into the spare bedroom to look at the paintings he'd caught a glimpse of last night. They were of full moons—and wolves that looked disturbingly familiar. Brother Wolf wasn't awake at all to agree, but Rifter was mesmerized.

The paintings were signed with the name Annie Woodall. A relative or just paintings Gwen liked?

He moved in to study them more closely—caught the scent of smoke. Fire. Sifted through them until he came to one that showed a wolf chasing the moon and felt dizzy again. Humans knew of the Norse myth, of course, but this painting felt . . . personal, as if the artist knew that what she was creating had special meaning.

He swore he could hear his mother repeating the oft-told story in his ears as the moon in the picture seemed to take on a life of its own.

The legend said that in the beginning, there was a Norse god called Loki, a shifter who had a wolf son named Fenir. Fenir had twins: Skoll, who chased the sun, and Hati, who chased the moon.

When Fenir was killed by the god Odin, Hati created two beings in his image who would become known as Mother and Father Wolf, Dire wolves born in human form so they could walk among humans without fear, but change to their true form at will. He reveled in their worship and their protection and instructed them to breed, and they did, creating a race of Dires. The race of Dires worshipped him as well, and chased the moon with him.

But as the packs of Dires grew, they became unmanageable and jealous of what the humans had—power, wealth, respect—and they became hard to control. They began to kill humans, and Hati grew very upset and warned them to stop or they would pay.

Every once in a while, a Dire was born with special gifts, and the Dire wolves weren't sure if they should fear or worship them. Knowing that Hati was becoming angry with them, the Dires decided to sacrifice the four with abilities to Hati in hopes that he would be appeased by this gift.

Hati took those four Dire wolves and made them the Elders—a high council of Dires who would govern their people. So they'd once been living, breathing Dire wolves, now suspended in time and the otherworld; Hati made them all-powerful and put them in charge of the earth-bound Dires.

You'd think that would make them slightly more sympathetic to the remaining Dires, but no, it actually made them harsher.

There was Leifr and Meili, who was said to be a brother of Thor. Eydis was the lone female of the group. Legend said when the fourth was outvoted on an important matter concerning Dires and their abilities, Hildr asked to be killed rather than go against what she believed in.

To this day, the Dires didn't know the hows or whys but always hoped that one day they would.

Thankfully, a knock on the back door pulled his near-hypnotic attention away. Vice and Jinx were there, Vice handing him clothes and pushing his way inside. "I thought we decided we were laying low during the day."

"I'm not out running the streets," Rifter muttered, shutting the door behind the men. "Waiting for night blows. Might as well be a fucking deadhead."

It had been their word for Vamps for as long as he could remember, wasn't sure how the Grateful Dead followers had gotten hold of it. Granted, there were a lot of vamps who did follow the Dead back in their day . . .

"Earth to Rifter." Vice was waving a hand in front of his face, and damn, the drugs were still making him loopy.

"Why were you out running alone? What the fuck, Rift?"

"Drop it," he told Vice, noting that Jinx was uncharacteristically quiet, like it was taking all his strength to keep himself in check. "I've got to check on Gwen. Something's wrong."

Brother Wolf whimpered as he began to stir. *Calm down, boy; you'll be fine in a little while.*

"Dude, we've got a sitch here," Vice continued to push.

"So do I."

"Mine's bigger," Vice said steadily.

"Get off my ass!" Rifter roared, a damned impressive sight, even for those who knew him well. He could be a miserable son of a bitch, but he kept his temper mostly in check.

Vice appeared unimpressed, but Rifter noted he kept his mouth shut all the same.

"She's in trouble—I feel it," Rifter said more quietly, because Jinx did not look good.

Vice could hold himself in check for only so long. "Oh, Christ. Look, we're supposed to help Weres, not humans," he started, but Rifter cut him off.

"Where's Stray?"

"Guarding our problem."

Rifter dressed and took pity because of Jinx. "Talk."

"Don't bite the messenger, hear?" Vice told him.

"Why not?"

"It's about Harm."

That one name was enough to send Rifter reeling, but he stopped himself since this wasn't his house. He was sure Gwen wouldn't appreciate claw marks on her walls.

It helped that Brother Wolf was still out of it, because it took everything Rifter had not to shift and run and kill anyone and everyone in his path.

Vice continued, "We found him last night. He killed about twenty weretrappers—shredded them. He's still got silver ill, so he's not answering any questions."

That fucker was back, and blood would run hot tonight. Right out of Harm's body. Rifter would take great pleasure in his pain. Revenge seared through his body like a blazing poker, and he was aware that the two Dires watched him carefully, would take their lead from him.

It took everything he had not to shift and really wake Brother Wolf. He could be home much faster and tearing into Harm. The satisfaction that would bring was better than any goddamned orgasm.

That's why the Dires had been so frantic to get him home. "There's gonna be hell to pay."

"Always is. We figured Stray's the one least likely to do damage before you get there."

That wasn't true, but Rifter didn't bother to correct Vice. None of the wolves other than Rifter had seen Stray's temper, and it was far from pretty. And he wanted to head straight home, but he couldn't shake the scent of Gwen being in danger. Brother Wolf was having the same problem now that he was waking up. "First things first. The human—Gwen—I've got to go to her."

"Not smart," Vice muttered.

"Not dark out yet either." Jinx spoke for the first time.

But the need overrode everything, including wanting to go to Harm and rip his head off his body. Something was definitely wrong—with him, with her, with this entire situation, and he didn't have time to sit down and figure it out. "Drive me to the hospital."

He was heading to the truck as he spoke, leaving Vice and Jinx to follow. But it was Jinx's words that stopped him.

"You took off the dream catcher," Jinx said, and Rifter touched his bare neck and tried not to look guilty. But he was still shaken from the dream, no matter how well he'd hidden it from his brothers. It had been the most vivid yet and took away any and all comfort he'd gotten while running with Gwen last night.

"Did you dream?" Vice asked, and Rifter nodded.

"Anything different?" Jinx pushed.

"I saw souls rising this time. I think I died and rose from the dead," he admitted, and Jinx swore. "I think I'm seeing the Extinction happen through my father's eyes. At the end, I think it was he who turned to me and said, *Save us, Rifter.*"

"What the hell? Did they not pass over?" Jinx rubbed a hand over the back of his neck and continued without waiting for a response to a question only Rogue could really answer. "Where's the catcher?"

"With my bike in the woods."

"You're so far from okay," Vice said.

"None of us is, if my dreams are any indication," Rifter shot back.

"Vice and I will go out tonight and hunt," Jinx assured him. "You limit your sleep."

Rifter promised nothing—because he couldn't.

"Are we really doing this? Because I'd think he'd be way more interested in Harm than this human." Jinx was snarling as he watched Rifter stride toward the truck and get inside. Vice fully expected to find a wolf in front of him at any moment.

"He bit someone—I smell it on him," Vice said. "That, and the human."

"If that were true, she wouldn't be alive," Jinx pointed out.

"He did something to make her come," Vice said bluntly, then muttered, "At least someone got to come last night."

"Don't think about getting lucky tonight—we definitely have to go hunting and figure out what the hell's going on with the dead Dires Rifter's dreaming about."

"Shit." Vice paused. "Do you smell witch?"

Jinx took a deep sniff and then nodded.

"This is gonna suck," Vice said as they followed Rifter into the truck.

Chapter 9

It was dark by the time Gwen left the hospital, dragging a large bag filled with the extra clothes and scrubs from her locker. She'd forgone stopping by HR to sign the final paperwork for her dismissal. They could hunt her down if they needed her.

The failure hung on her like a too-heavy coat. She was a little dizzy, which she attributed to hunger, and all she wanted was her bed.

She was nearly to her car when she spotted a guy lingering by it. She'd parked in her usual spot under one of the large lights that illuminated the lot and was close to the woods that separated the streets between her house and the hospital. She often ran through those woods, the trails not as defined as in the park across town, but it was quiet and lovely in there. She'd never had any trouble, despite the reports of gang activity she'd mentioned to Cordelia.

Cordelia. She'd already had enough trouble today, almost turned away from the stranger, but he looked weak and pale, and he was also sweating. Feverish for sure. There was something in his eyes that made her instantly move toward him.

"Are you all right?" she asked and nearly added, *I'm*

a doctor, but bit that back, because now it would've felt like a lie.

"I'm . . . you need to come with me," he said, his voice rough, but he wasn't meeting her gaze, instead stood like a soldier, as if he was holding something back and scanning the lot. For what, she had no idea.

"Come on, let me get you inside to the ER," she urged, dropping her bag to the ground and reaching for him, since he'd started to sway.

When he grabbed her back, he was surprisingly strong. "Not here," he said, but he didn't attempt to pull her in any other direction. "Please, Doc, I need your help."

Doc. "You can go to the hospital—"

But he had other plans, had pulled the knife before she'd finished speaking. Still, he didn't grab her, simply motioned for her to get into the car.

She dug through her bag for the keys, trying to buy time. "I'll give you money to pay for the ER visit, no questions asked."

"No. I can't."

God, his eyes were glazed, and there was fresh blood on his shirt. If she went willingly with him, he'd probably be too weak to do anything to her.

Could she take that risk?

She didn't see an immediate choice, beyond fighting, and the knife was big. The young man, bigger.

She pulled out her keys and attempted to click the alarm button, cursing her shaking hands.

"I just need stitches, okay?" he growled from behind her, although it somehow sounded apologetic.

"Leave her alone, Liam."

Both she and Liam turned toward the voice, which Gwen recognized instantly.

Cordelia. There was no way this was a coincidence. "Is he part of your monster-hunting group?"

"He's one of the monsters," Cordelia said.

Even though Liam was trying to kidnap her, Gwen didn't believe Cordelia, hadn't since the moment they'd met. But Cordelia had both a gun and a syringe she'd no doubt stolen from the hospital, and Gwen knew the woman would hurt her if given the chance. She threaded her keys through her fingers so the sharp edges stuck out when she made a fist.

"Gwen, let me help you," Cordelia continued.

"I don't want to be part of your group."

Cordelia smiled, a chilling thing, before she raised her gun and pointed it squarely at Gwen's chest. "You're not. You're one of the monsters too."

"Why? Because I went home with Rifter?" Gwen asked, totally confused. But before Cordelia could answer, Liam jumped between them. Cordelia's gun clattered across the lot, and she went down.

Gwen started back toward the hospital, but Liam grabbed her, dragging her, and she didn't know if she was being saved or kidnapped.

Both.

There was no one to scream to for help—change of shift had long passed and the lot was packed with cars but no people.

She screamed anyway, heard it echo across the lot, bounce off the trees, and reverberate in her own ears.

From behind her, Cordelia took one of Gwen's arms in a viselike grip and attempted to drag her away from Liam. Normally *not* staying with the slightly crazy, could-be-on-drugs person would be the right thing to do.

But that's how things had been going, and she was tired of fighting it. She punched Cordelia in the face, the keys quite effective at making the woman loosen her grip as blood poured from a gash in her cheek.

She jerked away from Cordelia, who snarled, "Stupid

girl," and came after Gwen again, surprisingly fast, knocking her sideways with a blow to the side of her face.

Gwen jumped up and went back at her, her nails raking Cordelia's back through her shirt as the anger welled from deep within until she could no longer see straight. Something snapped inside of her, and it was all painful and brilliant at the same time, a snapping, unholy light that she felt could somehow give an end to the torment of the last years.

At some point, Liam stepped in between them and lunged at Cordelia. Gwen stumbled back a little and realized the hospital was farther away than the path through the woods that led to the police station.

She was fast enough that she took the chance, but when she looked up, Liam was in front of her already, which seemed . . . impossible.

"Watch out," he called, and she ducked and turned in time to miss Cordelia, who was still brandishing the needle. Liam shoved Gwen back and dragged her farther along into the woods. She heard footsteps following them and knew Cordelia wasn't far behind. Everything was happening in fast-forward and she could barely catch her breath, even though she felt surprisingly strong as well.

"Keep running," he told her, and he stopped. She continued on a few feet but turned and stopped as well, couldn't leave him behind in danger. Cordelia was gaining, and Gwen doubled back toward him in time to see him circling Cordelia's prone body. The needle was sticking out of her thigh and she was still alive—for now.

Gwen's phone was buried in the bag she'd left by her car, her keys still clutched in her hand.

"I'll stay with her; you get the police," Gwen told him,

because she couldn't let a woman die in front of her. She had no idea what was in the syringe.

But Liam wasn't listening; he looked at her and panted, "Get far away from me."

He shifted from foot to foot, fisted his hands. His skin was covered in a fine sheen of sweat, his lips stretched in a grimace.

She should be scared, but facing death obviously took away her fears. Looking back, she'd never really been afraid of much anyway. She'd lost those closest to her, and after that, she refused to get close to anyone. And when you didn't have anything to lose, you had nothing to fear. "I can't. You need help."

"*You* need help."

Why was everyone telling her that? "This was self-defense—you won't be in trouble, but if you do anything else to her—"

"Get back—keep far away from me."

It happened like a flash; she'd been too close and got thrown to the ground in his frenzy. The man was gone, and she caught a blur of brown fur and harsh breaths like she'd never heard before. She lay where she'd landed, several feet from him, momentarily stunned, and then pushed up on her hands and knees and saw the actual four-legged creature in front of her.

And he was growling.

This wasn't the wolf from last night's dream. This one looked darker, and it was angry and scared.

And now you're comparing dream wolves to real ones.

"Whoa, boy, calm down." And now she was an animal whisperer.

She'd pretend to be anything if it kept her alive.

The wolf growled, low but somehow nonthreatening. It was looking around and then gazing back at her.

Is that what he was doing? Protecting her?

God, she was losing it. The strange, floaty prodrome of the seizure started to take her. The wolf whined and then jumped toward her as she fell back on the ground.

When she looked up, she saw the wolf—*the wolf*—on top of Cordelia, his teeth gleaming as he howled toward the sky.

This isn't happening.

She ducked her head before he tore into Cordelia's throat, curled herself into a ball, the strength and non-fear from seconds earlier totally dissipating. But when he turned back in her direction, she sensed it and knew she'd have no choice but to fight for her life.

Rifter was out of the truck and halfway across the parking lot, looking for Gwen's car, when he caught the scent of Were.

Young. Uncontrolled.

"Brother, I need you," he said quietly, and a low growl hummed in his ears.

Brother Wolf helped him catch the other scent in the air. *Gwen.*

Rifter wasted no time getting to the woods and shifted without bothering to strip. This time, he didn't care about ruining the leather he wore.

He heard Vice and Jinx behind him—they hadn't shifted and were discussing finding Gwen's bag abandoned by her car—and he raced ahead, the scent of blood calling to him.

When he reached the clearing in the woods he rarely ran through, thanks to the close proximity to the hospital and the lack of tree coverage from the road during winter, he saw a young woman dead on the ground.

His heart lurched, but it took him only a moment to

scent that it wasn't Gwen, but rather, the witch who'd attacked him earlier.

No doubt her death was the work of the young wolf he'd scented and possibly done in front of Gwen.

He stopped and listened, heard her voice, soft and steady, and he stealthily threaded through the trees to find her. When he broke through a thick bramble of bushes that ran along the partially frozen lake, he found her.

She and the young wolf were circling each other—Gwen was holding her hands out in front of her and talking, as if she could reason with the wolf. And she wasn't doing a bad job, because the wolf seemed ... confused.

Most humans would be running away, screaming by now.

Most humans would be dead by now too. A moon-crazed wolf attacked first and never asked questions, bore the brunt of the consequences later, depending on his or her pack. With this wolf, something was off.

Brother Wolf agreed and jumped in between Gwen and the young Were. Gwen started and Rifter hoped she recognized his wolf from last night.

No doubt she'd think she was having another medication hallucination. But this situation was far more serious than that. And as though Gwen read his mind, she ran.

Leave her—you'll scare her, Brother Wolf communicated with his brothers, who were ready and waiting. Not that his wolf presence had smoothed shit over, but she was his to calm.

His. There was no doubt. She was a part of him as much as Brother Wolf, and the thought flooded his body with both elation and complete fucking fear.

He left Vice and Jinx to deal with the moon-crazed

wolf, and he went after Gwen, who was running disturbingly fast for a human. Fear laced with adrenaline was no doubt whipping through her veins, and the last thing he wanted to do was have her hurt herself. He dialed it back a little to let her think she was losing him, wanted her to get to her house safely. He ran parallel to her and ended up arriving at the edge of the woods facing her house first.

She burst through the clearing at top speed, obviously not hurt, which was good.

Not so good was the Crown Vic parked in her driveway.

He hadn't heard sirens behind him, and hopefully Vice and Jinx would take care of the mess at the park before the law found out about it. Gwen could be implicated, because they couldn't let a wolf take the blame, no matter how much he cared about this human.

Brother Wolf was ready to howl at the moon, which would make her appearance within the hour. Gwen's slim figure raced onto her porch as he waited, hidden. Sniffed the air and caught the scent of fear—of treason.

These men weren't cops.

Chapter 10

Gwen could barely believe what she'd seen. All she could do was run. The woods were a blur as her muscles stretched, her blood churned and her feet flew across the ground.

She heard voices behind her and she picked up speed, frantic to get away, get home, wake up . . .

Hallucinating.

Maybe . . . or maybe she killed Cordelia. Or maybe Liam did.

What about the wolves?

She was at her front door in what seemed like minutes, but she wasn't alone. What looked like an unmarked police car sat in her driveway, and there were three plainclothes cops next to her on the porch. Before she could say anything, they flashed their badges and she bent forward, palms on her thighs, to catch her breath.

She smelled Rifter.

She looked up but didn't see him anywhere. Scrubbed her hands over her eyes, hoping to find herself still in the hospital bed, hooked up to meds.

"Ma'am?" One of the officers touched her arm and sounded genuinely concerned.

The rustling sound from earlier began again in her

ears, like someone was balling up tissue paper, and then it stopped.

Don't trust them.

She stood and pushed the man's hand off her.

She was losing touch with reality very quickly, and she couldn't tell them what she had seen because she couldn't be sure herself. "I'm fine."

"Do you always run like you're being chased when you're fine?" the second officer asked.

She backed toward her door. "You can go now."

"No, we can't. We need to know about Cordelia Smith," the third said firmly.

She blanched, thought about how she'd left the woman back in the woods. "She attacked me."

"Where is she now?"

How would they know about the attack so fast? And why were they here, instead of scouring the woods. "I don't know."

"You'll have to come to the station with us."

She realized then that she didn't recognize them at all—and they hadn't shown her ID. The town wasn't that small, and even so, she'd met most of the force, and some from the neighboring towns, in the ER. She had two officers' cell numbers on speed dial—they'd given them to her more for social purposes than for business—but her cell phone was back in the hospital lot and wouldn't help, damn it.

The keys still clutched in her palm might.

It was then she noticed that the second man held Rifter's leather jacket in his hands. "Why were you in my house?" she demanded, then reached out and ripped the jacket from his grasp.

He grabbed at her wrist in retaliation, and she was tired of people grabbing at her, stopping her. Scaring her.

"Let's go," he told her.

"Fuck you," she said. She was angry and she'd lost her job and she was about to literally lose everything.

Which meant that she had nothing to lose.

She realized that, in some form or another, she'd been fighting her whole life. First there was the illness, and then she'd been fighting for her career in spite of the illness.

Fighting to live.

Giving up was not in her—even as she did so, she knew she was prolonging the inevitable, but she had too much to do in a short time. It was as if something inside of her had decided to revolt.

"Get off me," she heard herself snarl as the anger throbbed between her ears, white and hot, and she dropped the jacket and backhanded the man who refused to release her.

He fell back, harder than he should have, but pulled a gun on her from his position on the ground. That only increased her ire, especially when one of the other men tried to subdue her from behind.

Without worrying about being shot, she jabbed an elbow into his ribs and turned in his grasp, shoving the base of her palm up toward his nose; she heard a satisfying crunch when she made contact.

He let her go, and as she dropped to her knees, she was vaguely aware that the other officer had fired his gun several times. But at what?

The weakness was gone, and she was too busy taking out her aggression on this man to care.

"Don't kill her," the downed one with the bloody nose cried out. She almost laughed that he was worried about her when the only thought in her mind was killing him.

She jumped up after the firing ended and dropped

him to the ground after her key hit his carotid. She still had two more men to contend with, and she wasn't going to be able to stop—doing this felt natural and right, and she was so strong . . .

"Get her in the van and call Mars."

She growled as they circled her, and then she realized she wasn't the only one growling.

The beautiful wolf from last night was next to her, looking a lot more deadly. When it leapt toward the men, there were screams and they scattered.

She swore she still smelled Rifter, heard the rustling in her ears again. She remained behind the wolf because, like the one in the woods, he was protecting her. And when she saw one of the men come up behind the magnificent wolf with a knife, she charged his back without thinking, clawing and kicking, even as she prayed this was all a dream.

Vice shifted, tearing the shit out of his clothes, and his Brother Wolf roared, catching the young wolf's attention and stopping him from following Rifter.

Either way, the young wolf was a dead man. It was never good to see a wolf lose control without the lure of the moon, like a rabid dog, and there was a body to prove he'd done so.

The young Were backed off farther, as though he would run as well in the opposite direction, and then the bastard turned and charged at Vice, attempting to grab his wolf by the throat.

Stupid, stupid Were.

Vice's wolf rose on his hind legs and let out a howl so fierce it rang his ears. He lunged and pawed, and in one hard, fell swoop, Brother took down the wolf like the pup he was.

A soft whimper rose from the dark brown wolf. Magnificent coat, stately animal. He stared into Brother Wolf's eyes with chocolate brown ones of his own.

Intelligent. Not moon crazed. But he'd been hurt recently. Drugged. And his chest was bleeding.

Vice's wolf nosed him, an order to shift. And even though the younger wolf hadn't bared his throat in submission to the Dire, something that would've normally found him flayed, Vice's wolf wasn't insulted.

The shift happened fast—the young man lying pinned under him. He was sweating and pale, and under different circumstances, Vice would've let him stay in wolf form to heal. But they couldn't risk anything—who knew if the trappers had alerted the police anonymously about the murder?

"Is she okay? I tried to save her—," the young guy croaked out. "She was in danger."

He was talking about Gwen. About saving humans. But he'd killed a weretrapper, and Vice couldn't fault him for that.

Vice told his Brother Wolf to take a backseat, and the wolf reluctantly allowed him to shift back, without moving off the boy first. The young man, who was probably close to twenty, stared at Vice, who now lay squarely on top of him, demanding, "Who's the dead girl?"

"Witch. She was working with the humans—the weretrappers. You're a Dire."

"No shit. What was your first clue?" Vice drawled, watching the young man squirm nervously beneath him. Jinx was taking care of the body and checking out the area to see if they were still safe or if the chick had a team behind her.

"Why were you protecting a human from a weretrapper?" Vice demanded of the boy, who started but didn't back down.

"I don't know. I just sensed . . . no, smelled that she was in trouble. I think I hurt her instead of helping."

"We stopped you before you could. Actually, you saved her." Vice stared at him. "Now, who are you?"

"I'm part of the NYC pack."

"You're an outlaw?"

He blinked. "The outlaws tried to kill me because I'm Linus's son."

Vice didn't say anything, the enormity of the situation too much to handle, with the naked young man who would be king wounded in the middle of the woods.

This was Liam, next in line to take over the Weres, at least before the pack wars had started. "Who's the witch?"

"I don't know. But the outlaws are still after me. And I have to survive for the sake of my pack," Liam whispered, and for the first time since encountering the young wolf, Vice scented his fear.

Vice didn't know whether Liam was talking about the weretrappers or the outlaw pack, but it didn't matter. He stroked a hand through the boy's hair. "'S okay. I'll get you someplace safe."

Vice got off him and helped him to his feet, ended up carrying him to the truck and leaning him there while Jinx tied the witch's body to the roof rack.

"What's the deal? We gonna perform funeral services?" Vice asked him.

"It's Seb's sister."

Liam paled even further, and Vice whistled and shook his head. "Brother, we've got more trouble than we can handle. I'm probably the only one looking forward to it."

Vice dressed quickly—there were always extra clothes inside the trucks, for obvious reasons—and he took the driver's seat so Jinx could fix up Liam as best he could.

He'd called Cyd on the way to pick up Rifter's Harley from the woods, if the trappers hadn't taken it already. He found a text now from the twin saying it was safe and sound, and being checked out for bugs and explosives before being brought back to the mansion.

Now he barreled toward the human's address, then slowed with the lights off as he got close and saw the car in the driveway. Muttered, "Fuck me," as he caught sight of Rifter's Brother Wolf taking out some were-trappers.

What he hadn't expected was the human woman fighting alongside the wolf. Hadn't expected the goddamned house to explode either, but that's exactly what it did while he and Jinx watched helplessly and Liam slipped into unconsciousness.

The fiery blast blew Gwen off the front porch and into the yard, her body's fall cushioned by fur. It slammed just the same, though, rattling her enough that she couldn't catch her breath.

The smoke from the fire didn't help, and she crawled away with the wolf urging her onward—half dragging, half pushing her—and she felt the sticky blood as her hand touched its hind leg. And then just as suddenly she was alone and there was a truck barreling toward her, stopping less than a foot away, causing her to jump to her feet.

She felt like running again—but where?

There was no one left to trust.

Trust the wolf, the rustling seemed to say. Her heart pounded and she felt the familiar aura of the seizure. In seconds, she'd be helpless.

He won't hurt you. But she couldn't be sure of anything, even her own mental health. Besides, the wolf was gone.

Oddly, the seizure never materialized, but she was still light-headed. She was picked up gently, but as with Liam earlier, the strength of this grip was something she couldn't break. A strange combo.

Still, she turned to try to see the face of the man carrying her.

"Don't bother fighting, sweetheart. Besides, I'm on your side," the husky voice told her, and she smelled chocolate and whiskey and sin. The man's eyes were piercing—black-ringed silver framed by spiky white-blond hair, tattoos covering his entire neck that she could see, and his smile was wicked, rounding out the look.

Trust it.

"I'm Rifter's family," he continued as he walked her calmly away from what was left of her burning house. He was certainly of the same giant ilk as Rifter, so she could believe it.

There was another man to help her into the back of the waiting truck. He was also as tall as Rifter, dark blond hair and beautiful green eyes that looked like the forest on a fall day, with flecks of red and gold and brown. "Are you bleeding?" he asked, and she stared down at her hand.

The man who carried her had been slightly taller. She looked between both of them. "It's not my blood . . . the wolf was hurt . . ."

She didn't mention killing a man.

"You're having a reaction to the medication the woman who attacked you gave you," the second man explained as he wiped the blood from her hand.

But Cordelia never got close enough to her with the syringe, had she?

"Cordelia didn't get me with the syringe, but she's been following me since last night—she saw me with Rifter and came into the hospital for me to stitch a bite," she said to the green-eyed one, but he simply said, "We'll get you to safety."

She wasn't about to argue. She hadn't realized how far the wolf had gotten her from her house, but she was back near the woods on the edge of her property. And while the soot was still in her mouth and nose, she couldn't feel the heat from the fire any longer.

And she still had Rifter's jacket tucked under her arm.

"Where's Rifter?" she asked as the darker blond man handed her a towel to wipe her face.

"He'll be along shortly. I'm Jinx. And I know you're a doctor. Can you help Liam with me?" he asked, and she turned to see Liam lying on some towels, paler than he'd been before.

Liam. *Not a wolf.*

She decided not to mention that last part to these men.

He was naked and his chest had been cut by a knife down the center, like someone had tried to flay him. She'd been battered, but she was breathing. The young man in front of her was barely doing so—and she moved toward him quickly out of instinct.

"Are you kidnapping me to take care of him? Or because of what happened back there?" she demanded, her gaze flicking back and forth between Liam and Jinx. No matter what their answer was, she wasn't going to fight them on this. She'd done too much of that today, and ultimately, these men—and the one dying—saved her life tonight.

Why they'd put it in danger in the first place was another story altogether.

"Little of both," the man with tattoos along his neck said without a hint of apology . . . or an introduction.

For some strange reason, that gave her comfort. "Then let's get out of here—the fire's freaking me out."

"Will do, boss lady." The tattooed man smiled a little, and she swore his eyes changed colors.

She wondered if she should admit that she wasn't allowed to practice medicine any longer and decided they wouldn't care about that. She was still damned good at what she did, and she would prove it now, to these men, and to herself.

Chapter 11

Once he'd gotten Gwen to the safety of his brothers, Rifter shifted back to human away from her. Now Vice was untying something from on top of the truck as Rifter raced toward it. The house was pretty remote, but they had only minutes before the real police arrived.

Vice pointed to the jeans he'd left on the hood of the truck, which was parked far enough into the wooded area for a quick escape and out of sight of the emergency vehicles in case they pulled up faster than anticipated. The windows were too dark to see through, but he could smell Gwen even now.

"What's that?" he asked.

"Witch. We've got to burn her," Vice said, motioning for Rifter to come look at the body. When Rifter pulled himself to the roof of the SUV, Vice uncovered her face.

Cordelia.

"Jesus Christ." Rifter continued to curse, checked her thigh and saw his bite from earlier. Seb would not take kindly to the death of his sister by wolf at all. "I bit her earlier, in the woods."

She'd been spelled when alive to look like a young woman. In fact, Seb's sister was much older, with white hair past her shoulders.

When Cordelia died, the spell had worn off. She was easily recognizable now as that old woman, a fate that Seb had escaped by refusing to practice black magic. Seb didn't look a day over thirty, if that, much like the Dires. Then again, the witch was now practicing the dark arts himself, and his looks could be masking a wizened visage like Cordelia's.

"Burn her," Rifter agreed. There would be hell to pay for this. And he was half tempted to do the burning right outside Seb's door because the witch would not take kindly to the Viking funeral pyre.

"This human's brought nothing but trouble with her, Rift. Cordelia didn't start circling you until last night, when you went home with Gwen—she admitted that herself," Vice told him as he hauled the body over his shoulder and held up Gwen's hospital badge, which he clipped onto the front of Cordelia's collar. "This will literally kill two birds with one stone, at least for a while."

Rifter nodded and watched Vice bring Cordelia's body close to the flaming house before heaving her into the fire. When Vice came back, sirens sounded in the distance.

"You still think Gwen's weretrapper bait?" Rifter asked, didn't wait for the answer. "Who's the Were?"

"Liam. The outlaws tried to kill him too—Gwen's busy saving his ass right now."

Rifter blinked hard. "Son of a bitch." On both counts. She was far too involved in their lives . . . and Brother Wolf was rising and demanding it be that way, thanks to his Father Wolf instincts. "We are a caravan of some bad shit right now."

Because Gwen was coming back to the house with them . . . where they had Harm shackled. The young heir who would be king of the Weres was currently dying in their truck, and, oh yeah, there was an entire pack of Dire alphas who weren't supposed to exist—and soon they'd all be under one roof.

Add a dead witch who'd been following Gwen since last night, and it was a recipe for disaster.

"You sure you want to bring her back with us?" Vice asked. "Because she said she saw wolves. Jinx tried to convince her that Cordelia shot her up with drugs, but this one's not buying it."

"She's dying," he told Vice, and that made the man go silent for a long moment.

"You're sure."

"Yes. And she's all alone."

"How do you know she doesn't have anyone else?" Vice demanded.

"I know." He could sense the deep well of loneliness because he'd felt it far too often. He had men he considered family. She had no pictures displayed in her house, just a small photo album tucked in a drawer and some wolf paintings.

He knew interns were busy, but her whole life revolved around work and her illness. "She'll die with us or without us. I'd rather her have someone there."

Vice nodded, and then, ever practical, said, "It'll take care of the problem of having to kill her ourselves."

Rifter shoved Vice viciously against the truck, so hard it shook. "Don't talk about her like that."

"You're still wearing her scent," Vice told him calmly, so much so that Rifter slammed him harder. "That explosion was meant for *her*, not you."

If Jinx hadn't stuck his head out and pointedly said, "Police," they would've fought until they bled.

Vice's eyes had turned, and Rifter wasn't sure his had ever reverted from the earlier shift.

"She almost died because of me tonight, and all she

wants to do is really live," he snarled at Vice before he released him.

"So show her a good time, then," Vice said, because *that*, he understood. "But tell me this—how the hell did she survive the blast?"

Rifter had no idea, because his body ached from being thrown. She should be unable to move, but once he climbed in the passenger's seat, he saw her moving around Liam's prone body in the back of the truck.

She didn't seem to notice him or the fact that Vice gunned the truck through the back roads, because she was busy giving orders.

Jinx was following those orders from Gwen, only because it was Liam, Rifter knew. And if he died, the packs would fall further into chaos than they already were.

These Dires rankled at the idea of following any orders, except those of their king. It had made their years of military service interesting.

"When we stop, use this to stitch him," Jinx told her, holding the roll of black wire all the Dires used when helping a Were to heal quickly.

"This is too thick," she argued.

"Use it," Jinx said, and leaned back when Rifter turned to him. "He's ripped out stitches before—trust me."

"You're a doctor?" she asked.

"Medic. Army. Combat medicine's a lot like the ER."

She nodded and began to give him the respect she would a colleague. "This is infected—that's why he was acting strangely."

"Must be," Jinx muttered, and Rifter shot him a look. The truck swerved and Gwen held her own, balancing herself with the grace of someone used to rough ambulance rides with dying patients.

And no doubt, Liam was dying. They could all smell it. Christ, they couldn't let that happen.

*   *   *

"We need a hospital," Gwen told Jinx, then glanced up briefly at Rifter.

She'd known he was close before he'd gotten in the truck. He'd never gone far from her—she felt him like a warm tingle along her spine. And the way he looked at her . . . it heated her all over.

He glanced at his leather jacket, which she kept close, like it was some kind of good-luck charm. She'd resisted the urge to put it on, but only because both her hands were currently holding Liam's chest together.

"My house has a clinic—we'll be there in a couple of minutes," Rifter told her, and she nodded crisply, wondering why they would need a private clinic.

The gang thing was looking more and more likely. "I need more gauze, then," she said, and Jinx produced it. The truck was stocked like an ambulance as well. She packed the wound, and Liam groaned softly at the pressure. "I'll stitch him once we stop. He might need a transfusion."

"We can do that," Jinx said, his voice low, his eyes not leaving Liam's newly opened ones. He put a hand over them, told Liam, "Close them and rest," and when he took his hand away, Liam had.

As they zoomed up the private drive, she couldn't make out more than the outline, thanks to the fog. The moon still looked full tonight, seemed to hang low over the house, though, shining a path for them.

At the same time, she heard a garage door opening, noted at least ten Harley motorcycles lined up and several Hummers, and this place had to be huge.

The clinic was in the basement, which was through a series of doorways down a wide hall, right off the attached garage they'd pulled into. Although she hadn't been able to pay attention to much beyond holding the gauze in place when Jinx picked Liam up and put him on a stretcher another young guy wheeled out for them, she noted that the place wasn't sterile looking.

Somehow, despite the lack of windows, it felt warm.

They ended up in the last room on the right, which had all the makings of an OR. Jinx swiftly grabbed what she needed, and together they worked nearly wordlessly, hanging fluids and blood, stitching Liam with the industrial wiring Jinx had suggested, all the while without the use of any pain meds.

If Liam felt it, he didn't complain. His heart rate was higher than she'd like it to be, though. "I still think he needs—"

"He's allergic to everything—too much risk of complication," Jinx cut her off, then said, "You're doing great."

She washed the mud and Betadine sterilizing solution and blood from Liam, careful not to turn or wake him. He was covered in bruises, all in different stages of healing. She couldn't turn him without risking opening the wound again.

"How old is he?" she asked.

"Twenty-two," Jinx said.

"Did Cordelia do this to him? I mean, they were fighting, but I didn't see a knife." *I did see a wolf, though* . . .

Rifter chose that moment to stride in, looking even more massive in a pair of jeans and a black ribbed sleeveless undershirt. She caught sight of a tattoo below his collarbone along his shoulder, and then she completely lost her train of thought when she saw him holding a bloody towel pressed to his biceps.

Instead of Jinx answering her question, Rifter posed one of his own. "How do you know Cordelia?"

"She came into the ER today with a nasty bite. She was asking me about you," she admitted. "Rifter, I don't understand any of this. Are you and your brothers in some kind of gang?"

"Is that what Cordelia said?"

"She inferred that. She also mentioned . . ."

She stopped short, felt way too foolish to say the word *monsters* or to tell them Cordelia accused her of being one too. "She's part of some take-back-the-night program."

Jinx snorted, and Rifter shot him a look.

She was locked in a house with men who were . . . killers. And no matter how they tried to hide it, they knew exactly who Cordelia was.

She wanted to ask about the men impersonating the police, wondered if they'd been in on the explosion. Did Rifter and his family know who they were?

She assumed someone would tell her eventually. Rifter knew she was in no position to rat them out.

"She seemed like a jealous ex at first," she said, her gaze locking on Rifter's. The air stilled between them, and he said, "She's not an ex."

"I'll let you two work this out without me," Jinx said, then smirked at Rifter and exited the room, calling over his shoulder, "Let me know when Liam wakes up."

"Let me take care of that for you," she said to hide how flustered she was, pointing to his arm, suddenly feeling foolish for acting jealous herself. With everything else going on, her love life should be the least of her concerns, but she couldn't get Rifter out of her thoughts; his scent wafted past her constantly.

Rifter didn't argue when she ushered him to the second stretcher on the other side of the room behind a movable curtain. He sat and waited while she found the supplies she needed. When she got back to him, she unwrapped the cloth that was wound around the huge biceps and stared at it stupidly for a long moment.

"This is a bullet wound."

"Yes."

"Were you near my house when those men started shooting?"

He nodded, and she wanted to ask why, but she didn't. It seemed almost rude, considering he'd saved her life. The female in her also gained satisfaction that he'd wanted to see her again.

"I already took the bullet out—just needs to be cleaned," he told her.

"Now you're a doctor too?"

"Little bit."

She cleaned him up and bandaged the round wound, which was already on its way to healing. "There you go. This needs to be changed daily."

He was watching her with heavy-lidded eyes that were deceptively lazy. This man was anything but.

"Thanks for saving my jacket."

She felt her face flush. "Those men were holding it. I just . . . freaked."

"I guess it was your good-luck charm."

No, that's turning out to be you, she wanted to say, but she held that back because it was too soon to tell.

She had nothing to go back to, and her stay would be short, no matter what. Maybe she could get used to being a biker chick. God knew she wanted Rifter. So she could be freaked or spend the rest of her time living, and doing so above the law seemed both appropriate and appealing.

"I obviously have some kind of brain tumor, and that's why I'm hallucinating things I can't have possibly seen. I also can't fight you and your brothers. I won't go to the police, and I know you don't trust that. But they wouldn't believe my story anyway. I don't even believe it. But those men said to put me in the van and to call Mars," she told him. "Where were they going to take me?"

"You're safe now, Gwen," he said, and she couldn't accept that non-answer. The next confession came out of her mouth before she could stop it, but maybe it would make him understand why she needed to know everything.

"My mother was killed by fire. So were my aunt and uncle. Now my house explodes, right after a strange woman chants and shows me a pentagram. So I really hope I'm losing my mind or else—"

Or else the possibilities were too frightening to say out loud.

"I'm a dangerous man to be around. But you knew that already," Rifter said.

She couldn't deny that she knew it, not when it drew her to him like a moth to the flame. Literally, at this point. "And I feel like I'm a dangerous woman to be around," she countered.

"This isn't about you. I have a lot of enemies."

"And now so do I."

"As far as the rest of the world's concerned, you died in that fire," he said bluntly.

"There's no one in the world who'd care," she said quietly, hadn't expected him to drag her toward him or hold her tightly.

"I goddamned do." His voice was gruff, the emotion behind it real. Her body pressed against his hard one. She fit between his opened thighs, her head level with his chest, and she looked up to catch his gaze.

It was smoldering. Her body was tugging her down a dangerous path as his erection pressed her—and he looked completely unashamed about that as he repeated quietly, "I goddamned care."

She wasn't really aware that she'd started to trace a finger along the tribal tat near his collarbone until he actually shuddered a little under her touch. She wanted to trace it with her mouth and fought that urge, instead moving her hand to the outer square of the bandage.

When she looked up at him, he was watching her with a heat in his eyes that ripped through her body like a fire.

"You gonna kiss it and make it all better, Doc?" he breathed.

Yes, she thought she might. And when he brought his mouth down on hers, she melted for him. This was so easy, probably the easiest thing she'd ever done. Her tongue played against his as the kisses deepened. She was ready to climb him, to let him take her the way she'd wanted to last night.

His hands roamed her body, brushing her breasts over her shirt, and she squirmed impatiently, allowing his hands to move underneath the fabric. Her own tugged at his shirt as well, and she touched her palms to his warm skin.

God, she felt like she was touching fire . . . and she liked the burn. He didn't seem to mind either—his body seemed to quake at the touch.

He'd pushed her shirt up, her bra aside and took a nipple in his mouth, sucked hard enough to make her stifle a cry of pure pleasure. Her hands held his head and she was climbing his lap, aided by a strong arm wrapping her waist.

Straddling him on the stretcher, his face buried against her chest, her face buried in his hair, she felt the orgasm start to rise in her. Her body was strung as tight as a bow and it wouldn't take much. He played her easily, his mouth suckling her nipple, and the wet between her legs called for his touch.

She wanted to be naked. Right now.

"Rifter," she murmured into his hair. His response was to grind his arousal against her, the rock-hard erection pressing between her legs, the scent of pine needles and cold air and a tornado of complete want spiraled out of control.

She felt the orgasm in her womb—deep contractions that rocked her with the same kind of pleasure she'd felt that morning. But this was better because she wasn't alone.

Rifter started to take off her jeans, but Liam picked that moment to stir, the monitor beeping alerting them. She and Rifter broke apart quickly, and she tugged her shirt down and went to Liam's stretcher. When she took his hand in hers, he opened his eyes and stared into her face for a long moment, like he was trying to remember who she was "You're all right," he managed finally.

"You're okay too. Just try not to move too much. I stitched you, but they won't hold if you try to go out and save random women."

He smiled a little. "Didn't mean to freak you out."

"Feeling better, Liam?" Rifter asked, and the younger man nodded. "Good. Gwen, you can go with Cyd—he's waiting for you in the hallway and he'll get you food and a place to rest."

She turned toward the door, which was still closed, but she heard voices in the hallway a bit too clearly.

"They're coming for him," she heard Jinx say, and realized they were talking about Liam. She heard muttering and caught bits of conversation among the cursing.

". . . knows he's alive."

". . . trappers working with the outlaws, like he said."

When she turned back around, Rifter was staring at her.

"I need to stay with Liam," she told him.

"Your stomach's growling and you're exhausted. And

my brothers and I have to talk some business with him—
we'll call for you if there are any problems."

She relented reluctantly. "Don't wear him out."

Rifter's lips curled, like he was holding back a laugh,
and she pushed past him into the hall, still feeling his
mouth on hers.

Chapter 12

Neither Jinx nor Vice commented when they saw Rifter, partly because they were focused on Liam, but Rift knew they'd smelled the arousal in the air. No doubt they'd caught his scent on Gwen.

He was marking her—subtly—but it was there. And he couldn't have stopped it if he tried.

It was frustrating because he needed to have her, and he knew that could never happen. Brother Wolf was pissed about that because he'd been marking her too, in his own way. Because as strong as Rifter's urge to mate with Gwen was becoming, Brother Wolf's urges to become Father Wolf were far more primal. For Brother, a mate was a source of more wolves, and that would make him truly complete.

Stray had remained with Harm, Jinx told him in passing, which Rifter was grateful for. But he wasn't sure how long that wolf would retain his self-control—he would head to see Harm for himself as soon as this conversation was over.

Now they circled Liam's bed—the stubborn young wolf was trying to sit up, but Jinx stopped him with a hand on his shoulder. "Relax—your wound was nasty."

Liam stared down at the line of black stitches at the

wound, which already appeared to be healing. "I have things to do."

"You need our help, so start talking," Rifter told him with a low snarl, because the young wolf looked ready to bolt.

"I need to get back to my pack—to lead them. There's chaos among the Weres now, and I have to stop it before it spreads outside of New York." Liam was growing frustrated, but he remained respectful.

Chaos was an understatement.

There were werepacks scattered across the United States and the rest of the world. The main pack, which would now fall under Liam's control, was in New York City, with the other large packs being in Texas, California and Wisconsin.

Discontent among the pack members was normal. For the most part, the alpha orders were to be followed without question, but living so close to humans and their ways had put a different spin on their lives.

Alphas would run their own packs while still following the rules of the king. But the main problem the outlaw pack had was that they found the old ways Linus adhered to far too restricting.

Join the goddamned club, Rifter had growled when Linus told them that. Rifter had also been privy to several werepack meetings about the subject, listening in from outside to ensure that the Weres all spoke their mind.

Teague and Tals, along with Walker, were the major problems.

"We're wolves—we're supposed to hunt and kill," Teague argued. But Linus had quashed their talk of rebellion without the Dires having to do much but remain in town. There had been little to no talk of the outlaws until a couple of weeks ago, when Linus and Liam had been kidnapped, their wereguards left dead around their New York City brownstone.

The outlaws hadn't publicly taken responsibility for any of this thus far. "Have the outlaws tried to take over your pack?" Rifter asked Liam now.

"That wasn't their first goal."

"What was?"

"The outlaws wanted to turn the Dires over to the weretrappers," Liam said quietly, and Rifter felt a collective, palpable pain rise from the Dires that surrounded the young wolf, whose father had died for them.

"Who?" Vice demanded.

"Tals. Teague. Walker." Liam shifted in the bed, his eyes lupine as he spoke of the wolves who had murdered his father. The death was so fresh it burned in his eyes, and the Dires waited, giving him the time to regroup and stop the imminent shift.

Total control over his wolf was not something a Were could ever have, but if Liam was to lead, he would need more of it than the average Were, especially under this kind of pressure.

Weres turned younger—at sixteen as opposed to the Dires' twenty-one. An imperfect system, Rogue had always said.

After several tense moments, Liam's eyes returned to full human, even as a thin sheen of sweat covered his chest. "They started quietly recruiting rogue wolves from other packs to join their cause—they believed that if my father sold you to the weretrappers, the Weres would be left alone. This was their plan—my father was trying to tell you, right before he got kidnapped."

"It's one thing for them to say it, another to actually do it," Rifter said.

"Either way, I've got to start taking back control by calling those three out," Liam countered.

"They won't respond to the old ways," Rifter told him. "Besides that, it's too public. And we've got enough of the humans breathing down our necks."

"Or with their tongues down our throats," Vice muttered, barely getting the last syllable out before Rifter threw him across the room. Vice hit the wall with a satisfying crack of plaster meeting skull and rebounded, landing right in front of Rifter, but with a few respectful feet between them.

"Wolf, I will take you out right now," Rifter warned, his voice low. "We have too many problems for infighting."

Vice nodded, and a hand on his shoulder from Jinx helped. But Rogue was somehow the only one who could fully control Vice and his many excesses.

Rifter turned his attention back to Liam. "Linus had been challenged before. He'd always fought and won."

"The outlaws blindsided him this time. He was murdered in front of me. If I don't take the pack over . . . ," Liam started.

"You're in no shape."

"Then get me ready," Liam challenged, and Rifter had to push him back down because Gwen would have his ass if the stitches split.

Since when do you worry about a woman's opinion?

He shook his head, and Vice looked at him strangely. "What?"

"Just waiting for you to react to what Liam said about the outlaws selling out Weres to the witches and trappers for profit. Because once we're under the weretrappers' care, so to speak, there's nothing to protect the non-outlaw Weres from selling their own kind out."

"Is that true?" he demanded of Liam.

"My father confirmed it in the week leading up to his death. At first, the outlaws wanted to out the Weres to the human population. They believed it would take away some of the weretrappers' power because they also want to out the witches. My father disagreed. They knew they wouldn't be able to do it without his consent, and that's why they killed him and planned on taking out the entire council. Tals and Teague were having private meetings, telling the rogue wolves, 'Why should the witches get all the benefits? We didn't start this—the Dires did. We shouldn't have to take on their burden while they're off partying.' They're angry wolves, more intent on killing than following the old ways, which makes them quite dangerous. The Weres like killing humans and have taken to selling their own kind to the weretrappers in exchange for protection. Some of them have started to work as bodyguards for both witch and weretrapper."

"Rebellion—using the weretrappers to get what they want—could they be any stupider?" Vice asked.

The trappers had started as good humans, but their purpose had evolved over the years. When the pre-Extinction Dires killed human families, the families bonded together, intent on keeping humans safe from the wolves. When the Dires were taken out by the Extinction and the Weres were created, the weretrappers began hunting them, not caring about the difference in breeds.

Over time, the trappers began to realize the power they could have if they were able to harness the power of the Weres. Now they regularly captured Weres and experimented with ways to keep them under their control.

Rifter knew the Weres were in far more danger than the Dires were—and since the Dires were sworn to protect them, they knew the fate of the pack leader who sat in front of them in the hospital bed. Sincere and strong, but inexperienced, and facing the fight of his life. "We'll need to make some confirmation of our own about all of this," he said, and Jinx nodded.

"I'm going with you," Liam said, and Rifter stared at the man who would be king.

"Tomorrow night. Tonight, you rest and heal."

Liam nodded, seemingly satisfied.

"I'll keep an eye on him tonight with Cyd—I don't think we'll need to call in Doc E," Jinx said.

"And Gwen's here. She's awesome." Liam looked pale, but his eyes were bright.

"You saved her, she saved your life, so you're even," Rifter told him.

"Still can't believe you brought her back here," Vice muttered.

"We should get her the hell out of town and warn her to forget all about you," Jinx added, stepping in front of Vice. Liam just watched all of them carefully.

"And let the weretrappers take her?" Rifter asked.

"Why would they want her?" Jinx looked confused, the way Rifter felt.

"Because of me. I can't leave her vulnerable," Rifter said, trying not to roar.

"At some point, she's going to figure out the difference between dream and reality," Liam said, and they all turned to him.

Rifter had to admit, the young wolf had balls of steel, because he didn't flinch at all. In the presence of the Dires, most young wolves pissed their pants at the very least.

He was most definitely Linus's son.

"So why did you go out of your way to help her?" Vice demanded of Liam, still not seeing the benefits of any human.

"She was in trouble—Cordelia was coming. And she's sick . . ." Liam trailed off as if he couldn't quite explain his actions.

Rifter interjected. "He probably sensed her seizures the way I did."

"Great, we can rent ourselves out as seizure-alert wolves if we need scratch," Vice said.

"Why wouldn't we be able to sense seizures?" Jinx asked, ignoring Vice, which wasn't easy to do. "I mean, it's not like we've had the opportunity, but it makes sense that we could."

"In all these years, I've never scented a seizing human," Rifter said. "But at first . . . it smelled like a shifting wolf."

"I have—and it does scent like a wolf shift. Difficult to tell them apart," Stray added.

Rifter frowned. "That can't be good."

"It's not like we're supposed to be out do-gooding individual humans. We have our own problems," Vice pointed out. "What good can a human with no gifts of her own bring to us?"

"She's a doctor," Rifter reminded him.

"Human. She bleeds," Vice argued.

"So do you."

"Cut us both and see which one survives."

Rifter didn't move, but his tone was deadly enough when he said, "I'd make sure you didn't."

"So we've got a wolf with a target on his head living with us. We're housing a human, and Harm's back. Merry fucking Christmas," Vice muttered, but he held up his hands in mock surrender.

"We'll have to train him if he has any hope of controlling the New York pack again," Jinx said quietly, his gaze on Liam.

"Oh fuck." Vice threw the hand-rolled smoke he'd lit seconds earlier to the ground. "Are we running a halfway house for these wolves?"

"What the fuck do you think you are?"

"I'm way more civilized." He bared his teeth even as he said it, exposing the gleaming white, longer-than-normal canines.

Vice was telling the truth—as odd as it seemed, Weres had no control over the wolf they became when they turned, making them hard to reason with. Brother Wolves could control a turned Were, but the Dires hadn't wanted to take control of the werepacks. They had enough trouble with the weretrappers and the witches.

Vice ran a frustrated hand through his hair and pointed at Jinx. "You'll have to train wolf boy the way you're training the twins. I've heard three are as easy to handle as two."

"I'll just bet," Jinx muttered. "And this one's all yours."

"Seriously?" Rifter eyed Jinx. "That's not going to end well."

"Yeah, but for which one?" Jinx asked with a smile.

Chapter 13

Cordelia burned.

Seb's own forearms and chest blistered with painful, third-degree burns, and for a half hour, he writhed on the floor, unable to do more than scream.

He'd hated her with the same intensity he felt during her dying moments—Cordelia had always known that her younger brother couldn't stand her. This blood-bond binding spell was her way of ensuring he kept his word and worked with the weretrappers after she was gone. She'd lost her immortality when she'd sold her soul.

He'd felt her die earlier—felt the sharp, stabbing pain at his throat and lost the power of speech. Whatever Were had claimed her life had surely taken a piece of his as well. And although the last breath left Cordelia's body long before she burned in the fire, her spirit hadn't surrendered until her bones were ash, a long and tortuous process that left him prone on the floor and barely breathing.

It took hours, but Seb literally died and regenerated behind the closed door.

When he woke, the blisters and pain were gone, and so was his sister.

Making Rifter pay had never been his top priority. It

would have to be now. It was the only way his coven, who'd joined in with the weretrappers—and the trappers themselves—would have it.

Seb had to remind himself that there were still good witches out there. Hopefully, the majority of the white witches would remain strong. Once the lure of the weretrappers and their promised power began to spread, it could cause complete chaos. Which, of course, was the weretrappers' plan. Start in one state, take it over, and once they controlled the New York financial markets, there wouldn't be much that could stop them from continuing to dominate other states.

There was a time he'd considered the Dires—especially Rifter—as more of a family than he'd ever had. His own had been long abandoned—he'd left his coven at twenty for refusing to practice the black arts. While it interested him as a student of serious magic, he knew the consequences. Black arts could turn men—even witches—mad. He wasn't willing to risk it, not the way Cordelia had.

When she first approached him about coming back to the coven, he knew he wouldn't be able to resist for long. As powerful as he was, black magic was much harder to outrun.

Good might prevail over evil in the end, but most of the time, it was pure dumb luck. And so he'd taken off and he'd run. Figured that maybe splitting entirely from the wolves would be enough to satisfy the coven that he was completely neutral.

It wasn't. The witches sent demons who chased him throughout the world, and Seb lost track of time, spent the majority of the last six years running, living like a hermit, trying to find someone he could pass his powers on to.

The only way an Adept, or master witch, like him

could die was to release his power into an unsuspecting child. Then he would become mortal and he could kill himself.

But to burden someone else—there was no way. One other witch he knew had done so. The rumor was that she'd branded a young girl the weretrappers now watched carefully, waiting for her powers to unfold. Passing powers on was such a risky proposition at best, and if Seb did so to the wrong person . . .

No. He could trust himself only to do the least amount of harm. And that was still, unfortunately, a great deal.

The binding spell his coven placed on him ensured he was bound to them, which meant he was bound to help the weretrappers as well. And so he worked spells that would help his coven and avoid the searing pain he endured every time a witch in his coven, or a weretrapper working with them, was killed by a wolf.

Now, after months of searing pain, he was beginning to break apart. He may have given his mental strength too much credit. By selling his soul in return for access to the black arts, he'd allowed the dark side to own him. He was no better than any of the demons he tried to get to do his bidding.

Their plan was so horrifying. He knew the Dires would survive, or maybe they wouldn't, but there was no way to let them in on the scope of everything without hurting himself beyond repair.

Beyond the curse, the coven threatened him with possession if he tried to stop or leak information to the Dires. Possession was worse; to not be in control, to do irreparable harm—he couldn't bear the thought.

His immortality was also now a curse, which the coven felt was a fitting punishment for abandoning them for the Dire wolves. And he was none too slowly going insane, losing any sense of humanity he had. The pain of

death each time was nearly enough to make him re-
nounce any and all wolves.

Seb was definitely being forced, but that detail
wouldn't matter to Rifter. To the wolf, loyalty was everything, no matter the cost. But if Seb hadn't taken this
curse, the coven would've given it to Rifter. And although it was impossible to tell if a cast spell would take
on a Dire wolf, Seb wasn't willing to take that chance.

Seb would never tell Rifter any of this because there
was nothing Rifter could have done to free him. Pain was
a powerful motivator—pain without the hope of any end
could drive a man insane, no matter how strong he was.

The less the Dires knew of the black arts—or had ties
to it—the better. It was the best Seb could do for his old
friends before he was roped into trying to take them
down the road to hell.

He was sure Rifter would have done the same for his
wolves. Even as he thought of his onetime friend, the
man he'd served proudly next to in the Navy, his body
rejected the thought.

The Dires were memories of a distant time he did not
want to be reminded of, because he'd been happy then.
Today he knew happiness was the biggest illusion of
them all.

Finally, he opened the door, behind which the weretrapper named Marlin Shimmin—aka Mars—waited
none too patiently. He had to have heard Seb's screams
but was at least smart enough not to mention it.

"The wolves are growing in number," he told Mars
without a greeting.

"So are we," Mars snapped back.

In reality, the trapper groups were spread too thin to
be truly effective. They were attempting to gain force
and rebuild the center the Dires blew up after Rifter and
Rogue escaped, where the scientists could continue to

experiment on wolves. Most of the trappers' smaller efforts to that end had been semisuccessful in pushing their agenda forward. A few well-placed Weres in local government offices they could control was an experiment that was going well, but now Mars wanted more. His ultimate plan was to use the demons Seb raised to possess other government officials, no matter how many times Seb told him that demons were tricky to control once let loose.

Mars told him it would be Seb's head if they weren't controlled. Seb knew he wasn't kidding.

Mars's relatives traced back to Viking times, to those slaughtered by the Dire wolves. Those early weretrappers didn't have the vision the group had today. Back then it was all about vengeance and honor—keeping the world safe.

At first the goal of these humans had simply been to destroy wolves. Over time, that morphed into a power play in which the leader and his followers wanted far more.

Today it was about glomming all the power and glory for their own group, and using the wolves to do so seemed the perfect revenge.

The weretrappers were now a paramilitary organization with human volunteers trained in the art of capturing and killing Weres. They'd been trying to do the same to the Dires, but that was a pipe dream. The methods they used, and their purposes, were secrets handed down over hundreds of years. During that time, they'd also kept the fact that there were such things as witches and werewolves to themselves, propagating myths and making sure that no traces of these real-life creatures were discovered. In time, to avoid detection, the individual weretrapping groups were forced to become as insular as the wolves they hunted.

"The world is too crowded," Mars would tell them. "We need a simpler way of life. A better way to protect our country's boundaries, since the politicians can't seem to do their jobs."

He would always get applause at rallies when he brought politics into the mix.

Currently, their main trapper cells were in California, Texas and Wisconsin, and of course the biggest group was in New York, mirroring where the largest Were packs were located. Smaller factions were scattered throughout other states as well, mainly wolf watchers who scouted areas and scoured the Internet for any chatter about wolf sightings from ghost-hunting groups and the like.

The Dires were the most slippery, despite their size. That was until Harm's true Dire nature was discovered, thanks to Cordelia. She'd followed Harm to his current lover's house and discovered that while the woman was human, Harm certainly wasn't.

Humans had far too much greed and hubris—and the kind of power Mars wanted would drive him into the ground faster than he realized. Everyone around Seb was using black magic to take things further and making deals with demons. If they thought they had control over their decisions, they were truly insane.

"We need the girl," Mars seethed now. He'd been practicing black arts with the coven for years, and he'd sold his soul for paranormal powers. That had turned him over the past year into an entity Seb no longer recognized. "And we need the Dires."

"The house spell cannot be reversed," Seb reminded him. "They're protected."

Mars moved closer to him, and Seb forced himself not to shudder under the man's touch. Mars massaged his shoulders, and the pain of the regeneration made it ache more than comfort.

The demon who wrestled with Mars for control of the man's body loved him, wanted him, body and soul. Sexually. Seb understood because the lure of his blood bond was now much like the fateful siren song. Like Vice, the Dire, no one could resist.

At one time, Seb thought he could use it to his advantage, to get Mars to help him leave the coven if he promised to help with other dark magic not related to the wolves, but the curse Cordelia placed on him wouldn't allow it.

"Do what you're supposed to and there won't be any more punishments," Mars murmured. "I don't like seeing you hurt."

If only it were that easy. "Linus's son lives."

"Liam will turn himself in for his mate." Mars was confident in that; Seb less so. Liam was king and could not be expected to act like a silly fool for love. Rifter, on the other hand, seemed to be doing exactly that for Gwen.

It would be the Dire's undoing. And that made Seb sadder than he'd ever thought possible.

Rifter walked up three flights of stairs, pausing at the second landing, where Gwen's scent lingered. He realized he'd be able to track her easily now. He didn't think she'd try to escape, but his brothers would no doubt have their reservations.

Having her here would be tricky. Letting her die alone wasn't an option.

He climbed the last flight and didn't knock before entering the room in the middle of the hallway, where Stray watched over Harm. He'd had Stray move him up to Rogue's floor earlier, when he knew Gwen would be staying with them. No need for her to stumble on anything to arouse further suspicions.

Stray wasn't surprised to see him. "I've been trying to rouse him."

Rifter noted the Taser in Stray's hand, as well as the burn marks on Harm's neck and arms. Stray appeared calm and unruffled, but in actuality, he was probably the roughest of the bunch, a street urchin who'd done whatever it took to survive on his own. He was used to being a loner and was still having trouble with the pack mentality.

But Stray did understand that the pack was necessary for his health. He'd been grateful to find wolves like him. He'd been exploited by Weres and humans when he was younger and living on the streets.

He didn't elaborate much about that to anyone besides Rogue, because that man knew how to keep secrets. And at the thought of Rogue—of the capture—the calm Rifter forced himself to have so he wouldn't lose it in front of Gwen or Liam dissipated. He picked up the unconscious wolf without compunction and threw him to the ground hard enough to dent the floor. He wanted to kill this wolf, but Rifter knew he needed Harm awake for it to be any kind of a satisfactory mauling.

It didn't stop Rifter from picking him up and slamming him to the ground several more times. Stray Tasered Harm for good measure. Twice. The Dire's body shuddered, but nothing else happened.

Harm looked the same as he had when he'd been trolling stages all over the world, hypnotizing the masses with his golden voice.

Bastard had always been too handsome for his own good.

"You call me the second he wakes—I don't care what else I'm doing. I want first words with him."

Stray nodded. "You'll be at the moon celebration, yes?"

He nodded. "We have two guests here—Liam, Linus's son, and a human, but she's sleeping. She saved Liam."

"She's the human from last night, isn't she?" Stray asked. "You know I'm not the only one who'll be asking."

Rifter nodded. Not only would the weretrappers know, but the outlaw wolves would as well.

She was in danger with him—and without him. "We're in some deep shit."

"Let the moon celebration ease you," Stray urged.

The party was always the day after the full moon. Until they had a proper way to vent their human urges, they would be too riled up to do much good for anyone. Full moons were for running wild. Moon celebrations were for feeding their primal frenzy, which followed when they morphed back to human form. The Elders knew they needed it badly, and it was a tradition the Dires continued to follow.

Stray would be relieved by Jinx because he was close to snapping. His calm countenance didn't fool Rifter at all.

Too bad the only release Rifter wanted was with Gwen.

"Mistake," Stray said, and Rifter pinned him to the wall.

"Cut that shit out."

"You can walk through my mind but I can't return the favor?" Stray asked.

"How long have you been able to do that?"

Stray didn't answer directly. "It comes and goes. Feelings need to be strong, and yours are strong."

Rifter pushed an arm across his throat. "Stay out of my head."

"You do the same."

"Did you forget I'm in charge here?"

"Then prove it."

He would give Stray some rope because he'd been watching Harm. Even though the wolf hadn't been with them when Harm left them originally in the early part of the eleventh century, he'd been privy to Rifter's and Rogue's capture, and the lone, rogue wolf inside of him was taut with untamed anger. "I'll prove it and you won't be happy, Stray. Watch your tongue and respect your elders."

Stray's eyes searched Rifter's but he said nothing more. Rifter left, but not without a last look at Harm.

When he headed downstairs, he heard the first strains of the music start—no doubt Cyd and Cain had grown impatient with waiting, and the Weres who'd been invited would be equally impatient to party with the Dires.

Inviting the wolves was a bit like inviting sin to come out and play. Beyond Vice, whose extremes could never be ignored, both Dires and Weres were simply examples of walking primal needs. They exuded it without trying— it was part of their makeup as wolves, and they saw no reason not to revel in it.

Like the extraordinary strength and speed they possessed, it was simply a part of who they were.

Humans didn't understand the power that lurked literally at their doorsteps, that if the Dires, no matter how small their numbers, decided to drop their tightly knit control—and that of the Weres—they'd wipe out a good deal of the population before anyone knew what happened.

It was much easier to play full human.

Sure, they'd all pushed the boundaries—dated movie stars, mingled with A-listers—but the charade and lack of resolution left them bored. It was easier to let the wolves have fun their way instead of reveling in the ways of humans.

But now the war of the Weres, the witches and the weretrappers was settling on them with a ferocity they couldn't ignore.

"We could just get the hell out of here," Vice would often say. "Not everything in life is our responsibility."

But it wasn't that simple. The Were packs had grown tremendously over the past hundreds of years. Unfortunately, so had the human population, as the area had become something of a trendy hot spot. They would need to move farther upstate soon, but some of the packs balked. Wanted to stay and instead thin out the humans.

That would be the worst thing they could do.

Linus had agreed, and he'd been killed for his views against the dissenting outlaws. And although the Dires had long stayed out of Were politics as much as they possibly could, the pack war threatened to expose them all.

But tonight all of that was put aside—a celebration of the moon, because they knew no other way.

The event was tied in with Rifter's dreams now, and he willed himself to forget how those ended . . . and he hoped he wasn't having any kind of premonition.

As for Gwen, he knew his brothers were right. Although she wasn't going anywhere, he couldn't risk her discovering what they actually were. He needed to make her think she was losing it a little—if she continued dreaming of wolves, she'd be less sure that what she saw was real . . . plus, he wouldn't be able to help it.

Chapter 14

Gwen showered in Rifter's black marble–tiled bathroom. The house, from what she'd seen of it, was far more decadent than she'd expected for some kind of Hells Angels gang. It was almost more like a rock star's palace—all of the rooms were circular, and she'd caught a glimpse of the large kitchen in the center of the house, with a huge brick fireplace and leather couches and a white shag rug.

Somehow, it looked both modern and expensive. And pretty damned clean for a bachelor pad that housed giant men.

She wondered if the windows were bulletproof. Or at least fireproof.

She highly suspected no one was sneaking in here to plant a bomb. Still, she was glad she'd shared her worries with Rifter and told him the basics of what happened to people around her.

She'd been eight when her mother died, seventeen when her aunt and uncle's house burned to the ground, destroying everything in it and killing them. She'd asked the judge for emancipation—couldn't bear the thought of foster care for the year—and it had been granted.

There hadn't been much money—no insurance because the adjustors claimed the fire was suspicious, believed her aunt and uncle had set it on purpose to avoid filing for bankruptcy. And so she'd started out alone and with nothing. Her high school counselor helped her get scholarships and loans for college. Gwen did the same for med school, but she was still pretty broke, except for a small savings she used to rent her house.

Now, as she washed the shampoo from her hair, she thought about the things she'd lost in the fire. There had been only a few things salvaged from her aunt and uncle's house. Some paintings had made it through, albeit with scorch marks across most of them, nearly obscuring the curious wolf-and-moon theme her aunt was obsessed with. Now they were completely destroyed.

Maybe they were cursed. Or maybe she was, as she'd always suspected. If so, these men needed to be far more worried about her than she was about them.

And she'd keep repeating that to herself until she believed it.

Finally she stopped smelling the smoke on herself and she shut off the water and walked out into the mirrored bathroom. There were clean white towels and she wrapped herself in one and searched for a shirt to wear.

Rifter had left one out for her, along with a pair of sweatpants that would never stay up. Since the T-shirt was thick and came down to her knees, she figured that would work well enough for now. She washed her underwear and hung them to dry.

Somehow, she'd have to get more clothes.

When she came out of the bathroom, she found an overflowing tray of food on the edge of the bed. She sat and ate until her stomach was satisfied—and until her head felt a little woozy.

Food coma. Coupled with all that had happened today, she was surprised she hadn't crashed earlier. Until now, she hadn't thought about seizing, and although she felt light-headed, she was able to lie back and relax.

She didn't know if it was hours or minutes later, but she found herself walking through the halls of the mansion. She'd never been a sleepwalker, but this didn't feel exactly like a dream. No, she was slightly suspended between reality and this floaty state that propelled her toward the music.

She stepped outdoors, the snow falling on her like some kind of fairy dust, the icy grass tickling her bare feet. She wasn't cold in the least—on the contrary, her body seemed to radiate enough heat to melt the snow as it touched her skin.

There were lanterns hung, strung along the porch, and people wandered around, coupling off. The music was sensual, and she found herself swaying to it a little as she watched, trying to get her bearings.

Jinx was here, as was Vice. There were other big men too, and lots of women. She swore she recognized some of them from around town, but faces were fleeting, like there was some kind of haze over the whole scene. She wanted to push away the gauzy curtain, but rubbing her eyes didn't help.

It was a party of dangerous men and beautiful women. The air was ripe with lust and sex, and there was no pretense of what this party was about.

Something surged inside of her—maybe something the meds suppressed, or maybe they weren't out of her system yet. Or maybe it was simply being anywhere in Rifter's presence.

Because she'd smelled him on the towels, the sheets, the shirt she wore. She smelled him on her when she was naked and just out of the shower, which made no sense. And she scented him now without question.

She wondered if she was supposed to be here, but

there was no way to make herself invisible—men especially noticed her. Vice looked her way, bared his teeth even though he looked relaxed. Jinx was standing with his back to the wall, a woman trapping him in place, looking like she was prepared to kneel between his legs.

There were weapons everywhere she looked—knives and guns—and none of the women seemed as worried as she felt. As it was, she was slightly terrified but way more fascinated. Because, along with the weapons of destruction, there were flowers and drinks and beads, like it was Mardi Gras. Someone put a few strands around her neck from behind, but when she turned she saw no one. She fingered the silver and pink beads and breathed it all in.

It was a party made of magic. Even now, standing at the threshold, she couldn't be sure if it was merely a dream. And she wasn't sure if she wanted it to be so or not.

As someone brushed by her, she felt a prickle on her skin. Saw Vice's easy smile again, this time directed to the man and woman standing with him. Heard him ask if they were afraid of the big bad wolf.

"I'm guessing you do more than huff and puff," the woman said, and the man moved behind Vice, laughed before kissing his way down the big man's spine. Vice pulled the woman in close and kissed her, and Gwen looked up and saw Rifter similarly surrounded by two women, but he wasn't kissing anyone.

He was staring straight at her.

Her skin prickled, tight and warm, like she had a fever. Maybe she did. She was light-headed, dreamy. Couldn't be sure this was reality and didn't care.

The women next to Rifter touched his bare chest, his back, stared up at him longingly, and she let the growl rip from her throat without care. They turned to her and Rifter smiled.

God, it was really the first time she'd seen that. It was beautiful.

The music was pounding, the air smelled heavy with perfume and musk and she wanted to dance. The women moved away from Rifter as she walked over to him and tugged against him, their bodies melding in time to the beat.

"What's the celebration for?" she asked him.

"The moon." He looked up at the sky and she saw it, nearly full and luminous.

"Everyone's looking at me," she said.

"Let them. As long as no one touches you."

"As long as no one touches you either."

"Feeling protective?" he asked.

"Why didn't you invite me?"

"You're here, aren't you?"

She got up on tiptoes as he bent his head to hers, and she kissed him—or he kissed her, tongue exploring, his erection pressing her belly. His hands splayed along her back and his posturing was nothing short of possessive—and protective.

All around them, it was half-naked bodies rubbing together under a nearly full moon, like a midsummer's night party except there was snow on the ground and the steam rose off the bodies.

"What are we celebrating?"

"Being alive," he murmured against her neck, then licked his way along her jawbone until she shivered. "Dancing with our inner beasts."

"I don't think I have one."

He spoke languidly. "Sure you do. I feel it." His hand strayed between her legs, her sex naked to his touch. "Your heart's beating down here. I feel it."

She flushed, rubbed herself on his hand. Might have

been embarrassed, but everyone seemed too caught up in their own frenzy to notice.

Still, she wanted him alone. In his big bed with the dark sheets. His hand was getting bolder.

"Come on—need you naked," he murmured.

Yes, she wanted that, and he picked her up, carried her like she weighed nothing. He cut through the crowds, went up the stairs and into his room. Put her down in front of the bed and skimmed her T-shirt off and stared languidly at her nakedness. Took his time, ran a hand down her shoulder, stopping at her breast. She gasped when he thumbed a nipple and still didn't take his eyes from her face.

The doors to the balcony were open behind the filmy curtains, and this all felt both illicit and romantic. *Dirty hot,* she thought as he flicked her nipple hard. That sent a shiver that shot straight through to her core like nothing she'd ever felt before.

She reached forward and undid the button on his black leather pants, and he rewarded her with another smile. Fingers on her other nipple as she ran a teasing finger of her own across the hard ripple of his abs, wondering why she had the sudden urge to nip her way down his broad body.

His hand moved between her legs and stroked slowly—she needed more. "Faster."

He complied, brought his mouth down on hers, his tongue mimicking what his two fingers were doing inside of her. Her hands ran along his shoulders—his skin was so hot, almost electric, and she wrapped a leg around his to give him more access to her. Loved the feeling of his rough hands on her . . . in her.

She moaned against his mouth, his name at first and then just incoherent things as his fingers took her more intensely. She was going to come—wanted to. Needed to, and the orgasm rocked her so intensely she wouldn't have been able to stay on her feet if he hadn't been holding her.

After a few long minutes, her head pressed to his shoulder, her body trembling, he picked her up and laid her on the bed. And then he stripped off his jeans, and she heard herself sigh appreciatively.

Everything about him was big, exactly the way he'd looked in her dream. He was extremely proportionate, built like he could take on the world. He was meant to pleasure a woman, from his looks to his hands . . . to his thick, jutting cock, and she spread her legs wantonly while she waited for him to cover her.

Finally, he moved forward onto her. She slid along the sheets, the material silky along the back of her thighs. His skin was rougher on the front, the crisp hairs tickling her. His mouth lowered to hers again; his arousal pressed her sex.

She wondered if she should mention her virginity, having nearly forgotten about it as her body took over. But then Rifter pulled away and murmured, "Make me forget," and she had no idea who or what he was talking about, but all she wanted to do was comply. Didn't want anyone or anything on his mind but her, wanted that with a possessiveness that was all-consuming.

Chapter 15

"My, what a big dick you have," the female Were named Chloe—or Carol or maybe her name didn't even begin with a *C*—told Vice, but when she started going down on him, who the hell cared.

Sex was an obvious pleasure. Wolves were primal creatures. Vice got to double his fun thanks to his bisexuality. Man, woman . . . it didn't much matter as long as he got off.

He was probably the only one of the Dires who didn't exactly hate the pain after orgasm.

The male Were he'd brought to his room hadn't even introduced himself—not formally, anyway, and he remained with his mouth pressed to the back of Vice's neck, sucking on the spot the Dire liked, alternately biting, and Vice's body was strung far too tight not to come immediately.

Since his Brother Wolf had missed his run last night, the wolf was restless, and a restless, irritable wolf living inside a volatile human body was a bad sitch altogether.

Vice had jerked himself off several times before the party in hopes of some relief—short-lived as it might be. Afterward, the ache made him nearly double over, even as his body asked for more.

It would never be enough, which was why, most of the time, Vice didn't give a fuck.

Which wasn't to say he didn't have fun. Even if he didn't want to, he couldn't help it; it was a built-in piece of the Dire nature—primal and strong. To ignore it was futile—Brother Wolf wouldn't allow it anyway.

No, being a Dire was all about finding balance, and when his needs were called out, they responded in kind. Vice let those needs course through his body—they were never far from the surface, but tonight they pulled him taut, a bow ready to snap, and he knew once the frenzy took him over, it wouldn't stop. And he was more than ready to throw himself into it.

The woman straddled him and writhed as she rode his cock. Vice lost any last semblance of control. Safe within the confines of his house and the moon celebration, he let himself revel in the blatantly carnal display.

Beautiful bodies, hot mouths, everything he wanted—and by morning, none of it would have mattered.

It never did.

Now the two Weres were fighting for his attention, which was exactly the way Vice liked it. The male Were tugged his nipple piercing, and Vice welcomed the pain. The Were ran his nail down Vice's back and he shuddered. Even now, as the pain surged after the orgasm waned, the new sensations built, tightening his balls. He closed his eyes and let the two bodies work on him, mouths and teeth and tongues, and they'd just moved to the bed when he heard someone at his door.

The knocking made him want to kill. Anything. The two Weres were fair game and they knew it, so they stilled.

Vice rolled out of bed naked and growled softly. He'd planned on using them all night, kicking them out before dawn and sleeping alone for the rest of the day.

Obviously, Jinx had other plans. "You in there, Vice?"

"Coming. Literally."

"Get them the fuck out of there."

"Taking your life in your hands," Vice called back, but Jinx opened the door anyway. Vice didn't bother to dress, stretched his arms out wide when Jinx rolled his eyes.

"You gonna huff and puff?" Jinx asked.

"Is he joining us?" the male Were purred.

"Fuck off. Vice, get dressed."

"Turning you on?" Vice asked. Jinx snorted and threw pants at him.

"We're missing a young one," he said, and Vice had no doubt whom Jinx referred to. Reluctantly, he pulled the female up and tossed both her and the male their clothes. They were obviously disappointed, and yeah, join the goddamned club.

When they left, escorted downstairs and out by Cain, who waited in the hallway, Jinx said, "We need to get him before Rifter kills him."

"Or me," Vice added, and Jinx nodded. The little fucker was out of the house and ruining Vice's moon celebration, blowing it to hell. Vice yanked on jeans and boots and a black T, satisfied that at least Jinx was coming with him. Because if his night was ruined, so was the man who suggested he be in charge of Liam, the little boy who cried wolf king. "Where's he headed?"

"He took Stray's Harley—Cain tracked him to the cemetery."

"Didn't know he was a ghost hunter."

"Cain's heard rumors that's where the outlaws are taking meetings. He's watching Liam, but I told him not to get too close," Jinx said, and Vice grabbed his jacket and followed his fellow Dire down the stairs and into the truck.

The Weres in New York had all been trying to join with the Dires for years.

"Why bother with the young and inexperienced when you could have us?" Vice had heard Teague demand of Rifter last year. Unrepentant and untamed, he was someone the Dires could respect if he'd controlled his part of the pack better.

Linus had kicked him and several others out when he'd discovered they'd been undermining him.

Now the outlaw pack was out for blood.

"You know, we should let them kill one another," Vice said as Jinx pulled out of the driveway, and he readied the rifle in case they ran into any trouble along the way. "None of them have the self-control they need."

"Funny, you talking about self-control. Besides, that's why we exist," Jinx reminded him, and Vice began cursing a diatribe about the fucking Elders, knowing full well he'd pay for it.

"How much worse can it get?" he'd ask, because his body was always strumming with want and need, no way to ever fully burn them off.

The pentagram tattooed on the front of his throat was a direct parody of the wolf-man movies. He touched it now and let the semirational part of his brain come into focus.

The packs were in ruins. Without their solidarity, it made them all easy fodder for the weretrappers.

The weretrappers would use them and eventually wolves would be outed, and then humans would freak the fuck out for sure. They'd have a Were army coming after them—one the witches would help to control through black magic.

Their great white wolf hope was twenty-two and recovering nicely from his near-death experience . . . and putting himself in goddamned danger.

He lit up a rolled cigarette, the blue smoke drifting around him, clinging to him like a lover and illuminating his illicit beauty, which had gotten him out of trouble for centuries.

Vice's old Marine sarge used to remind them that, in order to get out of a jam, they should confess to something illegal, immoral or embarrassing.

Vice took it a step further and would actually commit the illegal, immoral, embarrassing act and then confess to it. Because hell, if you were going to confess to the crime, what was the point if you didn't get the enjoyment from it?

When vice was in your nature—when vice *was* your nature—it wasn't hard to be a part of the pack lifestyle he'd grown up in. From the time Vice was born, he'd fit right into the Viking mold. Had been accepted, so the Running for him had been more of an annoyance than anything.

Today the story on the Vikings was that they weren't crazy or barbaric or pillaging, but the reality was that they had been. And Vice had reveled in that, so much so that the Running gave him less freedom than he'd had within the pack that lived among the Viking humans.

Their Dire culture had trained the young men and women as warriors from the time they were born, knowing that they would need physical strength if they had any hope of surviving their first several shifts into wolf form. Once those shifts were completed, the young males were allowed to run free in the world, to try on their independence and see how well they could blend in with the humans around them. It also marked them entering adulthood and enjoying more of the primal nature their wolves insisted on.

During his Running, Vice had been with humans who were far gentler, and he'd had to be careful. He'd been relieved when the time was over and he could return to his pack, only to find that, while he'd been on his Running, the packs had defied orders from the Elders and had in fact massacred humans in direct opposition to the beings put in charge of them by their creator, Hati, son of a Norse god who chased the moon.

Vice had been the most devastated by the Extinction of his Dire kind the Elders had wrought. How could you discover that your kind had been annihilated for the very excesses that your entire being was built upon and be all right? And one that you could do nothing to modify, no matter how hard you tried?

There was no answer to that for him other than to live forever.

———

Chapter 16

She can't handle you.

But Rifter's body didn't care. Gwen's skin tasted like black cherry, fizzing under his tongue as he licked along her neck like an explosion, and everything else melted away.

Only a dream.

But it felt far more real than it should. She was splayed under him, begging for more with every touch, every moan. And he was still too far under the pull of the moon to be this damned close to a human, but she was so willing . . . and he wasn't made of stone, no matter how much he'd tried to be.

His body longed for hers—there was no other way to describe it. He'd always been sexual—primal—but he'd never, ever wanted like this. It scared and excited him at once.

She ripped his shirt off and went for his nipples, suckling them, biting his pecs, taking his hand and putting it between her legs. "Please, Rifter."

"Gwen—"

"I'm not asking—I'm telling you that I need this."

"You don't know what you're telling me."

But he took her anyway. Before he could stop himself,

he was pushing inside of her. Her sex opened slowly for him—she was tight and hot, but welcoming as hell. He held her hips and thrust hard, once, twice, and she groaned, called his name and began to work into a rhythm with him.

So tight . . . this couldn't be her first time, though. She was getting too much pleasure from it, and from what he knew of virgins, that didn't often happen.

She was at his mercy, pinned beneath his big body, and she wasn't scared at all. "Now, Rifter."

He was no longer dreamwalking. He didn't know when they'd crashed back to reality, but he was fully inside of her and there was no way he was pulling out now.

She wouldn't have let him, clenched around him, her legs wrapped around him, heels digging his back hard.

Don't hurt her.

"Harder, Rifter," she begged. God, if he complied . . .

But her nails raked his back and for a second, he swore he saw wolf's eyes.

He must be seeing his own eyes reflected in hers, so he squeezed them tightly shut before she noticed, buried his head along her neck.

He forced back a growl. The air changed, and he took her then, plunged into her, stretching her, taking her with the ferocity he craved. Speared her with his cock, her wet heat sucking him in, and he took her hard, rode her until she came with a shudder and a cry, and then it happened.

If she noticed she didn't let on. Rifter thought she was too deep in the throes of the orgasm . . . but he was locked inside of her. Mating with her.

Up until this point, the mating was only something he'd heard described, but he'd certainly never experienced it firsthand. That was impossible.

All of this was fucking impossible.

But he couldn't have pulled out of Gwen if he'd wanted it. And he didn't want to.

You can't mate with a human. A dying one at that, and maybe it was the meds she was on or maybe he was for sure losing his goddamned mind, but he continued thrusting and they both had multiple orgasms that lasted longer than he'd thought possible.

Afterward, he waited for the familiar pain to hit him. Nothing could be that good and not make him suffer for it afterward.

But it didn't.

Something was happening—his body began to tingle, the way it would at times before a shift, and he smelled the shift.

Had he lost that much control or . . .

He pulled back and looked at her. She seemed to be lost in pleasure, her eyes closed, her body responding to his, but he needed to stop. With a herculean effort, he pulled out of her, and it seemed to take a few minutes for her to open her eyes and realize something was wrong.

"What happened?" she asked, her voice slightly hoarse, her eyes unfocused.

Lie to her . . . don't make her feel bad. "You seemed . . . different. I thought I was hurting you."

She blanched visibly. "Shit, I'm sorry. I think I must've seized."

He kissed her to stop her from saying anything more, for apologizing for something that didn't happen—something that, if it had, certainly wasn't her fault. He pulled back and said, "I must've brought it on—I came on too strong."

"You came on just right." She buried her face in his neck and hugged him, and they lay together, wrapped around each other, the strains of music drifting in through the open window.

The party would last until dawn, with some lingering through breakfast and a few lucky women past noon. Gwen would be here long after that—it was a definite first for him. "It's okay, Gwen. You told me what was going on the first night we met."

Granted, that seemed like years ago, rather than less than forty-eight hours earlier.

"It's not every day I get attacked and rescued like this," she said. "Normally I'd be scared."

"I don't want you to be." No, he wanted her final time to be peaceful. Didn't want her going anywhere, and for the first time he wanted to rail against the unfairness of it all.

God, this was embarrassing. Sex and seizures most definitely didn't go together. And if Gwen didn't know better, she'd have thought it had all been a dream, except she was wearing the beads someone had placed around her neck at the party.

Rifter played with them now.

Maybe you are really dreaming.

But the ache between her legs told her something real had happened, even if Rifter's unmistakable presence wasn't telling enough. And still she said, "Tonight seems . . . unreal."

He glanced at her, the silver and pink beads still twined around his fingers. "The celebration always feels like that."

"You have them a lot?"

"Once a month."

Would she be around for the next one? "Am I here because you feel sorry for me?"

"No. But the thought of you being alone through this—"

"So then, a little sorry?"

A smile brushed his lips. "I want to spend more time with you."

"You know I have nowhere else to go. Judging by what happened tonight, that probably works out well for you."

"Doesn't hurt."

That should probably sting a little more than it did, but she appreciated the honesty. Maybe there was more where that came from, so she took a chance. "Will you answer some questions for me?"

"Some." He stroked a hand over her cheek. "You need some food first, because I can barely hear what you're saying over your stomach rumbling. Again."

She punched his arm playfully—it was like punching steel. She studied his muscles for a long moment while he made a quick call downstairs and turned back to her. "Food is on the way."

She settled back, the sheet barely covering her. "Thanks."

"Why don't you tell me more about your parents—and your aunt and uncle. You seemed pretty convinced that you're—cursed, I think you said?"

"My parents were . . . it's a long story."

"I didn't realize we were out of time."

She fingered the tribal wolf tattoo that ran from Rifter's collarbone toward his pec—it appeared as alive as the one on his back, even though the look was totally different. He watched her intently as she touched it, and she felt his skin ripple under his touch. Maybe the tattoos made his skin more sensitive? But he didn't tell her to stop, was waiting for the rest of her story. "They're dead."

"So not really that long of a tale after all."

She smirked. "Wiseass."

"I've been told that."

"By all the women who follow you?"

Rifter looked around, then back at her. "You're the only woman with me."

Something in the way he said it made her not want to question him further. "My dad ... my mom said she didn't know who he was."

She didn't want to expound, but she had a feeling he'd understand. "I think he might've ... raped her. She never wanted to talk about him, always seemed really angry if anyone brought up my father in front of me. I was born in England and we lived there until she died. I was ten when my aunt and uncle took me in and brought me to the States. I stayed with them until I went to college."

"My parents died when I was young too."

"Did you go into foster care or did family take you in?"

He shook his head, and for a second, the shaggy, handsome wolf from last night's dream came roaring back to her. "Neither. I went out on my own."

"Was that hard?"

"Sometimes." He wasn't giving her more than that — not now, anyway. "Did you ever stop to think that it could just be a shitty coincidence that people die around you?"

"Coupled with the fact that I'm dying as the ultimate irony?" she pointed out as she threaded her fingers together. "No, it's not a coincidence."

"And so you went into medicine to try to make up for it?"

"It's not that simple."

"Nothing is."

"I was fired from the program today," she admitted with a casualness she didn't feel. "At least I got to do some good for Liam."

"Why did they fire you?"

"You know, the whole falling, seizing, dying thing."

She looked at him pointedly. "I'm sure that wasn't what you expected last night. I'm guessing that's why you left—you were probably scared."

"Do I look like there's a lot that freaks me?" he shot back. "Who do you think put you into bed? I stayed with you until I was sure you were asleep. I didn't leave until close to five in the morning, Gwen."

She didn't want to believe him. "Sure you did. I'm sure it was a real turn-on for you."

"Why are you so hard on yourself?" he asked. "You're beautiful. You're sick, and it's not your fault. I wish I could've been there when you woke up, but I had work to do."

He just looked at her, no pity in his eyes, but she knew he felt bad for her. Time for a change of subject. "You know, I dreamed about you after you left. Or maybe while you were there. I felt you. And I liked it."

Now she looked up at the dream catcher hanging on Rifter's headboard. She'd noticed it earlier—it was bigger than any she'd seen and quite intricate.

She reached up and fingered the delicate feathers now.

"It's a dream catcher," Rifter said.

"I know. My aunt bought me one—I used to have these really . . . odd dreams. I still have them sometimes."

"About what?"

"I'm running through the woods and it's really dark but I can see and hear everything." *Sort of like what happened earlier,* she thought, but didn't say that out loud.

"Doesn't sound bad."

"That part's not. But then something starts chasing me—or a few somethings. I wake up before they get too close because it's like I know I'm in danger." She paused. "What kind of dreams do you have that you need one of these?"

"Let's just say it's doing its job."

She wanted to find comfort in the thought of sweet dreams, but somehow she knew he was lying about it. And then the events in the woods and at her house came rushing back at her, full force. She sat up, felt dizzy. "This is all too much to take in. I don't even know how I'm supposed to feel. I'm here in your bed, partying after the man I just saved killed a woman in front of me. And then you . . . God, you killed those men."

"Gwen, I think the meds are—"

"I'm off them. I might be hallucinating, but people died today. And I killed one of them."

Chapter 17

Liam moved through the cemetery, careful not to step on the graves as he wove through the complicated coordinates he'd memorized a week earlier, when he and his father had their last meeting in secret.

He forced himself to keep putting one foot in front of the other before grief threatened to bury him. The fate of the pack weighed on him heavily enough already, and that was the only thing that had gotten him out of bed and down the driveway of the Dire mansion.

He'd waited until the music started before he attempted to get off the stretcher. The scar would remain forever, but the stitches were already disappearing. He was still weak, but he didn't plan on fighting tonight. No, it was about recon and it couldn't have waited another second. And it was too private to spill it to the Dires, no matter how much he owed them for saving his ass.

His body had naturally pulled toward the moon-celebration party but he'd forced his wolf out the door and down the long drive, his hair wrapped in a bandana, a borrowed black leather jacket and boots letting him blend in with every other Were wandering the property.

He scanned the passing wolves—no outlaw should have dared to come to this party—but Liam didn't put anything past Tals and Teague's group any longer. Hoped the Dires were too caught up in the moon celebration to worry about him, used one of the Harleys parked outside—hot-wired it and took off for the cemetery two towns over.

If the rumors panned out, he'd find out tonight.

His father had died because he had this intel. Word was no doubt already out that Liam had lived through the attack—if he wanted his proof, tonight would be his last shot before the meeting place was moved. That's if the original Were informant had the correct information to begin with.

He was downwind—the scent of Dire and of Gwen lingered on him—and he watched the stone mausoleum, innocuous and just like the others that surrounded it.

The stone would stop him from hearing much of anything—the witch's spell would take care of the rest. But he needed only his sight for this to know for sure.

Twenty minutes later, he had his answer.

She exited behind Teague, and Liam's throat threatened to close. He bit down so hard he thought his teeth would break, closed his eyes and reopened them, hoping the scene before him would be different.

It wasn't. Max let Teague take her by the hand and lead her away from the meeting place . . . and she was smiling.

He really had no one left.

The betrayal sliced him worse than the knife the outlaws had wielded against him. Dying would've been so much easier than this. He cursed his weakness, felt the shift start to take hold, which would split his chest back open.

"Hold it together." Vice's low growl, a command that Liam's wolf responded to. He became aware of Vice's viselike grip on his arm, the only thing keeping him from shifting and barreling into the group of outlaws.

They stood there as he calmed—Liam vaguely aware that Jinx was behind him as well—and watched Max and Teague and a few others disappear across the cemetery, followed by two humans who walked along the same path.

Weretrappers. Possibly witches, but Vice and Jinx wouldn't let him get close enough to tell.

No, Liam was on the witch shit list as of now because of Cordelia.

"Who's the chick?" Vice asked.

Liam opened his mouth but the words, *my mate*, lodged in his throat.

Mating was complete bullshit. "Grab her," he managed instead.

"Not here," Jinx said.

"She works at the hospital," Liam told them.

"Tomorrow," Vice said.

"Alive," Liam reiterated.

Vice sighed. "I've really got to teach you not to play with your food."

"You know she's human?" Jinx asked, and Liam nodded. It had been a shock to him as well.

And Max knew he was wolf. Knew who his father was. She knew everything about him, and even though she'd never truly fit into his pack, he was determined not to give her up.

And she'd obviously used him. What other explanation could there be? Hanging out with the outlaw wolves who'd killed his father . . .

He bit back a fierce curse as he thought about the guilt he'd felt hiding from her this past week so he wouldn't bring danger to her doorstep. They'd hidden their relationship for the last year from anyone but their closest packmates, although his father had known about it from the start.

Max, with her long dark hair and icy green eyes . . .
the tattoos down her arm that originally drew him to her
in the bar that night a year earlier.

Broaching the topic "I'm a wolf and howl at the
moon" had been easier than he'd thought. She hadn't
spoken to him for two weeks after that, not until he'd
serenaded her outside her window and made her laugh.

"We can be normal," he'd insisted. "My job is with the
wolves and yours is in the hospital."

For a while, it had worked. Now he knew better.

He let Vice and Jinx flank and lead him to the edge of
the cemetery where he'd hidden the Harley. Watched
Jinx walk it into the back of the van and load it up. He
got in the middle seat between the large wolves.

"She's my mate," he told them finally when they
pulled into the Dires' garage.

"No shit," Vice said. "Like an idiot couldn't figure that
out."

Gwen stared into his eyes, waiting for Rifter to try to
convince her she was losing it. Again.

But this time, instead of brushing off her questions, he
told her, "People did die tonight. Bad ones."

"I guess I'll need to believe that." She paused. "If
those men at my house weren't the police . . ."

"They weren't," he assured her.

"I'm supposed to help people." She put her fingers to
her temples and tried to breathe through the room spinning. God, she should at least have had one drink before
that happened.

"Self-defense is still allowed in this country. I'm going
to get you a washcloth for your head and run a bath for
you to soak in. You have to be sore from what happened—I see the bruises." He got up and went to the

bathroom. She glanced up and saw his back, and things began to click into place.

The wolf ...

Unmistakably a wolf tattoo that took up his entire back ... and the eyes ... it was as if they watched her. Fierce but beautiful.

It was the wolf she'd seen last night. The one that saved her from the fire.

Had she seen it the other night before her seizure and her subconscious processed it into her dreams? That was the only rational explanation she could come up with.

She wanted a closer look, found herself padding toward him even as he turned to tell her to get back to bed.

"Please, I need to see this." She pushed a little and he complied after he turned the water on, standing patiently, head up as she traced the wolf with a finger first, like she was afraid it would bite her if she got too close.

When nothing happened but Rifter letting out a stuttered breath, she grew bolder, ran her hands over the tattoo, and he shivered under her touch. The eyes ... they were looking at her.

"This explains it," she murmured.

"What?" He looked over his shoulder.

"I dreamed of this wolf the night I met you ... must've seen it somehow." But that wasn't possible. "He's beautiful."

Rifter nodded, like he'd heard that before, and she could've sworn the ink moved under her touch, undulated, but it must just have been a trick of the light, the way Rifter's muscles bunched and shifted as he moved.

"But I keep seeing them," she continued. "Tonight— Liam ... and then on the porch of my house ..." She noted that the bullet wound on Rifter's biceps had inexplicably healed, rubbed a finger over it but didn't comment.

He turned to her. "You've had a rough day."

"To put it mildly."

"Come on—bath's ready." He picked her up and lowered her into the warm water. The jets bubbled around her sore body like a panacea.

Rifter watched her, and maybe she should have felt shy or scared, but she'd given up on those feelings for now. They were getting her nowhere, and since he already knew basically everything about her past—and present and non-future—she decided that she'd take all of this on like the gift it was.

"Lean back and relax." His voice didn't leave any room for argument, and she did as he asked, letting him place the cool compress on her forehead. Still, she couldn't shake the feeling he was hiding something important.

Maybe she didn't want to know what it was—shouldn't want to, at the very least, but the logical side of her pushed through to force her to ask the questions she knew she should. "Suppose the police come looking for you because of what happened last night? You must be on their radar."

"Don't worry about me. I'll take care of the police. No one's going to hurt you or take you from me."

"Why are you doing this? You just met me."

"I don't know. Sometimes, it just . . . is." Rifter paused. "Is there someplace else you'd rather be? A hospital?"

"No—God no. It's just . . . I don't know what it's going to be like . . ."

"I'll take care of you, no matter what. Jinx too. You'll be comfortable."

"Not Vice?"

"He's a good bodyguard—he won't let anyone get close to you."

A ready-made family, willing to shield her from the police . . . although, granted, she was in trouble because of them in the first place. But still, these men were willing to take care of her during her last days. "This last seizure felt different. Like I was conscious. Only this time, I woke up and I wasn't alone."

He stared at her. "You won't be again."

This time, she chose to believe him.

Chapter 18

Once they got home, Vice forced Liam to eat, although that was the last thing the young wolf wanted to do. Jinx called him a mother hen and ducked before Vice could box his ears.

"Don't you have two teenagers of your own to raise?" he asked.

"They both got laid," Jinx replied as he shoved half a sandwich in his mouth. "My job here is done for the moment."

The sun had long since come up—and he and Jinx would need to check out the mausoleum again for supernatural activity. There had been rumors that it was where Seb conducted spells, but when Jinx checked a month earlier, he'd found nothing but a few ghosts who weren't helpful. If it proved to be only outlaw Weres meeting there, well, they'd take care of that too.

The Dires should've been outnumbered, but even with immortality on their side, they kicked ass. The weretrappers couldn't keep up, which was why different werepacks requested the help and expertise of the Dire brothers.

They were like the mercenaries of the wolf world, as evidenced by Harm taking out twenty weretrappers in no doubt the space of ten minutes without anyone inside the bar noticing.

These men had been born warriors; shifted or not, they worked in tandem with their wolves. They'd had hundreds of years to perfect themselves, but in truth, Vice had to admit it was mainly instinct.

"Are you telling Rifter I left?" Liam asked.

"Yep. We don't lie to him unless it benefits me," Vice said. "He needs to know about your mate."

Liam's face hardened. "I get to take care of that, according to tradition."

That was true, and Vice had no intention of interfering. Although he'd never mate himself, he certainly understood the formalities associated with it. Granted, he didn't respect any of it all that much, but hell, he didn't respect too much of anything. "Why didn't you tell us about her?"

"Her name is Max," Liam said, and it was obvious he didn't want to say more about her right now. "She no doubt thought I was dead, killed when my father was. Or at least I thought—maybe Teague and Tals told her I'd escaped."

"They might still think you're dead."

"Part of me wishes I was." Liam stared at Vice. "Teach me the ways."

"Yeah, okay, just give me a week, wolf." Vice snorted. He lit another blue smoke, offered it to Liam, who refused.

Probably the smartest thing that kid did all day. Because even staying alive was pretty fucking stupid. Plenty of people were going to try to kill him daily, for the rest of his life.

Someone would eventually succeed.

From the look on Liam's face, Vice knew the young wolf would never forget the sight of that slaughter. Vice knew he'd never been able to shake the sight of the aftermath of the Dire Extinction from his, and that was centuries ago. And still, "You hid."

"I was there—I saw them skin him alive. They cut his head off—it's still in their clubhouse. He hasn't gotten a proper burial and I have to live with that," Liam said fiercely. "My father made me swear on my mother's grave that, no matter what happened, I wouldn't reveal myself. He said I'd be the only hope—that I needed to find you. That the Dires would train me."

"You've never killed before?"

"Not humans."

"You killed the witch," Vice pointed out.

"She gave me no choice—I tried to just stop her."

Vice shook his head disapprovingly. "I'll have to teach you a hell of a lot more about the world."

"I'm not sheltered—I know things. I want to take control of my pack."

"Too young," Vice said, and Liam shot across the table at him. Found himself under Vice's boot, but it was a hell of a good try. Took a lot of balls. "Like I said, junior— too young."

"Then, teach me."

Vice rolled his eyes but let the young wolf up. "I'm not old enough to be a parent."

"Thousands of years. Seems like you should be somewhat mature by now," Jinx said, and Vice bared his teeth at him.

"We need to bomb the mausoleum," Liam continued, ignoring the sparring between the Dires.

"We're declaring war, then," Jinx reminded him quietly. A war in which they might have only partial help from the Weres and could bring the police—and the rest of the human population—onto them. The Weres who might be talked into helping would be wary of helping the Dires and bringing attention to themselves.

"I can get recruits," Liam said confidently.

"Young ones like you?"

"Young. Strong. Clean slates," Liam said, and Jinx shot a look at Cyd and Cain, the two young wolves who were already better fighters than many older Weres, simply because of the constant company they kept.

"It's our fight, not theirs," Vice argued.

"Then I'll make it ours," Liam said.

"I know where some of them gather weekly," Cain offered, and all the men turned to stare at him. "What? I'm not allowed to do recon?"

"We made the right decision to walk away last night—if we did anything, they'd know we're onto them," Jinx reasoned, and Vice knew he was right. Let those words of wisdom attempt to take hold in his brain, in place of the rapidly building rage.

"We have to get the leaders of the outlaw pack to talk," Liam said.

"They would take death over dishonor," Jinx said. "And death is absolutely what we'll give them."

"But not until we put the plan in place."

"What is the plan?" Vice muttered. "So the pack starts selling black market Weres to the trappers. What do they gain? A promise to make their pack powerful? Why would the trappers—who hate wolves more than any other supernatural group—agree to that?"

"They probably didn't. I have no doubt this is Seb's doing." Jinx looked grim, and Liam paced uneasily.

Black arts wasn't a subject to be taken lightly. Weres and Dires didn't touch the stuff—they already had enough problems.

Vice was so up for a fight. If wolves were selling out

their own, they were all in more trouble than they thought.

"If we fight, you can't participate," he told Liam.

"Fuck you."

Vice leveled the young wolf with a gaze. "Dude, you're the Weres' great fuzzy hope. If we lost you, Rifter would kill us."

"I'll call Rifter down here," Jinx said. "He'll want to know all of this—the outlaws and Max."

"Did you ever stop to think she could've been a plant all along?" Vice demanded of Liam.

"She's human—she didn't know wolves existed until—" Liam stopped suddenly.

"Ah, now the little boy gets it. Weretrappers are human, right? You never considered that?"

"No. Never," Liam said staunchly, although there was a slight waver in his tone now.

Wolf instincts weren't often wrong, but in this time of trapper and witch, you couldn't be too careful. And Vice was never one to mince words.

Liam moved faster than Vice thought, jabbing a quick punch to Vice's jaw. It glanced off him and it made Vice laugh at the surge.

In seconds, he had Liam pinned. "Stupid move. I know you've heard the rumors about my self-control."

"Don't you talk about her—she's mine to deal with."

"She's your biggest vulnerability. You want to lead, you need to get rid of that shit."

"What would you know about a mate?" Liam snapped, and Vice did as well, throwing the young wolf across the room into the plaster wall. Liam yelped in pain and slumped to the floor.

To his credit, he struggled to get to his feet, but Vice didn't allow it. Slammed him down hard, again and again.

Liam got up each time—shakier and wobblier, with blood coming from his nose. "Is that all you've got?"

"You do have a death wish." Vice clenched his teeth as he tried to stop his switch from flipping completely.

The man had amazing hands. Gwen sat forward in the bath, arms wrapped around her knees as Rifter remained behind her, rubbing her shoulders. He massaged the kinks from her back and her neck, and she fought sleep because she didn't have enough time left. Sleep was not on her short list of things to do, but spending time with this man was.

"Shit, these bruises are bad," he muttered, more to himself than to her.

She looked over her shoulder. "Must've happened at the house."

"I knew I was too rough."

"No, it wasn't you," she insisted. "It was a tough night—my house exploded. I've been bruised since then." He'd been rough during sex, yes, but he hadn't manhandled her to the point of bruising, for sure. But since he didn't seem reassured, she decided to do so for him.

She stood then, the water rushing off her body. He started, holding the towel but not handing it over. The fire in his eyes was like a lit switch, and she liked it.

He leaned in, brushed most of the dripping water from her body, but he left her damp. And before she could stop him, he lifted her like she weighed nothing at all and placed her bare ass on the top of the tall wooden dresser. She struggled for a second because of the height, always a fear of hers, but when Rifter spread her legs and dipped his mouth to her sex, that fear was forever erased, replaced by something far more pleasurable.

She grasped his shoulders, pushed her ass so it balanced on the edge of the wood. She was helpless, open to his mouth and his tongue as his hands balanced her hips and the sensations shot through her. It was almost too much, a shock to the system, like last night, and she willed herself to stay in the moment, to not let her illness take over.

The first orgasm blossomed almost too quickly for her to enjoy it—her body tightened and she needed more. Rifter knew it, didn't stop, laving and licking until her body was poised on the verge of coming again. Buried his face inside of her and tried to make her forget everything and anything . . .

One hard flick of a tongue on her clit and she did, yelling and clawing at Rifter's back. This time, he kissed along her thighs for a few minutes as she caught her breath before taking her down and holding her back against the dresser.

His sex pulsed between them—but he was most definitely holding back. And she wasn't about to beg, understood he was worried about hurting her. But God, her body craved him like a drug. She was already intoxicated by everything about him—his scent alone drove her crazy. They couldn't go on like this for much longer—her body wouldn't be able to handle it. Something feral inside of her was ready to snap, and hard, and he seemed to understand, nodded a little at her unspoken thoughts. Pressed his body to hers as the last of the orgasmic tremble ended and the pure, unmitigated exhaustion hit her.

She put her face to his chest and breathed him in, and he, in turn, carried her to the bed. Sometime when she was in the bath, the sheets had been changed. These were just as comfortable and still smelled like him.

Rifter turned his head to the door at the same time she heard voices. To her, it was a mash-up of different voices, but he listened intently like he was hearing every word clearly.

She'd learned in med school that sometimes people who had migraines had heightened senses—and migraines were along the same nerve path as seizures. Lately, every sense was on overdrive and she couldn't shake the feeling that she was somehow getting stronger, not weaker. Which meant she was in total and complete denial. And she planned on staying there until the end. And in this bed too, police or no police.

"Is everything all right?" she asked.

"I think my brothers are arguing," he said as his phone began to ring. He grabbed it and immediately rose from the bed and pulled on jeans. "Food's on its way and I'll be right back."

"Are you . . . leaving?"

"Not the house—just have some business to take care of downstairs," he told her. "Will you be okay for a little while?"

She shrugged, for the first time realizing that she was, in fact, a prisoner here, despite the nice trappings. "What choice do I have?"

"Jesus, Gwen." He pressed his lips together and his stance tightened like he was preparing for a fight.

She wouldn't give him one. "I don't like being controlled, but I'm here and I'm safe. And when I think about what happened with the fire . . . if everything had gone as planned . . ."

"Nothing ever does," Rifter told her. "And you still ended up in my bed, just where you belong."

Chapter 19

Rifter left Gwen with a tray of food Cyd brought up and more content than she'd been. He hated that she thought she was in a prison, because capturing and holding anyone wasn't his bag.

Except for Harm—he'd hold that fucker, preferably with hot tongs.

When he strode into the kitchen, he found Vice and Jinx there, with Liam and Cyd and Cain. Stray came in behind him, holding a small video surveillance camera so he could keep an eye on Harm.

He flashed the screen Rifter's way for a second so he could see the bruising on Harm's forehead from where he'd been dropped the night before. Rifter nodded in satisfaction, took the cup of coffee Cyd handed him as Vice told him, "The outlaws are definitely in bed with the witches and weretrappers."

"Do you think the outlaws are spelled?" he asked after downing half the caffeinated drink in one gulp.

"I think they're doing more than casual dabbling into black arts," Jinx said.

If so, it made them vulnerable and put them all at risk—the witches could turn a spell around in ways an unpracticed wolf couldn't. And since Seb's coven was rumored to be conjuring demons, the danger had been turned up more than a notch.

"We're as much at risk with that human upstairs," Stray said, with his annoying habit of reading Rifter's mind, and Rifter wondered why he simply refused to acknowledge his ability outright.

There was always a fucking reason, but Rifter didn't have the time or patience to deal with him now. Instead, he raked his claws against the wall next to Vice, who, for once, attempted to look contrite even though he hadn't said a word.

And then he turned to Jinx and Stray and ruined the moment. "Told you he was hooked on the human—she's like heroin to his wolf."

"Let's focus on the real danger," Rifter told them, and finally he got no argument. He turned his attention to Liam. "We did some real damage to the weretrappers' main building after Rogue and I were rescued. We burned the facility to the ground—razed it and left before the police and firemen arrived to investigate. It's in the weretrappers' best interest not to attract the attention of the law. It's the only thing that's stopped this war from growing out of control, and we need to keep it that way."

But the weretrappers were by far not the only worry. The pack uprising and subsequent war were brewing, and it left them all vulnerable. Having the wolf who would be king added yet another wrinkle to an already impossibly complicated situation.

"You could step in and lead them," Liam said.

Rifter had him pinned to the ground in seconds, the boy wolf under him, his throat bared in deference to the bigger, badder wolf.

Smart boy. "Don't you think of ordering me again, Were."

The guilt over the fact that stepping into that position

would simplify things was always in the front of Rifter's mind, something he and the young wolf's father had discussed.

But the thought of overseeing a pack where Weres happily mated and had families, while the Dires had none, was too troubling. Better to stay separated.

"If you won't lead, then you need to let me," Liam growled.

"You are nowhere near ready."

"I don't have the luxury of time." The young wolf paced as soon as Rifter let him up, the refrain now familiar to all of them. It wasn't a hollow request or one made because it was expected of him. The young wolf wanted to live up to the responsibility of becoming king. "If I cannot take back control soon, my pack will be lost, absorbed into the outlaws. And then, who knows how many will turn to the lure of the trappers? There are stories of outlaws turning in my pack members to the weretrappers for money and power—that's hard to resist for young Weres who have no leadership."

The young wolf turned back to Vice and said simply, "Train me."

It was a command, an order that should have made Vice break him in two, and Rifter watched with interest to see what his brother would do.

Vice simply nodded, realizing as Rifter did that the passion in the younger man was impossible to deny.

And then Stray was up so fast his chair was knocked back. "Harm's awake."

Rifter turned to Cyd. "Bring Gwen up some more food and make sure she doesn't leave that room for any reason until I tell you otherwise."

Rifter was the first wolf in the room, followed closely by the others. He'd barked for Liam to stay behind with

Cain, and the Weres complied, no doubt because of the ferocity of the order.

Now he stood over Harm as the large wolf blinked several times and attempted to get his bearings. Rifter allowed it because he wanted Harm fully aware of what was happening when he ripped him to shreds. Already, his canines were lengthening and it was hard to keep Brother Wolf down.

In time, you'll get yours, he promised, and that appeased the wolf momentarily.

"Rifter." Harm's voice was hoarse, fear mixed with pain, and his eyes went lupine. The silver chains would stop his shift, but he was suffering. "Is she . . . okay?"

She? Why the hell would he be worried about Gwen? "I'm not answering your questions, you bastard. You fucked us good—turned us in, and now you're going to pay in a way no Dire's ever paid before. And I'm going to have a hell of a good time doing it."

"I did it . . . to save . . . her. Gwen." Harm paused, took a deep breath like he was trying to get a strong hold on his wolf. Rifter couldn't stand it any longer, grabbed Harm by the throat and slammed him against the wall, the chains pulling taut on his legs. With his strength, it wouldn't take much to rip them off his body, but he needed to leave something for the others.

He put his hand back, and one of his brothers handed him a knife. He brought it up to Harm's cheek. "I don't want to hear anything you have to say."

But Harm's arm shot up, chained yet, but his wrist closed on Rifter's, pulling it slightly away long enough to croak, "She's my daughter."

Rifter's mouth dropped open, and he squeezed Harm's throat harder until the wolf turned blue and struggled against his bindings nearly hard enough to shake Rifter off. Harm would be hard to take down completely, but he'd inflamed Rifter with his lie.

What if it's not?

Rifter's world had already shifted on its axis. Now it spun completely out of control and threatened to never right itself again.

He'd really lost his fucking mind.

"Bullshit," Vice growled from behind him. "No female Dire has ever been found, so there's no fucking way. Let me have him, Rifter."

"No." Rifter backed away and stared at Harm, who coughed for a few minutes. "Who's her mother?"

"Human."

"There's no way."

"Apparently there is, King Rifter." Harm hadn't lost his cocky sarcasm—it was what drew millions of screaming women to him and made him and Rifter spar constantly when they were on their Running.

Selfish fucking bastard. "Her mother couldn't have been human."

"Don't you think I would've known if she wasn't? She was an artist—a painter—a good one until she got pregnant and went on the run with Gwen."

"How did she survive?"

Harm shook his head, like he was refusing to answer. Finally, he said, "I made sure she did—for a while. Then she lost my track and got killed, or at least I thought that's what happened. Later, I found out that Seb's sister, Cordelia, had been tracking me for years."

Had Harm loved someone?

No way—the man was too selfish to love anyone but himself. "Tell me Gwen's the only one."

"She is."

"And she has no idea?"

"Her mother was killed when she was ten. Gwen moved to the States with her aunt and uncle with a sizable settlement from me. But they never touched the money. I don't think they ever told her about it."

He recalled Gwen's words about her parents, about never knowing her father. If her mother made that up to keep her safe . . .

"This is impossible. And that makes no sense for her aunt and uncle to never touch the money." He turned to his brothers, who were all equally stunned, although Vice still looked skeptical.

"Maybe they knew what Harm was . . . maybe they knew a way to keep her safe," Jinx said, his eyes the most feral Rifter had ever seen them as they locked Harm in their gaze.

"Or they thought they did," Rifter said. "Her aunt and uncle were killed in a fire—Gwen was supposed to be there. The weretrappers have obviously been tracking her for a long time, with Cordelia's assistance."

Gwen had been right—people around her dying by fire was no coincidence. And that meant the weretrappers had had the witches helping them for longer than the Dires had originally thought.

Had Seb known?

"Wolves didn't kill them," Harm said. "The weretrappers and witches made it look that way. Or else they made Weres do it . . . maybe moon lust."

Rifter turned. "Why not take her sooner?"

"They were waiting for a shift that never came," Harm said. "She'd been medicated in hopes of preventing it from happening."

"The seizures," Rifter breathed.

"Yes—the medicine helped stop the shift," Harm said. "But the seizures are killing her."

Harm's grim proclamation made Rifter crumple the knife in his hand as if it was made of powder. Smoke rose and blood ran down his arm and the floor, and his brothers just stared at him.

He didn't wipe his hand, remained silent. He'd welcome the tight pain that would come with the shift his body so desperately needed, but he forced himself to stay in the present.

"She's not taking the meds any longer," he said tightly. "She's still having . . . episodes." During sex, which was a sure sign of a Dire shift coming down the pike.

How could he have been so fucking blind to this? The smells, the changes . . . her need to run. Her appetite.

"The bruises," Rifter breathed as Jinx shot him a look. He pictured Gwen's back as he'd looked on it a short while ago and realized that what he'd assumed were bruises from the earlier attack were now gathering in a very distinct pattern. "Her wolf glyph's coming out."

He traced around the edges of her Sister Wolf in his mind. Brother Wolf howled at the thought that she'd been trapped for so long, but Rifter soothed him.

He recalled when his own glyph began to appear, the pack pride that accompanied it. A month later, he was out on his Running. He hadn't been able to return home after that, because there'd been nothing left. Total and complete destruction. He'd walked through the rubble, wept over the dead men, their Brother Wolves slain with a slash across the men's and women's backs that rendered their wolf glyphs completely destroyed.

Cutting out the glyph was akin to killing the wolf in those days. Today it would do nothing to the surviving Dires.

"If she doesn't shift, she'll die," Jinx said. "And if she does shift, she might die anyway."

"No." Rifter spoke as if his will could command it.

"The weretrappers won't give up—neither will the witches," Harm said.

"And what—we should turn her over to them because of that? We know that's how you roll, but not us." Vice had Harm pinned to the wall, his mouth at the other wolf's throat, and for a long second, Rifter considered letting Vice do what he needed to.

But there was more to hear. And Rifter had to know every last, bitter truth. "Vice, off."

Vice complied, slowly. Licked his bottom lip and shuddered as he tried not to shift. A flash of lightning lit the room, while overhead, thunder rolled across the sky like a bowling ball hitting all the right pins, and Rifter swore the house shook. A chill went through him, stronger than any electrical current. March in upstate New York was not the time for this weather.

"I say we give him to the witches in place of Gwen," Rifter said. "It's what a father would've done in the first place."

"You don't think I tried that? They wouldn't take me," Harm insisted.

"So you picked us."

"Seb asked for you. I had no choice. You could survive the witches and the trappers. Gwen would've never made it out alive. The experiments . . ." Harm shuddered, and Rifter's fists tightened. The urge to kill Harm hadn't dissipated in the least.

"You have to believe me. I offered myself. I went there—put myself in chains," Harm insisted.

"Why the hell wouldn't they take a Dire offering?" Vice muttered. "This makes no sense."

Rifter could sense that Gwen had fallen asleep—peacefully so—and he was pacing and growling because he needed to get inside Gwen's mind and check on Sister Wolf, but he needed Harm's information just as badly.

"Vice is right. So talk." It came out as a wolf's growl and it made Harm bare his teeth. Spending the majority of the last fifty years around humans hadn't muted any of the man's instincts.

Harm came as far as the chains would take him—inches from Rifter's face—and Stray and Jinx and Vice all bared their teeth too, their canines lengthened, eyes changed, and the testosterone in the room was off the charts.

Harm knew exactly why, swallowed hard before he spoke between the booms of thunder. "She's got the power to kill us all."

Vice tried to hold it together, but his shift came with a hard howl and his Brother Wolf bounded for the window. Three floors down was a long trip, but for the adrenaline that raced through his body, it was nothing—the cuts and bruises he'd suffer only fueled him further, and when his paws hit the wet grass, he skidded and ran on bloody paws until his body ached so fiercely he could barely stand it.

And then he ran some more.

Chapter 20

Rifter hadn't moved in what seemed like hours after Harm's announcement and Vice's impromptu, uncontrolled shift and subsequent dive out the window.

"Not safe for him to be out alone," Rifter finally growled, and Stray shifted and followed him. Jinx refused to leave, although Rifter heard his harsh breathing behind him like nails on a chalkboard. And then he turned his full attention back to Harm. "Explain."

"There's something about her blood—Cordelia discovered it. I'm sure Seb knows too. That's why the trappers won't stop until they have her." Harm blinked hard and Rifter remained frozen, trying to stop the storm of emotions threatening to take his much-needed logic away.

"And her blood can really kill us?" Jinx asked, and Harm nodded.

Gwen was the very key to ending their immortality . . . and that of the Weres as well, at least those opposing the weretrappers and witches.

Without the Dire wolves and Liam's pack to enforce the order, the weretrappers and witches would—and could—run wild and take over the world far more easily than they could now.

Part of their ultimate punishment for being born Dires was that they needed to stay alive to save the humans. Vice was correct that the wolves weren't meant to save the humans on an individual basis, but rather, the race as a whole from whatever supernatural force threatened them.

Before Rifter could say anything, Vice came in with Stray, both in human form, and naked and dripping wet, panting slightly from the rapid shifts. Vice's eyes still glowed, the anger and confusion in them hard for Rifter to take.

"We need to kill her," Jinx said, his words cutting Rifter to the bone. Vice's nature would no doubt make him agree. Stray was a crapshoot.

"No," he told his brother.

"She puts us all at risk," Jinx persisted.

Mine.

Brother Wolf howled, threatened for the first time Rifter could remember to shift without his consent, and all for the sole purpose of fighting for his mate.

Mate. "Gwen's mine."

"You mated with her?" Jinx asked. "That is not possible . . . yet."

It wasn't—not fully, since he and Gwen would've had to have slept together three times and Gwen would have had to shift in order for the mating ritual to be completed—but the process had begun and Rifter refused to turn back.

Mating for the Dires was complicated—ceremonial, dictated by the old ways and unlike that of the Weres, who were not tied to any kind of mating ritual.

In order for the mating to be effective, the Dire male had to be chained, and the female would shift uncontrollably after they'd had sex. Mating therefore equaled danger for the male—he needed to be able to prove he could handle his female wolf.

Mating on the third time Dires slept together was an old custom, since they didn't encourage sex without mating. This was why the aftermath of sex had been painful and unsatisfying for the Dires since the Extinction, since it went against their mating protocol.

Once the Elders had been created by Hati, the maker of the Dires, the wolves would go before them to have the mating blessed. This was a fairly new custom created in the years before the Extinction, put in place by Hati.

It was said the Elders could deny a mating, even if the other rituals had been completed. Whether they had or not was something Dires had often gossiped about in hushed tones, Rifter remembered.

"Not your concern," Rifter told them all now.

"You are fucking kidding me. This is all of our lives," Vice said.

"A life you don't care about," Rifter pointed out.

"That's never been our decision to make," Jinx said when Vice went silent.

Rifter caught him by the throat, the next words he uttered taking everyone by surprise, including himself. "Gwen is mine. Do you understand? Mine."

"Yeah, okay, Rift, she's all yours. Put the big wolf down and go get her before the others do," Stray said, his voice oddly calming, and Rifter dropped Jinx, watched the wolf gasp for air.

"Bastard," Jinx wheezed. "You fucking bastard."

Vice pulled Jinx back as Rifted commanded, "Stray— give me the keys to the cuffs. And all of you, leave—I need to speak with Harm alone. Now."

"Now he wants to play at being king," Vice snarled, but the three Dires did as he asked, leaving both wolves who would be king alone.

Harm was staring at him—half father, angry at the

daughter's mate, half unsure of what to do at all. "You can't complete this mating."

"You don't tell me what to do."

"You can use Gwen to poison us—we can finally be free, Rifter."

Rifter moved toward him—as Harm tensed, Rifter merely used the key to unlock all but his left ankle. He looked at Harm and told him, "Don't ever let it be said I don't fight fair. I'm going to let the rest of them rip the flesh from your bones when I'm done. You can regenerate in hell."

"Take her blood and then let her die," Harm said, speaking in the old language, as if that would appeal to Rifter more. "Don't curse her to the life we have."

Rifter fisted his hands and growled, but the warning didn't stop Harm.

"You know I'm right. Would you rather be that selfish and keep her?"

She's mine.

Brother Wolf was in full agreement. They'd both been waiting forever for a mate. Had been sure they'd never get one, and now Rifter had to evaluate the sanctity of her life. And even as Rifter fought the urge to rip Harm's throat out, his claws emerged with a tight snap. Then he gave up the fight and the satisfaction of claws ripping flesh, not caring that the silver burns he experienced wouldn't abate.

Rifter didn't bother to fully shift. Instead, he and Harm rolled on the attic floor, both men getting out a lifetime's worth of hate and anguish.

This man had fathered the woman he loved. How the hell could any of this work?

After Rifter shut them out, Vice broke off from Jinx and Stray, went into the second door on the right. He closed it behind him and, naked, battered and bloodied, sank down next to Rogue.

"We're in trouble, man," he whispered, and nothing. Frustration rose again, and with no way to battle it down, he began to smash things in the room. Nothing hit Rogue—no matter how much control Vice lost, he would never let that happen.

And when his emotions pushed him to the point of complete calm, he sat among the ruins of the room and wondered how much longer all of this could go on.

He wasn't sure he wanted the answer.

He'd thought about death for thousands upon thousands of years, but when faced with the real possibility of it, why did it freak him out so badly?

"This wouldn't bother you," he whispered. Spirits were drawn to Rogue because he was an *other*—a supernatural being like they were. He could see them as clear as day, and sometimes it drove him crazy.

It had been easier when Rogue was actively helping. Now a part of Vice felt as dormant and helpless as Jinx did. Witches practiced ceremonial magic and conjured spirits to help them do their bidding—and now that of the weretrappers. That's where Rogue's and Jinx's relationships with the spirit world came in mighty handy.

"Hey." Jinx was in the doorway, nowhere near as calm as he appeared—not when his eyes were lupine. "Get dressed—we've got to go. Lots of activity tonight."

He barely looked at Rogue—Vice knew it was getting harder for him to do so with every day that passed, which was why Vice spent enough time in here for both of them.

He'd clean up all the shit in the morning.

It was fortunate Vice's extremes never let him remain in any one mood for very long—in a way, it was damned balancing. Much like being a goddamned schizo without hearing all the voices.

Except Brother Wolf's, which he didn't count. Much. Ah, fuck it, they'd deal with this shit at the house after the ghost crap.

"We need Seb's grimoires—we destroy that book of magic spells and he's got nothing," he said as he toweled the mud off himself and grabbed for a pair of black leather pants he'd left on the floor. He grabbed a black shirt and his black leather jacket and boots and followed Jinx down the stairs.

"If it exists, it's spelled," Jinx said over his shoulder. "Do you really think Rifter was right about mating with Gwen?"

"Seems pretty attached to her—it would explain a lot," Vice said. It certainly wasn't a full mating, though— there was more to it than onetime sex. But Rifter was acting like a possessive-as-shit, mated alpha, and that meant trouble for all of them.

Weres could have more than one mate. Dires mated for life. To find his mate after all this time and have her ripped from him . . . well, that was gonna be one hell of a wound.

They stopped talking when they found Liam waiting by the truck. The young wolf had his mind set on grabbing Max, and hell, Vice couldn't blame him. Obviously, women were really nothing but trouble, and they needed to look no further than their own house for evidence.

Still, the idea that they could end their lives with Gwen was certainly appealing and had apparently shaken Jinx to the core. He didn't say anything about it, but Vice had known the guy for three hundred years.

"I'm going," Liam stated the obvious, getting into the back of the truck even as Jinx told him, "We're grabbing Max afterward—you don't need to be there."

"I do." Liam shut the door and Jinx let the discussion end.

"Think Harm's okay with Rifter?" Jinx asked Vice instead.

"Not at all. But he promised to leave a piece for each of us." Vice climbed into the driver's seat and pumped up AC/DC for the drive.

"We're going back to the mausoleum," Jinx said as Vice maneuvered the truck out of the garage—he was definitely the steadier one tonight, and only because thoughts of Rogue centered him. And he would do anything for his Dire brother.

Still, he asked. "Why?"

"Because I felt something last night," Jinx said, and Vice didn't question it further. Jinx's and Rogue's freaky shit was something he didn't completely understand, but they all respected one another's gifts. "Something big's coming down the pike."

"It's already here," Vice said.

Chapter 21

The talking woke her—Gwen shushed whoever it was a few times because her body needed more sleep desperately. When she opened her eyes, she realized no one else was in the room with her.

She pushed the sheets aside, threw on a long T-shirt and the too-big sweats that she had to roll and tie to make them barely stay on and walked toward the door, the voices continuing. The men were talking—Rifter and Vice—and a voice or two she didn't recognize. It wasn't exactly English either, but she had no trouble understanding it.

The rustling blocked the voices for a long moment. *Listen. Learn.*

She opened the door and found the hallway empty, let herself be guided toward the voices.

"... should let her die."

"... kill her."

They were talking about her—she was sure of it. Had she been that much of a fool to think they'd keep her here safely forever? She was a witness—to what, she still wasn't entirely sure.

She continued listening as she made her way up to the third floor of the house, didn't understand or hear everything being said—just bits and pieces—but it was enough, especially when she finally heard her name. And a part of her wanted to shrink away from the conversation, sink back under the covers and pretend this had never happened.

The angry part of her reared its head—and won. At least long enough for her to stand in the open doorway and see Rifter, battered and bloody, but not beaten as badly as the man chained to the floor. Rifter said something in a language she only half understood, and he left out a side door. She backed out, but the floorboard creaked in the now-silent room and the chained man whipped around and looked at her.

"Gwen, what are you doing here?"

"How do you know my name?" she demanded as she backed away. The heavy chains he wore clinked when he sat up, but he didn't come toward her.

"Gwen, let me explain . . ."

"I've had too many explanations, none of them rational."

"This world isn't the way you've been brought up to believe it is. Forget your cold, hard factual science. There are things that exist that you can't even imagine. Nothing is beyond the realm of possibility here," the handsome man said, and something inside of her shuddered . . . and inexplicably wanted to embrace what he said. But logic won out—it always would with her—especially when the clinking of the chains around his wrists reminded her of where she was and what kind of people she was with.

"Why is Rifter's gang keeping you here?" she demanded.

"Rifter's gang?" he murmured with a snort—far too sarcastic for someone who was a prisoner, although he was as giant as the rest of them. Where did they grow these people? They should be studied—if she lived, she could ask them if she could write a paper on them for a medical journal.

"They're keeping me here too," she admitted. "Maybe we could help each other."

"No one can help me."

"What did you do to them?"

"Long story," he started, and suddenly she wanted no part of it.

She had to leave now, and she didn't know why. The restlessness took her by the throat, and she quickly exited the room and headed back down the stairs, not stopping until she got to the sliding glass doors past the kitchen.

It was dark and quiet down here. And she'd had enough.

As she ran across the lawn, the icy grass raking the bottoms of her bare feet, her brain was reeling.

And all the while, she couldn't shake the feeling that she should be running toward Rifter.

Gwen knows the old language.

Gwen's half Dire.

Gwen is your mate.

Watching her run down the hall away from him triggered every prey instinct—and a mating one Rifter didn't know he had.

His wolf was gonna howl tonight. The moon was past full, but staring up at it made his body throb with the need, the undeniable hunger that pulsated through every fiber of his being.

He tore his shirt in half, heard the low keening rise from his throat. Caught halfway between man and beast—which was how he lived his entire life—he finally let the beast out.

The beast was the only way to deal with Gwen now.

Daughter of the man who'd imprisoned him, who'd sold out the Dires and was responsible for Rogue's coma.

Gwen knows the old language.

Gwen's half Dire.

Gwen is your mate.

He waited until he heard Gwen run across the lawn, and then he shifted and went out the window Vice had broken earlier.

Gwen tripped on a tree root, caught herself before she tumbled headfirst. Before she could continue her run, she heard the growl and looked up to see a wolf's eyes watching her through the trees. She backed up and turned to run only when the eyes disappeared.

She ran until she hit the edge of the property, far more dark and foreboding than she'd ever seen. Torn between past and future, she hesitated before plunging into the woods—and it cost her.

The low growl from behind wasn't vicious—it was more of a warning for her not to run. She said a brief, silent prayer, and when she turned, she found herself facing the huge wolf she'd dreamed about last night.

The same one tattooed on Rifter's back.

How long he'd been behind her, silently stalking her, she had no clue, and she nearly went to her knees as he came toward her.

Once directly in front of her, he gave a howl that shook the earth—and her.

She slowly backed up with a strange sense of déjà vu. The wolf was cornering her, and she found herself up against a tree trunk. And the wolf kept coming.

"Why do you keep following me?" she demanded. "I'm trying to be strong, to do all this with dignity, and you're determined to make me think I'm losing my mind."

The words were spoken in one long, stuttered breath. Oh great, she was pouring out her heart to her hallucinations now.

And the wolf appeared to be *listening*.

"Please just let me go."

But as she watched, the wolf began to change. It happened in under thirty seconds but seemed to happen faster—a blur of fur to skin, four legs to two . . .

And then Rifter was standing in front of her, naked in all his glory.

It was too real for it to be a dream. The other possibility was a brain-tumor-induced hallucination, which seemed far more probable.

Because Rifter *could not be* a wolf.

"You're a . . ." The word *wolf* died in her throat. Maybe he'd fed her hallucinogenics, which would explain her dreams the other night.

There had to be something else beyond the simple explanation that Rifter was, in fact, a werewolf. Because those monsters didn't exist. Couldn't. Science couldn't explain them. And she believed in cold, hard fact.

But when Rifter turned into a wolf again, fiction stood before her, panting in all its huge, shaggy glory. And she swore that the damned wolf smiled at her before it turned back into Rifter.

Yes, she was definitely out of her goddamned mind. "I don't understand this."

"It's not something to understand—to analyze. It just *is*."

"I heard you and your . . . brothers . . . friends— talking. About wanting me dead." She stopped trying to move backward now, wanted to see what he'd do about the accusation.

He didn't tell her she misunderstood. All he said was, "There's more to it than you know."

"If you're going to kill me, then do it," she challenged, walked toward him and slammed her palms against his chest as hard as she could. He didn't move at all, and so she did it again and again, and he did nothing to try to stop her. "Go ahead, you big, bad wolf—do it!"

He grabbed her wrists instead and held her steady, so close to his body that the heat radiated. Even as she attempted to move, she found herself pulled back into place with a force she'd never felt—and it was only Rifter's hand. It wasn't hurting her, but there was no chance she could free herself. "You bastard—you said I was safe with you."

"You are."

"I know what I heard—you all want to kill me."

"I won't kill what's mine."

The wolf had taken over him now—she could see that clearly. And she should be scared—more than a little of her was—but his scent was easing her, lulling her into a place more befitting a seduction than anything. "I'm not yours."

"You're on your way, Gwen—don't tell me you can't feel it. And you don't want me to kill you," he said with a low growl. Her borrowed sweatpants were ripped off . . . and as she stared at Rifter she noted that Rifter's eyes were still those of the wolf, glowing nearly amber—the color of whiskey served neat—and she trembled because she knew she'd pushed it too far.

"This is what you wanted, little one," he told her, and she shook her head mutely and he laughed, but it came out a growl. "You didn't want me to stop last night. This time I won't. Can't."

And as angry and confused as she was, she couldn't resist him, not when he pressed her against him so the heat from his body turned her blood molten.

She tried to get the word out this time. "You're a . . ."

"Wolf." He wasn't interested in talking anymore. And since she'd just discovered that she wasn't going crazy, she accepted his rough, punishing kisses that heated her, spearing pleasure to her core. Her body was demanding Rifter, and he was readily accepting her.

Her fingers threaded through his hair. She could still smell the wolf on him—primal, animalistic—and as his fingers found her sex, she groaned and he . . . howled.

"Are you going to hurt me?" she asked.

"Never," he told her. "I don't break my promises. I will never hurt you." As he spoke, he tore her T-shirt from her like it was made of tissue paper and bared her naked body to him.

She knew he was telling the truth. "Rifter, what's happening here?"

"Same thing that happened last night. Same thing I wanted to happen the first night I met you, Gwen."

She trembled even as her body called to him. She scented him in the air, more strongly than ever despite the fact that they were outside, and every reserve she had gave way to raw, primal need.

This man was talking about killing you.

But as predatory as he was, she wasn't protesting. Couldn't. Not even when he took both her wrists in his and bound them together with what was left of her T-shirt, then pushed her down on all fours to the ground.

"I'm a wolf, Gwen . . . and you're just like me," he told her, right before he buried his face between her legs.

It couldn't be true—but even as he said it and his tongue found her sex, she knew with certainty that he wasn't lying to her. That she could escape if she wanted . . . that he would never, ever hurt her.

He's right . . . he's yours, the rustling told her, and then it was overpowered by her moans.

She was bared to him and there was nothing she could

do but remain open for him, on all fours as his mouth took her. Her clit throbbed as he worked it with his tongue, sucked it while she gasped and tugged at her wrists because she wanted to touch him.

She whimpered, but as he promised, he wouldn't stop. Not even when the keening moan left her throat and rang through the air, echoing in the still of the night.

But she was coming, dripping, her juices lapped up by him, and she came a second time in the space of seconds. She twisted and the bonds broke easily, despite how well knotted they'd been, and she stared down at them, wondering how she'd been able to do that.

And then, when Rifter turned her and prepared to take her with his cock, she no longer cared.

Her back crackled the leaves under her and she should've been so cold. Instead, his skin heated her like an electric blanket and there was steam rising from his shoulders as his body covered hers and he took her there, rocked into her hard and fast and left her breathless, with no quarter. His body seemed massive now that he was naked, and her legs fought to wrap around his waist.

He stopped for a second and put her leg over his shoulder, which left her open to his thrusting.

He was caught between man and beast—no, that wasn't true. He was man *and* beast and he reveled in it. He was forcing her to celebrate it as well. Naked in the woods, wrapping himself around her in a sensuous dance, readying to take her under the moon.

It should've been uncomfortable, but the grass was like a soft, warm blanket against her back, the rain a sprinkle of cool against her overheated skin. Something unfolded inside of her, a stirring that made her spread her legs and welcome the big man between her thighs . . . and when he pressed inside of her, she told him, "More."

He complied with a groan and a wicked shift of his hips that made something jolt inside of her.

This was all necessary. And right. She rocked against him, urging him farther inside so she could feel him in her womb. Her fingers dug into his shoulders, her legs wrapped around his body and ...

"Let it go," he murmured roughly, muscles bunching under her palms, cock throbbing between her legs.

"Take me now," she said in response, because it was so much simpler than thinking. His mouth captured a nipple between his teeth, flicked the end with his tongue.

Every sense was heightened, almost to the point of straddling the line between pleasure and pain. And even though he was not gentle with her, he was by no means too rough.

He was giving her exactly what she wanted.

Chapter 22

By the time Vice got them to the cemetery, the storm threatened, the sky heavy with clouds, the air singing with moisture. A harbinger of a disturbing and definitely out-of-place weather pattern.

Near the mausoleum they discovered they weren't alone in their ghost hunting, although the group of teens was there for a different kind of ghost. If they ever saw the things Vice had, they'd shit their pants for sure.

They had beer and weed, the boys trying to act brave for the sake of the girls, even though Vice scented the light fear.

"Who's afraid of the big bad wolf?" Vice murmured and went toward them.

"Vice, leave them alone," Jinx said, but it was too late. Vice was already jumping out and scaring the hell out of them. They all ran, except for one girl who started to, but doubled back.

"You're too sexy to be dead," she purred, although she didn't get all that close. Not until he spoke, anyway.

"Sweetheart, you have no idea." He smiled because she smelled damned sweet, and at heart, he could relate to this. During his own time of wildness, he would've joined them.

But that was long gone, and for three hundred years, serious business had taken precedence. And so he let his canines come down a little and bared his teeth and growled.

The girl who'd told him he was sexy dropped her beer and opened her mouth to scream, except nothing came out. When Vice smiled again, his teeth were normal, and these teens, by morning, would be convinced it was the beer and pot that made them see things—or they'd have a damned good ghost story for their friends.

Now that they were alone—so to speak—Liam slunk toward the mausoleum to see if there was anyone—human, wolf or witch—in there tonight.

Through the ghosts and spirits in the area, they'd been trying to get the gossip as to what the witches were conjuring, and looking for ways to help Rogue as well. Talking to Jinx was like a hen party for said ghosts.

"Lots of activity." Jinx squinted at the sky, the half-moon hanging over the cemetery like a painting.

Vice felt it long before Jinx said it, a jolt of static electricity up his spine. He hated this ghost shit, but being close to the twins, he'd started developing his own sixth sense.

"Don't let them party in your body, man," Jinx warned. "Make yourself an inhospitable host."

"That's impossible. Hospitable's what I'm built for," Vice reminded him.

The ghosts and spirits—good and bad—fucking loved him for his excess, like he could be their party in a box. He felt a ghost circling him, and then a darker spirit, and he chugged the Kettle One the teens had left behind before following Jinx.

"Nothing good can come from a demon. Don't let it get inside you again or I'll have to slap it out of you," Jinx warned, but it was too late—wolves and vodka had never mixed, and no matter how often Vice tried to build up a tolerance, it didn't happen. Besides, he was so used to dealing with this world, he found it more fascinating knowing he'd never actually make it into that realm.

Hell, at least he could make a visit now and again.

"That doctor from UGH—Eidolon—he's a demon," he pointed out. "Granted, he's a sex demon and these are just mean motherfucking not-getting-laid-anytime-soon demons, so I see what you're saying."

Jinx stared at him. "You scare the shit out of me sometimes."

"Try being me."

"No, thanks." Jinx stopped and stared at something behind Vice, who turned quickly and stood near his brother. "What the hell are you doing here?"

The apparition stepped forward out of the mist, held the top half of its body's shape. Jinx took a step back into Vice, who nearly had to hold the man up. "Jinx, dude, what's the issue?"

"He's my—"

"Son, you need to rescue us," the apparition said, and oh yeah, talk about an awkward family meeting. This was Jinx's father—his dead, crossed-over father who'd been killed during the Extinction, so really, neither Jinx nor Vice should be able to see him. So something was really wrong here.

"How can you see them, then?" Vice demanded. "How can I see them—I thought we could only see the earthbound?"

"That means they are," Jinx said grimly. "We're late to this party."

"Betting our invite didn't get lost in the mail."

"Really not good," Jinx muttered. "Necromancy. Black magic in its worst form."

The apparition persisted, repeating, "Son, you need to rescue your kind."

"From what?" Jinx pressed.

"We're being raised."

"For what purpose?"

"To fight our own kind. It's an army."

"Just like Rifter's dreams," Vice said quietly. An army of the dead—how very *Lord of the Rings* of them. These spirits were being brought back unnaturally and forced to fight—bound by an afterlife contract Seb was no doubt controlling. "Have they succeeded?"

"That's what I'm going to find out."

Vice felt certain he would be the one to find it out the hard way, but he let Jinx try things his way.

"When's this army coming?" Jinx demanded.

"Start of the blue moon," his father said, his voice an eerie echo in the dark.

Vice knew what it felt like to not be in charge of his own body and its urges, but he could get it all under control most times.

The army of the dead . . . they had zero say. Had they never been resting comfortably?

"You must not go where you're led," Jinx told him.

"We are bound by him who has raised us. We have no recourse, unless Rogue—"

"It cannot be so," Jinx said in the old language, slipping back into the vernacular easily.

What a hell of a ghost story this was turning out to be. Especially when Jinx's father morphed into something far more disturbing.

Vice heard the gargle and then the growl, unlike any wolf he'd ever heard. Instinctively, he backed up, but it did no good. He and Brother Wolf felt the spirit well up inside of him, and, fuck, it best have some damned good intel.

Dark storms swirled the sky—electric lightning pierced the windows, making the air smell like the sizzle it left behind.

"Man-made," Jinx confirmed, and Vice felt the energy run through him, tingling his piercings with an electric shock that turned him on as much as the air freaked him out.

He could smell ghost and witch and wolf, the supernatural world rising to revolt the way it often did at night. But this was extreme—and unnatural, even for unnatural beings like themselves.

"The spirits aren't happy," Jinx muttered, backing up and pushing at an invisible force with both palms, like he was being surrounded.

The chill hit Vice like a brick wall. He barely had time to draw a breath, never mind warn Jinx that he'd been invaded by something big and bad.

Talk to it, Rogue would tell him, but this thing was attempting to make him walk toward the mausoleum.

"Vice, no." But Jinx's voice sounded far away.

Don't fight . . . too late . . . we need you, son.

Vice let the thing continue to invade him, take him over until he could barely think straight. But for Rogue and Jinx's parents, Vice would do it, because from everything he'd heard about them, they weren't total assholes.

Jinx and Rogue had been doing this shit from the time they were ten—they were performing exorcisms by the time they were fifteen. This seemed the goddamned least he could do.

Vice felt the cold air of the demon rush through him—the thing hung on long enough for him to get a read on the type, which was the not-good kind. Seb had used black magic to raise the Dire spirits and would no doubt put a demon in charge of them, the fucking, fucking bastard. Vice's temper surged, until he wanted nothing more than to find Seb immediately and rip his head off. He could barely restrain himself from running off to hunt the witch.

You want to die, Vice . . . you've always been an aberration of your kind. Why don't you end all your suffering now that you know you can?

Yeah, yeah, the demon knew all his doubts and fears and would use them against him. Vice was stronger than that shit. "You're going to have to do much better than that."

The one you love will never love you back.

Okay, ouch, motherfucker. His anger pushed the demon out—the holy water Jinx threw on him helped. Burned the fucker, but it didn't go back to hell where it belonged. It lingered, and Vice wondered if he should let it or not.

But tonight, it was a drop in the bucket. And as he tried to catch his breath, the sky broke open with a deluge of biblical proportions.

"We've got to get home," Jinx called over the rushing water, and Vice held his hands out and let the water soak him in seconds flat.

"You do that," Liam told them. Vice had almost forgotten the young wolf was there, witnessing everything. "I'm going to get Max. If we don't grab her, we don't know what part she's playing in all this. She could have intel."

Jinx glanced at Vice, wiping the hair from his face. No deterring the young prince. "Hospital, then home," Vice yelled over the din of the water.

"I'll call Rift and tell him to stay inside," Jinx said as they hustled back to the hidden truck. Liam grabbed towels for them and they dried off as much as they could. Jinx dialed Rifter as Vice drove through the rapidly rising water.

"Stray, what's going on?" Jinx listened for a moment and mouthed, *Fuck*. "Well, find them and get them inside. There's gonna be trouble tonight for sure."

He hung up and turned to them. "Gwen ran—she and Rift are somewhere on the property."

"Does she know?" Vice asked.

"I'm betting she will by the end of the night," Jinx said.

"What about Gwen?" Liam was concerned. "Is she okay?"

Jinx glanced at Vice and then admitted, "She's a wolf."

"A Were?"

"A Dire," Vice corrected. "Half a Dire."

"Holy fuck."

"Couldn't have said it better myself, wolf. And if you tell any of your little pack this, I'll break you in half. Literally."

Liam wouldn't—the Dires knew they had his complete loyalty. He didn't understand the significance of what had happened, but he certainly knew parents coming back from the grave was no good. Shit, they'd all studied *Hamlet* in school, and look how things had turned out for that dark prince.

Chapter 23

Lightning and thunder roared overhead, but they were protected under the cover of the thick trees and the hunter's blind overhead that Rifter had made sure to roll them under.

The storm was nowhere near as dangerous as he was to Gwen. He watched lightning strike the air like a hot ripple of ribbon, snaking down to earth with a hard touch.

Supernatural storm for sure. The snow melted; the temperature was closer to sixty than the normal twenty. And right now, he didn't give a shit—was prepared to take Gwen, right there on the grass under the moon.

But the mating . . .

Brother Wolf howled. Father Wolf wanted the mating, would not want it to happen this way. Anything could go wrong.

I wouldn't be chained. And we don't know if the old ways apply, Rifter told his wolf.

The shift could kill her, Brother Wolf snapped back.

That was the only thing that stopped him. Churned his gut, actually, as he lay tangled with her, a thin sheen of sweat along his body—a glow on hers. Mating made Dires stronger—mating would ultimately give Gwen the strength she needed to survive. It was too dangerous to try to mate with a new wolf: The shift would be too hard and new wolves were uncontrollable, and after the shift—if they even survived—they could kill their mates.

He saw a few bruises on her from the other night and he moved to check her back again.

The pattern of the wolf was clearer now that he knew. This meant her shift was imminent; usually a week from bruising pattern to full glyph of her Sister Wolf—something exclusive to the Dires—and then the change would occur.

He brushed a hand down her bare back and she shivered a little. "Did I hurt you?"

"No, you didn't."

You didn't because she can handle you—because she's like you.

If he couldn't believe this was happening, he couldn't imagine what she was thinking right about now.

She started hesitantly, "What you said before... about me being like you ..."

"It's true. I didn't want to see the signs... never thought it could happen. But the fact that you survived the explosion, the seizures smelling like a shifting wolf."

"It's true, then?" she asked, rubbing her arms like her body was a stranger to her. And, in many ways, it was until she acclimated.

"You're a Dire wolf, Gwen—just like me. Except you're half human. And you're the first one of your kind. The first Dire female for centuries."

She blinked—hard. To her credit, she was remaining calm. "But you're ..."

"Human? No, this is just another form my wolf takes. I'm the product of two Dire wolves."

She nodded like she understood, but she wouldn't yet. "Is it true—that you want me dead?"

"No."

"But Vice and Jinx do," she said. "I told you I wasn't going to the police—that I can't . . ."

"It's not about that, Gwen."

"Then what?"

How could he tell her what kind of harm she posed to them?

How can you not?

Not now—it was already too much for her to bear. "Let's get you inside and I can explain more."

But she wasn't making any moves. "I was born this way?"

"Yes, but Dires don't shift until they're twenty-one. Because yours was held off so long with the drugs, that's why you're having the seizures." He had to be careful here because he honestly didn't know all the implications of what would happen to her when she did shift.

"And Dires are different from . . . other wolves?"

"Yes. Liam is a Were. We're Dires—me and Vice and Jinx, Rogue and Stray."

"And the man chained?"

"Harm," he said tightly. "Yes, he's a Dire. Until you, that's all we had—six Dire males."

"The rest are extinct?"

Rifter looked up at the moon and thought about his creation—wondered if Hati was up there chasing his moon . . . wondered if the Elders still cared.

How could they not, when they were once like him and his brothers?

He told her about the Elders and the Extinction of his kind—her kind. She listened carefully as he spoke of the old legends, and his heart grew heavy, as it always did when he thought about the past.

"The Elders council was created six years before they instigated the Extinction, and they told the Dires to revere the abilities found in some young Dires, not fear and destroy them. They were told that Harm would be their new king and that they should not harm any more humans. But the Dires didn't heed the warnings ... and the Extinction was put upon them."

He couldn't talk about what that actually entailed now. And thankfully, Gwen didn't push that, simply asked, "So you were left alive because you have ... abilities?"

He turned from the moon and looked at her. "We were spared because the Elders asked Hati to do so. We work with the Elders to keep the Weres in line and to help the humans our kind once hurt—and we also keep Hati happy. The Weres were created to continue to worship Hati and chase the moon with him. The Elders would remain in place, watching over the remaining Dires and the Weres."

"This is a lot to take in," he said, moved off her slightly, and she sat up, her body glistening in the moonlight. "You're so fucking beautiful, I can't stand it."

She blushed, but she didn't cover herself, not even when his eyes raked hers. There was so much more to explain, but for right now, there was other, more serious business to attend to, as the hair on the back of his neck stood up and a chill ran down his spine.

Brother Wolf alerted him to Stray's presence outside first, but Stray wasn't alone. No, there were Weres here. Maybe weretrappers too, but Rifter was too turned around from the second ritual mating to tell immediately.

He scanned the property, saw Stray by the sliding back door near the house. The Weres were coming through the south side. And no doubt Vice and Jinx weren't home—it was the only reason Stray would leave Harm alone.

It was problematic at best to leave Gwen out here unprotected, but there was little choice. He wouldn't get her to the door in time.

He signaled Stray to send Cyd and Cain out as soon as he distracted the outlaw Weres. Turned to Gwen and helped her pull what was left of her shirt on. Her pants were destroyed and he smelled the cloying scent of a potential first shift, that scent always more potent than for the shifts that followed.

"Gwen, you can't . . ." What? Can't shift? Because he knew that's what her body was telling her to do, and the second mating hadn't helped. "You have to be strong."

"I don't understand any of this."

"Just stay in between these trees and don't move. Cyd and Cain will come for you—as wolves. Both dark brown—one with yellow eyes, the other, green. They'll get you into the house safely."

She nodded, biting back the fear he saw etched on her fine features, and goddamn it, he wanted to wipe that pain from her forever.

But his fear was that it had only just begun.

"You'll come back?" she asked as she glanced between the men that had begun to emerge on the lawn and him.

"Always. It's not easy to get rid of me."

"I'm beginning to realize that," she murmured, touched his cheek with her palm and kissed him. A send-off to battle.

His blood surged—the battle was a part of him as much as the wolf. He backed away reluctantly, wove through the woods behind where the Weres came in so he wouldn't give away Gwen's position, and then he prepared to kill the outlaws threatening his way of life, his family . . . and most important, his mate.

Max worked her usual double shift. The amount of death and destruction—and crazy people—coming through the ER was twice what it normally was, and it was well past the full moon.

She knew far too much about the underbelly of this town—this world—and her connection to the supernatural one used to not freak her out like this. But she'd lost so much and she could possibly lose so much more if she wasn't careful.

She didn't want to be careful, wanted to run from this place, to find Liam and beg forgiveness. But he'd never understand and there was no way she could blame him.

She'd been recognized tonight—had denied it and got a laugh from the on-call resident as the older man insisted he knew her from the neighborhood.

When he left, she'd stared in the mirror and realized that hair color and makeup did nothing to cover up her sins. They never had, but she'd fooled herself for the past year.

Inside, she was still that same street punk, a mobster's kid who'd left Brooklyn when she was twenty to avoid marrying into that same lifestyle.

Running from your fate never worked—she was living a prime example of that fact. And she'd tried it twice now.

Her phone buzzed in her pocket. Teague. She took it behind one of the curtains as she restocked a cart.

He didn't wait for her hello. "Cordelia's dead."

Her mouth went dry and she tried hard to pretend she cared. "What happened?"

"Liam happened."

Liam killed the witch and she was happy. Cordelia made her blood boil—it had been so hard for Max not to slam the woman across the room earlier, witch or no witch.

They knew she was Liam's mate. They also knew about her past. So many ways to blackmail her, and they all made her furious.

In the past, no one would've dared to screw with her this way. No, they would've paid dearly.

Her thirst for blood back then scared her now. Some nights, she'd look in the mirror and wonder who she was, why her conscience would wake her up at night with a pounding heart and a pending panic attack.

As her temper grew, so did her need to control it. Liam understood so much, had from the very first night they'd met in the Were bar last year.

Funny, she'd always referred to her temper as the beast. To watch men and women shift into real ones . . . to have that undeniable freedom stirred jealousy in her.

She wished becoming a Were was as simple as the movies made it out to be, that all it took was a bite.

She was human. Mortal. Fragile. And Liam loved her anyway.

She'd never learned how to accept love without screwing it up. This time would prove no exception.

"I'm sending Weres for you now—be ready," Teague said, and he was her future whether she wanted him to be or not.

She knew it was time to go for good. But she'd walk out of the hospital like it was simply change of shift and not her last day. And so she pulled a black hoodie over her blue scrubs, put her bag over her shoulder and went out the back exit.

Tried to, anyway. The man waiting for her in the shadows of the hallway was pierced and tatted and huge. She pulled a knife from her pocket, knowing it was completely useless despite its pure silver blade, and he smiled. Widely.

"Sweetheart, don't bother. Just come with me." His voice was rough gravel, and it took her a mere second to realize which of the famed Dires he was. Vice. Perhaps the most dangerous of the grouping—and the most legendary. Even standing near him, she could feel the pull of desire, thanks to him.

She knew all about them from Liam, who'd coached her on Were—and Dire—culture, trying to help her fit in. "You don't understand—I can't. They're waiting for me."

"The Weres? Not anymore." He smiled then, and she noted the change in his eyes, the canines lengthening. The smell of a fresh kill enveloped her, and she wanted to celebrate, but she'd gain nothing from that. She wanted to beg but the words died in her throat as the brutally handsome man shook his head slowly. Held out his hand and told her, "Come on, now; don't be afraid of the big, bad wolf."

The door opened behind him and another large Dire said, "Cut the crap, Vice."

She looked out the door behind the second wolf and saw Liam standing there, watching her.

The first time they'd met, she'd been fighting and he'd saved her—she just hadn't known it at the time. Now she didn't bother to fight any longer—or at all, compared to her old self. Instead, she put her head down and let the wolves lead her into their truck.

Liam didn't say a word to her on the drive. She sat in the back next to Jinx while Vice drove with Liam next to him. Liam, the man she'd sworn to love for the rest of her days.

He'd taken her in, knowing she'd age, that she'd more than likely die long before he did. Made love to her, let her watch him shift. He'd made himself vulnerable to her and, in the end, he'd accuse her of using that against him and his family.

And he wouldn't be wrong.

Chapter 24

The uncomfortable elephant-in-the-backseat car ride from hell took forever, even with Vice doing close to eighty on the old back roads. He heard the human's harsh breathing, and it took a lot not to rip her head off for what looked like a major betrayal.

But she was a human, so he didn't know what the hell Liam expected. Shit, if he was going to train this kid, he would tell him what his Marine sarge had told him—*If you were supposed to have a wife, we'd have issued you one.*

"Hang on," he told them as he yanked the car on a hard right turn into the driveway and pulled into the Dire house's garage. Just before he pulled in, he noted Rifter coming at the Were pack surrounding the back property.

"They'll come through the woods on the north side," Jinx said as they raced through the house, leaving Liam to get Max inside.

"Secure her," Vice told Liam, "and then come and fight."

He stripped his shirt, as did Jinx, and they found Stray standing on the back porch, watching Rifter posture. Granted, the man could so back it up. Since the Weres appeared to forget that, Vice was ready to help remind them.

"Harm begged me to let him fight," Stray said, his voice harsh with anger. "I put the silver chain around his neck."

Vice clamped a hand on his shoulder. "Good man. We'll take care of this and then see what Rifter wants us to do with Harm."

"He's Gwen's father," Stray said. "I'm thinking he's going to be sticking around."

Jinx remained stoic, watching the Weres approach Rifter, counting and calculating the fight in his head with the precision of a master fighter, which he was. Vice was all anger and rage when he fought, but Jinx—and Rogue—they were both fierce and beautiful during the fight, the way a warrior was supposed to be. Even Stray was prettier than Vice in battle.

Vice shuddered then, as Jinx watched him. The demon spirits hadn't exactly left him—he could feel some leftover energy making him hinky as hell. He shuddered a few more times, and then something was burning.

His skin.

"Jesus Christ, Jinx . . ."

"Hey, you let it in." Jinx held the bottle of holy water and watched Vice's body smoke from where the spirits had been. Black smoke rose from him, and he felt the demon slowly loosen its claws.

"Dude, wait—let it stay and keep an eye on me," Vice told him, and Jinx's hand remained poised to throw more holy water on him. "Some of those Weres are spelled too. You need some demon on your side tonight, for all our sakes."

As Gwen watched from her hidden position, Rifter roared out of the woods, surprising the twenty or so men who'd been walking toward the Dire house.

Rifter moved toward the group bare chested, jeans

half undone and looking like some kind of primal god on the hunt. She could almost see the swagger of the wolf as man and beast melded to work as one. He wasn't rushing, gave off the aura of a man who couldn't be taken down.

The confidence helped to keep her breathing even, but the enemy was coming toward Rifter now. She counted twenty men on the opposing side, and while they weren't as big as Rifter or his brothers, they were nothing to sneer at.

She had a feeling Rifter and his brothers had been outnumbered many times before this . . . and she had so much more to learn about all of them.

Wolf . . . yours.

Mine.

Lightning flashed overhead, making Rifter look powerful and giant.

Invincible. Something inside of her clawed, wanted to run and fight alongside him. It took everything she had to stay put and watch.

She checked behind her and saw only darkness, turned back to watch the enemy advance.

It was then she saw the other men emerge from the house.

Are all these men . . . *wolves*?

Like you, the rustling whispered, more loudly than ever.

She would soon find out.

Rifter's brothers—Vice and Jinx—were there, along with a third man she hadn't met before. They were all shirtless as well. Vice was tattooed everywhere—he looked far more deadly than he had last night. You'd never know there was a gentle side to him at all.

Right now, she was glad to see all their ferocity.

"Back down," Rifter warned as the small group surrounded the large one. "Or perish."

It was that simple. But the Weres were moving forward despite his words. At first, they met in the middle of the lawn as men, and then arms and legs gave way to fur and claws as the Dires and Weres began their battle.

The fight scared her . . . but somewhere deep inside, she felt a thrill of excitement. It was like watching a gladiator match. The men's bodies, coated with a mixture of sweat and rain, impossibly perfect bodies, muscled and tattooed. And when the transition happened, she could finally watch and know she wasn't losing her mind.

It was . . . fantastical. If she wasn't so frightened . . .

The shift happened instantly—if she'd blinked, she would've missed it. One minute, Rifter was running toward the group of men, and the next, the handsome, fierce wolf was in his place, flying through the air.

One and the same, the rustling told her.

I have that inside of me. Struggling to get out all these years. She clutched a hand over her heart, which beat so fast she was sure it would burst through her chest.

One by one, Rifter's brothers changed. Vice was a shockingly beautiful pure white, and Jinx was a dark auburn, like a slow-burning fire.

The other wolves were smaller—it was easy to tell them apart, but there were so many more of them than the Dire wolves.

She watched Rifter with pride.

He's mine.

She felt like she should run out there and fight. Felt as though she could jump in there and put up the good fight. Her skin was tight as she watched from her position of safety behind the tree.

Rifter's wolf howled after throwing the broken-looking bodies of two Weres to the ground near where she'd hidden.

As she watched, the Weres turned back to human—the men were obviously dead.

They were going to hurt you.

The sky was so dark, the moon stood out in stark relief, looked like a cutout, and she let the rain pound her nearly bare skin as she watched the fight. There were growls—they sounded like nothing she'd ever heard before.

When the two wolves came up silently on either side of her, she forced herself to check their eyes. Yellow. Green.

Cyd and Cain, the young twins she'd met in the kitchen earlier. Their ears flattened, like they were trying to tell her not to be afraid. And then the yellow-eyed one—Cain—moved close and nudged her toward Cyd and the house. Slowly, almost reluctantly, she moved away from the fight and toward the safety of the house.

They'd come just in time, since the Weres had crashed through the woods where she'd been.

They scent you.

She broke into a mad dash for the doors, hoping she'd be safe inside. Liam was waiting by the door, let her in and closed and locked the sliding glass behind her. He had a high-powered rifle in one hand and looked like he'd be more at home in the military than here. His chest was bare and she could see the thin red line where his chest had once been ripped open.

The heavy stitches she'd put in earlier were dissolved.

"You all right?" he asked, without taking his eyes off the fighting outside.

"Fine."

"There are towels behind you," he told her, and she grabbed one and wrapped herself in it. "Can you work one of these?"

He pointed to a rifle on the table to her right—that one looking more like the standard hunting rifle her uncle used to use to hunt buck. "Yes."

She picked it up and held it against her body, her finger loose on the trigger.

Cyd and Cain remained in wolf form, stood pacing outside the sliding glass door while she remained inside, watching the scene play out in front of her like some CGI monster movie.

Except—were these men really monsters?

The Dires had fought as a team since the Extinction, learning early that they needed to stick together. And so they trained, far more stringently than they ever had with their packs, in order to work like a well-oiled machine. When Stray joined them, they worked him into their battles and he integrated well.

Now, without speaking, the men each took on the wolves in their trajectory—a close-quarters battle. This was in their blood. The fight made Brother Wolf's inherent viciousness take over both their sensibilities, until Rifter couldn't see anything but Were.

These were trained men, but not the leaders of the outlaw pack. They were sent in as a sacrifice, and that upset Brother more than anything. He ripped the head off a Were who'd grabbed his back leg in his teeth and threw the body away. Held the head in his teeth before shaking it off into the woods.

Some Weres were easy to kill, but some of these wolves were different. Off. Spelled.

Vice was taking on several Weres at once, his white wolf speckled with the blood of the enemy, his silver eyes lighting the night. Now, as a Were flew straight toward Rifter, it was met by Vice—large, snarling—and it hit the first wolf hard, slamming it far from Rifter and right to the ground.

Rifter knew that, for Vice, this call to excess during his fight could be terrifying and exhausting, and that was just for his brothers watching him. Vice was an out-of-control killing machine. Harm's singing could probably soothe him, Rogue's voice definitely would, but right now, there was neither. His Brother Wolf was so pulled to anger, there would be no stopping him until the job was done.

Vice's Brother Wolf roared over Rifter again—now his fur was muddied with red blood, since he'd caught the Were by the throat and rolled him the way a croc would its prey.

After the death roll, there was no doubt the Were was dead. The white wolf howled as two more Weres came toward him.

These wolves were beyond spelled—they were demon bound. Vice had a demon inside of him as well, and it was pissed. Rifter hoped to high hell Jinx had holy water available.

Chapter 25

Twenty minutes later and Gwen could still feel the static electricity along her skin. Liam's anger washed through the room in waves. She could literarily smell his anger and frustration as he pressed a palm against the glass. "They won't let me out there, and this is my fight."

"What do you mean?"

"They're here for me," Liam growled. "They didn't finish the job the first time."

But they were also here for her, according to Rifter. She kept that to herself and continued to watch the massive fight outside. The howls chilled her—the thunder rocked the solid-as-anything house, and she fought the rising fear to stand her ground.

"No one's coming in here," Liam told her, and she believed him. But she didn't lower her weapon.

There had been at least fifty of the outlaws at first, although their numbers were greatly reduced now. "Why are they after you?" she asked Liam.

"I'm next in line to be king of the New York pack—alpha of all werepacks. The outlaws killed my father. When you helped me, I was recovering from nearly dying at their hands. And now there's a war among the Weres. It threatens all of us. Makes us too public, and we have no desire to come out to the humans." He raised his chin proudly. "I didn't mean to bring this trouble here."

"Neither did I," she said with a quiet dignity she hadn't been sure she could muster, let alone truly feel.

Liam nodded and looked back out at the fighting. There was blood and dirt everywhere—the smell would forever be embedded in her nose, and although she was used to it from the ER, this was different. There was a mystical quality to it, and she knew for sure she'd passed somehow into another world, a portal, thin as it may have been, between the rational world of science, where none of this existed, and the supernatural one, where all of this was possible.

Suddenly, shots rang out in the air.

"Teague," Liam said fiercely. "He was a sniper before he got dishonorably discharged from the Marines. He's hiding in the trees."

She put her hands against the glass like she was about to push and leap through it. Palms flat, she scratched helplessly against the glass as Rifter's Brother Wolf sustained a bullet wound that ripped through his side.

She was so busy staring out at the fight, which was finally waning, when the Were literally came out of nowhere. Maybe he dropped from the roof, but when he landed between Cyd and Cain, she took a step back and Liam moved forward as the two young wolves who'd saved her went at him. The Were was gray, its fur matted, and it looked at her through the glass with eyes more demonic red than anything she'd seen from the others.

It was up close and personal, bloody and vicious, and she'd never been more grateful in her life. And when Vice's white wolf joined in the fray, the red-eyed Were met a quick end.

Cain and Cyd howled, a whooping sound that echoed

through the trees, as the Dires did the same, celebrating the spoils of victory.

It was over, at least for now. Four naked men stood in the field, surveyed the bodies littering the ground. Several Weres had run off, and she watched Cyd and Cain bound away through the trees, governed by some unspoken command to check the property, as the Dires walked back toward her, stopping outside the house and pacing restlessly, waiting for the young wolves to come back.

"None if this seems . . . normal. I mean, beyond the wolf thing," she said, more to herself than to Liam.

"There's some kind of spell at work. The magic dissipates when the sun comes up," Liam explained. "A lot of it, anyway. And a Were shifting to fight during the day is rare, anyway."

"Because of the moon?"

"Because of the police." He stared past her, his eyes on the sky, brow furrowed. Checked his watched and looked out again. "Six in the morning. Even with a storm, that sky's not normal."

Not for daytime, she agreed. It was still pitch-black out there, the sky a mix of heavy clouds and clear spots with no stars. No sun either, and still the hint of the moon, which she was sure could not be good for beasts pulled to it and by it.

You're one of those beasts, she reminded herself.

The dead Weres' packmates would have to come pick up and bury their own. Until then, the bodies would remain in the woods as fresh kills, trophies to show the Weres and witches and trappers that you couldn't fuck with the Dires and not expect to die in the process.

But the Weres had definitely been spelled. Rifter wasn't sure if it was the weather giving them their demonic edge or if he was still off from the second mating, but they were much harder to kill than they normally were. And he knew he wasn't getting weaker.

Fucking witches.

Jinx probably already had some idea of it, because he'd already said, "We need to talk," as soon as what was supposed to be dawn rolled around and the men shifted back on the lawn under the too-eerie cover of night to recoup and assess their injuries.

Thunder and lightning still reigned in the sky, the moon barely visible, and yet still her pull was indescribably strong. And when he'd finally gone inside, satisfied the battle was over for now, Gwen had been talking to Cyd and Cain, and the young wolves looked pretty damned enthralled with her. A look from Rifter made them back off, albeit with the cocky grins only teenagers could get away with. Liam had been there too, rifle in hand, ready to strike.

Now Liam, Cyd, and Cain remained downstairs with Gwen. She wanted to talk to him, but Rifter knew he needed to find out what the hell was going on with the witches and trappers first, and that took priority.

The Dires gathered upstairs, wet and partially clothed, having grabbed towels from the linen closets in the hallway. Rifter wrapped a towel around his waist, pressed another to his bleeding side and listened to Jinx's story about seeing his father's spirit as they sat among the ruins of Rogue's room.

They always held meetings here out of respect for him, but this time, Jinx looked uncomfortable. He paced as he spoke of what he'd seen in the cemetery, and Rifter tried to process all of it as the storm raged outside.

Rifter's throat tightened. "Seb's raised—and enslaved— our dead Dire packs?"

"Appears he's trying. He hasn't fully succeeded yet, but he's getting close. All of this"—Jinx turned to wave at the sky—"is part of it. A supernatural pull. Seb's behind it."

Jinx hadn't stopped pacing since his return. Rifter fully expected him to shift and run any second, but the man remained in human form. Muttered a prayer in the old language, and they all bowed their heads out of respect.

If successfully raised, would the army of passed Dires be forced to fight their own kind? Would they know what they did but remain helpless against that kind of magic? It sounded that way to Rifter, and Jinx agreed.

"I think it's been in the works for a while," Jinx continued and then stared at Rifter as the realization dawned on him—on all of them, judging by the dead silence.

Finally, Rifter said, "My dreams. Fuck." Bits and pieces of the nightmare flashed before him—his father asking to be saved—the battle, the souls rising.

"They never passed over?" Vice asked. "Wouldn't Rogue have known that—or you?"

"It's not like they've ever visited," Jinx said.

"Wouldn't the Elders be concerned enough about this to tell us?" Stray asked.

"Again, I don't know if Seb is actually bringing them back or if they've been hovering. And the Elders never tell us shit." Jinx's voice was bitter, as Stray's had been.

Vice was sitting on the floor next to Rogue, the fight having mellowed him to the point of extreme calm. It was unnerving, given the circumstances, but not abnormal. The pendulum would swing in the opposite direction all too soon. "How can we fight against the dead—especially our own kind?" he asked as he blew the smoke from his hand roll so it drifted over Rogue's head.

Rifter half expected Rogue to reach out and take the cigarette from Vice's hand and take a long drag, the way he'd done so many times in the past. But nothing happened and he pulled his mind back to the present, and Vice's damned good question.

It was a true concern, especially for the Weres. Tonight had been only the tip of the iceberg. If enough Weres were possessed, trained to do anything the weretrappers wanted, battles would not be as easily won as tonight's was. The minds of the Dires were harder to penetrate, but maybe with their own kind . . .

Jinx said, "I can try, but the dead . . . that's just not really my thing."

He shifted a glance to Rogue, and Vice continued to smoke among the ruins of his own making.

Rogue's mattress was far more comfortable than the floors they'd been chained to during the three-week imprisonment. Rifter didn't have to close his eyes to picture the cells with the silver-lined walls and matching bars, could still feel the ache on his ankles where the silver cuffs had sunk down to the bone.

"You should be more angry with your own kind," Seb told him during his one and only visit to Rifter. He'd been surprised the witch had the guts to come around at all. It had been the impetus for Rifter to escape—had forced the anger to well up past the drugs long enough to rouse Brother Wolf and formulate the plan to dreamwalk in a guard's mind and escape. Through that same dreamwalk, he'd discovered where Rogue was being held, a mile away underground, and rescued him. After he'd carried Rogue out, Vice blew up the facility behind them.

That had destroyed years of research. Killed eighty weretrappers and some feral Weres that had been experimented on to the point of no return. Rifter comforted himself with the fact that he had cost the weretrappers a hell of a lot.

It had cost the Dires more.

Rogue. Damn it. As tough as nails, the way they all were, but always more sensitive because of his gift, because the dead were always bothering him. Had Seb known what he was doing? Was Rogue purposely spelled?

The demon doc Eidolon didn't seem to think so. But now, with the possible rise of the Dire ghost army, it was looking more and more likely. "Why dream of this now? Seb's always stayed out of my mind because it was too dangerous for both of us. He wouldn't start now and give away his plans to me."

"Maybe he can't stop you," Jinx said. "Maybe Rogue's manipulating this."

They stared at the prone man, sleeping peacefully. Whatever was going on in his mind, Rifter would bet it was anything but manipulation.

"Are you sure Rifter isn't causing this with his dream-walking?" Stray asked. He'd taken one of Vice's hand rolls, and he'd lost some of the jitters that came with the shift and the fight.

"No," Jinx said. "But he can see it happening, which means he should be able to see into Rogue's mind."

All that swirling blackness would envelope and choke him—and yet, there was no other way. "Then there's only one thing left to do. I have to get inside Rogue's head and see if he's the conduit."

"You've never been able to do it before," Jinx said.

"I'm going to have to try harder."

"And you might not come back," Jinx pointed out.

"Are you more afraid you'll find out that your twin's the one fucking us over?" Stray asked suddenly, and Vice had his teeth on the man's neck before any of them could utter a word.

"Yes," Jinx said simply, and Vice let go of Stray. "It's a risk we have to take. Rogue knows things. He might be using whatever strength he can to keep Rifter out ... or maybe he's been waiting for us to figure it out and let Rifter in."

"Jesus, Jinx," Vice muttered, but Jinx continued.

"Things are goddamned falling apart—there are supernatural disturbances like I've never felt—things are falling apart. Weird murders. The weretrappers are trying to enslave humankind and the Weres."

"With the help of witches and demons," Stray added.

"No matter what, the weretrappers are stronger and more insidious than they once were. They're becoming as inhuman as the things they've called upon," Jinx said.

"You think they sold their souls?" Rifter asked, and Jinx nodded curtly.

"Fucking, fucking humans," Vice shouted at the ceiling, as if the Elders would hear it and come down to what—help?

They could, of course, but the Elders had long claimed they wanted the Dires to have free will. Rifter and his brothers were told the big picture, the right thing to do. But there was seemingly no end in sight for their redemption.

Maybe doing what they were doing was supposed to be its own reward? After all, how long is too long for a human life?

It was something Rifter had never been able to answer.

In the meantime, the Dires had seen it all, done it all, but there were always new challenges. Getting close to humans without shifting was one, but that required a special skill set.

If he was right, there could be another race partially destroyed, the rest enslaved. And if the mutant super-wolf Dire army created by the weretrappers took hold, humans were fucked.

The wolf world was large, underground. Meeting places for groups of packs took place in the mountains where humans couldn't easily travel. This happened infrequently, but when Linus had called, Weres listened.

Now it was a crapshoot. Loyalties were split and broken.

"If Rogue's the conduit for the Dire ghost army, we need the spell broken. We need a witch."

"Yeah, they're going to be so helpful to us," Jinx said.

"We'll have to be persuasive." Vice's eyes glinted with more than a hint of Brother Wolf behind them. His chest was smeared with blood and the tattoo over his heart seemed to beat with a life of its own.

"Even if we do that, Seb can use Gwen to kill us. We're too hard to study. Unstoppable. With us out of the way, he can reproduce her DNA and use the Weres. Even on their worst day they can outmatch an army of humans." Rifter balled his hands into fists. "I need to talk to Gwen—about her shift. Her parentage. Everything. I think you should all be there."

"You might want to ask her that first," Jinx pointed out.

"While you do that, Liam and I are going to have a nice talk with Max," Vice added.

"If you've already had a second mating," Jinx started, and Rifter held up his hand to stop him from saying anything further.

The third mating was literally the charm. She would shift—and there was no way Rifter could let that happen now—not until they figured out how her body was going to react.

There were a few half humans, half Weres. Most were significantly weaker than their lycan counterparts. It was looked on as a disability, a liability, and usually those halfs weren't totally accepted into the pack.

That wouldn't be the case with Gwen. He wondered if the Elders knew this.

"They know everything," Stray said bitterly, and Vice and Jinx looked between Rifter and Stray questioningly.

"I'm not going to finish the mating." Not yet.

"You're going to have to explain a lot to her. You're going to have to tell her about Harm," Stray continued. "I'm thinking that killing her father isn't going to go over well."

"He deserves it," Vice snarled, and nearly snapped Stray's head off, but Stray was fast, hit the other side of the room and prepared to strike.

"Not now—we've got to stand together," Rifter said. Alphas were all too used to having all their orders followed without question; this situation should've been next to impossible, but it had worked thus far.

Vice muttered, "Sorry," and Stray shrugged, and Rifter left them to clean up and went to find Gwen, but not before he stood over Rogue. He stared at his brother's closed eyes and wondered what kinds of hellish secrets Rogue was keeping now.

"Rogue, we need you," he muttered, amended, "I need you," because Rogue would know what he went through. The experiments, the nightmares both he and Brother Wolf suffered as a direct result.

But Rogue remained silent, as he'd been, disturbingly so, among the ruins of Vice's earlier tantrum.

Chapter 26

The Dires went upstairs after the fight—battle debriefing, Gwen supposed, although that didn't stop her from pacing as restlessly as the others, all of them keeping an eye on the property.

Liam held the rifle, and Cyd and Cain, now shifted back to human form, carried guns as well. None of them talked much, except for an occasional comment on the weather.

Gwen remained more toward the interior, where Liam had asked her to stay, rifle still in hand, and she hadn't been able to let her guard down either. She heard the talking upstairs, gruff male voices, and the rustling continued in her ears.

Rifter would explain more to her; she knew that. Patience had never been her strong suit, though, and this was pushing all her boundaries.

Suddenly, she heard a creak coming from inside the room to her right, and she went in, rifle up, because Liam wasn't close by.

The window was open and a figure was going out instead of going in. Were or not, she didn't know, so she pointed the rifle and said as firmly as she could, "Stop and turn around—hands up."

The figure stopped dead—and Gwen caught sight of a familiar ponytail and then the flash of a bare arm covered in tattoos. When Max turned around and saw Gwen, she looked anything but relieved.

No, her eyes were swollen—she'd been sobbing, apparently. And she was handcuffed as well. A wooden chair lay destroyed in the corner.

"Max? What's going on—why are you here?" she asked, instinct telling her to keep the rifle pointed on the woman, whom she considered a friend, the one whose phone number was still in the pocket of her jeans upstairs.

Max opened her mouth to speak, but nothing came out. She turned and tried to go back out the window quickly, but not wolf quick—Gwen could already tell the difference. Her bare feet slapped against the floor as she put the rifle down at her side and grasped the back of Max's shirt, pulling her down.

"Let me go," Max pleaded.

"It's too dangerous out there. You have no idea."

"It's more so in here for me—you have no idea." Max struggled and Gwen pinned her against the wall.

"Stop, Max—I don't want to hurt you."

"What's going on here?" Liam demanded from behind them. When Gwen turned, she saw his eyes were half lupine and she let go of Max and backed up.

"She was trying to go outside—I didn't want her to get hurt," Gwen explained, couldn't tell which one of them Liam was mad at. "Why is she here?"

"Shit, forgot about the hospital connection," Liam muttered. "Who the hell were you going to meet?" he asked, his voice rising to a near bark at Max, who swallowed hard but remained still. "I don't recognize you anymore. What the hell happened to you?"

She flinched at his yell, and he backed up, shaking his

head. It was as if he was seeing a ghost, but Max was most definitely flesh and blood. But now the wolf tattoos on the young nurse's arm began to make a bit more sense to Gwen. "How do you two know each other?"

"She's my mate," Liam bit out. "Although not for much longer."

Max was shaking and Gwen took her arm and led her past the broken chair to the couch, the chain between the cuffs clinking. "Why not?"

"She betrayed me. When a mate betrays her mate, it's grounds for death." His words were blunt, his tone, anything but, and Max drew in a harsh breath as if she'd been physically slapped. "What do you know about what's happening out there?"

Max finally spoke, not able to meet either of their eyes. "Something big—I don't know exactly what. It almost sounded like another pack was coming in to help them take over."

Liam turned away and Gwen wished she could leave the two of them alone. But Liam insisted that she stay. For both Liam's and Max's sakes, it was safest, but to watch the pain etched on their faces . . .

Her relationship with Rifter was just starting—theirs was ending with a terrible, and brutal, finality.

"I know where the outlaws are staying," Max admitted. "I had to get close with them."

Liam's eyes blazed, but this time Gwen watched the young woman stand her ground as he demanded, "How close?"

"They were going to kill me." Her words were a partial plea but also a statement of fact. "They knew, as your mate . . ."

"It would hurt me the most—which meant they either left me alive on purpose or their aim was to pick on the old pack ways."

"I didn't do anything with them. I avoided it."

"You shouldn't have bothered." Liam turned to walk away.

"She had a reason," Gwen said with a sudden, unerring clarity. She wasn't sure if she sensed it or smelled it, because the wolf inside of her was slowly trying to rise, but she knew what Max was hiding. As Max stared at her, Gwen walked forward, sat next to Max on the couch and asked, "How far along are you?"

She heard Liam's sharp intake of breath, and Max said, "Thirty days. They were going to kill me—I couldn't let them experiment on this baby after I died."

"Do they know?"

"I don't think so. I didn't want them to find out. Can you understand that?"

A wolf's mating instincts were strong, but her mothering instincts were more so. Gwen knew there was far more to this story, but she was in the way here. Slowly she stood and walked past Liam, who remained so still she figured he must be in shock.

She closed the door behind them and slid down against the wall next to the door, curled into a ball. The stress of the day—of the past days—had begun to take its toll.

What kind of life will you have?

You were born and bred to deal with violence. And she had to admit that truth—she'd always veered toward working in the ER—which was the most bloody and violent of all the internships. And she'd been good at it.

Liam felt the shift coming on and did everything in his power to stop it. He heard Max talking to him, telling him to remain calm, and if he remained in human form it would be a goddamned miracle. Much like the baby Max was carrying.

His baby . . . could it be? The timing was right if she hadn't betrayed him—the big *if*—because the typical gestation period for a wolf was sixty-three days and they'd been together in January for sure.

He breathed deeply and shoved his wolf down. He'd never lead the pack with such little control over his own personal life. Vice was right about that.

Even though Max was human, the wolf DNA in the baby would influence the gestation. She must've been so confused by it all—the pregnancy would be as hard as anything on her body.

It all made perfect sense, or at least Max's inability—and refusal—to fight the way she normally would have. In the past, he'd watched her take out much bigger and badder than her human self should've been capable of when she'd been threatened, and with that, she'd gained a lot of respect in his world. At least from those who knew about her. Hanging out with Weres was a dangerous proposition for a human. Because of that, only a few close pack members knew she was his mate.

Apparently, the cat was more out of the bag than he thought.

He'd met her inside Howlers. It had been a hot summer night and his body was twisted up, readying for the full moon. The first five years after the change were the worst, he'd been told, and so far year four hadn't been any better than year one.

Strange cravings ran through him, and although there were other female Weres there—pretty ones too—Max caught his attention because she was flirting shamelessly with another wolf when said wolf's very angry Were girl-friend and her friend confronted her.

He'd been prepared for Max to go down quickly, but she'd taken out two female Weres and had been halfway to taking out the male when Liam stepped in and dragged Max away.

It was for her own good. The male had been about to shift, and at that point, Max thought Weres existed only in horror movies. The jukebox blared Meatloaf's "You Took the Words Right out of My Mouth" over the outside speaker, with the singer appropriately asking about baring throats to wolves with red roses.

"Calm down—I'm not going to hurt you," he told her as she struggled worse than anything he'd ever wrestled. He had nail marks on his forearms and neck where she reached up to grab him, and she said, "I'll hurt you, then."

"I'll bet you say that to all the boys," he said.

He'd had to let her go, afraid he would really hurt her. She punched him in the jaw—hard enough for him to see stars. He grabbed her wrist and pulled her to him, and then he was kissing her, despite the stunning pain radiating thanks to her right hook.

Danger. Adrenaline. The forbidden, all mixed together with the beautiful, strong woman, and the best part was, she kissed him back.

His lip had bled and she'd run her tongue across it, like she could heal it. Wrapped her arms around him and held him close, like she wouldn't let him go. She was as protective as any female wolf he'd ever been with.

"Thought you wanted the guy you were all over in there."

"I thought you'd never notice," she admitted. For the next month, they were inseparable apart from his full-moon run. Her temper was bad, her attitude at times equally so, but never with him. At times, she seemed to melt, like he'd been the only person in the world she could be herself around.

He'd discovered early on that she was a mob kid, as in

the Italian Mafia. She'd run from her family and that life and ended up in one surprisingly similar in terms of danger. "I couldn't have ratted on any of them, and that's what would've happened—I was being forced into doing something I didn't want to. I came here to get away—to get out of that way of life."

It had stayed with her, though. Growing up in it embedded it in her.

Lying in bed, in Liam's arms, she'd confessed her dreams for a different kind of life, and he'd felt as guilty as hell.

He could offer her only more of the same. The pack wars were gearing up and he was intensifying his training with his father and his wereguards. It was going to get ugly.

When he'd finally worked up the courage to admit to her what he was, she hadn't believed it. He'd shifted for her under the moonlit sky while her mouth hung open in astonishment. And when he'd shifted back, she'd responded, "You can offer me love, which makes it so different from anything I've ever had."

But she was completely weirded out, nonetheless. She'd run from him, and although he'd be able to track her easily, he didn't.

She'd come back on that cold spring night last year and she hadn't left since.

And now Teague called her "Liam's pet." Liam had heard him say it as he remained hidden, listening to his father die.

Those screams and Max's betrayal—no matter the reason—would be forever and inextricably linked in his mind.

"If it was just me, I'd fight. But I couldn't because . . . if anything happened," she told him as if reading his thoughts. Hands on her belly, she turned away.

"Max—"

"You know my temper, how hard it is to control. You of all people know!" She fisted her hands and stared at the ceiling and breathed. "I'll kill anyone who tries to hurt this baby once he's born. Until then . . ."

"Him?"

She settled her gaze on him. "A boy. Next in line. You have to understand . . . I didn't know what else to do."

"You could've come to me—we could've found a way around it," Liam spat.

"How?" Max's eyes blazed, her hand going protectivel—instinctively—to her belly. He hated the silver circling her wrists. "I thought you were dead. They would've taken me in—studied me and taken the baby. I could never have forgiven myself."

"So you were going to let them take Gwen?"

"It was either that or abort the baby. The boy is the next leader, Liam. To do that . . ." She shook her head. "I went to the bar—spoke with the owner about getting Rifter's number to tell him what was happening. I know they help humans. And when Cordelia said Gwen was with Rifter two nights ago . . ."

Liam left the room before he completely lost control. Closed the door behind him and tried to block out Max's pain and the sounds of the Dires meeting in the kitchen with Gwen.

Chapter 27

Gwen had pulled herself together by the time Rifter finally came down the stairs, alone. He silently motioned for her to follow him into the kitchen. She did so with the fresh towels and medical supplies she'd collected in order to give herself something to do, plopped them all down on the table.

"Sit," she said, and he scowled a little but did as she asked. He wore a towel wrapped around his waist and there were marks on him that were already beginning to heal. But the medical professional in her couldn't simply let that go without giving them some kind of attention. "I saw you get shot."

"I'm fine," he told her, obviously irritated by the attention she was paying to his wounds.

"I'm just making sure. You'd do the same for me, right?" she asked, and he couldn't argue with that. The bullet had grazed him—she saw the long line that had already started to heal on its own. She checked the rest of his torso, her fingers tracing a bite mark along his back, right above the wolf's ear. "The fight was intense."

"You shouldn't have worried. You've seen me fight."

She had—and in wolf form. But it had been a blur. Wolf against man and seemingly no contest—even bullets couldn't bring him down. "Do you win in human form too?"

A small, well-deserved cocky grin emerged. "Always."

She didn't doubt it. With his size alone, who would be foolish enough to go up against him?

Beyond his brothers, of course. She went to the sink and wet a washcloth with warm water and moved it across his face first, getting rid of the dirt and blood more gently than necessary.

The big man practically purred under her touch, and she continued her exploration, down his neck, along his shoulders. All the while, his eyes never left hers.

Their relationship—which was supposed to have been a one-night stand—had gotten so complicated, she wasn't sure where to begin, but she needed to. She bit her tongue for a few more minutes because she liked being close to him—and anything she said was sure to break this comfort.

She traced the healed bullet wound from yesterday, gently patted down a long scratch next to it with a cotton ball dipped in peroxide. It had been deep—she probably would've stitched it under normal circumstances, but nothing about this was normal, and so she left it to the air.

When she'd finished with his upper body, she knelt at his feet and began to clean him. He growled, softly, and she looked up, surprised.

"You don't have to do that."

"I know. I want to," she said softly, and no, she never thought she'd want to do this. But barring the fact that she knew he wouldn't follow her up to the shower, she did the best she could here, washing his calves and thighs. His arousal tented the white terry cloth, and there was no ignoring it. She breathed in the smell of night flowers—musky and unmistakably male—and the familiar achy need spread between her legs again. Visions of riding him on the kitchen table made her wet—and then made her blush.

She refused to meet his eyes, concentrated instead on toweling him dry now instead.

"It's all normal, you know," he said in a voice as heavy with lust as she felt.

"What's that?"

"Your needs. They'll be stronger than human ones—and nothing to be ashamed of. Wolves celebrate them. Revel in them."

Like the party. Finally, she met his eyes and wondered if hers looked remotely lupine. "I still can't believe any of this."

"Come here." He helped her up and she sat in the chair next to him, the intensity between them more electric than the lightning flashing through the windows. He glanced toward it, his brow furrowed, and then looked back at her, but didn't say anything.

"There can't be any more secrets—please," she told him.

"I'm just trying not to scare you."

"More than being a wolf scares me? I don't think so."

Rifter gave a wry grin, and she realized that the bond she'd felt earlier was far stronger since they'd made love.

There was so much more she wanted to know, and she believed Rifter was ready to relent. She stared into his eyes, which were completely human—for now—and repeated, "No more secrets."

When Rifter relented with a sigh, ran his hands through his still-damp hair and waited, she continued, "The first night in the bar—were they all wolves?"

"No. We mix with humans. Most of the time, they don't know it. We just stay away from them around our moon call. Because we'd hurt them otherwise. We're too strong, need too much sex. Too much of everything."

"I didn't seize during sex last night, did I?"

"No, I guess you didn't."

"So what's happening to me?"

"It's a long story."

"About a little girl born a wolf."

"Technically, half wolf."

She tried to get up, but he took her wrist and kept her in place with an easy hand. "You wanted me to think I was crazy."

"The truth wasn't an option." His tone was unapologetic, but his eyes told a different story. "I have to protect my family—they're all I have."

That stung, but . . . "You protected me too."

"Yes. I had to."

"I can't wrap my head around this." She started to pace. "I'm really . . ."

"You're a Dire wolf. And there are a lot of implications that go along with that."

"And you're going to share them," she said, but he'd stopped talking and was in fact listening for something she couldn't hear. Actually, that wasn't true, because the second she began to concentrate, she heard it too, a low rustling. Movements so quiet she shouldn't be hearing them, the way she couldn't have possibly heard the conversations on the third floor when she was on the first.

It's the wolf, the rustling told her, and then that was silent.

She looked up and saw the other Dires standing in the kitchen with them, and instinctively she moved to back away. Rifter caught her and shook his head. "It's not like that. There's something in your blood that can kill them. And in centuries, that's the first thing that's ever promised to end a Dire's life."

"You live . . . forever?"

"Yes. So they want you dead—they're confused as to

whether they want themselves to die," he explained. "So far, immortality's been a bitch—and not ours."

"They want to die?" she asked, and he shrugged. "And you?"

"I used to want that, yes."

"And now?"

"Not a chance," he told her.

Dissension among the Dire brothers because of Gwen was something Rifter couldn't allow to happen. It appeared she didn't want that either because she told them, "I think I need to hear everything."

"If she's one of us, she deserves to know," Vice agreed.

Slowly, the Dires moved forward and stood around the massive kitchen table, watching for her next move. When Gwen nodded and sat, they joined her in doing so. Rifter took the seat next to her, because if he remained calm, perhaps she would as well.

There was so much to take in—so much to tell.

"These men are my cousins—my brothers," Rifter started, and Gwen looked at each of them.

They all looked basically the same, not really aging over thousands of years, just changing their style. Vice looked the most changed with the piercings and the tattoos, although he'd been doing that long before it was the fashion.

"You grew up together?" she asked.

"We were all part of different packs scattered across Norway—we've known one another since our Running," he explained. "It's when young wolves are sent out after their transition in order to learn to blend with humans. We have six months to play—go wild without letting on what we are—before we return to the pack for more serious business."

"You always go back?" Gwen asked, and Vice shook his head.

"Not all. Some decide to stay away," he said. "At the time, Rifter and Jinx and Rogue and I planned on going back. Harm had already broken away and left us."

She cut her gaze to Stray questioningly.

"I was alone until fifty years ago—they found me in Texas," he said quietly. "My original pack was in Greenland. I was on my Running when the Extinction happened."

"And so it's only the six of you," she said.

"Until you, yes," Rifter answered. He didn't want to go back to those days, but for her sake, for the history she needed, he would. And then he would tuck it away in those deep, dark places memories slid into and not think on it again.

He'd set out after his first three shifts, alone, with a single bag and some cash tucked into his boot. Headed toward the more populated cities, he'd had a sense of fear and excitement.

The Running was a six-month experience to see if the young wolves had learned enough to mingle in the world among humans without exposing what they were. Like spies in a game of covert ops, the men and their newly emerged wolves mingled among humans, took their pleasures and then would return to their packs to mate. And most of those deemed alpha wolves would lead their own packs.

Rifter was an alpha—son of an alpha and expected to mate Roslyn when he returned. They would move to another area and create their own village of Dires. And while Rifter knew what was expected of him, he'd felt so damned young and inexperienced.

"That's what this shit's all about," Vice had told him when he'd first met the wolf on his way to the city. He'd stopped for the night under the half-moon and found Vice stripping and preparing to shift.

Vice couldn't wait to go back, he'd told Rifter. Harm, whom they'd met in the woods the next night, told them he had no intention of returning.

They'd both recognized Harm as the wolf who would be king of all the existing Dire packs—he'd been hand-picked by the Elders to take over for the current alpha, Jameson, once he returned from his Running. With Harm's magnetic charm and skills as an orator, it had been easy to see why he was the best choice.

But the Dire had never been comfortable with the idea of staying with wolves. Always more comfortable around humans, his plan was to remain among them. That would leave Rifter, the next in line, to take over as king of all the Dire packs. It was a job he was uncomfortable with because of his curse, but a role he would accept as his destiny.

However, Jameson wasn't happy about giving up the throne at the Elders' behest. He wanted dominion over Dires and humans, didn't want to follow anyone's orders but his own. Rather than follow the orders of the Elders, he'd led the packs on a massive killing spree of humans that threatened to expose the Dire wolves.

Rifter supposed the Elders had no choice but to follow through with the Extinction. Still, it had come as a blow to the young Dires.

The wolves returned to Rifter's village, the first stop from their Running together, where they discovered that the Dires had been slaughtered, throats slashed, villages burned to the ground. The devastation was apparent from miles away.

They'd gone in cautiously, helping Rifter look for his family, for any remnant of his former life, and found only more death and destruction than they'd ever wanted to see.

There were no survivors. It was apparent to the young wolves, and it hit Rifter harder than a punch to the gut.

There was nothing left for him there. Rifter couldn't speak as he shifted and picked through the smoking wreckage and the bodies of the men, women and children he'd grown up with.

"Rift, we can't stay here," Rogue told him quietly but firmly, led him back to the other three.

"Suppose they're all like this," Vice said, voicing what he couldn't hold back the way the others had. "The Elders did give the warning about the Extinction. Maybe our packs rebelled?"

There had been some talk of rebellion before the young wolves left for their Running, done in hushed tones. The young Dires had assumed it was merely a few disgruntled pack members, that Jameson would never risk the future of the entire race.

They all shifted again and headed to Vice's village. They watched him, numbly, and subsequently, Jinx and Rogue, discover that their packs had been dealt the same cruel hand of fate.

"It's only us," Rifter said after they'd visited the last of the villages. They were the only surviving Dires, along with Harm. The only wolves, as the Weres hadn't existed during the age of the Dires. And the four of them decided it wasn't safe in their old country any longer, gathered up what supplies they could and took off on horseback with as many provisions as they could carry for their human selves.

That was so many centuries ago, when they'd all been twenty-one years old.

They hid among humans and after a while found it

suited them best. The Elders didn't make themselves known for another year. But one night, when there was blood around the moon, the Elders appeared and Rifter asked them one question.

Why?

But they'd already known the answer.

"The warning," Rogue whispered. "They didn't heed the warning."

Of the four, he'd been the most angry at that. Self-control was something he'd prided himself on. He'd worried while they were on their Running, but Jinx had soothed him.

But Rogue's contacts with the dead had forewarned him months earlier—he felt most guilty that he hadn't been able to get any of his pack to listen.

Vice had taken it the hardest, though. He was tied to excess, and those extreme, primal urges on the part of the Dires—which led to coveting what humans had—was what drove the Elders to destroy them.

And even though Rifter alerted Harm immediately after they'd discovered the massacre, Harm still refused to come back. Whether the guilt of what had happened was too much for him or whether it was pure relief that he had no responsibility of kingship, Rifter was never sure.

None of them ever understood why the Elders didn't enforce any rules on Harm, and they'd been smart enough not to question their ultimate authority. Not to their faces, anyway.

What would happen to them had been unknown. They were supposed to come back from the Running and be mated. Raise families. Live until they were one hundred.

At the time, it had felt like forever.

If they'd only known, Rifter thought wryly. If they'd only fucking known.

From that moment on, Rifter traded one family for another. They mourned. Planned. Ran with the full moon, that celebration more like a funeral, but their wolves necessitated the change.

And still, the Elders hadn't come to them. Not at that time anyway, and the young wolves mourned for their families. It wasn't so much that there was love lost. No, it was different with the Dires. Bred for battle, not hearth and home, the pack was more hierarchy than hugs. And although they'd all mourned the loss of their packs, it was more about loyalty and vengeance than love.

It took the Elders four months to pull the remaining Dires to a meeting, and they told them then in no uncertain terms what the Dires already knew—they'd been the ones to smite the pack.

"We were cold and starved, waiting for a death that never came," Rifter now told Gwen, who had been listening intently. She continued to as he told her how they'd mourned and hovered at death's door for what seemed like forever. "We had to repent. We've been doing that for thousands of years, but it's not doing any good at all."

No, they were forced to wander nomadically, dragging their fortune and spoils behind them like the albatrosses they were.

"We've lived everywhere. Done and seen everything." Rifter sat back and looked at his brothers one by one, their faces shadowed by the low light in the room and the lack of any from outside, despite the nearly noon hour.

They'd combed the earth, searching for more like them. They were sure they couldn't have been the only Dires out on their Running when the Extinction occurred.

Finding Stray had confirmed that, but he'd claimed he'd never met another Dire since the Extinction.

"I can't imagine." Gwen's eyes shone softly—a simple show of emotion from a woman who'd thought she'd lost everyone related to her as well. With that story alone, she relaxed, but she didn't stop questioning. "I'm well past twenty-one, so when will I . . . um . . ."

"Shift," Jinx offered. "Normally, I'd say blue moon, but with all this paranormal activity, it's going to happen sooner than three weeks' time. You already said her wolf is coming out, right?"

She turned to Rifter as well. "How do you know? And what's the blue moon?"

"Blue moon's rare—happens once every few years, and it's the second full moon this month. And I know your wolf's coming because I've seen the bruising on your back—it's going to turn into something like my wolf."

Gwen asked, "Is that what's aching?"

"Yes—it's like a bad burn for the week before it emerges," Rifter said.

She'd thought maybe her back had some light burns from the explosion, but when she'd looked in the mirror, she'd seen only the bruising. It was the oddest feeling, like something was under her skin.

Now she knew that something was. But as long as they were on the topic of burning . . . "What's the significance of the fires? I mean, my mom, my aunt and uncle and then my house . . ."

"It's how they used to kill witches. They burned them. Sometimes they burned Weres too. But typically, Weres didn't get caught. Witches started retaliating on the Weres who refused to help by giving them the same treatment," Rifter told her.

"Revenge," she said softly. "The witches killed my mother?"

"I think it was someone who wanted you to believe it

was the witches," Rifter said. "Most likely the weretrappers, before they dragged the witches to their side."

"So those men at my house tonight—they were witches and weretrappers?"

"They were full human," Rifter confirmed. "The only witch who's been in recent contact with you is Cordelia."

She blanched. "How long had she been watching me?"

A look passed among the Dires, and she knew they were still holding back. She waited a long moment until Rifter finally admitted, "At least six months."

"How can you be sure?"

"They started following you again in earnest just before Rogue and I were captured," Rifter admitted.

"I didn't know you were captured as well," she said, and he nodded. "How did they know before all of you did? About me, I mean?"

Again, the men gave each other sideways glances, remained silent for a long moment. Vice muttered, "Fuck," and Jinx pushed away from the table and stared at the dark sky. She started to wonder if there would ever be daylight again, or if this Alice-down-the-rabbit-hole thing was simply going to continue for the rest of her life.

Which was still pretty damned precarious.

"Please," she said. "I can handle whatever you need to tell me. But if I don't know everything about my own life, that makes me vulnerable."

Rifter glanced at her, his face a tight mask of pain. "I hate that they're after you."

"Earlier, you said they were after me *again*. Which means they've known about me for a long time."

"You were well hidden with your mom for ten years, and with your aunt and uncle for much longer. You became vulnerable, but the witches thought you were sick too—they were pretty sure you wouldn't make it through the shift. And now there are people who want to hurt you because of what you are. To use you. Some Weres are turning their own kind in for profit." Rifter was incensed. She couldn't blame him, but humans had been turning against one another since the beginning of time. Why should wolves be any different?

But obviously they were.

"You said Weres. So why is Harm chained up if he's a Dire, like you?"

Rifter shook his head. "Not now, little one. You've got too much to process already."

"Yeah, see, that might work on your wolf groupies," she started, and he looked a little too pleased at that. "Tell me what Harm did. Because I heard him tell you that you should've let me die."

The anger flashed hard and fast in his eyes again, but then he smoothed it away with a control that astounded her.

Gotta get me some of that.

"He's saying it for your own good, even though every fiber of my being protests agreeing with him ... for many reasons."

"Why? I don't understand."

"We don't know if you will be fully like us. Immortal."

"As in, living forever? So I've gone from immediate death to immortality?"

Something flickered across his face. "We don't know anything yet—about your shift ... what could happen."

"Liam's a Were. You're Dires. What's the difference, besides the wolf on the back?"

Jinx spoke first. "Transitioning to a Were is easier on the body. You've got to be strong to survive a Dire shift, especially the first three shifts. And with you having human DNA ..."

"Plus, I'm weak from the years of meds."

"They affect a wolf's metabolism differently."

"It explains so much, but I still have so many questions," she murmured, more to herself than to them. "I'm a Dire who might not survive. And even if I do, I might not be immortal."

When she said it, Rifter's heart twisted, and he turned away before she could settle her gaze on him.

Chapter 28

Seb ran now, through the woods in the driving rain he'd had a hand in creating, having shifted into a small coyote, like the Native American shamans had taught him. He'd done this with the Dires too many times to count, loved the freedom of the change, the lightness of his body.

These days, there was nothing light at all. Worst of all, he wished Rifter had let him die during the witch trials in the 1600s. Seb had been alone on the platform, with the rough wood planks under his bare feet, heavy twined rope twisting around his neck—already tight enough to make him dizzy.

That noose was much like the invisible one he wore now.

Then the crowd surrounded him, their venomous hate enough to make him weak. And the young wolf that broke through the humans, the only one brave enough to save him, and all because Seb had saved a local child. He'd used natural herbs, not magic, but they'd tried to kill him anyway for his witchery ways.

He hadn't hated them, because of their ignorance. But now a hatred burned through him, stronger every day. He paused to stare to the heavens. The sky was hidden by bands of treacherous rain meant to intimidate and harm. The air smelled like sulfur and fear, the moon a ticking time bomb.

Tonight, Seb would make sure the moon was full of voodoo pasted on an inky sky.

Rifter would know the weather wasn't natural—his dreams had been interfering with Seb's work for months now.

And unnatural things should never be raised. The dead should be left dead. He'd learned that lesson a long time ago—he thought his family had too. But once they'd given themselves over to the dark side, it was too late for them to come back.

Being good was just as difficult as being evil, maybe more so. Now he'd been on both sides of the coin.

It had all started before he met Rifter. Seb could still remember the screams in the middle of the night emanating from his parents' house. He and Cordelia both lived close on the property in their own houses, and although he and his sister had never been close, they'd both been committed to the close-knit coven they lived near.

Except Cordelia had married a mortal and had a child with him—had done so against all the advice from her family and coven, because, although they were white witches and hence immortal, her husband and child would not share that same gift. It was handed down only through immediate family members and only if she married another white witch blessed in the same fashion.

When her husband and daughter were killed when the river they were crossing on horseback flooded, there was no consoling her.

"I have to bring them back," she'd said, her eyes wide. Seb had known it was far more than the grief talking and had prayed that after a few days, when the initial shock wore off, she would reconsider. That his parents would stop her.

But nothing could.

"I can't watch her like this," his mother had whispered to him.

"You've got to stop her," Seb had told her. But his parents caved as weeks passed and Cordelia begged for their help.

Seb left home the night they conjured the spell to raise her dead. Retained his white-witch status and the immortality that came with it. He became very powerful in his own right. Much more than his coven could hope to attain on their own, even with the demons' help Cordelia called upon. Good conquered evil then. But not forever.

Seb's magic was elemental. Spiritual. Natural and practical. He was strong because of his goodness, not in spite of it. There was no way out of what he was forced to do. The spell Cordelia had rendered was too powerful, the punishment too severe. He couldn't use his white magic to protect him—he had to fight with some dark magic, and a part of him began to turn dark and ugly as those powers grew.

Necromancy in and of itself wasn't evil—no, many psychics and seers regularly called on the spirits for divination. But the dark arts raised the dead in order to use them for their own purposes, to control them and force them to carry out wicked deeds.

When Seb cast the first spell for the selfish purposes of the weretrappers, the goodness he'd been cloaked in from birth began to slowly dissipate. He felt it leave his body in increments, like wings of an angel brushing against him. By the time this was all said and done, his soul would be as black as night, like his sister's.

Cordelia's husband and daughter tried to kill her when they returned from the dead. Although they looked like her family, they were shells. Unnatural things that *did* unnatural things. She ended up having to banish them to hell.

She'd been haunted by it for the rest of her days, hence her haggard appearance.

He shook that off and finished his run, his mind still full of dark visions. When he walked inside his room at the top of the tower they'd chosen to lock him in most of the time like some fucking twisted fairy tale, Mars was there. The invasion of privacy rankled him, but since his entire coven was always at risk, he bit back a sharp rebuke and reminded himself of his plan to extricate from the weretrappers.

In time, they would all be free. But for now . . .

"The Weres you sent to the Dire house are dead," he told Mars. Most practicing witches of some caliber had animals who helped and protected them when casting spells, and Seb was no exception. Earlier his familiar raven had reported to him by flying in and perching on the top of the mantel. Some of the outlaw Weres had already been spelled by Cordelia, a special army of nearly uncontrollable wolves whose main job was to keep the Dires busy.

"Are you sure? They were strong."

"Mars, in all these years, you haven't learned? Dires are never going to let you go through with your plan without a great toll on all of us," Seb said.

"When we have Gwen, they'll have no choice. But you're really screwing this up. The spell to raise the dead didn't take," Mars said.

"The sky is still under my control. They dead are very strong—they'll resist." Seb shook the water off himself and grabbed for a towel. Living among wolves for hundreds of years made his more primal instincts emerge, but Mars was human, and those sensibilities didn't mesh well.

"Rogue is resisting as well," Mars told him, and Seb fought the urge to backhand the shit out of the little man. It made Seb physically ill every night to recast that particular binding spell.

A deal with the devil was no deal at all—Seb had learned that the hard way. No, he'd known that going in, but still. Seb hated performing necromancy—it was as if Cordelia made sure he got a taste of the hell he was unable to stop her from doing.

The feel of the dead around him; vicious, violent, ground-rotting beasts who would not be controllable once unleashed. But Mars didn't listen to him—no one did.

"Rogue's brother is interfering with the raising. He would have been much more valuable than the king," Mars pointed out. That was indeed the truth, and Seb was forever grateful that Harm had a lick of sense left in that metal-addled brain of his.

Chapter 29

Rifter had stayed deadly quiet, and finally he'd risen and walked out of the room after Gwen mentioned her possible mortality. It was easier for her to talk about it, she supposed, since she'd always been mortal.

Vice and Jinx and Stray remained, though, with Jinx watching her carefully, like she could shift at any second.

If she thought about that long enough, she'd have a panic attack for sure. She took another shot of whiskey instead.

"Why isn't the night ending?" Stray asked.

"If Seb's spell is good enough, it could be night until the blue moon—a supernatural cornucopia," Jinx said bleakly.

"This is fucked," Vice stated. "Gotta do something. Because humans are going to notice this shit, and we're all in trouble then."

She couldn't help but agree, even though technically, she was dead in the eyes of most of the town. "I'm really the reason behind all of this?" she asked tentatively.

"Not the whole reason, but you're sure as hell not helping," Vice offered with what she was beginning to see was his usual candor.

As long as he was up to answering questions ...
"You're immortal but Weres aren't?"

"They live a long time, but they're not truly immortal, no. We were the unlucky ones granted that." Vice put his feet up on the table, his size-twenty-two feet a dead give-away that this man was a vice all his own, if you believed the old wives' tales about the size of a man's feet being equal to the size of his ... "Since there were no Dire females, there were no mates for us."

"What about female Weres? Why can't you mate with them?"

"They can't handle the mating," Jinx said. "We're all wolves, but we're different breeds."

"But we do fuck them," Vice added. "What? Brother Wolf needs to get some too."

"You said Stray was found later," she said, and Stray nodded. "Does that mean there could be others?"

"We looked."

"Not in hospitals. Not for half-breeds. We didn't know they could exist," Jinx said. "Now we don't know if we've unwittingly let other Dires die because they couldn't shift."

But would she have actually died? Would her human side have prevailed over the curse of the Dires' immortality? "If I'd been alone when I shifted, would I have been a danger to humans? Are you?"

"Only if they annoy me," Vice said with a shrug. "Other than that, humans don't interest me. No offense to that side of you."

"None taken." She paused. "But you can tell the difference between a human and a witch, right?"

Vice shrugged. "Humans taste like chicken. Witches taste like rotten chicken."

"You ... eat humans?"

He looked at her like she was the stupidest person on

earth. "No. We kill them. They don't taste good enough to eat. Because I don't like chicken."

Jinx shook his head. "I'd apologize for him, but it wouldn't do any good."

The man called Vice was taller and bigger than the others, and she supposed that was fitting, since his ability was tied to all the extremes a person—or wolf—could have.

He looked like sin, and she was pretty sure he could take anyone he set his sights on down the wrong path, and down to their knees. They might even beg for it, and from the curl of his lip, she knew she was right.

But although she didn't mind looking at him, the spark in her belly burned in pure relief only for Rifter. Rifter, who'd just come back into the kitchen to shoot Vice a disapproving look. She guessed that if she was starting to develop supersonic hearing, then Rifter's must be much stronger.

Her eyes wandered to him, the lust rising inside of her, and she could smell it on him too.

It's the animal inside of you—give in—what's the harm?

So far, she'd found no downside. But obviously, the Dires had been around for a long time before her, and they'd found one.

She put her own questioning aside for the moment and let the men get back to what Rifter referred to as *pack business*, muttered it under his breath as he took his seat next to Gwen again.

"We don't hurt humans—we protect them against moon-crazed Weres and we try to make sure the Weres keep the peace among themselves," Rifter told her, wanting to kill Vice for his *humans taste like chicken* comment. Although he wasn't exactly wrong.

"We need to stop thinking about being lone wolves in

light of recent events. Our pack's growing," Jinx pointed out.

"The twins are alphas—they'll lead their own packs one day," Rifter said.

"Yes, but those packs could work in tandem with ours to make sure a capture never happened again," Jinx said, stared at Rifter, a direct challenge that, at times, could be dangerous.

"It won't happen again," Rifter said, and it was taking all his control not to think about that time in the snare of the humans.

The chains, the drugs . . .

"They hated us, wanted us destroyed, and I could understand it. Respected it, in a way, after what our kind did to theirs. But then something changed and they decided to use us for their own purposes. They think if they can control an army of wolves, they can rule the world."

"Could they?"

Rifter stared at Gwen, his eyes Brother Wolf's. "Yes."

That shook her. "We—you—have that much power inside of you?"

Again, he simply told her yes. She stared down at her own hands, the knowledge of the power she held overwhelming and heady all at once.

"We can't let it happen," he said.

"How many Weres have they slaughtered?"

"Too many to count. We've killed weretrappers as well, but with the help of the witches. The Weres are easier to spell. Especially the young ones. The trappers capture the moon-crazed ones and use that to their advantage, try to reprogram them. So far, they haven't been successful. Weres they've tried to fix, so to speak, haven't survived."

"What do the witches use?"

"Drugs and spells. Wolves don't fare well with

either ... our metabolism can't handle the drugs. The spells ..." He shook his head and tried not to let his body shudder at the thought of what they'd tried on him.

"Why did Seb agree to help them instead of joining forces with you against them?"

Rifter had never been able to figure out a satisfactory answer for that—he'd long pondered it, but thinking on it and talking about it were two different things.

There was a time he considered Seb a brother. Vice and Rogue had always warned him to be cautious, but Rogue never elaborated as to why, and Rifter dismissed it easily. He'd served side by side with the man. That created a brotherhood all its own.

"Seb's an Adept—a master witch. Beyond time, although he looks human and lives among humans like us. He was charged to go back to his own coven, who'd made the pact with the trappers. Cordelia was the head witch of the coven and she wanted him back in the fold. I know he was worried he'd bring the wrath of witches on us, but he didn't give us a chance to help him. He just left, damn it. And then he's been selling out Weres ever since."

"I understand that the witches weren't working with them until recently. But how is it that they didn't grab me between the time they joined forces with the trappers and now?" Gwen demanded. "You keep skirting the question. I've been vulnerable, so why wasn't I found earlier?"

"Harm made a pact with Seb—they were watching out for you, until Seb left us and went to the coven," Rifter finally said, and she stilled.

"Harm—the man chained upstairs. What, he's my bodyguard?"

"No, Gwen. Harm is your father."

Chapter 30

If she hadn't been sitting, Gwen definitely would've fainted. As it was, she turned really pale, and Rifter found himself holding her semi-upright while Jinx brought her soda and told her to "keep fucking breathing, Doc," which she didn't appreciate if her "fuck off," was any indication.

It made him feel better, though. When she pushed away from him, she downed the Coke. "Stronger."

Vice got up and went for the Jägermeister, because they'd finished the Jack Daniel's Green Label. Poured her some neat and she did three shots before she spoke again. "Why is he chained?"

"Because he's the one who turned Rogue and Rifter over to the trappers—in exchange for your protection," Vice said.

For once, Rifter was grateful for Vice's lack of impulse control—no way in hell would he have been able to get those words out. The look of hurt on her face was hard enough—better he hadn't been the one to put it there.

Well, technically, he had.

It was his turn for drinking—he grabbed the bottle and downed half. It took his wolf a lot more to get hammered. That would barely take the edge off.

"How long have you had him here?" she asked.

"Since the night I met you," Rifter said. "So I'm guessing none of this is really coincidence. He killed twenty weretrappers outside another bar—they were headed your way."

"Rogue is hurt—you were hurt . . . because of me," she said, repeated it a few times like she was trying to burn it into her brain.

"It's not your fault."

"Kinda is." She took the bottle from him, but only to stop him from drinking more. "What's going to happen to Harm?"

"We don't know," Rifter admitted.

"Does knowing why he did it change anything?" she asked quietly. "I mean, I just found my father. And I'll have to lose him."

Vice walked out of the room, which was probably for the best. Jinx followed, and Stray remained quiet for a long moment before saying, "He betrayed us long before you came along, Gwen. There's a lot more history there."

"I understand," she said quietly. But Rifter knew she didn't. Couldn't. "Can I at least talk to him?"

He couldn't deny her that; he nodded, and Stray slid off the counter and left them alone.

"They're angry."

"Yes. Wolves take loyalty seriously."

"So do I." Her eyes glittered with anger—and with tears. "But he's my family."

"So are they. Tonight's the first I heard of him being your father."

"He kept it from all of you?"

"We haven't seen him for a while." Like for thousands of years.

"Are you really going to let me talk to him?"

Better now, while he still retained all his limbs. "Why? What do you want to know?"

"More about my mother. Do you think my mother and my aunt and uncle . . . knew what I was? Were they killed because of me? Did Cordelia know?"

The floodgates were opened—there would be no stopping her from making the connections. And even though he hated the man, Harm had helped to create Gwen, the woman he and his Brother Wolf had decided to mate. "I think your aunt and uncle knew, yes."

"They were so good to me. But I didn't look or act like them at all. And then I was sick—a burden. They never said it, but how could it not have been?" She hugged her knees to her chest. "And now I'm finding out that they knew I was a wolf. Half wolf."

"What if they'd told you?" Rifter asked. "They probably thought they were helping you so you didn't make a connection between the seizures and the shift. I don't think they knew they were putting your life at risk by not letting you shift."

But that's what had happened nonetheless. And if Gwen's mom did know what Harm was, he would've told her about when the shift might occur for Gwen. "They were protecting you," Rifter continued.

"By killing me," she finished for him. "I can't blame them as much as I blame Harm. He knew—he could've stepped in at any time. But he didn't."

They hadn't had time to deal with Harm, to decide what they would do to him for the betrayal—and beyond. Sending him out to the weretrappers, however, would put them all in danger. He knew it as well.

But one day at a time. "Harm said he lost your trail for a while—your aunt and uncle hid you, which, in the end, served you well."

"The paintings—the wolves and the moon . . . you saw

them. The wolf looks like a Dire wolf, but not you or your brothers. Did you recognize Harm? Is that what he looks like when he's . . . shifted?"

"I knew there was something familiar about them. I was drawn to them, but I didn't have time to study them for long. I needed to get to you."

As much as she wanted to be part of a family—of this family—she was too much of a danger to them. "Rifter, was Harm right? Am I a weapon?"

"Don't think that—don't say it."

She would always be a threat to the Dires. The Weres too. And if Rifter was king and she was mated to him, what kind of queen would she make? Who would ever trust her? "I'd never be able to leave the house, go anywhere without the fear that they'd grab me and use me against you. And I could never live with that. Never."

Not that she would necessarily live—no one knew if she could even pull off a shift. Maybe nature would make that decision for her—survival of the fittest and all. "Even Harm thinks I should be allowed to die."

Rifter's expression was pained. "I can't make this decision for you. I want you here. Having to let you go now would kill me in every way except the one that counts. Immortality's a heavy burden, but we'd be together. Mated."

She'd already felt the pull—there was no denying its power. "This is all incredible. Unbelievable. My father is chained up because he tried to save me at your expense. I don't know how I'm supposed to feel about all of this. I need to . . . go somewhere. To breathe, away from all of this."

"You can't."

"Right, because for all intents and purposes, I'm a prisoner and a ghost." She spat out the words. "Maybe you should just let me die—would've been easier on everyone."

"Don't you say that. Don't. You. Dare." His eyes went lupine. Feral, like he'd flipped a switch.

"Why do you care so much?"

"Because you're mine."

"I'm not anybody's," she whispered. Because no one had ever wanted her like that, with an intensity that could burn her worse than the sun on a hot summer's day.

"You are mine."

"Because you say it?"

"Because you know it," he said fiercely, his voice ringing through her like an electric zing right before he split the kitchen table in two with a single hand and a roar, and walked outside.

Anger vibrated through him as he slammed outside, but it quickly turned to something else, an emotion he'd never thought he'd feel. One Rifter still wasn't sure he wanted to feel, although the choice seemed to not be his.

Would the Elders finally find them worthy of mates? And why now?

Because Gwen is dying.

Could they be that goddamned cruel? Of course they could. Even from his first meeting with them . . .

The young Dire sat on his haunches, staring at the moon. He bit back a howl, he and his Brother Wolf still trying to reconcile themselves as one.

The initial encounter with the Elders was something not every Dire experienced. In fact, many dreaded the thought of being called in front of their mystical creators.

He was no exception, wished he wasn't quaking with fear as he tried to remain still. Since then, things hadn't changed much.

The Dires met with the Elders only in shifted form— the shift occurring uncontrollably in their presence. It was humiliating as shit to have that kind of submission happen involuntarily, and even their Brother Wolves didn't like it.

And it came out of nowhere. A light flashed and the trio morphed in from a portal.

They took human form—all had wolves' eyes and ethereal beauty that you couldn't look at too closely. Looking at them was a bit like looking directly into the sun.

In the past months, Rifter had gotten down on his knees in the middle of the woods and begged the Elders to come down and help Rogue.

He'd gotten shit in response.

The Elders didn't like his attitude. They never had, and they berated him for trusting a witch. Like he wasn't doing that a million times a day on his own.

He'd been born into the most lethal pack the Dires had ever known—both feared and revered and eventually exterminated because of their inability to control the excesses they'd grown to crave. Wolves always had primal callings, and those were to be allowed, even cultivated. But their humanlike wants, like money and power, were things that the wolves shouldn't have been concerning themselves with.

But Rifter had been trained in those old ways, and that did not simply fall away. The desire to hunt, to rule, had been born and bred in him, would rise up with a fierce need that was nearly impossible to tamp down most of the time.

He would not be responsible for leading the men to a new Extinction. That wouldn't be an honorable death, no matter how badly they'd welcome it.

But now, with a mate, the thought of dying or even having to leave her behind made him want to rail at the moon—and the Elders.

Made him want to lock her in a room and not let her

out until they could keep her safe. Which would never be possible.

His mate was beautiful and strong. Smart. She made him laugh.

In the short time they'd been together, she'd made him care. She mattered to him in a way he hadn't been able to let anyone matter. Not since his brothers, but that had been a different kind of bond.

This was beyond fate—he felt like the luckiest man in the world.

He didn't want to lose her. He'd already lost so much, and he railed at the unfairness, mainly to her. Because all she wanted to do was live.

He'd thought about begging the Elders to spare Gwen, to take him instead of her, but they didn't bargain that way. Instead, he spoke into the silence that haunted him. "I'll be a king—a real king. Whether you spare her or not, I've decided to take the title."

The epiphany rocked him, the total truth in his words undeniable and long overdue. And they did nothing to lessen the pain he felt at knowing Gwen could leave him. He reeled.

A week of happiness, if that. A week spent possibly watching her wither and die, knowing there was nothing he could do to stop it.

The howl tore at his throat, strummed the air with a ferocious echo, and for the first time, he understood what it was like to truly mate. It was as if his heart was ripped from his body whole and held in someone's hand. He hadn't realized how incomplete he really was.

How utterly terrified he was at the thought of losing her.

Mated to a Dire who might not survive her shift, all he could do was remain still under the moon's pull.

*   *   *

As Gwen watched, Rifter stood alone in the rain, then went to his knees and howled, a mournful sound that rang through her, skittered up her spine.

Her belly tightened—fear and sadness—he was already mourning her.

He'd be devastated if she died during her shift. The whole time she'd been thinking about it as her body, her life . . . nothing about the fact that, according to Dire law, she and Rifter were halfway to mating.

It wasn't just about her any longer. And that was something she'd always wanted but never thought she'd be able to have.

She was throwing it away whether she meant to or not.

It was in that moment she knew she would need to survive. For herself, for Rifter—for their mating. Everything welled up in her—the sadness, the fear, the pain— and she let it go for the first time in maybe forever.

She would live because she and Rifter were meant to be together. To throw that away, when she'd fought so long to live, to find love, would be the most foolish thing she could ever do.

No matter the consequences, she was his. Had been from the second she'd met him, and not because of any strange mating ritual of old. Besides, they hadn't fully mated yet. And even if it didn't prove true, she'd never believe he wasn't meant for her.

There was no reason to deny it any longer.

Before anyone could stop her, she was outside, walking toward him in the rain. His back was straight and strong, and he stared up at the moon like it could give him the answers.

From the way he howled, even though he remained in human form, she guessed he wasn't getting any.

"Rifter," she called softly, much too low for him to

hear, but he did, because he lifted his head and turned it a bit. Of course he heard . . . he was a wolf.

Like you, her Sister Wolf said, quite clearly.

"Please, I need you to turn around and come back inside. I didn't mean to scare you . . ."

He rose from his knees and faced her, but there were several feet still separating them. She thought it best to leave it that way while she explained. "I haven't been part of a real family for a long time. I've been alone. And the thought of hurting more people who accept me, who I could love . . . I can't have that on my soul. People around me die—you already know that. You couldn't die, not before I came to light. And now you can, because of me."

"You'll need to shift," he said hoarsely. "I hate that you have to go through that pain."

"I know. I will. I want to—for you. For us."

At those words, Rifter walked to her, but even though he stayed close he didn't touch her. "If you stay with me and shift, you're not safe. After surviving all of that, you still won't be. If you leave, you're not safe."

"So I'm pretty much screwed, and not in the good way, right?" He finally broke a little smile at her words. "Thank God you finally liked a joke."

"It's a very serious situation, Gwen. You must know this."

"I do." But the surge of power running through her made her feel . . . indestructible. "I thought the house was spelled."

"Wolves need to run. We need space to do so—we need the outdoors."

"I can fight," she reminded him. "You can train me as well, the way you are Liam. I can be a warrior, like you."

"I don't want you to need to be."

"But I need to be."

"They will never stop looking for you," he continued. "For all of us, but you, you're special."

"To them—or to you? Because you're all I care about."

He stiffened at her words, obviously not too used to kind ones. "I've been waiting for a long time . . . I thought I'd wait forever. I'm worried I might still have to."

She hugged him, waiting for him to relent. When he did, his mouth sought hers in a brutally demanding kiss.

Exactly what they both needed. She reveled in the taste, the feel of him. The danger . . . and the comfort of knowing that finally—finally—she belonged somewhere.

And she belonged to someone. Now she just needed to prove to Rifter that he belonged to her as well.

Rifter kissed her neck, licked the water and Gwen's scent and fought the urge to bite her, to mark her, because she wasn't ready for that yet. But soon . . .

As if she read his mind, she murmured, "You can get me through this. I can get myself through. I promise, Rifter—I'll come back to you."

He wanted to believe her, had no choice but to do so. He embraced her more tightly and felt a newfound strength radiating from her, and he buried his face in her neck. She was all cherries and tart—sweet like sugar. "We'll do it together."

He carried her then, picked her up while she held tight to him, her face buried in his chest as if not wanting to break the skin-to-skin connection. The light rain pattered on their bodies, soaking them through to the skin, but Rifter didn't walk faster. This walk was part of his commitment to her as much as their time in bed had been—the cycle had begun and there would be no turning back for either of them. Not now, not ever, and he needed his brothers—everyone—to know it.

And then, just as suddenly as the rain began, it stopped like someone had turned off a showerhead. He looked up to watch the clouds dissipate quickly, revealing a day that had already nearly waned into night—but a clear night.

The bad energy was gone, replaced by a calm, clear evening.

He stopped and howled, and it was no longer mournful despite the hardships that lay ahead.

He'd found his mate. And he never intended to let her go.

Chapter 31

Vice and Jinx watched the interplay on the lawn, more for Rifter's and Gwen's safety than anything. Vice didn't mind being a voyeur, but this scene made his heart hurt.

At some point, Jinx turned his back. Privacy . . . and because he was grinding his teeth together. But Vice couldn't. And as Rifter walked toward the house, the sun broke through the clouds, the rain ceased and it was daylight again.

Jinx stared out the side window at the patch of sunlight playing across the floor. "Whatever the spell was, it didn't take."

"Do you think . . . Rifter stopped it?" Vice asked.

That gave Jinx pause, and Vice continued, "You heard Rifter say she was his. That the mating process had already started. Mating always made Dires stronger. What if it intensified whatever magic Rifter's got going on with his abilities? We don't know what that shaman did to him."

"If even that's true, it doesn't mean Seb won't keep trying," Jinx pointed out.

"We'll try harder." He thought about how shitty he'd been to Rifter when he'd told Vice that Gwen was dying and vulnerable.

Vice would be the only one to come right out to Rifter and tell it like it was. He couldn't help himself. The lack of finesse was his curse and his gift, what drew people to him instead of repelling them.

It was Vice's destiny, but none of them had quite figured out what to do with it, including him.

Jinx was staring at him.

"What?" he asked irritably.

"You really think the spell was broken because of whatever's happening between Rifter and Gwen?"

"I think love can do anything when it's strong enough."

"And you know what that's like?" Jinx asked, with a hint of sarcasm.

"I do."

It was the first time Vice had ever admitted to something like that. He looked at Jinx, who tried not to appear stunned and didn't succeed.

"Not a word," Vice warned, and Jinx nodded but still asked, "How do you handle it?"

"Obviously, not well." Vice's hands shook a little, and he stuffed them into his pockets, hoping Jinx wouldn't ask who.

He didn't, instead asked, "The mate thing ... do you think, one day, for us?"

"For me, never. I can't be tied to one person without cheating. For you, I hope so, brother. Goddamn, I hope so."

Even as Seb chanted in the spell circle, the candles around him flickered and the disturbance raced through his body like a fever. He paused and realized the rain had ended—the raising of the Dire army would not be completed tonight.

There was a far more powerful energy overpowering it, and Seb could imagine what it was. But when his familiar flew in the window, he knew he'd been right.

The damned raven had been following him since he was six years old. Had been there when he was running with the wolves. Looked at him sadly now even as it remained loyal.

"You're free to go anytime," he told it, the way he had every day since he'd been shackled by invisible chains that led to hell.

But the raven stuck around. Didn't understand that loyalty never got anyone anywhere but hurt.

Mars barged in moments later, although Seb had lectured him many times about not walking in during the casting of a spell, and the raven, who hated Mars more than Seb did, made a graceful exit. "Why did the weather change? I thought you could control this."

"The spell doesn't work if something the Dires do overpowers it. Good versus evil—it's all about the balance," Seb explained.

"I don't need this hocus-pocus shit."

"Then you shouldn't have brought witches to help you." His jaw ached from clenching so he wouldn't say more. He was dying here, and not all that slowly.

Mars touched a hand to his cheek, and Seb remained still even though he wanted to recoil from the touch. When it drifted to his neck and down his chest, he tried not to panic.

"I can try the spell again," he said, hoping to distract Mars. One of these days, that would no longer work.

"If this doesn't happen soon, baby, I've got to ask the witches to attach your curse to any weretrappers and Weres killed by the Dires," Mars whispered, an excitement in his eyes at the blending of sex and death.

Seb might as well really be dead if they did that.

"I think this might help you instead," Mars said, began to chant in a way that made Seb turn cold. It was the punishment long promised to him, a spell attaching a demon to him that could have come only from Cordelia. His sister was finding a way to reach out and hang on to him from inside her grave, and since Mars was half-possessed himself, the spell would hold—and Seb was powerless to do anything about it.

The demon wouldn't possess him—not in the traditional ways, because that would make it too hard to control Seb. No, this demon would be more like Seb's keeper, meting out punishments when Seb even thought about doing something wrong.

Seb cleared his mind of anything the demon might latch onto, felt the black smoke rise around his body even before it floated up around his face and brushed his neck.

"I know you'll do the right thing," Mars practically purred against his cheek. "This is just some added incentive."

Mars's eyes were nearly pitch-black. Seb knew, in a few days time, his would resemble them and he wouldn't care if he ended up in bed with Mars or not.

Chapter 32

Gwen was unstable — no doubt ready to shift. Max had seen enough young wolves in her short time among Liam's pack to sense these things, but it was so apparent a blind person could note it.

It would be tough for the doctor, although the Dires seemed to have accepted her.

Vice, on the other hand, wanted to rip Max apart. Maybe she should've tempted him enough to let him. Maybe her son would never be accepted by Liam or the pack.

She'd watched the horrific fight last night from the single, barred window that faced the large backyard. Even in the dark, she could make out the shift. The man-to-wolf thing had at first shocked her, and later, she began to understand the wolf's nature.

Liam could kill her easily, was supposed to, when she'd discovered his wolf status — it didn't matter that he'd been the one to reveal that secret.

Now Max looked at the secret swell she'd been hiding under her scrubs and sweats. She'd grown out of her jeans within two weeks' time.

It was lucky she was the only wolf in the hospital. The ob-gyn had given her an ultrasound, pronounced her very early on. Way too early for the doctor to have seen anything out of the ordinary. Another week into the pregnancy and the fetus would have shown anomalies.

But they didn't deal with wolf gestations, which took place over a much shorter period of time.

She was due in three weeks, her nesting instincts in overdrive . . . and she'd lost the leader of her pack and the man she loved in quick succession.

There was a place for her in the outlaw order. If Teague came now to rescue her, would she take his offer and leave with him?

It was a question she hoped she wouldn't have to answer.

"This can't be possible," the police officer was saying as he motioned to the dead girl's body when FBI agent Angus Young came on the scene. One flash of the badge and the local law scowled. "Really? You like AC/DC that much?"

"It's a family name," Angus said for the hundred millionth time in his life. The damned band never died—he'd be better off changing his name. Except it helped to get him laid and comped hotel rooms at times.

He was tall and angular—not exactly handsome, but he was rugged enough that women were drawn to him. He was convinced the opposite sex scented danger and were equal parts attracted and repelled by him. "Just tell me what you've got here."

"Nothing the feds should be interested in."

He stared at the man's badge. Officer Leo Shimmin. Now, that couldn't be coincidence. The paramilitary organization he'd been watching for the past ten years had a man with the same unusual last name. "Why don't you tell me anyway?"

"A young girl was found murdered in the woods."

If Angus investigated, he'd bet the woman's heart was missing. The MO would match the string of murders that matched heavy metal band Knives 'n' Tulips' year-long concert across the U.S. Angus had tracked murders through Europe and Canada as well, but he'd never been able to pin anything on his main suspect, the band's lead singer, named Harm. And he'd tried on many occasions.

He tried harder now that the murders hadn't stopped when the band broke up.

"Could be a crazed fan. Or a roadie," his longtime partner, John Paxton, liked to point out.

They were all young, dark-haired women. Definitely Harm's type, if the dating life sprawled across the tabloids was any indication. "Was she a brunette?" he asked now, and Shimmin nodded.

"Suspects?"

"Yes." He pointed to the young man in handcuffs. "We found him at the scene, standing over the body."

Angus looked at the young man standing there calmly. "He doesn't look bloody."

"We found her blood on his hands and the sleeves of his shirt. He claims he was walking home and was about to call 911 when we happened on the scene. I'm bringing him in for questioning," the officer said, showed him the kid's ID. According to his license, the young man, named Cain Chambers, was twenty years old, the address an apartment building off Fifth Street.

Angus made a mental note to swing by there later. "And you think he killed her and hung around, waiting to get caught?"

"Her body's still warm—I think we surprised him. Got a call from a concerned pedestrian who heard screams coming from this part of the woods." Shimmin shook his head. "Guy already lawyered up and demanded his phone call. Just kept repeating his lawyer's name and number."

Angus stared down the young man, who returned the gaze without fear, and wondered what kind of trouble Cain Chambers got into on such a regular basis that he had his lawyer's phone number memorized.

Chapter 33

Once Rifter had carried her inside, he'd gotten her towels and dry clothes. Gwen sat in front of the fireplace next to him and ate at his urging. It didn't take much, because her stomach was growling. The Dires and the Weres were in the house but giving them their privacy, and she and Rifter were mainly silent while they finished their food.

He'd kept a hand on her thigh the whole time, like he was afraid she'd disappear if he let go.

"It's like, how was there an entire underground, a sub-culture subsisting—existing—along with us?" she asked finally, her voice still tinged with disbelief even though she was now living, breathing proof of it. "I mean, maybe, when you kissed me that first night . . ."

"Werewolves are born, not made. That whole bitten shit's a myth," Rifter told her roughly. "If a wolf bites you hard enough, you die. You won't be lucky enough to turn into one."

These men were proud of what they were—they didn't skulk in dark corners because they were ashamed, but because of safety reasons. Because no human on this earth could truly accept them.

"Werewolves and witches and . . . ghosts?"

"Vamps too. All things that go bump in the night," Rifter agreed, and the scientist in her wanted to say no, it wasn't possible.

The wolf inside of her simply howled, like it was laughing at her confusion, though not unkindly. She had little choice—she could die on the pills or off them during the shift. "If my shift is . . . successful, then what?"

"You have to shift at least three times," he said. "After that, your Sister Wolf's stable. After that, technically, you have to go on your Running. But it's too dangerous to let you free in the world now."

"I'm not leaving you."

He gave a wan smile. "I'd go with you. We'll go when this has all calmed down."

"They say you're king."

"Only because Harm renounced the title. He always felt more at home with humans than with wolves. He always said that being king would be like a death to him."

"Your brothers don't seem to think you're second choice. Neither does Liam. They have so much respect for you as a leader."

"I didn't want the job, but I do it for all of them," he said. "I was the next choice in the mind of the Elders."

"I can imagine it's not easy leading," she said cautiously.

"Nothing about being dual natured is easy. It never should've been," Rifter said. "We pay for our primal urges."

She believed it, since she felt like she was already paying.

She could barely keep her eyes open, even though her mind was spinning.

"You should rest," Rifter told her. "We're going to have more company—with the paranormal activity, you've got to keep holding your shift off until we can eliminate some of this danger."

She nodded because she understood the severity of the situation, but whatever was happening inside of her was becoming constant and persistent. Her back was sorer by the second, and even the well-worn soft cotton shirt of Rifter's was bothering her. She planned on sleeping naked against the clean, soft sheets of his bed.

She let him lead her upstairs, the rest of the men planning on staying up all night to guard the house and the property. When they got into the room, the first thing she did was take the shirt off, and his gaze grazed her body appreciatively. "Goddamn it, I want you so bad."

"What's stopping you?"

"You. Sometimes it can . . . bring on your shift sooner. I don't want that to happen until we're more prepared."

"I thought the next full moon is at the end of the month—the blue moon."

"You won't last twenty-four hours. Your wolf's been suppressed for too long. Besides, Dire wolves never needed the moon for their first shift. It's going to happen soon. I recognize the changes," he told her. "It's in the way you're moving. Your eyes. Your skin. I can't believe I was so blind to it."

He turned her bare back to the mirror and she looked over her shoulder. The odd bruising was giving way to the shape of a wolf. Decidedly more feminine than Rifter's, but still large enough to cover her back. And the eyes—she saw an outline of them . . .

"Her eyes don't . . . shine."

"They will," he assured her. Ran a light hand over her newfound glyphs, and she shivered as something fluttered inside of her.

She wasn't alone in her body anymore, and it was strange and wonderful. "Tell me what it's like."

"It'll scare you."

"Then I'll ask your brothers—they'll be honest," she countered, and that was true.

"You can ask them tomorrow," he said, then literally picked her up and put her into bed. But then he joined her and she put her hand on the tribal wolf by his collarbone.

"Will I have one of these as well?"

"This is a real tattoo, not a glyph," he explained. "I got it so I would always be mindful of my ability, partly to remind myself that I'm both cursed and blessed. My brothers got the same one, in solidarity, even though they all were born with their abilities and I was literally cursed with mine."

"Why?"

"Have you ever heard of the berserker legend? It was reported to have started during the Viking times. Except there was no such thing. See, we fought next to the Vikings. The legend said it's men who went crazy during the heat of battle—the only thing they were wrong about was that it wasn't only men. There were Dires involved. They had the moon craze. The berserkers slaughtered the family of a skinwalker. He survived and cursed me with dreamwalking. It's something I can't control. I get pulled into people's dreams, feel their pain."

"Humans too?"

"Yes, but I'd have to know them pretty well, and that usually doesn't happen." He glanced at her with a wry smile. "I was given the powers of a skinwalker, which lets me dreamwalk and dreamcatch. Getting yanked into a dream that wasn't mine is really jarring—to feel the pain, fear, longing, is what twists me around the most. When I was young, it freaked my parents out—I used to wander in their minds when I was little. When I could talk about what I'd seen, things got really uncomfortable."

"That must've made for some interesting show and tell," she said. "Unless ... do wolves go to school?"

The corner of his mouth quirked up. "We do."

"With ... real people?"

He laughed at that. "We went with other wolves. But today's wolves blend right in. We don't moon phase until we're twenty-one. Weres turn at sixteen, which makes them a little harder to control, what with all the hormones banging around their bodies to begin with."

"So this dreamwalking ... that's what you were doing with me the first night we met," she said, and he nodded in confirmation. "And at the celebration—"

"Part dream. I was trying to make you think all of this was a dream, just in case ..."

"In case?"

"I didn't know you were a wolf. But I was hoping you wouldn't ... that maybe the doctors were wrong and you'd stick around."

"Would you have let me, if I wasn't a wolf?"

"But you are. If you weren't, I wouldn't have been pulled to you," he told her. "The dreamwalking bonded us more quickly."

"You don't just walk in dreams—you can influence them too."

"Yes. It's how I got the weretrappers to release me from my chains. I walked through a sleeping guard's dreams and convinced him to open the door and take the silver away. And then I killed him and everyone else I could find before I grabbed Rogue and escaped." He paused. "I'm violent, Gwen. It's in my nature."

What could she say to that? She'd seen it. And she had it inside of her too, along with her Sister Wolf. "It's necessary."

"You don't understand; I have that viciousness inside of me and I like it—don't mind being violent and dark. Destruction comes naturally to me. It's a part of who I am."

"What are you telling me?"

"I'm not built to be kind and considerate to humans."

She blinked. Was he pushing her away because of her lineage? "You've already been that way to me."

Rifter shook his head as if refusing to believe her. She touched her palms to his bare back, trying to calm both man and beast. "You're dark, yes. But you're not bad."

"Gwen—"

"I won't believe it. Not after everything you've done for me," she said finally, her Sister Wolf urging her on. "I'll do anything and everything to prove it to you."

He stared at her, his eyes slightly lupine. "You have already. It's just all so new. Talking about it . . . the capture. My family. I mourned for them even though I hated them for what they'd done."

"They taught you the ways of the pack."

"More than that. My family's responsible for my gift . . . and the beginning of the weretrappers. My father killed a shaman's family in cold blood, for the pure thrill of it. And that shaman cursed me, and his descendants vowed to rid the world of wolves." He stared at her. "My pack—my kind—is responsible for the scourge that's visiting us today."

Although she hadn't felt threatened by him, even when he followed her into the woods, the wolf in her knew Rifter was more than part beast. Feral, dangerous—and she knew instinctively that calming him, soothing him, was what she was meant to do.

"My kind too," she reminded him.

"Yeah, your kind." He stroked a strong hand through her hair—rough and so gentle. He was holding back from her, and if her scent was driving him half as crazy as his was her, he had near herculean strength. "The Elders' punishment makes a lot of sense now that you know this, right?"

"Yes . . . and no. It sounds like it's in a wolf's nature. How can you stop being what you are inside?"

"I don't think that's who the Dires were. Not at first, anyway. The packs got too much power. In a way, they're not all that different from today's weretrappers. There's a thin line between what motivates all our kinds."

She had to agree with that.

Her kind too. Rifter found himself praying that her wolf side was strong enough to override her human frailties.

"So the gifts . . . curses, you all have—they let you help humans and fight the weretrappers?" Gwen asked.

"It's our charge to keep the weretrappers at bay so we can save the other humans from them and any wolves they might produce for the sole purpose of hurting the human race as a whole," he agreed.

"So you're taking care of the human race," she breathed, and Rifter nodded. "Saving us from ourselves."

"Trying to."

"Like wolf superheroes," she added and meant it.

It certainly was no small charge—humans were impossible, wanted more and more power but had no idea what to do or how to deal with it once they got it.

The weretrappers were extreme examples, but they were certainly power hungry, terrorists in the strictest sense, ready to overthrow the government and run it their way. But it helped for all their sakes that it was in the trappers best interest to deny any werewolf existence.

"Why can't you get into Seb's dreams?"

"He wants me to stay out as badly as I want to stay out, for the most part. Sometimes, I can absorb traits and qualities of the person I dreamwalk with. Black arts is something I stay far away from." Still, someone—no doubt Seb—was determined to pull him inside of the dark magic, no matter how hard he resisted. "Obviously, I'm okay with my brother Dires. Even you ... but Seb, the black arts would become a part of me. I could gain powers I don't want and might be unable to control."

His brothers had been unwilling to let him attempt to break into Seb's dreams—and until now, it hadn't seemed a necessity. The witch was a formidable enemy. Trained ... talented ... Although the Dires couldn't be spelled, Seb knew too much about their foibles and ways to get around that. At one time, Seb had considered himself a brother to the wolves. But when his coven had been threatened, Seb turned his back easily on the Dires.

"They are my kind," Seb told him after he'd explained he was returning to his coven.

"Funny how for the past few hundred years, we were your kind," Rifter said, knowing he'd have to spend the next however many years hunting Seb as ferociously as he had the weretrappers. "Where was your family when the noose was around your neck? I remember you all alone and not nearly as powerful as you are now."

"You saved him from the Salem witch trials?" she asked with awe.

Rifter had jumped in, snapped the rope in two with the powerful jaws of Brother Wolf. Seb rode out of the stunned crowd on Brother's back, clutching the fur for dear life until they'd gotten to relative safety.

He'd exposed himself to the crowd. "You can still find the myth if you search online. They claim that all the people involved were experiencing a mutual hallucination."

"Why did you save him?"

"He was all alone," he said simply, and she understood. This particular band of deadly brothers had a soft spot for lost boys like themselves.

Of course, they'd never admit that, as evidenced by Rifter's next statement. "We figured he'd be useful to us as well."

"Sounds like he was."

"For a long time, we helped each other."

"And now that his sister was killed by Liam, because of me . . ." She trailed off, then asked, "Why did he leave his coven in the first place?"

"He refused to practice black arts," Rifter said. "And now he's conjuring demons. Ironic, isn't it?"

"He was your best friend."

"That ended six years ago." The betrayal still stung, and he suspected it always would.

"Why?"

"His coven was threatened. Ultimately, for him, blood was thicker than water."

"But they're evil still?"

He nodded. "That's why the weretrappers wanted him. Seb's the strongest witch the coven's ever seen. They need him. Worked his guilt."

But there were other ways for Seb to have solidified the coven's safety—Rifter was sure of that. Selling out the wolves who'd loved him like family over the years couldn't have been the only solution.

Would he have done the same for Gwen? For his brothers? He'd like to think not at Seb's expense.

"Maybe there was really no other way around it."

"There's always another way." Seb had simply let his family spin their webs and keep him close. "You never betray your own. Never. Not even under the threat of death."

He knew—because he and Rogue had been there and neither man had broken . . . no secrets had been given away.

Chapter 34

Rifter hadn't meant to fall asleep—one minute, he and Gwen had been talking; the next, the nightmare came on hard. He shot up out of bed, clawing at the invisible Dire army around him. Marching toward him, surrounding him until he couldn't breathe, couldn't speak, couldn't think.

They wanted him dead. He put his hands on them, touching air, trying to kill them. And he was bleeding. He touched his neck and felt the sticky warm blood.

It would always be on his hands, no matter how hard he rubbed them, and he wasn't aware that he'd woken up until he heard Gwen calling his name.

"Stay back," he whispered hoarsely, but she wasn't listening, was covering him with a sheet.

He hadn't been aware that he was shivering. His skin had the familiar tight feeling; if he'd shifted in his sleep, he could hurt her.

He looked down at his hands—they were clawed. Brother Wolf was so close to the surface, ready to protect and defend.

"Rifter, please—talk to me."

"Seb's doing something really bad," he said finally. "I'm connected to it."

It was the same dream—the massacre, the Dire army rising, but then there was something more. At the end, he'd been back in that cell in the weretrapper's compound. That had been totally different from the other dreams, and made this one the worst of all. "I walked through my capture again—I was trapped. It was like no matter how hard I struggled, I couldn't escape. And it was too goddamned real."

Being captured had been torture—there was no other way to describe it, and Rifter went out of his way not to.

Chains held his ankles to the floor when the shift came. They cut into Brother Wolf's flesh. With the aid of the drugs, Brother Wolf was constantly unsure and confused— Rifter spent most of his time trying to calm the wolf down, forcing him to sleep it off.

The weretrappers kept both his and Rogue's Brother Wolves down because they knew the wolves could—and would—rip their throats out. Rifter and Rogue went in and out too. The experiments were brutal.

"They tried to mate Rogue," he continued. "A female Were—she was as freaked as Rogue."

"You . . . watched?"

"Didn't have much of a choice. We were chained together during that particular experiment."

"Did they try with you?"

Rifter shut his eyes. "Yes."

"Rifter . . . baby . . ." She held him, comforted him, and he let her. "I'll never let them take you again. Because your mine."

Her alpha female instincts were really kicking into overdrive, and despite the horror of the dream, it turned him the hell on. Her too, obvious from the way she'd begun to move against him.

She knew they couldn't risk a third mating—not tonight. But her scent mingled with his, and in minutes, they would be too far gone to care.

"Gwen, you need to stop," he warned, his voice hoarse, but she didn't. Her hand wandered down his belly, stroked his cock, and he held himself back so he wouldn't throw her down and take her.

She bent her head and licked the head of his cock, then took as much as she could in her mouth and sucked. His balls tightened and his hands fisted the sheets. Her free hand stroked his balls, exploring him with tongue and hands, her eyes looking up at him as she did so.

She was pushing him to the brink of orgasm—and he let it happen, let her take over his body, and poured out all the anguish he'd felt earlier and replaced it with an orgasm that brought him off the bed.

He howled—heard it echo and bounce off the four walls and, no doubt, beyond.

He didn't wait to recover before he was up and putting her on her back. He wanted her—needed her—and he would have her. But instead of driving his cock inside of her, he kissed his way down her body and she offered no resistance. Opened her body to his kisses, his hands, and he buried his face in between her legs, her sex wet for him, the scent of her marking him . . . and him marking her.

He knew the exact moment she shattered, felt the clench on his tongue and left it there, feeling her body convulse around it as his mouth filled with the even sweeter taste of her orgasm.

She moved so fluidly, sensually . . . he could picture her running alongside him, for pleasure, the way they had in her dreams. And in the aftermath, she remained pressed against him, listening to the blessed quiet from outside.

No more rain. Whatever had happened between them

tonight had been that powerful, and no doubt connected to his mating intentions, but he didn't kid himself that it was over.

He wondered if Gwen's blood would make her more powerful than any of them, despite her half-human status, as he ran his hand over her back. She shivered a little under that touch. "It's more sensitive, right?"

She nodded. "I still can't believe this. I mean, how could my life change so completely in forty-eight hours?"

"I've asked myself that before a couple of times," he said. "I wish you didn't have to fear your shift. I want you to be able to revel in it."

He wanted to prepare her for the shift, but he didn't want to freak her out. He couldn't put it off forever, and it was probably better if he took control of it with her.

He remembered his own shift—after he'd been told about the curse, he'd wondered if his initial shift was made worse because of it. He'd been twenty-one, and the shadow of his wolf had begun to take shape on his already broad back over the course of two weeks following his birthday. At night, he'd stare at it in the mirror, craning his neck, waiting until he could see the wolf's eyes.

The first time he did, he realized that at that moment, his own eyes had turned lupine as well. The rustling sound in his ears became much clearer and he realized he was hearing a voice.

Brother Wolf's voice.

"This is going to hurt," Rifter had murmured, and Brother Wolf hadn't disagreed. Later, Rifter had gotten the shakes and woke, shivering and sweating simultaneously. His mouth was dry, his eyes burned and his cock was strangely hard.

"It feels like you're turning inside out," Rifter explained finally. "It seemed to happen really fast. But later, I discovered I'd been out for about three hours."

"Will it . . . hurt?"

"It's more like a relief. But the wolf will ride you hard. At first, it feels like it's taking more from you than you can give, but it never asks for more than you can handle," Rifter explained. "Giving in completely makes it easier."

Accepting her lot and the equal parts pain and pleasure that came with it was Gwen's job. The key to surviving the shift.

Her only hope in coming back for him.

Chapter 35

The banging on the door made Gwen start and Rifter jump out of bed with the grace of the wolf he was, his muscles rippling as he went to the source, unarmed and unafraid.

Would that be her one day? Would she be as much of a weapon as he was?

It was Jinx and Cyd, and both looked concerned. She wrapped the sheet around her as she listened.

"Cain's been arrested," Cyd said angrily. "He went out to recon the mausoleum. I went after him when I didn't hear anything, followed his scent to the police station. He's being interrogated by the FBI in conjunction with the murder of several humans in the woods by the hospital."

"I'll go bail him out," Jinx said.

"Won't he need a lawyer?" she asked, and all three men glanced at her.

"I'll do," Jinx said. "I've got the falsified paperwork to prove I'm an attorney."

"I'm going with you," Cyd said, and then looked to Rifter for the okay. Rifter nodded.

"You'll wait in the car," Jinx said.

"I'll go too. I'll recon around the station while you

play lawyer and see what intel I can get," Rifter said. "None of this is a goddamned coincidence."

She had to agree.

When he shut the door, he didn't dress right away. Instead, he went to the window and stared silently at the moon like it could spill the secrets of the universe.

Gwen wished with all her heart that was true.

"You'll be okay with Vice and Liam," he said.

"I'll be fine—go get Cain."

He nodded, went to shower and came out wearing all black. Her senses flared at the sight of him, the smell of him, and he grinned in spite of himself. She blushed at the fact that her hormones were as out of control as an eighth-grade boy's.

"Behave yourself," he told her before he left.

"Be careful," she murmured at the closed door, not sure if she was speaking more to Rifter or to herself.

Jinx drove them to the police station—Rifter sat in the passenger's seat and Cyd was trying his best not to drive them crazy. But twins were spookily close, as Rifter knew from Jinx and Rogue, so he cut the kid some slack.

"What was Cain doing out by himself?" he asked Cyd finally.

"He thought it best if he went alone," Cyd admitted sheepishly.

"Obviously, best if he stayed the fuck in the house," Jinx growled as they pulled up to the small police station.

The lot was teeming with cop cars and people in handcuffs, and they sat there and watched the scene outside in amazement.

"World's going fucking nuts," Rifter murmured.

This was like a supernatural zoo, and the humans didn't even realize it. His skin prickled as Weres and witches nodded to him—in deference and in challenge—

and although none of them would dare start anything in the middle of the precinct, it was still a bad sign.

This had been a bad moon—and the lunar cycle wasn't over. The blue moon only complicated things, making it the perfect month for some kind of wolf-witch-ghost-army apocalypse.

For a second, Rifter almost felt sorry for the humans, who went about their business without a goddamned clue. They were worried about terrorists abroad—or the cells inside the United States—when they had a far worse problem right at their doorsteps.

Jinx dressed conservatively for his role as Cain's lawyer—a buttoned-down shirt and pants of the highest quality, Italian and custom-made, making him look like the rich guy he actually was. His hair was tied back with a piece of leather, giving him that perfect blend of business and bad boy that made all the women in the station—police and hookers alike—stare his way.

While everyone was duly distracted, Rifter pricked his ears toward the interrogation rooms. Cain, not surprisingly, wasn't talking. The young wolf wasn't so much moon crazed when he'd arrived as...different. The Dires spotted that immediately. Cyd was far more uncontrolled, and Jinx suspected Cain was an omega.

In real wolf packs, the omega was the lowest of the low. With the Weres, the omega was far more powerful than that, part myth, part legend, something so rare.

Were wars were won and lost over omegas, which was ironic, since true omegas could help bring about peace and harmony to any pack graced with their presence.

The pack that kicked out the twins had no idea they'd let an omega go.

Cain had been right to keep his knowledge of what he was to himself. Anyone lucky enough to have him in their pack—and no doubt about it, it was the omega's choice as to which pack he would grant his presence—would have a definite edge.

"My client's fingerprints aren't at the scene. He was taking his nightly run, which, last I checked, wasn't against the law," Jinx was saying, his voice crisp and businesslike. "So either arrest him and set bail or we're out of here."

Impressive. Rifter would've snorted if the police weren't taking Jinx so seriously—and if the entire situation wasn't more so.

He waited for Jinx to walk into the room with Cain, and then he strolled around the large room seeing what other information he could pick up and caught sight of a raven perched outside on the windowsill. By the time he got to it, it was long gone, and Rifter knew without a doubt it was reporting back to Seb.

Chapter 36

After Rifter left, Gwen tried to settle back into the pillows and sleep. But she was far too restless, growing more so as the hours ticked away. She finally gave up and went to the window the way Rifter had. The thunder and lightning had stayed away, the night was clear and the moon lit the sky.

Something stirred in her every time she looked at the moon now.

She dressed and went into the hallway, saw Vice coming down the stairs. "Everything okay?" he asked her.

"Can't sleep."

"I was headed up to hang out with Rogue," he said. "Wanna come?"

"I haven't . . . met him yet."

He stared at her for a long moment and then motioned for her to follow him. For such a big man, he was so silent. The stairs seemed to creak only for her, as quiet as she tried to be.

They passed the room where Harm was staying. She wasn't ready to see him yet, even though she'd asked Rifter if she could. Just knowing he wouldn't stop her made her nervousness settle.

Rogue looked almost identical to Jinx, except for the

hair color. It was past his shoulders and his color was still the tawny golden tan she'd come to associate with the Dires. Even Liam had some of that cast, as did the young twins.

"He's beautiful," she said, her voice low.

"Yeah," Vice agreed without a hint of irony in his voice.

"He looks so alive. I wish there was something I could do," she said.

"He's been looked at by Eidolon—he's the demon doc in charge of UGH—Underground General Hospital."

"There's a hospital for demons?" Maybe they were accepting applications.

"There's a lot you're going to find out in the coming weeks," Vice said. She turned from where she sat next to Rogue to look at him. Vice made himself comfortable on the floor with a blanket and she realized that he planned to sleep here, with Rogue.

These men had been together for centuries. She'd known Rifter less than three days and it already felt like much longer.

Having Rogue be out of it must be akin to having a limb cut off for them. "There's got to be someone who can help him. If your . . . Elders can't help, isn't there another supernatural entity who can?"

"It doesn't work like that. Every supernatural group has a set of restraints on them, a higher power to hold them to a certain standard. We have the Elders. Witches, vamps—they answer to something similar of their own kind. The Elders hold all the cards," Vice drawled. "As evidenced by the fact that they massacred our race."

"I don't understand why they took out the whole race. Surely they could've made examples—"

"We were too powerful—threw off the balance of

nature. Weres and vamps are more equally balanced. Besides, my pack had been in talks to take over the human villages for years."

Her eyes widened. "Take over how?"

"Kill most of them. Enslave the rest. In reality, the Dire clans weren't much different from the weretrappers." He looked pained at having to admit that. It was never cathartic—the truth always burned. "It's more than ironic that we're now charged with protecting humans from wolves."

"Why were the six of you chosen?"

"We've figured it had something to do with our abilities. Not every Dire was born with them—and you know that Rifter's was given to him as a curse. The Elders were supposedly created because they were sacrificed by their Dire parents, all because they had abilities too. Hati was angry at the Dires for doing that and saved them, made them his eyes and ears of the Dire world, so to speak. Anyway, we don't dwell on what is. Nothing changes. Time moves forward and we move with it. We were always other. We didn't fit in—didn't want to."

"Why not?"

"With the humans?" he asked, as if that answered the question completely.

"Hey, let's remember I'm half, okay?"

"I remember," he muttered roughly. "They're uptight. When they give in to their instincts, they act as if it's the worst thing ever."

"I can't say you're wrong," she admitted. "So are there wolves—Weres—all over the world still?"

"Wolves are everywhere. We just don't make pests of ourselves. We want nothing to do with humans, but the weretrappers are obsessed with us. I'm sure you've seen sneakers hanging off live wires, right?" he asked, and when she nodded yes, he continued, "That's a sign. You see that, it's a sign that the weretrappers have found wolves in the area."

She turned in time to see Stray standing in the doorway. "All quiet outside."

"But the Dire army . . . they're still . . . trying to raise them?" she asked tentatively, and Vice nodded.

"How do we get them to pass back over?" she asked, and Vice cut a glance to Rogue. "Wait, Rogue can do that?"

"His gift lets him communicate with spirits, Jinx's with ghosts."

"I didn't realize they were two separate entities."

"Most don't. Ghosts are still earthbound and spirits have crossed over. So that's why their gifts work best in tandem. The Dires passed and were brought back, so Jinx wouldn't have much ability to help them find their way back. Rogue could summon the dead to help them. But . . ."

But Rogue remained helplessly incapacitated. She brushed a hand over his forehead. "Did Seb spell him?"

"Eidolon couldn't be sure. Rogue is in there, but whatever happened during the experimentation was too horrible for him to revisit. Rifter can't get into his dreams—at least not past the horror and fear part."

She touched Rogue's pulse point, checked his pupils again. Listened for his Brother Wolf, the way she could now hear Rifter's wolf, but she heard nothing. "There's got to be something else we can do."

"Fight," Vice said, his eyes a pale glitter, his countenance almost gleeful. From what Rifter had told him, Vice was a slave to his . . . well, vices, and she couldn't hold it against him.

"Ghost-hunting wolves?" she asked, wanting to understand it more.

"The spirits are a good indication of the supernatural

balance," Vice explained. "We monitor all of that. There are varying degrees of good and evil in our world—and even though we're often portrayed as all evil, that's just not the case."

Before all of this, she would've considered most of this so unbelievable.

"Jinx can talk to demons, but he doesn't have the kind of influence Rogue does. It's why they make such a good team. A twin yin-yang thing." He ran a hand through his hair and turned away from her.

For the first time in her life, she realized she wasn't just bringing danger on innocent people. That there was danger inherent in being who she was. "I wish I could do more."

"We might never have found Liam alive if you hadn't been around. What happened to bring you to us is fated for sure," Stray said.

"Even though . . . Harm . . ."

Vice turned and stared at her for a long moment. "I can't hold a parent's crime against a child."

A lump formed in her throat. Acceptance. She would have it here.

Chapter 37

It couldn't have been more than twenty minutes later when Gwen heard Liam yelling for help—for a doctor—and she ran swiftly down the stairs, Vice at her heels. When she got into the room, she found Max on the floor, curled on her side, and Liam pacing anxiously around her, his face ashen.

"She called to me and I found her hunched over. She said there's pain," he told them. Gwen noted he'd taken the handcuffs off her, as if attempting to make her more comfortable.

Max lay motionless and Vice growled, a warning, maybe. But without thinking about the fact that Max had betrayed her—indeed, Gwen's only thought was saving the baby—she rushed to her. Dropped to her knees and pushed Liam out of the way.

She felt Max's pulse—rapid and uneven. Her skin color was okay, and she pulled up each of the woman's lids to check her pupils.

"Do you have an ultrasound machine here?" she asked. "This could all be from stress but—"

She saw it in the men's eyes before it happened. In seconds, a knife went across her throat—scraped her skin dangerously as Max steadied herself behind Gwen.

The woman was strong. Gwen remained as still as she could, not sure who she was more pissed at—herself or Max.

"Let her go," Vice growled. "You don't know who you're fucking with."

"I know everything," Max shot back. "She's your queen. And if you don't move aside, she won't have a head."

Your queen . . .

"Max, don't do this," she said quietly.

"Stand up," Max told her, and Gwen did so as carefully as possible, the swell of Max's belly against her back, reminding her that any move Gwen wanted to use to defend herself would hurt the baby.

As Vice and Liam moved forward, she put her hand up slowly. "Let her take me. Don't hurt the baby."

She heard Max's sharp exhale—surprise, maybe—and then the woman held her more tightly. The knife cut her a little and she gasped, more from surprise than from pain.

Vice and Liam remained like stone statues, but their eyes . . . there was no denying their wolves would come out any moment if this continued.

"Max, if they shift—," she warned.

"I know this world better than you do," Max snapped.

The young woman was like a wounded animal, scared, lashing out at everybody. Gwen tried to remain calm, because defusing this situation would save her life. "You're making a mistake."

"I made a lot of them."

"Liam told you he'd let you stay until the baby came," Gwen reminded her.

"I don't believe him. I just want to go have the baby by myself. And then Liam can do what he needs to for pack honor, if he can find me."

Liam growled in low warning, and Gwen willed him to shut the hell up. She told Max, "Let me examine you and make sure you and the baby are okay."

"Why would you do that for me? After what I did?" Max sounded like Gwen was almost too stupid to comprehend. "Let's go—tell them to move—and point the way to the garage."

The men separated and let them through as Max walked them backward. Gwen felt the drip of blood run down her neck as she pointed down the hallway that would lead to the garage.

"You're too soft for your own good, Doc. I counted on that," Max told her quietly. Almost sadly. "Open the door."

Gwen did, willing her hands not to tremble. They walked across the smooth floors to the truck closest to the automatic door. Max pulled her along to the driver's side and turned her, but kept the knife to her throat.

"This is silver and it's the only thing that could kill a wolf. And since they don't know if your human half renders you immortal, like the other Dires, I think you should continue to be smart."

"Take the truck and go, Max. No one will stop you."

"You're my way out of here—and my way back into the outlaw pack," the woman told her.

Gwen had always known Max was tough, but this was the first show of real, albeit controlled, anger she'd seen from the young nurse. She also knew that if she drove off this property with Max, she was as good as dead. Or worse, if she got into the hands of the weretrappers.

She attempted to keep Max talking, to find some trigger inside the woman that would make her relent. "How long have you known about me and what I am?"

"Not for very long. At first, they told me they needed a doc to work with the witches. I told them you'd never agree to it, but when they were insistent on you, specifically, I got suspicious. I didn't know . . . half Dire. No wonder they tried so hard."

Gwen cocked her head. "Were you ever my friend?"

Max shrugged. "I never had anything against you. I don't really have friends—never did."

"What about Liam?"

"He was my lover, not my friend."

The words came out so brutally cold. Gwen saw red on Liam's behalf. Had Max used him and the baby as an excuse?

Then again, she hadn't fought—not once. She was truly protecting the life inside of her. She heard the rustling in her ears and her sight faded in and out for a second, even as every other one of her senses went into sudden, sickening overdrive.

Something took her body over—something vicious and kind at once. She blacked out for a second, and when she came to, Max was staring down at her belly and Gwen held the knife pointed straight at her baby.

"Gwen, we've got this," Vice told her. She looked up and saw the men on either side of Max, restraining her—and looking at Gwen strangely. "Bite it back, Gwen. Breathe and give me the knife."

When she did, Vice's hand burned—actually smoked—at the touch of silver, but he smiled instead of grimacing at the pain. Liam handcuffed Max's hands behind her back and yanked her toward the door leading to the house, and Vice held out his free hand and helped Gwen down from the truck.

"What's going to happen to her?" she asked, although Liam had already told her. A part of her was hoping what he'd said was being reconsidered.

"Dishonoring a mating is grounds for death. And after what she just pulled on you—"

Gwen looked into his silver eyes. "You're going to kill her?"

"It's Liam's job to do so," Vice stated coldly. "It's pack rules, Gwen, not mine. Traditions are made to be honored. If we lost those, we've lost everything."

She understood what he was trying to cling to—those ways had gotten the Dires through thousands of years. And death by dishonor wasn't a foreign concept to humans, either. "She's pregnant."

"She betrayed him—she needs to die," Vice said, because to him, it was that simple. Betrayal was punished with death—simple and effective.

Max turned toward them—she looked miserable too. Not the confident woman who ran the ER nurses with surgical precision, but when she leaned in to Gwen, the same spark shone in her eyes for just a second as she begged, "I know I can't be forgiven for this, no matter the circumstances. But please, let me have the baby safely. And then I'll banish myself."

"Do we look like a day-care center?" Vice demanded with a snarl.

"My son is still heir to be king of the pack, regardless of what I've done. The Weres respect that lineage," Max said, her chin held high even as regret flashed in her eyes. "Liam's son should not be punished for me. Will you protect me until the baby's born? Keep it safe?"

Gwen held her breath, wondering if Liam—if any of them—would refuse that. She doubted they would, or could, but the thought of Max being turned over to the trappers . . . the witches . . . the rival gang . . .

"Why would Liam want the baby of a traitor?" Vice asked, and Gwen took a few steps back from all of them.

She was in a whole different world here, didn't know any of the rules, and the rustling in her ears was so loud, she couldn't think. She covered them, knowing it wouldn't do any good, and she left the room with Vice at her heels.

Gwen leaned against the wall outside Max's room. Her body had broken out into a sweat, but she was shivering, like she had the mother of all fevers. She was vaguely aware of Vice's words, but they were a jumble, mixed together with Stray and Harm talking in the ancient language.

Talking about her—the shift . . .

She brushed off Vice's help and raced upstairs, the sinning wolf at her heels. She heard his muttering loud and clear, something about how women who could hear through walls were really goddamned dangerous.

She fell on the top step and Vice told her, "Don't do this, Gwen. Try to hold it off."

"I don't know how," she managed, but the chills stopped, long enough for her to stop shivering uncontrollably.

"That's it—just breathe and concentrate. Let's get you back into bed."

"No," she said fiercely, then picked herself off the ground and walked into the room where Harm was being held in time to hear the man who was her father beg, "Letting her shift is the biggest mistake you could make, other than not killing her."

And then Stray saw her and muttered, "Shit."

She might not have shifted yet, but her wolf hearing had obviously kicked in. She'd been three floors down and they'd been behind closed doors.

She took a step forward, even as she heard Rifter's voice behind her, calling to her, urging her to come to him.

That need was strong, but something pushed her to move toward Harm. She stared at him, processing things — no wonder he'd looked familiar to her before. Her father was the former lead singer of one of the most famous heavy-metal hair bands from the eighties.

And he was also, apparently, a wolf. How all of that worked was beyond her, but now wasn't the time for a father-daughter chat.

"Gwen," Rifter started, but she put a hand on his massive chest and pushed him out of the way. She heard a low growl emanate from his throat and was under no illusions that Rifter allowed her to move him.

But she was tired of being coddled. "You're really my father?"

Harm nodded. "I'm your father, yes."

Rifter growled again, and the entire tenor of the room changed. Because the man in front of her — his eyes — were different, and when she looked back at Rifter, his looked oddly similar.

They were wolf's eyes. And she had a strong feeling hers looked similar.

She got closer to Harm. "You want me dead."

"It's not that simple, Gwen. There's so much you don't know," he told her, and that was true. Her head began to spin and the familiar symptoms tugged at her.

She held out a hand, and Rifter caught it. "Rifter, it's happening."

"Another seizure?" Rifter asked.

"I smell a wolf." Vice sniffed the air. "A Dire."

There was dead silence, and it took her a long moment before she realized that it was her shift they scented. She was half blind, like they'd lowered the lights, and she stumbled, hands flat to the wall until she found the door.

Rifter was on her before she could leave the hall, his body pressing hers, hot and familiar. "Am I dying?"

"I won't let you."

If only it was that simple.

His voice sounded different—hoarse, huskier, and in the room they'd left came a howl that chilled her to the bone. "You're going to shift and I'm going to help you."

"I'm scared. Of the shift ... of you ..."

"You should never be scared of me," he told her. "I'd die if you were."

She wasn't. She knew on a logical level that she should be, but she put her hands on his shoulders. "Help me."

From what, she had no idea. All she knew was that the urge to run was overpowering. She needed to do so in the same way she needed air—there was no substitute or compromise. And when she ran, the stairs shifting in front of her like she was on an LSD trip, she heard Rifter behind her, telling her he wouldn't leave her.

Finally, she was outside. She took a deep breath— smelled fresh grass under the wintery ground and the incoming rain. And Rifter—he was with her. She spun in a circle—Rifter's wolf eyes glowed.

She was Alice down the rabbit hole and she knew she was dying, right then and there. Or at least a part of her was. Whether she'd be reborn into the wolf depended partly on her will and on a lot of things well out of her control.

As she watched, Rifter shifted impressively. The rustling in her ears got louder, like her wolf was trying to communicate with his.

"Rifter," she said, and the wolf turned to look at her with Rifter's eyes, the way they'd looked when he'd kissed her today.

He did love her. It was all that mattered.

She fell to the soft grass on her hands and knees, her skin tight and hot, and how she ached. She heard a growl, could've sworn it came from her.

"It's happening," she said, and the wolf was nuzzling her.

Your Sister Wolf is coming, the rustling said, and Gwen saw the blackness cover her eyes like a blindfold.

Chapter 38

Nothing happened like it was supposed to. Gwen collapsed, twitched a little, but she remained in human form. Unconscious human form.

Brother Wolf howled and tried to get some kind of response. Still nothing.

Rifter would have to dreamwalk with her, but not out here, with the sky darkening and the thunder rolling in. His skin felt like a thousand pinpricks as electricity crawled the air.

This was unnatural, but that was literally the least of his worries at the moment.

He shifted back to human form, saw Vice and Jinx waiting for them on the back porch. He picked Gwen up as gently as he could—goddamn, she was pale—and moved her indoors.

"Help her, Jinx," he said as he stood in front of the men he'd lived with like family for three hundred years and saw the same helplessness in their eyes that was no doubt reflected from his.

"Go to her," Jinx urged, then leaned in and took the dream-catcher necklace off Rifter's neck. He'd made Rifter put it on again as soon as they'd finished talking to Gwen the previous night.

"Suppose she comes with me into that nightmare?" Rifter asked over his shoulder as he walked up the stairs to his room. He laid her on the bed, on his pillows, as Jinx took the dream catcher down from the headboard as well.

"Better she's with you than alone," Jinx said. "None of us deserves to be alone."

Liam had watched the Dire wolves handle the outlaw attack with military precision. He'd known Rifter was trying to save the pack on his own, and he knew Rifter's brothers would never allow Liam to be captured without a fight.

Tonight, he'd repaid them by nearly letting his mate kill Gwen, the woman about to be mated to the Dire king. And as he watched Gwen run—perhaps even partially shifting—he knew that, in order to take control of his pack, all the training in the world wouldn't help him prove shit unless he confronted the demons he'd refused to face.

He still held Max by the arm in the corner of the garage. Her cheeks were stained with tears although she'd never admit to crying—never cried in front of him, actually.

He'd admired her strength at one time.

"If Teague came here tonight, would you go with him?" Liam demanded of her, and she jerked uncomfortably in his grasp.

"To save you—and the baby. That's all I wanted to do."

It still didn't make her answer go down any easier. Any trust they'd had over the past year crumpled. And here he'd thought he could hang on to something . . . anything, connected with his past.

It was all future now. And, like Vice said, women would only complicate matters. "Are you sure this baby's mine?"

Her face lit up with indignation. "Of course."

But something inside pulled at him hard not to believe her. If the outlaws had been planning their takeover for a while, what better way to infiltrate their newfound enemy than with his own mate?

Had she ever loved him? His anger rose hot and he knew what he needed to do. "So let's bring you to him right now."

He unhooked her and recuffed both hands behind her back. Not that he couldn't handle a human, but if she went at him, he might have a problem controlling her without hurting the baby.

He borrowed one of the trucks in the garage—a Humvee built like a tank and able to withstand the weather outside. The rain hit the windshield in sheets, and it was definitely difficult driving, but he made it across the bridge and past abandoned cars and finally pulled in front of Teague's house.

"This is a death wish," Max told him.

"For Teague—not for me." Liam had trained and sparred with Vice only once, but he'd learned several tricks that were mostly dirty—and effective.

This was war—and while he could utilize some of the old traditions, Liam was about to institute some new ones. He slammed open the door and pulled Max out with him—called to Teague with a rough howl that made Max wince next to him.

As the rain lashed at him, Teague came out of the house, his eyes already lupine.

Control, Liam, he ordered himself. In a time not too long ago, simply seeing Teague's anger would've brought about his own shift. Now that lack of control shamed him, even though he knew it was simply Were nature.

He would fight that—and continue to—if he was to prove himself a worthy leader.

This was for Linus, his father—for their entire pack

and its future. "You've betrayed me and the pack—I can't let you live," he told Teague.

"Young wolf, don't you understand? You can't survive this," Teague called back, his canines long, cutting his lip as he spoke.

Without warning, Liam pulled Max in front of him and held his knife to her belly. It was silver and it burned the shit out of his hand, but it would hurt her a whole lot worse.

Teague stopped cold. Max was frozen in his arms, and he waited and watched. "Come closer and I'll do it."

"Don't," Teague managed.

"What do you care if I kill my mate and my child?" he asked, because he already had his answer.

This baby wasn't his.

"Get back in the goddamned truck and don't make a move," he warned Max. "Not if you give a shit about that baby."

She moved fast as soon as he let her go, scrambled into the truck as he went forward to Teague. The man was no longer standing stock-still, but the initial shock gave Liam an edge.

Still, he threw the knife to the ground. This would be a fair fight—and a fair kill—just as tradition called for.

The men caught each other by the arms, turned in a circle as humans under the sky, which was as deceptive as Teague himself. A man he'd never called friend, but one he could've easily called brother.

To ask why—from either of them—would be futile.

The shift occurred for both men almost immediately after they completed the first circle. Liam wasted no time in going for Teague's throat. As a younger and slightly smaller wolf, Liam didn't have the advantage. But with the anger pounding through his body, he didn't need size or training.

This was avenging his father, and he tore Teague's throat out and then ripped his body apart, piece by piece, under the thunderous sky.

He killed Teague but couldn't bring himself to do the same to Max ... not yet, anyway. He'd already taken enough from her child as it was. And when he got back in the truck, leaving Teague's disrespected body out to be discovered by the other outlaws, he was soaked and bloody and barely able to stop himself from trembling.

But he did.

Max's sobs were muffled by her fist pressed to her mouth. He didn't look at her on the drive back through the rain—the truck barely making it over the bridge, water lapping at the tires.

When he pulled back into the safety of the Dire garage, Max was still crying softly. He'd need to have Gwen or Jinx check her out to make sure the shock wasn't doing anything harmful to the baby, even though he cursed himself for caring.

"You knew," he said quietly. "Knew the baby wasn't mine the entire time."

"*You knew* what I was from the start."

He had. "Loyalty was never your strong suit—you just pretended it was."

"That's not true—I needed to go with who I thought was the toughest—the unbeatable one. I didn't want to end up on what I thought would be the losing side ever again," she told him. "I'm farther along than I told you. You were away with Linus on pack business when it happened."

There was nothing more to say—they'd both been very wrong. And so he walked her inside, put her back into the locked room and went to find Vice.

He'd opened up a shit storm of trouble for himself and the Dires, and he was prepared to deal with the fallout.

Instead of Vice, he found Jinx, pacing anxiously in front of the fire. "Hey, where'd you go?"

Liam told him, keeping his voice from shaking — anger and pain were harder to keep out than he'd thought — and Jinx stared at him for a long moment. "Vice'll be proud as hell."

"The outlaws are going to come here looking for me," he said.

"Let them." Jinx's voice was firm, fierce and unwavering. "You're going to need to start assessing pack loyalty. And I know two young wolves who wouldn't mind being a part of your pack, if you'll have them."

"Cyd and Cain?" he asked, and Jinx nodded. "I couldn't think of two better right-hand men."

"Good."

But there were far more problems to be solved. "What do I do with this baby?"

Jinx didn't give him an easy answer. "Technically, she's part of your pack, so you do what your traditions tell you to. It's the best way to maintain control and your status as a leader."

Death to the mother; send the child away. Banished to a rogue life . . . no doubt he'd be dead before his conversion. A leader would make the hard decisions, do what needed to be done for tradition and pack pride.

If he couldn't . . . he would have to walk away from his pack altogether. There was no other choice for him.

"I'll grab you something to eat," Jinx told him.

"Not hungry."

"You'll eat anyway," Jinx said before disappearing. For a long while, Liam stared at the floor contemplating his past, present and future. When he looked up, Cain was in front of him, holding a plate with several large sandwiches.

His stomach growled in spite of everything. He ate quickly, thanked Cain.

"You've had a rough night."

"I've lost everything."

"You have your pack," Cain pointed out. "You have me and Cyd. Don't fuck up your opportunity because of a human and her frailties."

Chapter 39

Waking up would require work—Gwen's limbs were heavy, even while her head felt floaty and dizzy.

The rustling in her ears was incessant—she wanted to cover them and scream, but knew it wouldn't block anything.

She would have to accept the pain and let it in. She groped in the dark until she heard a familiar voice and turned toward it. "Rifter?"

"I'm here, baby girl."

Her body felt like she'd been beaten and lost the fight. "I thought I shifted."

"You didn't. You're . . . caught in the shift," he explained.

"That can't be good." She focused enough to see Rifter's face next to her. "Am I awake?"

He shook his head no and held her hand in his. "I won't leave until you are." He was her beacon, would make everything worth it. She focused on that. "Put your hands on me."

He did—his touch hot, electric. "More," she moaned, and then wondered if it was a good sign that she wanted him so badly, despite the pain.

His hands roamed under her shirt, along her rib cage,

and then they covered her breasts as his mouth did the same to hers.

She couldn't resist him any more than she could breathing. His mouth took hers in a way that discouraged any thought of resistance—she was wet between her legs, needed the weight of his body on hers immediately, here and now.

It appeared Rifter felt the same, since she found herself wrapped around him.

"Claim me," she heard herself murmur, and he did, with his hand. She wanted more, but he stopped her when her hands found his arousal.

"Gwen, we can't—gotta get you out of the shift first."

She acquiesced, only because his fingers drew her so close to orgasm she could do nothing but lie there and accept it. Reveled in it, as her hips drew up to meet his strokes, his lips dragged kisses along her neck and breasts, soothing the imaginary wounds and making her forget her troubles.

His fingers took her, moved rhythmically, his thumb circling her clit. Why was this so easy with him? There was no worry or embarrassment, only a longing for him greater than she'd ever known.

"More," she told him. And he gave it to her, brought her to a first and then second orgasm in quick succession while his tongue played on her nipple and her body soared with pleasure.

If she wasn't already unconscious, she would've sworn she passed out. But when she opened her eyes, everything was covered in that thin, gauzy film, the way it had been at the party. This wasn't the first time Rifter had walked inside her dreams, but now that she knew what was happening, she was definitely not comfortable with it.

Knowing she was stuck between worlds this time definitely added to her fear.

After her heartbeat returned to normal, she looked around. They were in Rifter's bed, not outside, which was the last place she remembered being. "I'm sorry . . . I tried to hold it off, but I got so mad—at Max and then at Harm."

Rifter stretched, his massive chest rippling when he shrugged. "That'll do it, especially when your wolf is young and uncontrolled."

Your wolf . . . "Does Harm hate me?"

"No. He doesn't want you to be immortal, to have to deal with what we've had to."

"His life doesn't seem so bad," she muttered.

"He's alone, Gwen. We all are—and I was." He paused. "Our mating gives them a hope they don't want. Because this might all be an aberration, a once in a lifetime. We were prepared to never have mates. So my brothers are pulling for us as hard as we are . . . and I hope the Elders let them experience what I am."

She let that soak in for a long moment. Stroked his hair, touched his lips with her fingers. And then realized that, if Rifter was in her dream with her, the way he'd been the first night they met, something could possibly be wrong.

"Rifter, did I . . . I mean, I felt like something was happening to me. But did I actually . . . you know . . ."

"Shift?" He took her hand and held it. "No, you didn't. I think you're trying, but it hasn't happened yet. You're in human form still."

"And asleep?"

"Unconscious."

Damn it. "What can I do?"

"Jinx is checking you—your breathing's a little shallow but everything else is okay. It might just take your body some time to give itself over to Sister Wolf." He paused. "Do you still hear her?"

She didn't, hadn't since the incident on the lawn. She concentrated, tried to hear anything, but it was terrifyingly quiet. If Rifter hadn't been here with her . . .

Suddenly, she heard Rifter's muffled curse and realized they were moving. It was like the first night she'd met Rifter—more like floating than actual walking, but they were outside and then they were someplace she didn't recognize.

She smelled blood—and fear—and there was confusion. She was behind Rifter but she was seeing the scene like she was living it. Like she should know where she was.

It took her a moment, but she did.

Battlefield. Rifter's pack. The slaughter. She was terrified, especially when she fell to the ground next to Rifter and a shadow passed over her. He held her hand tightly and they began to float up among other spirits.

"Don't let go," she told Rifter. He tightened his grip.

Thankfully, the spirits rose ahead of them while she remained somewhat firmly rooted on the ground with Rifter. But they were walking—not back to the warm, comfortable bed. No, they moved forward from the battlefield to inside—a hot, stifling place.

The walls—they *dripped*—blood, maybe? She didn't want to think about it—she was already light-headed and warm, like she had a fever that wouldn't break.

"Don't touch anything. Only make eye contact with me," Rifter warned, and she kept her eyes pinned to his back.

It was almost as if her feet weren't touching the floor, not completely, anyway. She was far more out of it in this dream than in the others. And yet everything was somehow much more real in this one, which made it horrifying.

"I want to turn back," she said.

"Me too. But I can't." They were both being propelled forward by an invisible force. What waited on the other side of that doorway was anyone's guess.

"Let go of my hand and wake up," she begged him. "You're being pulled because of me."

He didn't deny it, but he held fast to her hand as they reached a long corridor with what seemed like a million doors on each side. The hallway got smaller and smaller until she could only walk behind Rifter, not next to him.

He didn't let go of her hand once, though. Finally, he stopped at a door and paused, then opened it with a strong kick, slamming it and cracking the frame. She jumped and followed him into the room, which was so dark . . .

And they weren't alone. She squeezed his hand and he turned to her. "I've never been able to get this far on my own. I'm sorry—I don't mean to scare you . . . but we're close to Rogue—I can feel it. And it's going to get ugly."

"I'd rather be scared with you than alone and terrified," she said, and meant it, but when she heard the unearthly shrieking begin, she backed up and refused to go any farther.

She didn't ask any more questions, not when the heat hit her, followed by the screams. They were hollow sounding, mournful. They climbed into her soul and clung there, and she felt like she'd never, ever forget the sound, no matter how old she lived to be. "Is this where his mind is all the time?"

"I think so. I never knew if he was keeping me out or if I wasn't strong enough to get to him."

But with her, he was. She supposed this wasn't the time for the hows and whys, and so she forced herself to breathe, asked, "How can he stand this?"

"He hasn't had a choice."

It had to be hell—or a close facsimile. There were sharp rocks under her bare feet and she was sure she was bleeding, but she stayed close to Rifter as they moved into the complete blackness.

Flames licked the walls. She heard chanting but couldn't see the source.

And then she felt Rifter stiffen.

Rogue looked like Jinx except his hair was dark, like Rifter's. Rifter reached out and turned Rogue's head toward them, and she saw that the entire left side of his face was covered in a tribal glyph pattern.

From the way Rifter touched it with a shaking hand, she guessed it hadn't been there before. But Rogue's arms and chest were marked with black and red symbols that she couldn't interpret and Rifter didn't look surprised to see those. "This one," he pointed to Rogue's face. "New markings."

"And the rest of them?"

"They come and go—he calls them protection," he said. The ones on Rogue's face didn't look anything like the others. His voice was hoarse when he cursed, "God-damn it," quietly.

At that, Rogue opened his eyes. "Not smart to use that name down here, you know? And who's the human . . . whoa. What the hell's going on upstairs?"

Rogue was in hell, and it wasn't one of his own making. It was worse than being locked up in the weretrapper jail, and Rifter had to force himself forward. He wished he didn't have to take Gwen with him.

But to leave her behind . . . she was terrified. He wouldn't make things worse since she obviously couldn't see the mare sitting on Rogue's chest, keeping him in a constant state of sleep paralysis.

The mare was like a succubus, and now it all made

sense. There was no way to move her without killing the person who'd cast the original spell. It was probably Seb, and killing the witch could prove to be next to impossible. The mare kept her eyes focused on Rogue, not turning her head at all toward Rifter or Gwen. And when Rogue stared at him, there was a silent "we won't mention this part to Gwen" message sent between them.

"This is Gwen—she's Harm's daughter."

Rogue lay on a bed similar to the one at the Dire mansion, but this was ringed with silver, rendering him immobile. He blinked and looked up at Rifter. His voice was hoarse, familiar. "Lookin' like a king," he said, with a glance toward Gwen. "Sorry I can't greet you properly."

She moved forward, touched his forehead. "Does it hurt?"

"I'm used to it." His voice was rough, but it was the first contact he'd had in the six months since he'd been rescued from the weretrappers and brought back to the house unconscious, and Rifter knew he liked it.

Still, "I don't want you to be used to this shit." He took a deep breath, needed to remember why he was called here. "I need to ask you about something."

"The Dire spirit army? I'm not the conduit," Rogue confirmed. "But they know I can stop it."

"Is this Seb's spell?"

"Yes. You know how you can fix it."

That would be the hardest thing he could do—and not only because of his history with the man. The witch was immortal and no doubt guarded by black magic. "What about the Dire spirit army—how is he doing that? Can Jinx do anything to stop it?"

"Technically, the Dires aren't ghosts—they've passed already and been brought back, which is why he can see them, so no, that's my department. Seb's bringing them back and keeping them in hell," Rogue explained. "After enough time here, you'll agree to anything."

"What did you agree to?" Rifter demanded, but Rogue just stared up toward the heavens and said, "She's not going to wake up without help. The Elders refuse."

Gwen stiffened beside Rifter and Rogue. Although she'd suspected as much, hearing it with such finality made everything far more real.

She already hated the Elders for what they'd done to the Dires, but this made things worse. "The Elders are cowards."

Rogue shifted his eyes to her. "Don't say that too loudly—they have an awful lot of power, as you can see."

"They're not the ones holding you here?"

"No," Rogue confirmed.

"They could stop it if they wanted to. And they could wake me up," she added.

"So could I," Rifter told her, and by the look in his eyes, she could tell he was planning something that turned her stomach.

"No, you already gave up something for me. You spent time in their prisons because of me," she told him. "I won't let you go through that again.

"I'd go through it a million times if it meant keeping you safe."

"No."

"You wanted to live, no matter what—you told me that."

"That was before I knew all of this." She paced the room as Rogue remained silent. "We can fight them."

"Or we can give them a sacrifice."

"You'll bring about the downfall of the human race."

"They won't be able to replicate me," he said. "But they'll spend a long time trying."

"I deserve a say in this."

"Me too," Rogue said quietly. "What's happening with the weretrappers ... it's gone far beyond what it was ever supposed to."

"No shit—the world's in some kind of supernatural shit storm."

"They have no idea what they're letting out," Rogue said. "They think they're gaining power when they're really handing over any they had to the demons."

"And Seb's helping. Allowing it."

"He's bound like I am."

Rifter stared at Rogue. "You know that for a fact?"

"I'm pretty sure. Shit, Rifter, why the hell else would he do this? It's never made sense."

"He did it—that's all that matters."

"I'm telling you—that goddamned coven put some kind of spell on him."

Gwen knew Rifter wanted that to be true, more than anything.

"Then we can free him," Rifter said.

Rogue shook his head. "Way too late for that. He's fucked. You'll be saving something that's slowly turning unnatural."

"Some say we're unnatural too," Rifter pointed out.

"He's gone, Rift. Let it go."

Gwen could tell it was a devastating blow to Rifter. As much as he hated Seb, she knew a part of him still held out hope that Seb would return to the pack.

"Sorry, man. If I thought there was any way ..." Rogue trailed off, racked by some invisible pain. He gasped for air, cursed, and then he was still for a long moment.

She touched his forehead and his eyes opened. "You've got a nice touch."

Rifter growled and Rogue laughed hoarsely. "Relax, King, I'm not honing in on your mate."

Both men stilled suddenly, and Gwen swore she heard howling inside her head. And it wasn't her Sister Wolf.

Chapter 40

Rifter heard the howls in his ears. Something was happening in the other world—the real world. Rogue felt it too.

"Outlaws," he whispered. "You've got to stop all of this, Rifter. Figure out a way."

This was one of the worst places Rifter could think of being, and yet the thought of being pulled away made him sick. But the other world—the real world—tugged at him, and he knew he had to get back to his brothers.

In fact, if he looked hard enough, he could see them, standing next to him and Gwen, looking worried at the fact that neither was responsive.

Now he turned to look at Gwen and Rogue. Gwen was touching the silver along Rogue's wrists, trying to move it away from the tender skin so it would no longer burn him and standing far too close to the mare for comfort.

She'd already asked if there was any way to cut the silver bonds off.

Both Rogue and Rifter were worried because the silver didn't burn her at all. "Maybe the half-human thing—or a mutation," Rogue had whispered, and Rifter hoped that's all it was. He hadn't mentioned to Rogue about Gwen's blood and what it could do to them. Figured that was the least of their worries right now.

"I've got to go," he said.

"I'll stay here, with Rogue," she told him. "It's not like I can wake up yet anyway."

That was true, but he could lead her out of this place. And if she stayed . . . "I won't be able to come back here to get you out if you don't wake and shift. The only reason I made it this far was because we were together."

Even Rogue protested, telling her to go to a quiet place and concentrate on herself. "You can't stay here."

But Gwen was having none of it. "I'm not leaving a Dire in hell all alone. I can't do anything else but be here for him, so let me do that. I'm tired of being helpless. I won't be, not anymore. I'll be all right — I'm tougher than I look."

"Well, to be with Rifter, that I believe." Rogue looked at him and Rifter sighed.

The fact that Gwen would do that for his brother . . . what more could he say? "I will make this work. I won't leave either of you here for much longer."

Rogue nodded. "I believe you. I'll take care of her as best I can, see if I can help her get the hell out of the shift. Tell the others."

Rifter nodded, reluctantly released Gwen's hand once Rogue took her other one to keep her close.

The fact that she could stay like that, with Rogue . . . whether that meant she was too close to being a spirit already was something Rifter refused to think about. He walked through hell alone, leaving her in a place she might never return from.

Over my dead body. And it just might come to that if he could get the Elders involved.

But first things first. He roused himself and brushed a

hand over her cheek before he went upstairs into the room where Harm was held.

Vice scented them first, but Jinx was up at the glass door overlooking the deck before him. "Fucking mother-fucker," he muttered as he stared out into the woods, the multiple sets of wolf eyes impossible to miss.

"It's the second wave of outlaws," Vice observed.

"This could be in retaliation for Liam," Jinx said.

"Or meant to distract us so we can't blow the mauso-leum. Either way, it's all part of the same weretrapper bullshit, and we're surrounded. But I refuse to be trapped in this house for the rest of my goddamned life."

"If we fight, *we* can be spotted by the cops," Jinx re-minded him.

"I don't see any other choice," Vice said.

"We need Harm to fight," Stray said as he stared down the outlaws from the glass door leading to the deck. "It'll make things quicker."

"No," Jinx said firmly.

"Can't leave him chained forever," Stray argued.

"He'll stay that way until Rogue is freed," Jinx said.

"Now's not the time for this discussion," Vice re-minded them. "The longer this takes, the more police presence will show in this yard."

"Should we try to wake Rifter?" Stray asked.

"I think he's got his hands full," Vice said. "Leave him. The twins and Liam are ready for this."

Jinx and Stray nodded, and the twins and Liam looked pleased that the Dires thought to include them. Al-though none of them wanted this fight, they were anx-ious to prove themselves an asset.

"If you see Walker or Tals, leave them for me," Liam growled.

*   *   *

Rifter stripped and shifted out the third-floor window right onto two Weres who were hell-bent on killing Cyd.

To be fair, the kid more than held his own. When the two enemies were ripped to shreds, Rifter and Cyd moved in the opposite direction toward what appeared to be a sea of wolves, when the singing wafted over them like a warm breeze. The outlaws simply froze in place, but not the Dires. And one other wolf, whom Rifter had had his eye on from the beginning.

"Fucking Harm," Vice muttered. "Always has to show off."

"Good song, though," Stray said. It was an eighties favorite — headbanging metal — and Stray was shaking his head to the beat until Vice hit him.

Liam and Cyd and Cain were frozen too. No way around that.

"Finish this," Rifter told them. "I've got to check on something."

The wolf ran into the woods, too agile to be a Were. It was smaller than a Were as well, closer to a coyote. Something a shape-shifter would accomplish — or a witch.

He had run with Seb like this all the time — except they were running side by side, not chasing each other. This time, Rifter knew he wouldn't catch him, so he stopped, shifted. Called out, "Seb, I need to turn myself in to Mars."

The small wolf stopped. Turned warily and waited to see if Rifter would stay in place. When a few minutes passed, the figure blurred and Seb appeared. Fully fucking dressed. That was the one cool thing witches could do when they shifted.

They'd been friends for centuries, looking out for each other through the witch and werewolf trials. Rifter had always admired Seb for refusing to hide what he was.

Now he wanted to ask Seb *why*, but they were so far

beyond that. The man who'd been his best friend, who'd stood with him through mission after mission, during their SEAL days as well as before and after, was no longer on his side. No matter the reason—the damage was done.

"I need to turn myself in to Mars," he repeated. "I'm assuming you can facilitate that."

Seb didn't say anything immediately, and Rifter swore he saw something flicker across his face—sadness, maybe—and then his features hardened again. "What's the pay-off?"

"I need you to save Gwen," he said bluntly. "She's stuck in her first shift."

"Just because I get her through the first doesn't mean she'll live," Seb said.

"I realize that—don't repeat the lore of my kind back to me." Rifter's words were mostly a growl. "Tell Mars my terms. No tricks."

He turned his back on Seb, walked restlessly through the woods. If the witch had wanted to try something, he didn't need to wait for that. And Seb, for all his faults, had never been a coward.

"She's yours, isn't she?" Seb asked.

Rifter turned to see that Seb had silently followed him. "Save her, Seb. If you ever gave a shit about me, do this."

Rifter stared at the man with the short dark hair and amber eyes. He looked thinner. Pale too, but that's what happened when you hung out with demons. "Seb, you can still come back to our side, and we'll protect you."

"You don't mean that—you'd have my head."

Rifter nodded. "On a stick."

"My coven comes first," Seb told him.

"I would've helped you if you'd come to me first," Rifter tried again.

"You would've killed me," Seb said. "Maybe I would've been better off."

He hated that Seb could say that and mean it. His friend had always had melancholy, but he'd found a place with the wolves he'd been comfortable with.

Whether Seb would betray him again remained to be seen. Fool him once, shame on Seb. Fool him twice . . . the shame on Rifter would be nothing compared with losing Gwen. "Just make the deal with Mars. I'll wait here."

"I hope, for your sake, this isn't a trap." With that, Seb disappeared into the trees while Rifter waited alone.

Chapter 41

The remaining outlaw Weres were cut down easily as Harm continued singing. Although Vice wanted to mow the man down as well, he couldn't begrudge him the easy save.

But that was the problem—Harm always wanted the easy way out. Sometimes it wasn't the best way.

Still, they didn't waste time, killed the Weres easily as they remained frozen in place because of Harm's singing. His ability to soothe with his music—or conversely, rile the place up—was part of the reason he'd been chosen as king so long ago. A great leader needed an equal charisma that was almost hypnotizing. And while Harm couldn't do that with his speaking voice, when he sang, he could employ this ability at will and on a whim.

"Where'd Rifter go?" Jinx asked.

Vice shrugged. "Said he saw something—probably just patrolling the perimeters."

Jinx didn't look convinced and Vice wasn't either. But then Harm stopped singing and Liam and the twins unfroze and stared out at the sea of Were bodies.

"What the fuck?" Liam looked around and saw Harm up at the window. "His singing does that?"

"When he wants to," Vice said. "You have no

immunity—no amount of training will help. So be thankful he's on our side." For now.

The twins and Liam loaded the van with the Were bodies. Rifter instructed them to dump them into the river. The dual-natured body broke down quickly— they'd be dust within hours, but they couldn't afford to leave them on the property.

"Twenty-five in all," Liam said. "I knew all of them, damn it."

Vice clapped him on the shoulder. "Better to know the measure of a man's worth before you need to count on him."

Liam nodded and got into the van with the twins.

"Hey," Harm called from the window. "Get your asses up here."

"I'm so not taking orders from him," Vice muttered, but Jinx stared at the blond wolf.

"I think it's about Rifter's visit into the woods," he said, and Vice muttered a long string of very choice curses. "I hope Rift's got a good plan, because I have a feeling Seb was here."

They grabbed towels and clothing and headed up to find Harm, still watching out the window. He'd been left unchained except for an ankle, and he was humming under his breath as he turned around.

"No need to thank me, brothers."

"We weren't planning on it, asshole." Vice was too relaxed from the fighting to get worked up again immediately, but if Harm didn't cut his cocky shit, he could work something out with his Brother Wolf. "I'm guessing Rifter spoke to you before he jumped out the window."

"That he did. Said he's turning himself in to Mars."

"And you thought it was a good idea to let him?" Jinx asked while Stray grabbed the Taser gun from the table across the room.

"Wait a minute—I couldn't exactly stop our king," Harm told them.

"You've been locked in your bubble—you have no idea what it's like in the real world," Stray told him.

"King Rift has a plan," Harm said, his hands up as if in surrender. "He knows how to escape through the dream-walk. He wants to take them down from the inside once they save Gwen from her shift. He figures they'll be dis-tracted enough with him for the moment—it'll leave you free to take down the mausoleum."

"Won't that bring the police?" Stray asked Jinx.

"No other way to try to stop the Dire ghost army spell. The whole place is unholy ground. Blow it, salt it . . . and pray. If it's the center of Seb's spell, it can weaken it. If nothing else, it keeps Vice happy."

Vice agreed with that one. "Stray, why don't you get into the computer and alter Mars's rap sheet to include arson? Get the police to look in his direction and lead them to the mausoleum since it's his family's remains kept there."

"And Rifter's going to free himself once that's done?"

"Yep." Harm crossed his arms. "Once Gwen's awake, he'll dreamwalk through you all and let you know where he's being kept if he's got a problem. But he wants to kill Mars and use that as an example."

"If Seb's spelling the wolves, he's the one who needs to be killed."

"Rifter said he'll take care of that as well. But he needs his cooperation first."

"Yeah, because he's still hoping Seb will turn around and leave the trappers behind," Vice muttered, and no one bothered arguing with him because they knew he was right.

Gwen had watched Rifter leave through the doorway, which promptly closed and sealed behind him as though it had never existed. For the first time, she widened her view, looked around into the windows that surrounded Rogue. Through them, she saw real live scenes of incredible torture happening in front of her. *This must truly be hell,* she thought, as she watched men and women mouthing *help* and other things she couldn't hear through the heavy glass. But when they screamed, their mouths forming black, empty Os, she swore the sound ripped through her. Her eyes flicked back and forth between the images as if her mind couldn't stand to focus on one for very long, but the flayed skin and the burning . . .

"Focus on me," Rogue commanded. "Don't look or you'll go nuts."

She pulled her eyes back to him and took a deep breath. "I already feel that way."

"I hear you."

"Are you ever going to tell me what that . . . woman's doing sitting on your chest?" she asked finally.

Rogue stared at her. "You see it?"

"Yes. I wasn't sure Rifter could and I didn't want to upset him," she said. Rogue's explanation of the mare didn't exactly comfort her.

"Just don't look her in the eyes," Rogue instructed.

"Don't worry," she assured him. "Do you think Rifter can find a way to stop the raising of the demons and the Dire army?"

"Maybe. Depends on what kind of demons they're releasing."

"I always thought a demon was a demon."

"Not even close. And not all demons want the same things," Rogue told her. "You're going to be learning things you never thought were possible beyond Hollywood movies. Keep your mind open. You'll need it to survive."

Gwen stared at him. "Tell me the truth—I'm really

stuck and hovering between the world of the living and the dead, aren't I?"

"We both are—both stuck," Rogue explained. "The longer you stay, the longer you risk staying trapped for good."

She tried not to think too hard on that, stared at the red marks burned into Rogue's skin by the silver chains, visible since she'd loosened them. She hated feeling helpless, could only imagine what his brothers felt.

"This isn't so bad—hell week was worse."

"What's that?"

"SEAL training."

"Wait, you were all in the military?"

Rogue nodded. "Easiest way to get off the local radar. Every once in a while, a human knows something they shouldn't because of a careless Were. Before the modern military, we lost ourselves in whatever battles or wars were happening around the world. We were bred warriors, so it was a natural choice for us. Later, we all went into different branches. Our blood's normal and everything else is close enough to pass. Since we can control ourselves during the full moon, we were good candidates. We'd only get sick from all the injections."

"So you were a Navy SEAL . . ."

"Rift was too." He smiled. "Jinx was in the Army. Medic. Vice was a Marine."

"That doesn't surprise me." She paused. "Not Stray, though."

"Yeah, he went in after he met us. Army Ranger." Rogue looked at her. "You can still get out of here. You're not concentrating hard enough."

"I'm worried about you."

"Worry about Rifter," he told her. "Try to hear him. You're not fully mated, but you're connected as sure as I'm stuck in hell."

Gwen closed her eyes, although she kept her hand on Rogue's forehead. She listened for her Sister Wolf and the familiar rustling. It seemed like hours passed before she heard Rifter's voice, but she couldn't see him.

"I can hear him. How can I be doing this?" she asked Rogue, because she was here with him and yet somehow hearing Rifter as well.

"You might have a power; you might not. Until your third successful shift, we won't know, but it appears you're absorbing Rifter's—feeding off it. Mating—even the start of a mating—can make both Dires stronger." Rogue's explanation was rational—gentle—but his face was tight with tension and anger, no doubt a mirror image of hers.

"Harm said . . . he said my blood can kill all of you," she admitted. "It's why the weretrappers went after me."

Rogue stared at her for a long moment, and she waited for him to tell her to leave. Instead, he told her, "You're hovering between life and death. Healer and destroyer. This could get interesting."

Before she could ask how, he brought her back to the task at hand. "What's Rifter doing?"

She quieted and listened. Rifter was speaking the old language—fast, but she caught enough to understand.

Spell. Wake her. Me in return.

Who was he giving himself to? "I think he's turning himself in . . . in exchange for waking me up and leaving me alone. He promised he wouldn't. He can't—we can't let him."

"Can't stop him. He's doing it for you." It was obvious to her that Rogue knew Rifter was lying the entire time.

"But we're not even fully mated. How can this be?"

"In his heart, you are."

In hers as well. And she had a plan as much as Rifter—it broke through as clearly as the return of the rustling in her ears. And although she couldn't hear it as clearly, she suddenly knew exactly what she needed to do. "How do I kill Mars?"

"You're nuts," he muttered. "He's got a plan, Gwen. My brothers will get him out."

"I can't let that happen."

"Too late."

She hated the man next to her suddenly. Told him so.

"Not the first woman I've heard that from," he said. "Let him do what he needs to. You'll be free."

"And then what? One shift out of three," she pointed out. "And this brothers-freeing-you thing isn't working so well for you."

His face hardened. "He's got to fight the trappers."

"Did you ever stop to think that maybe I could be of some help? That maybe there's a reason I'm here? Beyond that, he's my mate. I refuse to let him suffer another second because of me," she said fiercely.

For the first time since she'd met him, she saw the trace of a smile on Rogue's face, even as he shook his head. "If you kill Mars, all bets are off. The spell could be broken and you'll be back here with me. Best case, you're all in a shitload of trouble."

"There's got to be another way."

"And suppose there's not?" Rogue asked her. "Can you live with yourself?"

"I guess I'm going to find out."

Chapter 42

Rifter knew Mars and his wereguards were on their way fifteen minutes before they showed up in his backwoods. They were either that cocky or that stupid.

Both, he decided. He waited there, naked and seemingly vulnerable, until Mars came through the trees.

He'd caught sight of the man before—seen pictures too—but in person, it was definitely easy to mark him as semipossessed. Anyone who was under the influence of the black arts showed the same signs—pale, eyes just a little off-color, and way too sure of themselves in situations like this.

Mars was facing a Dire wolf with Weres he knew Rifter could rip from head to toe. Granted, Rifter had a stake in all of this, and Mars must really be counting on that.

"Well, well, the king's surrendering," Mars said with a smile. "You're going to fit in nicely with our plans."

"You really think using wolves is going to help you rule the world?" he asked. "Because that's fucking nuts."

"I don't need to know what you think, Rifter. I just need your cooperation."

"What happened to your original mission of destroying us?"

"You're all aberrations of nature—don't really deserve to be alive. None of you can control yourselves."

"And you're going to give me that control, are you?" Rifter asked dryly.

"Yes, although I'm sure you won't like it."

"I'm sure I won't." He held out his wrists for the cuffs. Mars told him to turn around so he could be cuffed behind his back. The second he put his wrists together, the knife sliced into his chest, catching a lung. He doubled over in pain, and Mars laughed as he put the cuffs on.

"You don't think I trust you all that much, do you, wolf?" he asked. "Take him to the car," he told the Weres, who grabbed him by the arms and started to drag him toward the waiting van.

He gritted his teeth, closed his eyes and thought about Gwen. Doing this for her—freeing her—was the best sacrifice he could think of making. And if that made him an aberration—a sick freak of nature—then so be it.

He could think of nothing better to be than a Dire. "Just wake her up."

"Oh, we're not doing that," Mars said. "Seb wanted to help you, but I convinced him it's not in his best interest."

Rogue had been right. Rifter knew it, but how could someone who'd stood by him, fought with and for him, betray him so badly? Seb had been his only chance to help Gwen through the shift, because he couldn't count on the Elders.

Couldn't count on anyone but himself and his Dire brothers. And Gwen.

Gwen.

Rifter shoved Brother Wolf down hard as the pain screeched through his lungs.

If she's gone, you still have work to do, he told his wolf.

And then he looked up and saw the raven flying overhead before the second knife invaded his body.

The punishment would come the second the demon who watched Seb knew he was waking Gwen for a good purpose and not an evil one.

"If I can wake her, she'll come here looking for Rifter and we can capture her," Seb had reasoned to Mars after giving him the news about the king turning himself in.

Mars had reinforced stainless steel cages made. Seb didn't bother to tell him that he knew exactly how Rifter escaped the first time and it had nothing to do with brute force.

Now, as he fought through the scorching pain the demon inflicted on him to stop him from casting the spell, he chanted the incantation three times to pull Gwen from her first shift successfully. It was the best he could do before the demon took hold.

He'd pushed it too far, and he'd pay dearly now. Better that he didn't remember anything anyway.

The wait seemed like an eternity. Gwen channeled the panicked, nervous energy, replayed her plan in her mind.

"My brothers will try to stop you," Rogue warned her.

She would be faster than the other wolves—had to be. She would wake up and then she would need to stop Rifter from giving himself to Mars.

"You could come back here, Gwen—and then you'll be stuck," Rogue warned for the millionth time. "He doesn't want that."

"And I don't want him hurt either. At some point, I get a say." She glanced at him. "If Seb comes through on his end of the bargain, what happens?"

"You'll shift to wolf and then back to human—fast—

and you'll wake up," Rogue told her. "When you feel the pull, leave me, okay? Just go and don't look back."

"What about you? Isn't there still hope?"

"There's always hope, Gwen. Always hope."

The rest happened so fast she didn't have time to say anything else. One minute, she was next to Rogue; the next, she was blinking under the lamp's light next to Rifter's bed. At first, nothing worked right—she opened her mouth to call out for help, for anyone, but nothing came out but a low growl.

She looked down, saw she was now a wolf—vanilla coated—and immobile. Before she could panic for real, she blinked at bright spots that flashed before her eyes and pain overtook her again—she pressed through it, the rustling turning more to a wolf's howl inside her head.

God, it wasn't supposed to be like this. She was supposed to have shifted hours ago, should be running through the woods, not lying like she was already dead.

What if Rifter hadn't made that literal deal with the devil? She could be this way indefinitely.

They'd been right when they worried she might not be strong enough. The mind was willing, but the flesh was all too weak.

And then, within seconds, her breath came fast, bones felt like they were twisting and turning in ways they shouldn't and her face felt pulled into a grimace. She licked her lips and felt for the long canines that were disappearing. Her heart beat fast and she was so hot . . . and still, she couldn't move, couldn't scream, couldn't do anything but let whatever was happening simply happen.

Surrender, Sister Wolf told her.

Sister Wolf was pretty damned smart.

Finally, after what seemed like hours but she was sure had been only minutes, she stared down at her naked human body, her clothing in tatters on the bed around her.

Had she ever really shifted? It could've been part of a dream, except her hand moved and plucked some vanilla-colored fur off the black sheets.

And she could move, stand. She tested her voice by calling for Rifter once she'd pulled on the first shirt she wore. It smelled like Rifter.

She had her nose buried in the fabric she'd pulled up around her face when Jinx answered instead, came up the stairs at lightning speed.

"I'm okay," she told him, and he still insisted on her sitting down on the side of the bed so she didn't faint on him.

"You've been through a shift—you're not okay."

"Do you know why I woke up?" she demanded, and he pressed his lips together grimly but refused to answer her. "I know why too."

"Let it be, Gwen."

"I can't—you know that."

Jinx turned away from her to stare out the window at the storm currently raging at the windows, beating the house with its heavy, fat drops. She rubbed her arms and listened to Sister Wolf.

Tell me what you know, she demanded, and to her surprise, she got an answer.

Listen—he needs you.

She pricked her ears, knew what was happening. She was up off the bed and down the stairs like a shot, faster than she'd ever run in her life. She burst out of the back door into the pouring rain, which felt like a thousand needles piercing her skin, and still, she ran faster.

"It's too soon," Jinx called. "You're not strong enough to shift now—and you can't do what you're planning as a human!"

He was right about that part, of course. She ignored him as she ran, heard his curses behind her, his footfalls heavy. If he caught her, she'd never rescue Rifter.

She also knew he wouldn't leave the house unguarded with Harm inside—Rogue had told her that—and she hoped he'd been right.

She ran faster, enough that she felt her muscles taut with the strain, and she burst into the wolf within seconds and ignored the sudden, sharp pain as the fierce need to stop Rifter was all she could think about.

Consequences didn't matter. The rush of the change charged through her. She was like a moth to a flame, not caring about the burn. She caught Rifter's scent, stronger now, and then sighted him.

Rifter was handcuffed with silver chains that held his wrists behind his back. There were also two silver knives sticking out of his side, subduing him.

But his pain and anguish still vibrated through him, and she felt every inch of it. Nothing Rifter could've said or done would've stopped her, and she watched his face as she made a beeline toward the man standing in front of him, with his back to her.

The man named Mars turned at the last minute and yelled. A grace combined with indisputable power surged through her when Rifter went down with the silver spikes in his side and moved out of the way. It was pure animal instinct that pushed her forward, thick claws on front paws slamming Mars to the ground.

They both hit the earth hard. She heard several cracks, but it didn't seem to be any of her bones. Mars groaned as she ripped with her teeth at the arm holding the gun. He screamed and she knew it wouldn't be enough to stop him.

She was going to kill him. As much as she wanted to blame Sister Wolf for all of this, a part of her wanted this man to pay for trying to take her family away from her.

She could've been living at the very least with her father. The unspeakable anger charged out of her, and although she was a new wolf, her emotions made her a force to be reckoned with.

A heavy weight slammed her back, and she attempted to shake it off, felt teeth at her own neck even as she attempted to tear at the human's beneath her. She skirted out from between human and Were, Sister Wolf wild and wiry at the same time.

The Were bared its teeth and came at her; she didn't give him an inch, took him on and found herself surrendering everything to Sister Wolf—she knew exactly what to do. It was like Gwen sat back and watched, saw her wolf rip the Were's throat out—and the victory howl tore from her own throat.

Despite still being handcuffed, Rifter must've taken care of the second Were, because he was next to her, dead. She watched him work to fish the keys to the chains out of the dead Were's pocket, and a surge of relief ran through her.

It was short-lived, because Mars was down, not out. He was trained, and he struggled up, the gun pointed at Rifter, who struggled away with the silver embedded in him still.

The blood . . . my God.

"Don't, Gwen," Rifter told her, but Sister Wolf had other plans. And when Mars turned the gun on her and fired, she barely felt it.

But before she could take him on again, Rifter had him down, was holding the man down with a hand on his throat to subdue him. Still in human form, he moved his hands to the sides of Mars's head and turned it, fast and hard.

All hail, the bastard's dead.

But there was no time to celebrate, because Rifter collapsed then, falling off Mars onto the grass. Helplessly, she circled him, nudging him, trying to get any kind of response.

You have to let me back out, she told Sister Wolf. *I can help him.*

She stared at Rifter and forced herself to concentrate, pictured herself turning from wolf to woman, waited for the pain she'd felt before. Prayed for it.

Rifter groaned and spit out some blood. His eyes closed again and she cried out to him, except it came out a howl.

Concentrate. Surrender. We're one . . .

And she did. Closed her eyes and trusted. When she opened them again after the hot flash of pain, she was naked in the rain.

She dropped to her knees next to Rifter. Shook him until he opened his eyes and asked, "Tell me what to do."

"Taking out the knives would be a good first step."

"Sarcastic bastard," she muttered. "I knew that—I just didn't know if it would hurt your wolf."

She tugged at the first handle and realized she'd have to yank it out. She did so quickly, both knives, and Rifter passed out again, his breath rough.

Her head began to swim—the shift had been hard on her. And they were in the same position they'd started in. When he opened his eyes again, he asked her, "Why the hell did you do this? They woke you up. They were prepared to leave all the Dires alone in exchange for me."

"And then what?"

"I'd find a way out once you were all safe. I had a plan."

"You're not an island, Rifter."

"That's funny, coming from you. A one-woman wreck-ing crew," he practically roared.

"I saved you from yourself."

"Ditto."

"You've been around for centuries and that's the best comeback you've got?"

He grabbed her, pulled her down and kissed her hard, fast, until their bodies were practically melded together. It didn't matter about the weather—the pain—the fear. All that mattered was that she was in his arms again.

Finally he stopped, took his mouth from hers. "We can't stay here—got to get back and figure out how much trouble you just caused us."

Chapter 43

Vice commando-crawled toward the mausoleum in the dark. Sarge had taught him a hell of a lot about demolition, and he loved putting that shit to good use. It was gonna blow to high heaven and take a few weretrappers with it.

Sarge had died a few years ago—Agent Orange or some shit, they said. Vice had visited him once in the nursing home, although he'd worn a disguise and pretended to be there for someone else, because he couldn't have approached the man looking exactly the same as he had thirty years earlier.

Stray waited back in the woods—his lookout and backup. The street kid in Stray would never change—he was as tough as shit.

The thing was, if Rifter was going to give himself to the weretrappers to save Gwen, Vice was going to do everything in his power to blow the weretrappers off the face of the earth. And then he'd kidnap Seb and make the man his own personal spell caster.

Seb's place of demon worship was next on the list. But first things first.

He picked the lock easily—child's play to him—and creaked the heavy door open. The chill blew through him like a winter's bite in the ass. "Try to keep me out," he muttered to whatever the hell guarded the place and heard light laugher in return.

Fucker. He shifted around, content that he was wearing enough protective amulets to keep himself covered, and checked the place out.

There were single tables on the opposite ends of the two crypts. Otherwise, it was disturbingly clean and quiet for a place causing so much mayhem in the world.

When he looked up, he saw the spell circle on the ceiling. No doubt the charms were buried in the floor. Sure enough, he found what looked to be new concrete in the middle of the floor.

He narrowed his focus, channeled the rage he felt toward the trappers and Mars into this job. With precision, he wired the place to blow, in case he got stopped earlier than expected. He had just enough C4 to keep the blow from spreading too far, because he didn't need the other spirits whose graves he might disturb coming after him.

Hurry, son . . . need your help . . .

It might be the most his mother had ever spoken to him when he was alive, and it was just as annoying now as it was then.

Once the wiring was complete, it was time to take care of the supernatural shit. That was trickier than C4 and hand grenades combined.

Sweat poured off his chest and back—he'd stripped down to just jeans as he dug through the flooring to the fragrant earth below, and then he dug through with his hands, looking for the bones and the bag of charms that cast the spell.

The mausoleum was in a perfect position—a crossroads. Vice wasn't sure how they'd missed it before, but he saw it clearly now, the perfect cross of walkways converging on the gray stone building.

After Jinx did more research, they'd discovered it belonged to Mars's cousins, several times removed. Probably related to the people Rifter's pack had killed all those years ago.

He sprinkled the power along the ground—it would break any spell that was cast here. He salted the rest of it, in case there were any bones that he'd missed when he'd dug out the concrete floor.

Nothing good ever came from unholy ground.

He stood, surveyed his work. Texted the all clear to Stray and waited to hear from Jinx.

This was a house of cards—he had to time it exactly right or else he'd fuck up Gwen's shift but good.

They didn't hold out much hope for Rogue. In fact, it could make things worse for him, but they needed to get Rifter and Gwen out of trouble first.

His phone beeped. He stared at Jinx's *it's a go* text as he exited and blew the mausoleum to holy hell behind him.

Rifter insisted on carrying her back to the house. Gwen was already wet and cold, and he was faster, even hurt, so she let him. Figured she'd done enough damage and arguing would only make things worse. Plus, she'd overdone it for sure, and her body was feeling the effects, as Jinx had predicted.

But she wouldn't admit all that to Rifter.

She saw Jinx at the door, watching, but when Rifter brought her inside he wasn't there. Probably giving them privacy, which was good, since she was naked.

He put her in front of the fire wrapped in a blanket while he went to get her dry clothes.

When he came back, he remained stripped down, despite the other blankets available.

"Aren't you freezing?" she asked.

"Wolves are good in the rain," he said, shaking his body off and ignoring the towel.

"You're so angry with me."

"With myself," he corrected. "I'll fix this."

Obviously, he no longer felt her help was necessary. She contented herself with the fact that they were both safe and pulled the blanket tighter as the rain showered the house.

She fully expected to see Noah's ark float by—that was how biblical this rain was.

According to the radio, the town was flooding. Roads closed, buildings took in feet of water and emergency sirens wailed in the distance. The Dire house's power flickered eerily and stayed on, albeit slightly dimmed.

She'd never given much thought to the supernatural realm at all. Now it was in her face, all the time, and couldn't be ignored if she wanted to. It was as brash and obvious as Vice, and she wondered how she could've been so blind to it. How all humans were . . .

She knew that this storm signaled the start of bad things, but right now it was the only thing keeping the police—and possibly the weretrappers—from them.

She didn't think it was the right time to ask if witches could swim.

And then Jinx came in, and his news promised to turn the quiet Dire house into a scene of mass confusion shortly.

Jinx hadn't wasted any time before telling Rifter about Vice readying to blow the mausoleum and finishing with a blunt, "We're kind of fucked."

"Why did Vice do that?" she asked.

"He's trying to free Rogue—and you—and the Dire army. I stayed here in case Rogue suffered any ill effects," Jinx said. "So far, none."

"The police—"

"Already have our names—a safeguard, thanks to Mars and his paranoia. He'll keep the outlaws—and any new Weres who come his way—under his protection and safe."

"He's dead."

"He's got two brothers—one's a police chief," Jinx said.

Cain came in then, quiet as always, surprised them by saying, "Liam called Walker and Tals out. He said he'll take them on tonight if necessary."

"Jesus Christ," Rifter muttered.

"Liam's human needs to go," Cain said. "Not because she's human, but she's not loyal. I don't trust her."

It was the most Cain had ever spoken at one time. Rifter stared at the young omega—he and his twin had come far in the year they'd lived here and trained with Jinx. "That's up to Liam."

"I know that. I've already told him my piece. I can't be under a leader who doesn't listen to opinions." Cain jutted his chin. "Liam's cool with that. We've got some other Weres coming here—Cyd and I will vet them outside. If need be, we'll help you with this situation with the ghost army."

"Good job, wolf." Rifter put a hand on his shoulder and couldn't help but notice the small, pleased smile on Cain's face. It might've been the first he'd ever seen.

He turned his attention back to Gwen, who was staring into space. Shifting took a hell of a lot of energy, and he sat next to her now, took her hand.

"I'm okay?" she asked.

"You're awake and you shifted to wolf and back. Just took you a little while."

He took the cup of tea with honey Cyd handed him, and she took a grateful sip.

"How'd you know my throat would be so sore?" she asked.

"The howling."

"Oh."

"It gets easier," he told her.

"It almost killed me." Her words were blunt, and he winced. "Sorry. So how much damage did I cause?"

"Enough," he told her, although he kept his voice steady. "But you couldn't have stopped yourself if you wanted to."

"How?"

"You're a little moon crazed. New wolf is hard to control. In this case, it happened to work in your favor," Rifter wheezed. The silver weapon had caught a lung, and it would burn like a bitch until it repaired. His hands were burned. And Gwen's next shift could kill her.

They were alive but vulnerable. Forced to be hidden away while the supernatural world was about to be at war. Balances were shifting, and with Mars dead, there would be hell to pay. And he was no closer to Seb than he had been earlier, which meant Rogue was still trapped in hell.

"Have you healed?" she asked. He lifted his shirt— the bleeding had stopped but the wounds were still deep. It hurt to breathe, but he'd been through worse. Much worse, when he thought he'd lost her.

"Mars's police officer brother is rumored to be next in line to lead the trappers. He doesn't care if he outs the wolves," Stray told them now. "According to the trappers' site, they'd rather it be that way. Humans will be scared of us and the trappers will offer protection."

"Yeah, okay." Vice snorted but he didn't look at ease.

The noose was slowly tightening around them. Soon, they would be completely pinned down if they didn't act fast.

"Gwen's the top priority," Jinx told Rifter. "Bring her to the compound and let her shift."

"No, not now." God, who knew what kind of reversal spell Seb might be putting in place?

"Now or never," Gwen corrected him. And as much as he hated to admit it, she was right.

Chapter 44

When Rifter and Jinx put their heads together, Gwen went upstairs to confront her father.

This time, no one stopped her. That was good, because she felt like she was running out of time. Maybe Rifter did as well.

When she entered the room, Harm turned swiftly, as if ready to fight. His ankle was still chained, and it looked as raw as Rogue's ankle had. Her throat tightened, but she swallowed it because no one was getting off that easily today.

"You're bruised—what happened?" he demanded immediately, and her hand went to her neck. She'd forgotten that Mars hadn't gone down without a fight, although she couldn't be sure if the damage had been done by him or his wereguards. "Did Rifter do that?"

"No, of course he didn't." She paused. "I tried to kill Mars. Rifter finished the job for me."

Harm just stared at her like she'd lost her mind, so she continued, "Now he's really mad at me."

She expected Harm to keep staring or maybe tell her she was wrong. But his words surprised her. "He's used to doing the saving. He doesn't know how to handle a woman who can do that for him. He's never even had the hope of that, because he didn't think there were any Dire females left."

"I don't even know if I can shift again and live. And then I'm taking away Rifter's only chance at a mate ever, and I shouldn't do that. And I don't know why I'm telling you this . . . because I think I hate you. I should hate you."

"Yeah, you should." Harm gave a lopsided smile that had made him the hard-rock poster boy for many of her friends growing up. She thanked God at this point that she'd been more into classical music, because that would've made things really awkward now. "The first shift is hard. And yours, harder than most because you're half human."

The shift had been like a brilliant swirl of rainbow colors bursting—painful and exquisite at the same time. "I've killed people."

Harm actually looked . . . proud. "A wolf's got to be able to defend herself."

She stared at her hands. She'd learned a long time ago when she'd started dealing with doctors and hospitals that hands could cause both life and death.

Only to people who want you dead, Sister Wolf whispered. *You'll see.*

"Do you paint, like your mom?" he asked her.

She shook her head, confused. "I don't. Wait, the paintings were done by my mother? My aunt always said she painted them when she was younger, and they even had her signature on them."

"She was keeping you safe, like she was charged to do. I gave her cash and sent her away so there was no trail. I always knew where you were, though. I had guards— Weres—around the area. I knew you wouldn't have noticed."

She hadn't, of course, but she'd never felt anything but

safe with her aunt and uncle. "I miss my mother," she blurted out.

"Your mom . . . Lucy . . . she was so beautiful. Like you." She noticed Harm's fingers shake as he pulled a picture from his wallet. It was yellowing and wrinkled.

It was obvious he took it with him everywhere. She held the paper by the edges carefully. It wasn't the only picture of her mom she'd seen, but it was the only one the woman seemed happy in. "How long were you two together?"

"Not long enough. I was taking a break from touring. Three months in the mountains and she was there, painting." He had such a faraway look in his eyes that it brought tears to hers. "When I came back from the next tour, she was gone. She'd left a note—she was scared. Wanted to protect you. I didn't know the trappers had been following me because of a witch named Cordelia. I was so stupid."

At the mention of Cordelia's name, Gwen shuddered. "My mother knew what you were?"

"It was impossible to hide it from her. No, that's not true—I stopped wanting to. At first, she was terrified. Disbelieving. I explained that I couldn't be with her because of the wolf side, but she told me that she could handle anything. She did, but I was very careful." He paused. "I didn't know about the baby—about you—at first. When she told me, it was because she needed money to hide from the weretrappers."

"To hide me?"

"Both of you. Since she'd been impregnated by a wolf, she didn't know if they'd force her to carry more half-breeds." He stared at the picture from over her shoulder. "I gave her everything she needed, and the trappers still got to her. You're lucky you were at the hotel where your aunt and uncle were staying—your mom called them in because she was worried. Knew she was being followed. And they weren't really your aunt and uncle, but close friends who'd been told everything. And you stayed safe for a really long time."

"How?"

"Seb. It worked for a while—I made a pact without Rifter's knowledge. But when things turned bad between wolf and witch . . . shit, Rift and Seb were so close. I never thought . . ."

She wanted to tell him it wasn't his fault, but technically, that wasn't true. She wanted to forgive him, but she wasn't there yet. "She was very brave," she said instead.

"She was willing to do anything for you. In the end, she did."

"And you weren't."

Something dark and painful skittered across his face. "I tried. After Seb went to the weretrappers' side, I did everything in my power to keep you safe from them. But they wouldn't take me instead of you. I figured I was better served staying out and watching over you."

"Why didn't they want you?"

"They wanted Rifter and Rogue for their abilities in particular. I had to make a choice—my daughter or my brothers. They could fend for themselves. You would have never survived with them."

"And yet, you don't want me to survive. To shift. You hate being a wolf."

"I hate not being able to mate with anyone I want to—there's a difference. It's a hell of a lonely life. And I like humans, Gwen, more than I like most wolves. The fact that your mother was able to get pregnant by me— that was a goddamned miracle. And I couldn't be with her. It was so unfair." He stared at her. "I guess you won't have that problem."

"Don't you think, with so few of us left, you should try to make up with them? If nothing else, for my sake?"

"Never going to happen. They can't stand me because I like humans."

"I think you missed the mark on that one. They can't stomach the fact that you didn't trust them enough to tell them all of this. You didn't come back to help them. You have so few of your kind left and you turned your back on them. On me. I'm half human, so what's your excuse?"

Harm's mouth pulled into a tight grimace. "Right— you're half human and my daughter. Do you think they're going to treat you any better than me?"

"They already have," she spat.

"Because you can kill them. Once they take a step back and wrap their heads around how truly dangerous you are if captured . . . don't think they're going to treat you any differently than these silver chains." He pointed to his bonds, and his eyes looked lupine even though his tone was sad.

She stared at him, the anger making her head pound. How could Rifter not hate her? No doubt a part of him did, but she couldn't believe what Harm was telling her.

Or maybe she just didn't want to.

Chapter 45

The police cars lined the area around the Dire house, prepared to do a thorough search of the surrounding woods. They wouldn't come to the door and demand entrance, though, because they couldn't see the house. Thanks to a protection spell Seb had gifted them years ago, the only people who could see the house were wolves, and only those who hadn't betrayed the Dires. It was a complicated, irreversible spell—pure, unadulterated magic. Sometimes the Dires would sit there and watch the police actually walk through their house, unencumbered by the surrounding furniture and walls.

But the Dires still took nothing for granted and had built a space to go to during such emergencies after Seb went over to the dark side—and hired a Were bail bondsman who could get Vice and Stray out of jail, if need be. The underground lair was built on hallowed church ground—demons couldn't touch the place.

Hopefully, the police would look on them as troublemakers and not delve much further. The weretrappers had made a stupid move turning the Dires in—as dangerous for all of them as it was stupid.

The stakes were their lives as they knew them—it

would take all their strength and abilities, working together, to pull their asses off the line.

Rifter barreled up the stairs in time to see Gwen leaving Harm's room, a hand over her mouth. When she looked up at him, he knew Harm had opened his big mouth, talking shit she wasn't ready to hear.

"I'll fucking kill him," he told her. "Whatever he said, it isn't true."

"How can you even stand to look at me ... knowing I'm the reason for Rogue—for your nightmares," she started, but he pulled her close before she could say another word.

"It's not your fault. I'll take time proving that to you, but the police are here now, scouring the property. We've got to go."

"I've brought you guys nothing but trouble—how can all of you be so good to me?"

"It's not hard at all, Gwen. It hasn't been from the beginning."

"Even though I can kill you?"

"Yeah, even though."

She looked like she wanted to say something more on the subject, but she let it drop for the moment. "The police are here because of Mars and his brother, right? God, I messed everything up."

"No, you saved me. Always remember that. You have to calm the hell down—you can't afford to shift now. Come on, let's go now—we'll talk about this, okay?" He kissed her—hard. "You've done nothing wrong."

She took a deep breath, but her eyes were changing. He could see she was having a tough time holding it together, like any new wolf.

But she was far from any new wolf, and the agitation was rolling off her in waves. "Let's go."

He took her hand and led her to the basement, where

Jinx waited by the door, ready to seal it back when they passed him. It looked like a flat wall, and if tapped, wouldn't sound hollow. When Jinx opened it, he pulled her inside and they started to walk along the dimly lit corridor.

When the door slammed behind her, she jumped.

"It's okay—this leads to an underground compound about a mile from the house. We rarely need it, since the house is invisible to humans."

"It never was to me," Gwen told him.

"If you'd said that earlier, it would've been my first clue that there was something going on with you."

They walked in near silence, Gwen's harsh breathing jarring him with every step.

If she shifted here, it would be so dangerous for both wolves. He turned and held her—they had half a mile to go, but he couldn't go on with her so upset. He kissed her until she stopped resisting, until he felt the tears on her cheeks dry.

"Baby, it's okay," he murmured into her neck.

"Don't tell me you didn't hate me when you found out."

"No, I didn't. I couldn't. You're an innocent in all of this. Harm was trying to save you, the same way I did when I turned myself over to Mars." He paused. "I can't fault him. As much as I want to, there can't be any lies between us."

She nodded. "I'm sorry—you don't need my breakdown right now. Let's get to safety and you can make your plans."

He held her hand the rest of the way until the two of them approached what looked like a blank wall, until Rifter used his palm against just the right spot. He stood back as a door opened in front of them, and then he ushered her inside. He waited to turn around until it closed and sealed behind them.

The compound was large—all one floor with surveillance monitors and weapons and food. Enough to survive several apocalypses, which was ironic considering they could all just sit outside in lawn chairs and not worry about death.

Gwen was looking around as he checked the monitors, especially the ones leading to the house. He saw his brothers watching the police comb the property, and his gut lurched.

This was all too fucking public. Staying here would bring trouble beyond their wildest dreams.

But for now, he had to calm Gwen down—that was a kind of trouble they couldn't afford.

"Why are there chains here?" she called from one of the bedrooms. He walked to the door to see her staring down at the heavy silver cuffs attached to cement walls— they were double hinged and reinforced to the wall.

"If we've got a moon-crazed young Were, we can't always control his shift. But we can control where he goes once he's shifted. This way, he stays here and doesn't hurt anyone," he explained.

She picked it up even as he tried to stop her. Was by her side in seconds, watching her hold the chain in her palm, waiting for her to yell and drop it, or at least see some smoke rising from her palm.

"It's still not burning you?" he asked incredulously.

"Not at all." She touched it with both hands. "What does this mean?"

"Maybe it'll only affect you in wolf form." *Or maybe you're not out of danger with your shifts yet. Maybe you're not really a shifted wolf until silver burns you.*

Fuck.

They were cut off here, which was the point. But the proximity. The need . . . her scent . . .

"Your eyes," she whispered.

"Yours too." He took several steps back as the walls closed in. "Let me get us some food and we can . . . talk."

"I don't want to talk."

"Me neither. But you need to know about the mating . . . what can happen."

She nodded, placed the heavy chains on the floor and followed him out toward the kitchen.

Rifter was romancing her.

They were in the middle of a crazy battle and he was taking the time to cook for her. He poured her wine and made her spaghetti, and she ate because her body gave her no choice. Sister Wolf demanded fuel.

"Will my appetite calm down?" she asked.

"It gets worse—but you'll get used to it. You'll know how to manage it." He sat next to her at the big table.

"I can't believe you're doing this for me. It's like . . . a date."

"I've lived around cursed humans long enough to know their customs."

"But not understand them?"

He smiled. "I've begun to. Our mating practices are . . . different."

"Starting with the fact that we never use the term mating."

"Right, but it's just semantics. The point of dating is to mate, but humans are reluctant to admit that. Like sex is something to be ashamed of."

"That's true."

"But it's all around you—you use it on TV and in books, but you can't walk up to a woman and tell her you want to mate."

"That depends on the time of night and how much she's had to drink, but yes, I get your point." She took a sip of the red wine—it bloomed on her tongue much the way Rifter had—spicy, rich and almost as intoxicating.

Rifter had most definitely become like a drug to her. She wondered if that was all part of the mating ritual. "Back when you had a pack, what was the ritual?"

He finished his wine and poured her more. "Drink."

"That bad, huh?"

"Not bad—just different."

She narrowed her eyes. "I don't have to sleep with the other Dires, do I?"

His growl reverberated across the room. "Sorry. Brother Wolf doesn't like that question."

"Guessing that's a no."

"The wolf can be more protective of his mate than the human. Dires and Weres know not to touch mated females. Mated males are even more dangerous than the young moon-crazed ones."

"Protective."

"A nice way of saying jealous as shit." He smiled. "Mating was never arranged. The moon celebration is a time of mating and fertility. That's where you sought your mate. And then some of the Dires started taking more than one mate, which wasn't allowed under the old ways, and it got wild. Some wanted to get back to a more"—his mouth quirked to the side—"civilized way of life."

"But the others refused."

"Yes. They continued their pillaging. That's when the humans began to hunt us and the Elders sent down their first warning."

"But you can't be killed."

"No, we can't *now*. But our kind used to die. Silver poisoning's a horrible death. They would kill us—stuff and mount us."

"You became immortal after the Extinction, then?"

"Yes. We went on our Running. The Dires, led by

Jameson, defied the Elders' instructions purposely. The current king didn't want to give up his throne to Harm or to me. The packs went crazy and massacred villages of humans. Stole their money and possessions ... I don't know what they were thinking." He shook his head. "Like we told you, we're the only Dires left."

"And then the Elders created the Weres?"

"Yes. In our language, *wehr* means *man*—to the were-trappers, we were man-wolves. Dire or Were, as we know them, didn't matter. We were monsters to be destroyed. And later, we were monsters who could help them to rule the world. The Elders' warning never sank in, and we pay the price as best we can. But we've never thought the Elders would allow us to mate. We've never been able to before, and sex reminds us of that."

"What do you mean?"

"Sex is great while we're having it, but we pay afterward, with pain."

"So every time after sex, it hurts?"

"It's not pleasant, no." He paused. "It's tied to the mating. We're supposed to mate, not screw around randomly. After the third time with the same person, well, let's just say we're not supposed to be with them unless mating's our intention."

"Is that why you held off—in the woods?" she asked.

"Yes. Barely."

"Mating is something you want, then."

"With you, yes."

She bit into a strawberry, swore she could smell the dirt from the garden where it had grown. It tasted like earth, delicious and fresh. "Do you only have one mate?"

"Yes. But our mates are not ... predetermined. It's like when humans say, *you just know it's right.*"

"Humans get it wrong—a lot."

"Humans don't have our sense of smell."

That was true—Rifter's scent was so distracting to her—and none of the other brothers' scents came close. Although they did smell good. "So we're fated."

"You're mine. I know that as surely as I know I'm going to live forever. I know it and I like it—I want it. Since that first night in the bar I was drawn to you. The night I found you, I'd been riding around searching. You pulled me to you as surely as if you'd called out my name."

She had been looking that night, restless, unable to stand it any longer. "Is it because of what I am that you found me? Did you sense the Dire in me subconsciously?"

"Maybe. Think of it this way: Jinx could've found you that night—or Vice or Stray. They were all out on moon call. But they didn't. I went out to find you because I knew you were out there. Well, technically, I knew there was danger. And I guess I was right."

She clinked her wineglass to his and took a big gulp.

"It can't all be hard," he told her. "Our wolves won't let us shoulder burdens without equal parts pleasure."

"You have to know the happiness to know sadness."

He nodded, looked pleased at her understanding.

"What happens now?"

"We wait until the danger's over."

"I mean, between us," she clarified. "And sealing our mating."

"You need to shift right after our third time together. And it's not an easy shift—you're still having trouble, and the third shift is always the toughest on a new Dire. The mating shift is hard enough on its own even for an experienced Dire. It's not usually combined like this."

"It's going to have to be," she said firmly. "If we're fated . . ."

"In the old language of the Dires, *fated* is our word for your human word *love*," he said, and her heart began to beat faster. "That's why you can't mate on the first try. It

would be a goddamned disaster. There's no such thing as
a soul mate — it's about lust and love and attraction — all
the things that happen between humans. Wolves just
happen to make better choices."

"And so by the third time together, you know?"

"Yes. It's always worked for us in the past. If the mating takes, you shift right after."

"And you?"

"I'm chained so I can't shift and hurt you — that's tradition."

"But can't I hurt you?"

"Yes. "You have a choice not to be mated to me. Or
to anyone," he said. "You could wait. Shift. See —"

"There is no one else for me. You know that."

His nostrils flared as her scent did. "You could leave.
Find that out."

"Where else would I go?" she asked, incredulous that
he would bring this up now.

"You could live in the world alone," he said. "Stray
did."

"And was that easy? Was he happy?"

"No to both."

"And it's not like there's a cure for what I have."

He actually looked offended. "You'd want a cure?"

"I don't want to die."

He blanched. "That's not what I meant — I want you
to live. But I don't understand why you'd want to re-
nounce your wolf. It's an honor."

"You all want to die, but you don't want to be . . . human?"

"Never."

"How are you going to deal with me, then? Because
part of me still is."

"How well will you deal with the world of wolves?"
he shot back.

"I've felt the violence. Meted it out. You're fighting for your family. So am I," she told him. "I'm not here because I've been lonely, although I have been for a very long time."

She'd refused to admit that to herself before this. Pride or denial, she wasn't sure which, but now that she'd found someone who understood her, she wasn't letting go.

"You are magic to my logic," she told him. It was as simple as that. In many ways, they were opposites, but they completed each other.

"I love you, Gwen. Make no mistake about that."

She loved him too. He'd taken her into his world, walked her through it, and it was marvelous here. A dual nature was freeing. Whether her body would handle the demands well was a whole other story. But even if she didn't have immortality, neither would walk away.

Chapter 46

The third mating would bind them as mates forever, force her shift . . . and possibly kill her. But Gwen felt stronger than she ever had. She could do this. She would.

"I don't think we should put off the inevitable," she told him now.

He stared at her like she was nuts, said bluntly, "You've had too much wine."

"I've had just enough," she countered. "You need me—as your mate—to fight. Maybe my ability will be what you need to keep the Dire army away or to wake Rogue up."

Or maybe I won't make it through at all.

The unspoken words hung heavily between them, but she knew there was no time to waste. "We're here because of me. Because of my possible human frailties. Instead of babysitting, you could be back at the main house, helping your brothers."

"I'm right where I need to be. Where I want to be," he clarified, and his scent flared around her. Arousal filled the air like a mysterious dark spice, chocolate and cinnamon and other earthy flavors combined. She could almost taste it on her tongue.

She stood and started to strip her clothing; he gave a low warning growl she didn't heed. She stood naked before him, running her hands over her already hardening nipples, letting one slide down her belly and linger between her legs.

He can't deny you—that's part of the third mating. Ask—and he has to follow, Sister Wolf whispered.

Something mysterious and wonderful was taking her over—and yet she was still somehow in total control. "Come on, Rifter. Now."

He swallowed hard. By this point, he was a partial slave to his mate—until the mating was fulfilled, he would need to do her bidding. She could see he was trying to deny her request but couldn't. Slowly, he stood, his biceps bulging, his jaw taut, his cock pressing his jeans to the point of bursting.

She was wet, hot, between her legs already. She trembled a little at what she was about to do to him. But every nerve in her body ached for him, her muscles taut with a need so great, she wasn't sure it could ever be filled. But she damn well wanted Rifter to try.

She went to the first bedroom, with the chains, and noticed another set of restraints on the floor by the far side of the bed.

"Are these more wolf restraints?" she asked, fingering the leather straps.

"No, those are Vice's personal ones," he said, and she nodded, fingered the fine black grain and pictured them around Rifter's wrists.

She pointed to the bed. "Down, boy."

"I haven't been a boy in a very long time," he told her in a voice that was dangerous.

She didn't heed the warning because she could be as much so, if not more. And her body reveled in it now, as if she'd been waiting her whole life to come into her own.

"Take your clothes off, Rifter . . . and tell me how to tie you down."

He cursed roughly as he tore his shirt and jeans off. "Those will be purely decorative," he told her. "It's that ring that'll keep me from shifting and hurting you."

She turned and saw the collar on the floor—leather lined with pure silver. "This goes around your neck?"

"And the chains go around the bed." He pointed to the headboard, which was iron and bolted to the floor. "You need to lock the door and give me the key so you can't leave this room when you shift."

She paused, her resolve waning for a few seconds, until he said, "Do it, Gwen. Don't back down now."

She picked up the collar and waited for him to sit on the bed. She would do that last, putting it aside and snapping the leather cuffs on his wrists and ankles and chaining him to the bed. He was spread for her—massive and gorgeous—his eyes starting to turn.

"Hurry," he told her hoarsely. Hating to hurt him but knowing it was necessary, she picked up the collar and he lifted his head, allowing her to easily snap it in place.

He hissed when it went on and made contact with his skin. His eyes went back to human coloring, and he paled slightly.

"How will you be able to—"

"It's a mating collar—it's not meant to disable me," he told her. "We took it after the Extinction. We've never used it. This is the first mating since then."

Indeed, the smell of burning had ceased, and he was still rock hard and ready for her. But he wasn't looking at her. She climbed onto him, put her hands on his chest.

"Let me inside, Rifter," she murmured. "Still holding back from me."

"For good reason, little one."

"Not so little." She smiled and brought his hand between her legs to the wet heat, and his body jerked with pleasure.

"Don't tease, little one," he warned, but Gwen was hearing none of it. "Let me tease you—bring your pretty pussy up here."

She complied with his order, straddling his face, her hands gripping the headboard as he tongued her hot flesh, sucking and laving until she was coming with a cry that echoed through the four walls. Her throat was sore, her breath harsh, as a second orgasm grabbed her almost immediately.

Humans suspected the moon was responsible for many things that scientists tried to debunk.

They were wrong. The full moon spelled humans the way it pulled wolves, although not as strongly. But the more frailties the humans had, the closer to insanity, the stronger the pull.

Those were human favorites of the wolves. They walked the line, could see and sense the supernatural. Rifter almost felt sorry for them. Like the Dires, the insane were caught between worlds.

Humans were so fragile, he thought as he stroked Gwen's hair, then cupped one of her breasts in his hands, the metal chains clinking as a reminder of what had yet to happen. He traced a nipple with his finger, the dark pink nipple rising taut to meet his fingers.

Gwen smiled. Delicate, wrapped in strength. She was rebounding from the first of her many orgasms, stretching in deep satisfaction. His cock was aching for release—the thought of plunging in between her legs and claiming her was the only thing on his mind. His seed in her, his scent in her forever . . .

Would he break her? As that thought crossed his mind, Gwen reached between his legs and stroked him.

He hissed a harsh breath between clenched teeth at the unexpected caress.

She had no idea what kind of beast she'd awakened. The primal desires of the Dires tended to be uncontrollable. He lost control during sex, as much as he would during any inhibition. The collar wouldn't help much with that.

If the mating were successful, the postorgasm pain that would normally rock his body would be gone.

"Gwen . . ."

She wouldn't stop, was making her way down his legs as he remained as helpless as a newborn with the chains on his neck and ankles. Now he attempted to keep his hips from bucking wildly, the last vestige of pretending he had any control over the situation.

In actuality, he'd left himself too open to her advances. And when her tongue flicked the head of his cock, he found himself reverting to the old language, his wild urges rising to the surface.

It only seemed to encourage her.

She's part Dire, he told himself.

Part human, Brother Wolf said, but he told the wolf to shut up as she swallowed his cock. He came then. She wouldn't know he could come many more times with equal force within an hour's time span. That he needed to.

"Mount me," he commanded as she stared at his still rock-hard dick. "Now."

She stroked between her own legs as she straddled him. She took the head of his cock inside of her and she shuddered, her golden skin glowing. He'd love to use his hands on her, grasped the chains that held him fast.

When he was fully inside of her, she threw back her head and cried out with a deep satisfaction. And then she began to ride him as he watched the beautiful curves of her body, the graceful way she undulated.

He smelled her wolf. This was bringing out the wild in her; it was equally dangerous for him. If she shifted while he was bound, as he hoped ... she could do him some serious harm. It was always a tricky time, but that's why a mating didn't happen with a brand new wolf.

It was worth the risk.

Gwen lost count of how many times she took him. Hours passed as he remained buried inside of her, helpless against the chains. And she still hadn't had enough—no matter how many times she came, her body refused to be satiated.

"You want more?" Rifter asked, his voice hoarse from the chain pressing his throat. He was still hard. She didn't know how, but she wanted—needed—to have so much more.

"Please," she whispered.

"You do please me. Please yourself."

She began to rock back and forth, grabbed the chain around his neck as she did. He whimpered and she pulled back. It was the first true sound of pain he'd made the entire time, and she touched his cheek, willing his eyes to open.

"Should I take the collar off?" she asked.

"No—fuck no," he managed, his face contorted in agony. "This is supposed to happen. Worth it. Mating is ... complete on my end."

"And on mine?"

"Check your Sister Wolf—turn around and look," he encouraged.

She turned her back to the mirror and looked over her shoulder.

Sister Wolf's eyes shone back at her. "You did good," she whispered.

Back at you, the clear voice said calmly. *Hard part's not done yet.*

"I didn't shift," she whispered, more to herself than to Rifter. "I thought that needed to happen."

"It does," he told her.

She couldn't believe what she'd just done with him. To him. As he lay chained to the bed. She studied the perfection of his body. The scars he bore only served to add to it, instead of taking away from the beauty.

His chest bore deep scratches—and she'd made them. And it excited her.

"Keep marking me, mate. More."

His eyes were pure wolf. Strength radiated from him even though he was a slave to her with the silver collar.

The trust he had in her . . . had anyone ever held her in such high regard? "You were worth the wait, worth all the fear and pain and sadness. I'd do it all again if it meant ending up here."

"I waited forever for you, baby. I'm never letting you go," he told her, and the possession in his tone heated her like fire.

"I'm never letting you go."

"Take me again."

She did. Lost control—every sense—the room spun, and it was like a dream. But this time, the reality was something she didn't want to shy away from. Whispered, "I love you, Rifter," in his ear.

And then everything began to change inside of her.

As a physician, she should know that logically, scientifically, none of this could be real.

The wolf living inside of her disagreed heartily. But as she stared at herself naked in the mirror, she still couldn't see it.

Let it happen.

She rubbed her arms, turned around and stared at her back.

The switch was an exquisite type of pain, as if, by finally allowing her body to do what it needed to, it re-warded her.

She was scared, but a voice whispered to her. At first, it was no more than a rustle in her ear, and then she heard words—some in the old language.

Sister Wolf. Live as one.

It felt oddly normal and completely strange all at the same time. One minute, she could speak. The next, she could only growl or mewl. She supposed she could howl too, but she held off in favor of backing away from Rifter.

Sister Wolf didn't want to, though. Thank goodness Rifter was fast, unchained himself, took the collar off and shifted. His wolf was bigger than hers and oh so ready to play. But even as she tried to move toward him, Sister Wolf's legs buckled under her. The last thing she heard was Rifter's Brother Wolf howling in her ears.

Chapter 47

Gwen never switched completely to wolf form, no doubt thanks to her half-human side. Which meant the mating hadn't fully occurred.

Seventy-two hours later, Rifter still sat with her while she slept. He ate a little at Vice's urging.

She was dying, and there was nothing he could do about it.

Outside, the human world was being threatened, promising a battle of the immortals. It was only a taste of what was to come.

No sun again—for days, it was nothing but thunder and lightning across the eastern seaboard, a front that had weathermen frustrated and concerned.

Inside the mansion, Rifter paced as Gwen remained so damned still.

He'd been trying to get inside her mind since she'd passed out. But it was as terribly quiet as Rogue's, and that terrified him more than anything.

It was less than two weeks until the blue moon. The outlaws hadn't been back, but Cyd and Cain had been reconning, confirmed the trappers were up to something big. It had to center around the spirit army.

And Rifter needed to leave Gwen in order to come up with a plan. She would want that, he knew. But the thought of taking his hand from hers . . .

"Where are you, Gwen?" he asked out loud, probably for the millionth time. The thought of her wandering alone . . . the thought that she wasn't wandering at all.

"Rift." Jinx's voice. He turned to see his brother in the doorway. "It's bad. Seb's spell is stronger now. The mausoleum isn't necessary any longer."

Seb really had made a deal with the devil. Rifter wasn't sure his heart could break any more than it already had with Gwen, but it did.

"I'll try to go back in to Rogue. See if he can use me as a conduit. Or if that doesn't work, I'm going into Seb's dreams." They both knew where that would lead him, but for once, Jinx didn't argue. The fate of the humans their kind had hurt once had started all of this—it was Rifter's fate to end it.

He was about to turn back to Gwen when the flash hit. The brothers stared at each other as the unmistakable signs of the summoning from the Elders flared between them.

Rifter took it as a sign that he'd agreed to do the right thing for all concerned and prepared to face hell as he knew it.

When they'd been summoned, Rifter left Gwen in Liam's care without explanation. There was very little time. When the Elders pulled for the shift from human to wolf, their free will was left in the dust.

As their Brother Wolves padded cautiously into the woods past their property, Rifter felt a growing gnaw of trepidation.

None of them were rushing to the meeting place.

Rifter took the lead, and when they reached the spot, he sat with the rest of them in a V formation behind him. They all stared up at the moon.

It took ten minutes of tense waiting before the flash came and the three Elders—Eydis, Leifr and Meili—stood before them in human form.

"Quite a mess," Eydis told them. "I hope you're not expecting us to get you out of this."

Behind him, Vice growled. Eydis shot a flash of light from her hand to singe his fur—and the skin underneath—and he whimpered a little. But hell, he probably enjoyed it more than anything.

"Don't push me, wolf. I can make things so unpleasant, even you couldn't stand it."

Her gaze fell on Rifter. "We're allowing a single wish. It won't solve all your problems. If you don't choose wisely, you might even make things worse for yourselves."

Leifr said, "We'll be back to hear your answer soon. Don't make us wait."

Once the Elders were gone, the men were able to shift immediately. They stood staring at the place where the Elders had been as Rifter tried to process their sudden generosity.

If it was a trap, the Elders were determined to let the Dires set it and snag themselves. Rifter knew which wish he wanted, but it would most definitely make everything worse.

Vice spoke first. "Save Gwen."

Rifter stared at his brothers as they all nodded in agreement.

"I know Rogue would agree too," Jinx said. "And I'm sure as shit not counting Harm."

"There are other things . . . As king, I'm supposed to choose what's best for all, not for just me," he said.

"What's best for the king is what's best for us," Jinx countered.

"You could all wish for mates," Rifter told them.

"And take away yours?" Stray asked. "No. Save Gwen. We'll deal with the rest. We've got nothing but time."

Chapter 48

The woman before her was so blindingly beautiful, it hurt. Gwen roused and stared down at her still-human body, confused. "Who are you?" she asked without speaking, as she was still very much in Sister Wolf's form.

"I'm Eydis. One of the Dire Elders. And you have yet to complete your third shift," the woman said.

No shit, Gwen wanted to tell her, but Eydis lifted a brow and frowned as though she did.

Mind-reading Elders. Something the Dires forgot to mention. "Will I finish my shift?"

Eydis pointed toward the group of men who stood in the woods, talking. About Gwen. "We left the choice in their hands. So many other things they can choose—and yet, they're sacrificing their own wishes and wants for you."

Gwen felt the tears rise.

"What if the Dires can't save the weretrappers—and the humans—from themselves?"

"They don't have a choice. It is their charge. They must find a way."

"How long will you punish them?"

Eydis smiled, more chilling than comforting. "Include

yourself in that, Sister Wolf. You've accepted their burdens."

She had—gladly. "Then hurry up and save me."

"Impatient, just like the others," Eydis mused. "The Dires saved you. But you will always be a danger to them. Always. You'll have to live with that."

She stared down at the men, all too willing to accept her despite that major flaw inside of her, something she could never change. "I can."

"I still can't believe they respect you. A half human," Eydis mused. "Odd."

Gwen heard the growl rip from her own throat.

"Now, now, little wolf, it's not the time to fight me. You've got to get yourself out of this mess. We're not the ones stopping you. Never have been. You've always been in your own way. I'm here to help you with that."

Was that true? Gwen had never wanted to die, had made it clear she wanted to be with Rifter. So why would she stop herself from shifting?

"You haven't given yourself over to the ways. You want it to be on your terms . . . your . . . science, as you call it. Forget your old ways; surrender to the new ones."

"And I'll magically transform?"

"I've never understood humans' penchant for snark," Eydis sniffed. "Don't be so skeptical, human."

"Half wolf," Gwen told her.

Eydis smiled. "You won't be alone this time. I have great power, and I don't help just anyone."

"Why me?"

"You've proven yourself useful. Loyal. And the Dires need help now, more than ever." Eydis paused. "I was taken before my first shift—some call that lucky and say I'll never know what I missed. But I know what I missed. Sometimes, I force myself to remember what it was like to be one of them."

She put her hand on Gwen's arm, and maybe for the first time, Gwen understood a little bit about the Elders. They could fix things—some things—but not until their Dires made the necessary sacrifices.

Nothing good can be attained easily. And for Gwen, being with Rifter was the best thing she could do.

We've got nothing but time.

At Stray's words, the Elders were back, standing before them. But the difference was that there was no forced shift for the Dires. The men stood before their makers in their human form for the first time ever.

Eydis spoke. "Your Sister Wolf is strong. Not afraid to speak her mind."

"My brothers and I agree that saving Gwen is our wish. But you should be saving her no matter what," Rifter told them, pushing his luck to the edge. "We cannot be lone wolves for eternity."

Leifr smiled, but it was far more wicked than comforting. "There have always been more."

"Then why the fuck weren't we told that it was truth?" Rifter growled, and this time Vice was holding him back. Never a good sign.

"You were never not told. You continued to search, did you not?" Leifr smiled as Vice's Brother Wolf growled like it was ready and willing to attack. "Control your Brother Wolves, or I'll do it for you."

It was a command, not a suggestion, but Vice and his wolf had stopped taking either long ago.

"We never stopped looking, but every lead, every rumor was false. At least until we found Stray," Rifter said. "So there are more . . . beyond Gwen?"

"One of you has known that for a long time," Meili said, and, yes, Rifter would have to kill one of the wolves standing behind him for that.

"It's time for the Dire pack to flourish," Leifr intoned. "We can't allow Gwen to be taken from you. Not when the great war between the supernatural and the humans is upon us."

"Humans are performing dark magic. Lines are blurring. Prophesies long considered dead are being unearthed as true," Meili continued. "There need to be more of you to fight the weretrappers and the witches. You must protect those humans you've been sworn to over the years. You must not let the dark arts win."

Prophesies long considered dead . . . Rifter contemplated this before telling the Elders, "I will never let the dark arts win. And thank you for saving Gwen."

"Your intentions were finally from the heart," Eydis told him. "And so it will be done."

Rifter nearly collapsed with relief. Brother Wolf howled a grateful response. But there was a catch here— there always was.

Eydis told them, "She'll be immortal, and her blood will always be deadly to you. She's your mate—and your kryptonite, all rolled into one."

I understand, he told them. *Wake her up.*

Chapter 49

There would be time later to figure out who knew what about living Dires beyond their pack. For now, Rifter raced into the house toward Gwen, his brothers behind him.

The rain had replaced the snow once more, which meant trouble still lay ahead, and they moved through the water easily.

Once in the room, he found Sister Wolf curled on the pillows, her breathing shallow, and he swore his heart stopped.

"Hey," he said softly, and the beautiful female lifted her head and stared at him and then at his brothers behind him. "You're safe. You made a wolf shift . . . now come back to me, baby. I know you can do it."

He heard his brothers leave in order to give them privacy, and he knelt by the bed and waited. Put his head down and prayed, then lifted it when he heard the growl quickly followed by a whimper.

Gwen was curled naked against the pillows. She was so still that, at first, a wave of panic rushed through him.

But her breaths were even, albeit slightly shallow. She was pale. But she'd made it. His silent prayer of thanks to the Elders earned him what felt like a light touch to his forehead, followed by a light breeze on the back of his neck.

Whether the Elders would be watching out for the Dires more closely now remained to be seen, but Rifter could only hope.

The worst might seem like it was over, but he knew it had just begun. But with his mate by his side, he had every reason to be hopeful.

"I'm really awake," she said quietly after a few long moments as she stared down at her limbs, flexed her hands, which had been paws moments earlier.

"Did it hurt?"

"No, not really . . . it's . . . it felt right. Finally."

He brushed a hand across her cheek as color began to return. "Finally. Your wolf is beautiful."

She flushed with pride. "I can't wait to do it again."

"Shift?"

"Yeah, that too," she murmured. "Will you chain yourself down for me again?"

"Didn't think you were that kind of girl."

"I didn't know I wasn't really all girl." She grinned. "I made it through, so that means I'm okay now, right?"

"You're more than okay," he told her, his hand moving to touch the bare skin of her back, the unmistakable heat rising between them. "Do you need to . . . rest?"

"I've rested enough for a lifetime. I feel like I could run a marathon."

Her energy level would only continue to grow. Still half human, always would be, he supposed, but Sister Wolf would take over as much real estate as she could to protect Gwen. Sister Wolf would protect her as fiercely as his pack always would.

"The mating's been accepted. Blessed. Eydis told me," she said.

"We still have to do a moon run," he told her, even as

her hand found its way between his legs. Blood rushed to his cock, and its pulsating need for her overwhelmed everything else.

She obviously felt the same way as she stroked him, agreeing, "Yes. Run. Later." Then she tugged him in for a kiss and he stopped talking.

Everything felt different. It was different because she'd transformed. Her body had somehow turned into Sister Wolf and back, and all the pieces somehow fit together perfectly.

Forget your science, her wolf whispered. *Embrace your wolf.*

Gwen planned on doing just that, and to Rifter as well. His scent was so powerful, called to her in a way too powerful for her to resist.

Giving herself to Rifter again, now that the mating ritual was complete, made it even more satisfying. There wasn't danger in this coming together—there was hope. And so she undid Rifter's jeans and let her hand circle his hard, thick length with no barrier, watching his eyes grow heavy lidded with her efforts.

So different than the first night they'd met, and yet, the feelings that started then had been real on both ends.

"That's it, baby. Stroke me like that," he told her, and she complied, loving the way she was giving this man— her mate—pleasure. Sister Wolf howled and Gwen wanted Rifter so badly she ached.

Rifter knew. His hand traced a path down her belly until it rested between her legs. His fingers found her core, and she realized that everything was more sensitive. Her skin tingled and her arousal surged as though she hadn't orgasmed for years.

She needed one now. She straddled him and guided him inside of her, slowly at first, and then she pushed herself down hard so that he filled her completely. Everything about Rifter's body against hers was right. Things were complete, inside and out. And when he held her hips, bucked up inside of her, she cried out.

The sensations, the pleasures, all magnified, until it all became one blur of taste and sound and sight. In the middle of everything, his lick along her earlobe made her shiver.

When he bit her shoulder, she shuddered, cried out in surrender of what she'd once been. Came hard, contracting around him, pulling his orgasm into hers, until both their breath ran ragged, their bodies slick with sweat.

And he was still hard.

"Hours. I need hours with you. Days." He spoke to her in the old language, filled her with joy that she understood.

"We've got all the time you need," she told him.

"All for you," he told her. "Everything . . . it's been for you, my fated one."

"I love you," she said. "I know, it's the human word—"

"It's all a part of you. A part of me." He kissed her and she didn't know how he could be so gentle and rough at the same time, the combination instantly setting her on fire. "I plan to spend forever doing this—tracing every part of you with my fingers, my tongue. My cock buried inside you."

She couldn't think of anything better.

Chapter 50

Angus sat in his car, engine off, and lit a cigarette, knowing that smoking wouldn't be the thing that ultimately did him in. The job was a likely candidate, this one in particular.

He'd been shot at many times over the course of his career. Knifed. Kicked. Punched. Threatened to hell and back.

Four years earlier, Angus had found himself on the receiving end of right hook from Harm—a powerful punch Mike Tyson would've killed to have.

There had been rumors for years that Harm was into the occult, that he'd made some kind of deal with the devil to stay so youthful and good-looking. The success of his band was off the charts. The stories of drug abuse and infighting, more so.

Angus had been too embarrassed to consult anyone about his suspicions, but as soon as he'd purchased a book on the supernatural from Amazon, he'd been called into his supervisor's office.

Big brother was most definitely watching.

He'd learned about a branch in the agency he didn't know, and never would've believed, existed. A new world opened for him, one that made him go home and drink until he passed out.

Two days later, when the hangover finally passed, he went back in and found himself on some kind of crazy vision quest.

Harm had disappeared somewhere in this town. Angus had checked hotels, motels, inns. Hospital and morgue. Prison. No rental-car records or credit card activity. His bank accounts were strangely silent, and the money sat untouched.

How did a grown man—a highly recognizable one—disappear into thin air?

He pondered that some more as he stared out on the vast field of empty land where blood was found on the grass after calls of a disturbance by neighbors. Except there were no neighbors for fifteen miles in either direction, thanks to the woods. But it was an odd place for a clearing.

He needed to check with the buildings department to see who owned the property. Local law enforcement told him they were looking into it. Which meant they weren't cooperating with his investigation.

Speaking of, the black-and-white cruiser pulled up alongside his car. He got out his badge and rolled down the window, saw it was the same man he'd met at the earlier crime scene, where Cain Chambers had been arrested and then released for lack of evidence.

"I've got some information I think you'll want to hear," Leo Shimmin told him as he held up the picture of a pentagram.

Angus glanced at Shimmin and nodded.

Rifter stood with Gwen in the kitchen as they all gathered around. Three days had passed since the Elders had visited, giving them plenty of time to recover.

Gwen had also shifted another time and back, just to prove to herself that she could. Rifter was pretty sure this relationship stuff was going to be the death of him in some way.

"What did I miss?" Gwen asked, because she hadn't seen the brothers or Liam or the twins since she'd first awakened.

"We blew up the mausoleum. Liam killed Teague and put a bounty on Walker's head. The FBI and the police are onto us. Rogue's still out and the Dire army still needs to be stopped. Does that cover it?" Vice asked.

Rifter glanced at him. "And we need to find a witch strong enough to reverse Seb's spell on Rogue, since killing him's going to be impossible."

He'd told the Dires about the mare spell on Rogue, but not Gwen. There was only so much a new wolf could handle, and she'd taken on more than her share.

"Yeah, they're all going to be dying to help us," Vice muttered.

"I'll get us one," Jinx said with such certainty that no one said anything else.

He'd have to do it soon. The heat was really coming down on them hard. The wolves looked like they were part of a motorcycle gang and normally did nothing to dispel that rumor. This way, they were typically given a wide berth by humans, and generally, if the police were smart, they left the men to their own devices when they realized they weren't causing trouble by selling drugs or running guns.

No, the wolves were just running.

But now the town was in disarray, as were their lives, evidenced when Stray turned the monitor to face them and scrolled through wanted posters with all their faces on it. "We're in big fucking trouble."

Indeed, this level of outing had never happened. Technology was really a bitch.

"Liam's on here as well," Stray said. "Someone's done a hell of a lot of research."

"Has to be Mars's brother," Rifter muttered.

Harm cleared his throat guiltily and they all turned to look at him. He wasn't in the attic anymore like some fucked-up version of Scrooge's ghosts, but he still wore silver bonds on his wrists and ankles.

"I'm wanted," he admitted.

"We already caught you."

"The FBI's been trailing me—some guy named Angus Young. There have been murders that happened in every town the band played in—and then murders in every town I showed up in after the band broke up."

"Someone's been killing and putting the blame on you?"

"Yes."

"You sure it's not you and you're trying to put the blame on someone else? Because you're damned good at that." Vice snapped his teeth together, thinking how much more satisfying it would be to have Harm's neck between them, crushed like a paper cup.

Harm straightened. "I saved your ass from the outlaws and this is the thanks I get?"

"We were doing just fine without you," Rifter said. "We'll do fine if you're not here."

"Banish him," Stray said. "I know from experience, living without support is like a death."

"What's to stop him from taking another job in the limelight?" Vice argued. "He's already weaseled away from us too many times. Gave up his kingship."

"Rifter, you were always stronger. I couldn't do it," Harm told him now. "It was all too much, and they'd never have let me give up the crown any other way. The only thing I wanted to do was the music."

Gwen remained silent during this exchange. Now the

men looked at her when she asked, "Tell us more about the FBI."

"I found out that the current killings match a similar rash when I was touring in the eighties. An agent named Angus Young's been tailing me, and it's only a matter of time before he figures out I'm the same person—he's already asked me about it. And then he'll wonder why the hell I haven't aged." Harm looked at them. "I mean, plastic surgery makes people look good these days, but no way would he believe that I'm human."

"The problem is, I don't think they believe you're human at all," Rifter said.

"We're going to have to move," Jinx said. "I don't see a way around this."

"Not until this supernatural shit's under control." Local papers were reporting increasingly weird things in the area. Weres were affected—leaving now would be akin to desertion, and Dires didn't do that.

"You surrender once and you're fucked." Vice stood firm. "Even Gwen instinctively knows she was born for retribution."

Gwen nodded, that need hot in her blood. She had a family to defend, and she would never go down easily. But the fact that her blood could kill them . . . "How can my blood hurt you?"

"It's not as simple as you spill blood on us," Jinx explained. "It would have to be transfused in great quantities. That's why they wanted you—they could study your blood and re-create it in order to fell us."

"How do you know this?"

"I went through Mars's house, hoping to find the grimoire—the book of spells. Mars had it written down as part of his battle plan."

"We'd have to start killing the humans," Jinx said.

"And that's a slippery-assed slope, even if they want us dead first."

"Then we need to find the other Dires the Elders were talking about," Vice said. "Obviously, one of us knows something."

They all turned to Stray, the obvious choice. He didn't deny anything, stopped typing and shoved the keyboard away. There was a stubborn set to his jaw, and Rifter fought the urge to punch the hell out of it until it dislocated.

"How many are there?" he demanded instead.

"I only know one. My brother, Killian," Stray said through clenched teeth.

"After fifty years, you couldn't trust us?" Rifter asked.

"I respected his wishes. He's not out getting us in trouble or hurting people. But his ability will help us."

"And he'll do that?" Jinx asked.

"He owes me. He'll come when I call to collect," Stray assured him.

Rifter didn't want to ask any more, but Stray continued, "If I thought he could've helped Rogue, I would've called him back already. But his talent lies in another area of importance to us."

"What's that?" Vice asked.

"His ability allows him to plant suggestions inside people's minds. Kind of like hypnosis, the suggestion remains there and becomes more than a suggestion. Only works on humans." Stray paused, as if waiting for Rifter to question him further.

There would be a time for that, but it wasn't now. Instead, Rifter just growled, "Get him here."

Chapter 51

The ceremony formally mating him to Gwen took place during the waning moon. Since the police and the FBI were watching the property attached to the house carefully, Gwen, Rifter and his Dire brothers, along with Liam and the twins, traveled to the underground compound. On the other side of the place, there was a stairway that opened to a patch of nearly deserted woods that ran along the river. The moon shimmered, making everything look unreal, but Rifter knew how real it was. How much danger they were putting themselves in to make him and his mate one.

Under that moon, where the Elders could see and bless the union if they so desired, he and Gwen spoke in the ancient language, the promises of love and devotion the Dires used back in the old country.

It had been so long since he'd heard it, but Rifter made sure he'd never forgotten it. He had a feeling none of his brothers had either. And when the words were spoken and he and Gwen embraced, they shifted together, Gwen still taking longer than he did, making him hold his breath with anticipation.

And when they howled jointly, the rest of the men shifted as well, and he and Gwen ran together along the river, with the Elders, the Dires, Cyd, Cain and Liam watching over them. Howling at the moon as they returned.

After going back inside, shifting and heading to the house, they ate a meal together. Then Rifter watched Vice wield the tattoo gun easily in his massive hands, knowing from experience the buzz of the needle wasn't an altogether unpleasant sensation.

This was his brothers' present to her. Gwen understood the honor, and she'd been the one to insist that it be done that very evening.

Her tribal tattoo was smaller, more delicate, drawn along the inside of her wrist by Rifter and inked by Vice.

She'd chosen that spot purposely. "Where I can always see it," she told Rifter after he'd carefully drawn the marking.

She'd been marked in so many ways over the past weeks.

She was accepted, and that made Rifter's pride swell.

Liam, Cyd and Cain were equally marked—symbols of solidarity and protection. They were considered part of the Dire tribe, even though they would branch from it. With Liam as king and alpha, Cyd as an emerging alpha, and Cain as omega, the New York City pack would have a powerful new beginning.

It would be necessary to defeat the monsters headed their way in the form of the spirit army. The Dires had never had to fight against themselves.

Harm was there, although he hadn't been accepted back into the Dire pack—or forgiven by any of them. But he recognized that he needed to stay out of the limelight and away from the FBI, so he had little choice.

The tabloids were having a field day, calling Harm a recluse. His manager called nonstop.

Until Rogue woke, nothing could ever be the same.

So much unfinished. After living so long with so many loose ends, you'd think Rifter would be used to it by now.

When Gwen came and embraced him, he pushed aside those thoughts. "It looks beautiful, just like you."

"I love you so much, Rifter. Love you . . . forever."

For the first time ever, he was able to truly believe that was possible.

Epilogue

He'd gone into hibernation mode for most of the winter, waking only to run during the hot nights of the summer months along the shores of the old country. So alone, the way he'd wanted to be, needed it to be, for everyone's safety.

Now he was needed. He heard the call from deep inside, a blood bond of family unbroken by time.

His brother never called to him, not once in all the years since they'd separated. But there was trouble now, and Kill rose to his feet and prepared to make the long stretch to find Stray.

Acknowledgments

Writing a book is never a solitary experience and as always, I have many people to thank. First, to Irene Goodman, for listening. For Danielle Perez and Kara Welsh, for giving the Dires a home and for loving them as much as I do. For everyone at NAL for being so welcoming.

To my go-to people, Larissa Ione, Maya Banks and Jaci Burton. I couldn't do this without you. For Lea F., who's supported me from the start. For all my readers, whose e-mail and posts on Facebook on Twitter mean more than they could possibly know.

For my family—Zoo, Lily, Chance, Gus—thank you for letting me follow my dreams, and for understanding when it takes me a while to return to earth.

Don't miss the next novel in the Eternal Wolf
Clan series by Stephanie Tyler,

DIRE WANTS

Coming in November 2012 from Signet Eclipse

Two Dires will be born to aid in the great war between wolf and man. One can hear, the other influence. Brothers who, if they don't turn their wrath on each other, will cause destruction and ruin outward.
　　— Prophecy of the Elders (circa tenth century)

The prophecy that Stray had grown up hearing about him and his brother, Killian, was coming true. Now Kill was coming to town and would be expected to live up to his name, and Stray needed to run to lose himself. To hunt instead of brood, to stop trying to figure out if the prophecy wanted him dead or alive.

As part of a pack of what was believed to be the last six remaining Dire wolves, he was feared and revered. Currently, they called the Catskills in New York home, had come back here months earlier to aid the Weres and had found themselves embroiled in a shitload of trouble.

Still, in the woods outside the Dires' secret underground lair, there was laughter under the glow of the moon. Even if it was foggy, the moon shone to them as bright as the sun did to humans on a hot summer's day.

The nightly run would happen on the plot of land that

was protected by unshifted Weres. Under normal circumstances, the Dires changed their locale as often as possible, but this was anything but normal. The safe place was at the end of a tunnel that let out into a thicket of woods that was nearly impossible for most humans to pass through. Rifter, their leader, was there, with Jinx and Vice.

Jinx's brother, Rogue, remained in a supernaturally induced coma back at the house, along with Harm, the Dire who'd walked away from the pack thousands of years ago and had come back a week earlier, bringing nothing but trouble with him.

Gwen was with them as well. Rifter's mate, a half Dire, half human. Harm's daughter.

Stray watched Vice rib Jinx for picking up a were-chick the night before. Rifter and Gwen were nuzzling each other. Business as usual, despite everything.

Except Stray had an even bigger secret than the brother he'd been keeping under wraps. But tonight he was determined to shake off the maudlin shit and let his Brother Wolf run wild. And Brother growled in agreement, barely waiting for Stray to strip before the shift began. It was a pain-and-pleasure kind of thing, a change that pushed Stray to his limits every time his wolf took over.

"Stray's gone!" Vice called behind him, and Stray knew his shift would pull the others along. Sure enough, he was soon surrounded by the wolves as they disappeared into the woods, camouflaged in safety.

Stray wasn't the name he'd been given at birth. He'd adopted the moniker after he left his pack, because he refused to use or even think about his given name. Kill refused to change his. Maybe he was too proud or too stupid—or a combination of both. Stray could be stubborn too, but living like a hermit was his gig, not Kill's. He couldn't imagine how his brother had fared alone all these years.

Being a hermit was okay for Stray—it had been lonely as shit, but it was easier than reading people's goddamned thoughts all the time, which got old and exhausting very quickly.

The Dires had never pushed him to reveal his ability, nor had they mentioned the prophecy, but that didn't mean they didn't know about it. Fact was, Rifter and his Dire brothers might have suspected there were more of their kind out there after they discovered Stray. At one point, Rifter had asked him outright and Stray had denied it. But now that they knew about Killian, would they make the connection about the prophecy as it related to them? And when would he have to admit that there was another Dire pack, not immortal, living quietly in Greenland?

The Elders had never forbidden him to speak about them, but he was oddly protective of a group that had been anything but kind to him.

Stray had already given up more in the past few days than he'd ever planned to. But this Dire pack had kept him safe, had treated him like a brother for the past fifty years.

Maybe he should've let them in on all of it—the other pack, the prophecy—before now, and he couldn't tell if it was his guilt or their possible unspoken disapproval weighing heavily on him. And so he ran faster, breaking away from the pack, Brother Wolf craving a solitude he hadn't gotten since all the shit started raining down on their heads.

He felt his brother drawing near as surely as he felt the moon's pull. There was a darkness in Killian, one that Stray brought out—and was pretty sure he shared as well.

And soon, the pack that took him in would know too. *They all have abilities,* he reminded himself. But putting his together with Kill's could turn the brothers into beings beyond all control.

Power was a damned dangerous thing, but not as much as the freedom he craved. Freedom was as dangerous as shit these days to seek out, but Brother Wolf wanted to hunt. To seek, to stalk prey while relishing in the game of the chase.

He lost track of time and the trails, knew he was pushing it by running this close to the highway but didn't care. His Brother Wolf moved fast, paws crunching the packed snow.

He was searching. Scenting. The full moon had passed, but a second called the blue moon would happen in less than a few weeks. His body felt hot and tight and every run made things worse, not better.

Brother Wolf ran, paws treading the wet earth until he couldn't hear anything but his own breathing. Everything inside of him relaxed and he melted into the forest surroundings, because that's where he belonged.

He scented his prey and stalked it for miles. Sometimes, the thrill of the hunt and the chase were better than the catch.

This time, the catch was pretty damned good too.

Stray would be the last one in tonight. Vice shifted back and prepared to wait for him to show through the thicket of trees sometime before dawn.

Stray would come back bloody, the way Vice had. Not unusual, but since he'd confessed how young he was—seventy-five to Vice's centuries—Vice was impressed at Stray's self-control.

The kid was really a goddamned baby.

"We've got to find out more about Killian, 'cause I've got a bad feeling about it," he said to Jinx, who'd come up beside him.

"You shouldn't fuck with him," Jinx said after a long pause. "This brother thing . . . it's no joke."

He knew Jinx was speaking from experience, since his twin was currently all fucked up and lying in some kind of supernatural coma. Only the death of the witch who'd cursed him could break the spell—and since that witch was immortal, they needed a hell of a miracle.

He leaned against the gazebo that was directly over the tunnels the Dires utilized. The protected underground lair was built beneath hallowed ground. There had once been an old church here, razed before the Dires purchased the land. Even though the building was gone, the consecration would always remain.

Vice figured there had to be some religious types flipping in their graves over the fact that wolves were living on church ground. He wasn't sure why, other than the fact that they weren't human. But he'd never understood any organized religion. He'd fought in the Crusades, not just because he liked to fight, but also because he liked the idea that everyone deserved freedom.

Well, most everyone. The weretrappers had to get over themselves. Centuries was too long to hold a grudge.

This vendetta on the part of the trappers wasn't about what the Dires once did—over the years, they'd saved a thousandfold more humans than their packs had killed. It seemed like it would never be enough. But he'd be damned if he let those fuckers use the wolves to kill.

Because of that, the hunt for the witch who could save Rogue was on. The sky remained unnaturally dark, as it had been for days. The supernatural influence pulled at all of them, made them uneasy. Growly. Shifty. The pull would get more intense as the blue moon neared.

The supernatural storms that had invaded the town weeks earlier had receded, but they were all still vigilant, awaiting the storms' return. The weretrappers weren't about to give up this easily.

But Jinx hadn't been able to contact the Dire ghost army again—and they didn't content themselves that it had been disbanded. No, there was no doubt a far more sinister reason the army could not be reached, and the Dires were grateful they'd been able to make the initial contact at all.

Vice especially was getting tense—his shifts from one extreme to another would happen so fast his own head spun, and although he was never even close to being politically correct, the things that came out of his mouth surprised even him.

And Jinx was getting nowhere, except more pissed that he couldn't find a witch to help Rogue even though he claimed he felt her—and that she was close.

Stray, who had been getting more and more agitated as his brother got closer, found himself pulled out of the house during the daylight, as if searching for something.

Vice had taken to trailing him to make sure Stray wasn't getting himself into trouble. Between watching over him, training Liam and ghost hunting with Jinx, Vice barely found time to get into any trouble of his own. And hell, that in itself was too unnatural for him to deal with for much longer.

"Fucking witches," he muttered.

"Tell me about it," Jinx said. "Stray's coming—he just shifted."

They watched him turn from wolf to human about thirty feet from them, still covered by the surrounding foliage.

"You're sleeping out here with him?" Vice asked.

"Yeah, think I will." Jinx motioned to the covered porch. "We'll be all right."

Vice didn't think any of them would be, but for once he managed to hold his tongue.

*   *   *

Vice and Jinx were waiting for him. Neither said anything when Stray walked back to them in the field with blood still smeared on his chest. They were all predators, believed in survival of the fittest and enjoyed the hunt as much as he did. Wolves were meant for this, and as long as they were taking down animals and not humans, they were well within their rights.

Doing so kept their predatory instincts at bay—they'd all learned long ago how important that was, but no one more than him.

You're a beast. His mother's words echoed in his ear. Why would she be surprised at that? Why would his nature be so bad when they'd been created in Hati's image?

All he knew was that he didn't want to be locked up again. Couldn't bear it. And he hated the old surge of panic that rose up in him, a sign that the street mutt inside had not been exorcised.

If he thought too much about it, his scar began to ache fiercely. His heart beat a tattoo against his rib cage as he ran his hand over the long, knotted swath of tissue that ran diagonally across his chest, starting just above his heart and traveling downward, as though someone had tried to flay him open.

Someone had, just to see if he would die.

The only scars that won't heal on a Dire are scars made by another Dire.

Hell, dying would've been the easy part.

"Good run," Rifter said, with a smile and a hand clamped on Stray's bare shoulder. He'd been behind the gazebo with Gwen, who still hadn't gotten entirely used to being completely naked in front of all the men, and who already wore a T-shirt, though the rest of them were still bare-ass naked.

The Dires didn't get moon crazed, but they had grown up in a time when hunting prey had been easier and more acceptable.

For as long as he could remember, Stray had refused to be the prey, had outrun and outgunned most anyone or anything that dared to come near him. He almost went mad when Rifter and Rogue were captured and tortured, because he knew what that felt like all too well.

"Stray, this thing with your brother—how much of a fucking freak is he?" Vice asked without prelude.

Stray's way of answering was to jump toward Vice with a growl as Jinx got between them.

"Guess I've got my answer." Vice stared at Stray over Jinx's shoulder. "We need him, so don't fuck this up."

"Glad you agreed not to fuck with him," Jinx muttered, his hand shooting out to hit Vice across the back of the head.

Stray turned from them to look up at the sky as the two Dires tussled next to him.

The moon wasn't ready to relent her hold on the world just yet—these last few hours of dawn were some of Stray's favorites, the in-between time when most creatures were quiet and everything seemed at peace.

The solitude was what Stray enjoyed the most. He knew Jinx best understood, as they were the only two who consistently slept in wolf form. For Jinx, doing so blocked out all the ghosts who constantly needed his help.

For Stray, blocking out others wasn't that easy. His ability was developing at an alarming rate. At first, the wolf's emotions had to be really strong in order for Stray to hear his thoughts. Now, if he tuned in, he could hear just about everyone—Dire, Were, human, maybe even witch—and it made him feel like he was going nuts.

Hell, maybe he was.

Also available from

STEPHANIE TYLER

Dire Warning
An Eternal Wolf Clan Novella

AN ORIGINAL NOVELLA
AVAILABLE ONLY AS A
DOWNLOADABLE eSPECIAL

Immortal and invincible, Rifter is the head of the last surviving
pack of Dire Wolves—a band of Alpha brothers charged with
protecting the Weres. But now that witches have joined forces
with nefarious weretrappers, it's a perfect storm for double
trouble. When the murder of a human points to a wolf—along
with the threat of the packs being outed to the world—the
Dires fear that something even more dangerous is out there
hiding in the dark, something waiting for the right time to
show itself.

Available wherever books are sold or at
penguin.com